MAGICAL LOVE

*Fairy-tale romance can come true—with the help
of an open heart, and a little magic, the Prince Charming
of your dreams can become the love of a lifetime...*

Sea Spell

TESS FARRADAY
June 1998

*As a child, Beth fell into the churning sea, only to be lifted gently
out—by a dark-haired youth with a knowing, otherworldly smile—
who then vanished into the mist. Somehow the young girl knew her
elusive rescuer was a powerful, legendary selkie, who could
become the love of her dreams...*

"Tess Farraday is a magician and her pen is her wand. She's
created a hero who is a tantalizing mixture of pure sexuali-
ty and utter innocence. *Sea Spell* will leave you breathless
and begging for more! Mesmerizing!"—MAGGIE SHAYNE

Once Upon a Kiss

CLAIRE CROSS
July 1998

*A princess was born to a rejoicing land...But soon a cruel witch
came before the infant in a rage, and laid down a curse: "When
the princess reaches her full beauty, she will prick her finger and
fall into a deep sleep. Only one thing will wake her—the kiss of
true love." So it came to be, and the princess slept in her remote
castle, until twelve hundred years had passed...*

A Faerie Tale

GINNY REYES
August 1998

*According to legend, a faerie must perform a loving deed to earn
her magic wand. So, too, must the leprechaun accomplish a special
task before receiving his pot of gold. But the most mystical, magical
challenge of all is . . . helping two mortals fall in love.*

Sea Spell

TESS FARRADAY

JOVE BOOKS, NEW YORK

MAGICAL LOVE is a trademark of Berkley Publishing Corporation.

SEA SPELL

A Jove Book / published by arrangement with
the author

PRINTING HISTORY
Jove edition / June 1998

The Penguin Putnam Inc. World Wide Web site address is
http://www.penguinputnam.com

ISBN: 0-515-12289-0

A JOVE BOOK®
Jove Books are published by The Berkley Publishing Group,
a member of Penguin Putnam Inc.,
200 Madison Avenue, New York, New York 10016.
JOVE and the "J" design are trademarks
belonging to Jove Publications, Inc.

PRINTED IN THE UNITED STATES OF AMERICA

10 9 8 7 6 5 4 3 2 1

Acknowledgments

Sea Spell took me into so many uncharted waters, I needed many guides.

For teaching me to think like a poacher, I thank Captain Mike Wade, California Fish and Game. Jenny Osborn of the U.S. Coast Guard helped me look for bodies and Deputy Sheriff Steve Eich taught me how to commit justifiable homicide. Sue Andrews of the Marine Mammal Hotline shared seal pup expertise. Many others explained their devotion to protecting the fierce but fragile sea.

Thanks also to Dr. Ron James, who lived in the land of selkies, to Cathy Erickson for her ocean library and my beach wedding, to Lyndi Cooper-Schroeder for faith and to Elane Osborn. When I couldn't go to the beach, she brought the beach to me.

Chris Platt, Kathy Sage and Christine Patt remain critique partners with sharp pencils and soft hearts. Thanks, guys!

Thanks to Alice Orr, for counseling of every kind and to Gail Fortune, who probably never refused a childhood dare. And most of all to Cory. Your compassion for a seal on the beach told me all I needed to know about my selkie hero.

". . . Suffer a sea change
Into something rich and strange."

The Tempest
Act I, sc. ii

Sea Spell

Prologue

GREY GALLOWS BAY
JUNE 1985

"You can't do this to me." Beth edged toward the door, away from her stepmother. "Maria said I'd meet him on Midsummer Eve, and the sun will be down in two hours!"

Carol glanced up from her magazine. "Don't be so melodramatic, Elizabeth. Maria reads tea leaves for fun. She couldn't guess you'd have nothing to do but brood in this superstitious village."

"Grey Gallows isn't a superstitious village." Beth closed her lips and wished her father, slumped in his deep yellow armchair, a legal pad on his knees, would look up.

He didn't, and Carol didn't care if Grey Gallows was the only home Beth had ever known. Carol couldn't wait to move them to San Francisco.

Thunder rattled the cottage windows, though the sky beyond showed blue.

"She certainly didn't think you'd go out in such weather searching for a"—Carol's voice dipped with suppressed laughter—" 'soul mate.' "

"I don't completely *believe* in fortune-telling, but how

could Maria know Grey Gallows has legends about Midsummer magic?"

"Unfortunately, Grey Gallows hasn't cornered the market on ignorance."

The heart, the shield, and urgency. Maria had found those symbols in Beth's cup. They promised Beth would find her true love on Midsummer Eve, but only if she defended herself.

A gale of chill wind ruffled Carol's pages as Beth opened the cottage door. Her stepmother's blond eyebrow curved up a notch.

"I won't go into town. I won't even go down on the beach."

"Jack?" Carol turned toward Beth's father.

"Have fun." His gesture might have been a wave or a plea for silence.

"Take a coat." Carol frowned at Beth's cutoff jeans and tank top.

"I'll just walk to the edge of the bluff and look down at the seals." Beth let the door slam behind her. She ran and a sudden mist curled in her wake.

Silver splinters of lightning warned her back from the edge, but the ocean beckoned. *He* must be down there. Wrapped in fog, Beth poised above the Pacific Ocean.

Early explorers mapped this finger of land as the last outpost of civilization, a slender bridge between men and the ocean's mystery. Once in a dream, Beth had followed the tide's pull into nothingness. Now, since she could not see the water, Beth closed her eyes, listened to the language of the waves, then sailed off the end of the known world.

No one noticed.

Beth surfaced and sniffed. The cold dousing made her recognize the truth. She'd half wanted to give Carol a heart attack by proclaiming independence with one grand gesture of defiance. Not that it was an impossible dive. Beth had practiced for years. Now she could plummet safely into the cove without disturbing the seals.

Treading water, Beth used both hands to clear her eyes of

seawater. No seals basked in the cove. They frolicked farther out. Around the point, driftwood-littered Lyre Beach remained empty, too. Not that she'd really expected to see a tall, handsome man hailing her from the sand, but she felt oddly lightheaded, as if Maria's magic and a summons from the sea really had compelled her leap. Her soul mate's absence put a little crimp in her exhilaration.

Beth arrowed her hands into the waves and arched her body after the seals, swimming out toward Moon Isle. Slapped by wind, translucent gray waves crested atop each other. But a little rough water didn't scare her.

What *had* frightened her was their trip into San Francisco early that day. After a terrifying plunge down Lombard Street, the crookedest street in the world, her father had escorted Carol and Beth through weird alleys to Maria's candy shop, taken one look at the spotless walls and marble slabs, probably the same sort used in morgues, then he'd abandoned them. With his gray-blond hair shining above his denim shirt, Dad whisked Carol's BMW off for a session with Hal, his mechanic pal. Carol only kept that car to keep Dad. After writing, sports-car repair was Jack Caxton's passion.

"Remember, Jack! The tacos at that café across from Hal's disagree with you!" Carol had shouted after Dad. Then things improved.

Tying a purple paisley scarf over her wild ringlets, Maria had beckoned Beth into a world scented with black tea and candlewax, spiced by wild hope. In mere hours, Maria predicted, Beth would meet the man who'd offer her love for a lifetime.

Where the heck was he?

Beth dived through the base of each wave, stroking out, breathing sips of fog as it settled. Ahead, a raft of bobbing seals greeted her. Sleek and sable, they tolerated her invasion, swimming beneath the silvery blanket of fog while thunder lumbered overhead.

She wouldn't find her one true love out here. Not unless he were a fisherman, a seal, or one of the old villagers' legendary

selkies, the seal people who enchanted mortals with earthy,
eternal magic.

Wind swirled a window in the fog and the seals rose, rearing
back against the water, peering through. The sky glared gray-
green as lightning stabbed toward shore. The crackling threat
was still building when a faint lapping rocked Beth, and the
seals disappeared.

Beth followed, diving, kicking, pulling her body deeper beneath the waves. She'd never gone wrong imitating sea creatures.

Until now. One heartbeat before the concussion of thunder,
her eyes opened on a watery world of seals scattering through
the kelp forest. The undersea explosion rolled her in bubbles.
Flippers fanned past, and a leathery tail scythed across her leg.

Up. She had to surface for breath. Leafy amber cords of
kelp snapped, and her ankle went numb. A last seal rocketed
past. Beth's pulse slammed and her chest swelled with an insane feeling of fullness. She needed air. Now.

Glimmers above told her she'd wasted air swimming toward
the ocean floor. The numb tug on her ankle meant she'd tangled herself in kelp.

Don't panic. She surged against her tether, then forced herself to stop. Panic, then struggle, then the six minutes of re-
serve oxygen was wasted. In lifesaving class, she'd memorized
the stages of drowning, but it did her no good. She was sinking.

No. Beth's legs drew up with an instinctive jerk. She bent
double, staring past the black dots crowding her vision to slip
free of the kelp.

Dots still frenzied before her eyes, making her movements
wobbly as she settled toward the sea bed. Then all the dizzying
dots converged into a single black, luminous eye. A final chain
of bubbles fluttered from her lips. Then she saw two eyes.

A huge black seal lifted his muzzle beneath her chin. Beth
flopped, heels over head, and kept sinking.

Force smacked between her shoulder blades, compelling her
toward the surface. He swam behind her, beneath her. Every-
where.

Too late. Beth felt her limbs float free. She cartwheeled down through green darkness pierced by golden shafts of sunlight from a sky she might never see again.

The seal had turned into a gypsy boy. Of course, she'd never actually seen a gypsy, and the burn in her nose and throat testified to an overdose of seawater, but as Beth's eyelids flapped open, she was convinced he looked like a gypsy should.

Dark skin. Wet black hair twisted like commas around his face. A smile more dizzying than the gull reeling against the charcoal clouds above.

Beth closed her eyes. Waves lapped over her toes. Consciousness drained away like the sand, stolen out from under her as the sea tried to take her back. The seal . . .

Pummeling pain in Beth's chest revived a minutes-old memory. He'd given her CPR. He'd breathed for her and saved her life.

He still loomed above her, no seal but a boy, using the hem of her sodden shirt to wipe her lips.

"Get away from her, you animal!" Harsher than the gull which flew screaming into the air, Carol hollered. Her feet skittered down the steps cut into the cliff.

A siren wailed from the highway. Thunder rumbled, moving away, and the boy's smile flashed again.

Could a face be half-elfin, half-grandfatherly, entirely magical? Could the eyes of a teenage boy look black and mysterious? Could a smile move into your heart and take up residence, like a cat settling down on a rainy day?

Certainly.

If you'd sustained brain damage, anything was possible.

Beth brushed away sanity, letting his smile kindle glowing warmth inside her ribs. And then the gypsy growled.

Or something. He'd ignored Carol's whooping, but Dad's low "Hey!" made the gypsy's brown-black eyes narrow like a predator's.

Later, Beth tried to remember that instant he loomed above,

staring as if he'd memorized her. Had he touched her? Had he spoken? She couldn't say. She only envisioned, over and over, the shape of his lips as they formed the words, ''Remember me.''

One

Slipping through the alleys of San Francisco after dark was a dangerous pursuit.

Beth was genuinely good at it.

The theater door had just closed behind her when a foghorn lamented the thick night. Streetlights shimmered partway through the fog, defeated before they lit the sidewalk. A pair of tourists in shorts went shivering past Beth as she stood in the shadows, waiting for her eyes to adjust to the darkness.

She had two hours to invent a spectacle that would dazzle Phoebe's mysterious Mr. Gordon.

Phoebe, theater manager and Beth's best friend, had peered over her shoulder, realigning the seams in her black stockings as she delivered the command.

"Nothing fancy, just a few people on your balcony—"

"What?"

"—an informal fête, after the last curtain." In vintage cloche hat and flapper skirt, Phoebe looked like Betty Boop, but she was deadly serious.

"Phoebe! I won't do it. I run this playhouse—"

"Of course you do, dear. Now get your little butt in gear, or I quit—got it? Wear the black jumpsuit. And lots of mascara."

Five minutes later Beth stood at the mouth of the alley she dreaded the most, trying to work up enough adrenaline to take the shortcut to Rosetti's.

As she darted into the shadowy opening, her running shoes grated on broken glass.

It's lucky for Phoebe that I live where I do, Beth raged. Perched in a flat over the theater, with a Shakespearian production in progress below, Beth couldn't punish Phoebe by pushing her down the stairs. She'd been sorely tempted to do just that, even though Phoebe had presented a convincing argument in favor of seducing Mr. Gordon. Still, Beth could have done without the fashion advice.

A window screeched overhead. Something heavy ricocheted off the brick wall before it hit asphalt. Beth dodged, bumped her shoulder on a Dumpster, and sidestepped a mound she hoped was cabbage. And then there was light.

"I knew you'd come tonight." Maria Rosetti, whose white coveralls matched the netting over her salt-and-pepper hair, stood in the open back door. "I just made your tea."

Beth slipped inside, blinking back the glare off the shop's white walls and marble candy slabs.

"Can't stay for tea." Beth drew a breath heavy with cinnamon and chocolate. A tentative wisp of jasmine curled from the cup Maria stirred. "Really, Maria. I have to present an elegant 'après theatre fête' in"—Beth pushed up her pink flannel sleeve to consult her watch—"an hour and forty-two minutes. Phoebe insists."

"You're doing the chocolate and strawberries thing, I suppose?" Maria extended the cup, then tapped her lips with a fingertip, mentally sorting through her inventory.

Beth nodded and sipped. Phoebe's fundraising instincts made her inclined toward emergency parties thrown in Beth's flat. Arranged in a collection of antique sterling serving pieces, fresh strawberries and chocolate made a quick, elegant buffet. Next, she'd pilfer champagne from Carol's hotel cellar.

"It'll have to be truffles then. Drat, they really need two hours to come to room temperature. Remind me to find a curse in that girl's tea leaves the next time I read for her."

Maria Rosetti, candy maker extraordinaire, fancied herself a charm weaver. She credited local hotels' and restaurants' demand for her candy to magic. Phoebe believed implicitly in Maria's teacup fortunes. Beth tried not to.

"Don't be too hard on her, Maria. She claims to have cornered a man with big money, who also loves my father's plays."

Maria backed out of a walk-in cooler, carrying a door-sized tray of truffles. "Your father writes wonderful plays."

"I know he does."

All the same, Jack Caxton's career had peaked ten years ago, just after he won a Tony and before he married Carol. Fortunately, Carol's dowry included the half-block of San Francisco real estate that encompassed her hotel, Maria's shop, and a tiny gem of a theater, the Foghorn Playhouse.

Maria's gloved hands moved like pistons as she packed truffles into a shipping box. "There. What else?"

"You're invited, of course. About eleven o'clock." Beth took the box, balancing it against the waistband of her jeans. She squinted out Maria's window, stalling. "I've never seen fog like this. That spangly stuff must be ice crystals. Hey, you don't happen to know this Mr. Gordon, do you?"

"If I knew some wily investor, you think I'd be paying your stepmother's outrageous rent?" Maria gazed heavenward before narrowing her gaze on Beth's teacup. "What are you worried about?"

"Poor Mr. Gordon's obviously deranged." Beth bumped the back door with her hip, maneuvered through, then answered through the screen. "Phoebe says he was entranced by my photograph in the playbill and he can't wait to meet me."

Beth had minced past a clump of newspaper as it tumbled down the alley, when Maria called after her. "Dress nice, Bethie. He might not be so crazy."

In eleven hours she'd be on the beach, her own beach,

where dressing up meant pulling a T-shirt on over her bathing suit. She could hardly wait.

If she hadn't heard their squalling, Beth might have stepped on the cats quarreling over something skeletal and smelly. The fog was that thick.

She might have missed the rear entrance to Kung Foods, too, if a whisper hadn't beckoned. "Hey, honey, want to get lucky?"

The truffle box wobbled in her grip as a match scratched to light a cigarette and a smiling face. "Eddie, if you make me drop this, you're a dead man."

"Big party? Want me to tend bar?" Eddie Kung, seventeen and avid as a mongoose, shifted from foot to foot.

"Aren't you working tonight?" Exhaust from the underground parking garage clung to him, but Eddie considered himself a dandy, so Beth wouldn't think of mentioning it.

"Let 'em park their own damn cars." He knocked at one of the barred windows, then jerked his chin toward the truffle box. "What time?"

"Eleven, if you're sure you can make it. And I need a couple flats of strawberries."

"Kung Foods' Oriental Produce and Oddities aims to please." Eddie sketched an obsequious bow and hammered on the window, backhanded. "C'mon, Ma, open up."

Door chains rattled, a bolt slid back, and the door opened a crack. "Eddie?" queried a thready voice.

Eddie ignored both the voice and the aroma of steamed shrimp and ginger root which streamed into the night. "You wearing what you have on?" Eddie asked. "Or shall I dress up?"

"Jacket and tie." Although Beth was tempted to leave on that curt note, she couldn't. "Eddie, you don't happen to know a Mr. Gordon, do you? Rich guy? Not too bright?"

Eddie snorted. "Great big sushi-eating guy with weird eyes? I don't know about dumb, but he's one fast son of a—" Eddie's teeth clamped closed. "He's like a martial artist or something. Thinks he's real bad." Eddie shrugged and glanced at his watch. "Eleven? I better hurry. Oh, and if you see

Carol—hey, she's not coming, is she?—tell her I'm really sorry about the Mercedes.''

Fifty-five minutes left to snag a half dozen bottles of Carol's champagne, shower, and bring herself up to Eddie Kung's exacting sartorial standards.

The Bronze Iris Inn's hushed elegance provided a refuge from the fog-shrouded night. Couples drank brandy and idled over chess boards in the parlor. Glassware tinkled in the French Provençal restaurant. After a glance confirmed Carol was absent from the tranquil lobby, Beth left the truffle box at the concierge desk and hurried past.

The hotel shared the fragrance of furniture polish, lavender potpourri, and honeycomb candles with the Foghorn Playhouse, but it was the scent of fresh-baked sourdough bread that led Beth toward the kitchen.

She almost made it. Beth had managed to bribe a busboy to deliver a crate of champagne to her flat, she'd retrieved the truffle box, and was heading toward the door with thirty minutes to spare, when Carol turned from straightening a trademark arrangement of iris.

Carol's blue eyes widened in despair, apparently comparing her chatelaine's chic with Beth's pink shirt and jeans. ''Child, I vow, if there's a condition called fashion-impaired, you have it.''

''Tragically, it's untreatable.'' Beth shrugged. She didn't have time for baiting her stepmother. At the beach she'd have long sunny days without Carol. ''I'm leaving. I just stopped by to borrow a crate of champagne. Phoebe's sprung another emergency reception on me.''

''Who is it this time? Not another film star?'' Carol's distaste showed in the unconscious pat she gave her cotton-candy blonde coif.

''Actually, he's an investor interested in *Where Dead Butterflies Go*. Phoebe claims that could mean ads in *Variety*, guest-shot promotion, and an all-Equity cast.''

''How wonderful.''

Carol's rare excitement was contagious. Beth sighed. The reason she'd never truly hated her stepmother was that Carol hadn't married Jack Caxton as a celebrity or—recently—tax write-off. She clearly loved him.

In an unlikely sisterhood of silence, Phoebe, Beth, and Carol kept Jack's failure from him. He wrote while they manipulated finances and rights to classic plays whose repertory appearances supported his flops. But all three women believed his newest work, *Where Dead Butterflies Go,* had the commercial punch to make Jack Caxton a star again.

"Who is this investor? Why are you doing something so obviously spur-of-the-moment? I could have given a lovely little reception."

"And done it right." Beth echoed her stepmother's implication as the inn's front doors opened. Chilled, anxious over the time, but unable to consult her watch without dropping the box, Beth hurried on. "But he's in the theatre *now*, and Phoebe says he's not the formal type."

"Eccentric." Carol nodded to a guest in a moisture-beaded overcoat.

"Besides, I'm leaving town tomorrow." Beth backed toward the door.

"Come by for brunch first. You know how Jack loves a leisurely Sunday brunch."

"No time. My alarm's set. Soon as I can cram Peaches into his carrier, I'm gone. To Grey Gallows," she added, before Carol could ask.

"Jack's given you the beach house, hasn't he?"

Beth nearly dropped the truffles. She'd kept the secret from Phoebe, from Maria and Eddie. Her friends. How on earth could Carol have guessed?

"Quit gaping, Elizabeth. Jack can't hide anything from me. It's insane—what he's doing, when that property's so valuable. Still, he thinks you belong there, writing your poetry. I told him I couldn't fathom why you'd want to live among people who think you're a lunatic."

"That's an advantage that comes with the artistic license, Carol. Poets are allowed to seem crazy." Beth felt a twinge of disloyalty in the tender spot where she hid her poetry and her past. Spellbound, maybe, but not a lunatic.

Beth had spent dozens of library hours researching her "hallucination." Whether real or dreamed, she'd encountered a time-honored archetype. At worst, he was a primal memory, at best, wild magic.

If she'd escaped drowning in, say, Cornwall, where Celtic lore still permeated the minds of intelligent folk, she would have been considered blessed, not loony. Rescue by a seal who'd transformed into a boy, would have revived tales of selkies, a highly intelligent and handsome race whose magic allowed them to walk as men or swim as seals.

By the time she settled in San Francisco, she'd stopped explaining, stopped insisting, but she'd never forgotten.

With a subdued *bong*, the inn's grandfather clock marked a quarter hour.

"Come by later if you feel like taking a look at Mr. Gordon, Carol." Beth burst into the night at a wobbly jog, wondering if she'd retrieved her black jumpsuit from the dry cleaner.

Beth she was called. *Elizabeth,* but he'd known that for years. He'd tracked her, followed her, planned one-hundred appealing conversations and discarded every one. Now he stood on her balcony, unseen and a bit worried.

Since the storm, he'd seen her six times. Once at Grey Gallows, singing and drinking beside a bonfire with Junior and some of his loud friends. When he'd learned she lived in San Francisco, his Beth-sightings became more frequent. He saw her in Ghirardelli Square and several times with her father at a Mexican café. The time he'd followed her to the maritime museum, she'd grinned in shared appreciation for a model ship with cobweb-fine rigging. In October he'd remained a few lengths behind her as she swam in a rough sea offshore from Playland, a long-dead amusement park. But Beth hadn't required rescue.

In all those times, she'd never met his eyes before moving on.

Always, Beth brimmed with contained excitement, but yesterday she'd overflowed with it. He'd longed to catch Beth's exhilaration and shower it back over her, but he couldn't think how to do it.

An auto-body shop, filled with the racket of pounding hammers and whining power tools, muffled the conversation Beth had over tacos with her father, but suddenly she'd been standing, hopping and hugging Jack around the neck until his chair had only two legs on the floor.

Tonight, at last, Gordon would speak to her again.

He leaned back against the rail around Beth's balcony. He'd slipped into the flat before she returned with the chocolate, and his impatience wound ever tighter.

Winds off the bay nipped the back of his neck, tempting him to act, to move into the room and kiss her. Her apartment was dim, lit by candles flickering inside glass lanterns. She wouldn't recognize him, at first. . . .

No. His kind were hunters. They knew the value of observing, of quick-sinewed movement. He could wait.

Inside, the one called Phoebe smiled toward another room, greeting Beth.

"*Très chic*, girlfriend." Phoebe applauded from her perch on the arm of Beth's couch, which sat jade green and welcoming in a main room with pale walls and carpets.

"It was your idea. Where's your mystery man?" Beth's voice carried clearly.

"He got restless and decided to take a walk around the block. The cast is changing. Most of them will be up. Eddie's in the lobby, looking through the lost-and-found for a tie."

"He'll probably keep on walking." Beth crossed before the open sliding-glass doors. A breeze blew the curtains inward and she glanced into the night.

He remained still.

Beth's red-gold hair, fired bright by the lanterns behind her, fanned over her shoulders, then lifted on the breeze. Night hid her expression, but her head tilted faintly, as if she sensed him.

"Not a chance he'd take off," Phoebe assured her. "He likes your looks, babe. One peek at that portrait in the lobby—"

"The one with my dad? You said the playbill."

"Both. He had 'Eureka!' written all over his handsome face." Phoebe turned to the opening door. "Hi, Eddie. Nice tie."

Gordon resented the youth's intrusion. To curb his irritation, Gordon looked down on the city's dark meanderings. He watched a traffic light change from amber to red and heard the hum of a vehicle on tracks.

Would Eddie recognize him? Perhaps not, but Eddie's street companion would. Simon thrived on skateboard purse-snatchings. He'd just surprised a woman accompanying her young to the Exploratorium, when Gordon saw him.

Now Gordon's chest rose inside the confinement of his dark shirt, grateful Eddie had come alone. Simon would remember him. Gordon didn't like purse-snatchers.

Shifting for a better view, he saw Beth wore the most amazing red high-heeled shoes. Without appearing to balance, she leaned toward a table, hands hovering as they accounted for each item. Flashing with silver, with red berries and gold champagne, the buffet presented a fine appearance, but nothing tempted him.

Beth rearranged a platter, then the silken material of her jumpsuit flared away from her legs as she turned on Phoebe. "Is he *from* San Francisco?"

Now he saw her face. As before, her skin seemed a bit sunburned. She tossed her hair away from the silver loops in her ears, away from freckled cheekbones slanting beneath sea-green eyes. He remembered those eyes.

Apparently, she thought Phoebe too slow in responding. "Is he just in town on business? Where does he live?"

" 'Offshore' is all he'll say. I'm not joking about the mysterious part." Phoebe held up a palm to fend off Beth's suspicious expression. "He's genuine, though, at least in the money department."

Three actors burst through Beth's door. Laughing, they bracketed the food table. Beth moved to the door, searching the landing and the stairs.

"Maybe he owns an island." Under cover of pouring for the new arrivals, Eddie quaffed half a glass of champagne before Beth snatched it away and dumped the drink into a potted fern.

Phoebe touched her friend's sleeve, looking earnest. "Settle down. He'll be here, and you won't be disappointed. I'll tell you one last thing, shall I? It's a feeling I have, about Mr. Gordon.

"Have you ever heard of a hurricane party?" Phoebe's voice invited an audience. The actors and two women who'd just appeared on the landing moved to listen. "Hurricane parties are the most terrible, wonderful things in the world. When I was a teenager on the Gulf Coast, I went to every one I could.

"First, you race the hurricane, driving like crazy. Whoever called the party waits at the door and whisks you down to the cellar. With no windows and no light but candles or flashlights, it's eerie, but exciting." Phoebe glanced around Beth's apartment as if conjuring that alien environment. "Sometimes you play cards, or neck. You drink wine and eat whatever was in the kitchen when the radio announced the emergency.

"And then you wait: scared to death something will happen and just as afraid it won't." Phoebe's audience drifted away, leaving Beth to the tale's whispered conclusion.

"That's what Mr. Gordon 'feels' like. Don't wish him here any sooner than he wants to come. He sort of gives me chills."

Gordon pushed away from the balcony rail. Surfacing from the fog and darkness outside, he advanced toward Beth, then suppressed his speed. Frightening Beth would wound him like a shark's bite.

"Good evening, Miss Caxton." He took her hand—small and hot, a little sticky with champagne—and watched her face for remembrance. Beth's pupils pooled wide to take him in.

Self-conscious, he reviewed his appearance. He didn't always get things right. This time, he had. His hair was tied back. His shirt was buttoned and loose jacket *un*buttoned. He wore jeans and shoes. The mystery of human trappings, or their lack, often caused him trouble.

Beth's expression was surprised, not critical. The pulse in her fingers did not seem a fear response. If he judged by the surging where their hands joined and the pounding that traveled from his wrist, up to the crease in his arm, he thought she might feel attracted.

He cherished the possibility and his delight was only slightly carnal.

"Mr. Gordon, I'm so glad to meet you. I hope you enjoyed the play?" Beth's cool smile was meant to disguise her jittery pulse.

Politely he released her hand and instantly wanted to reclaim her arm or nudge her shoulder. He didn't. The social handshake had been a gift, prematurely intimate.

Human rules dictated he watch for a second opportunity. If she stumbled, he could steady her, but that seemed unlikely. He'd watched Beth maneuver through the trash-strewn alleys of San Francisco. She moved with unfailing grace.

"Phoebe tells me you're a man of rare good taste. You like my father's plays."

"And your portrait in the playbill." He'd misspoken, striking her still, drawing raised eyebrows from the others. But he'd found silence a great tool among humans. He didn't apologize.

"Thank you." Beth reacted with a faint chuckle, and he marked it as the first time he'd seen her laugh.

With jerky starts and short smiles, she introduced him to everyone in the quickly filling room. Rather than show displeasure at the crowd, he shook hands and dragged his feet a bit, hoping she'd tow him along by the arm.

He disregarded names, except for a gaudy-skirted woman named Maria who studied him with amusement. He noticed challenge in the handshake of a red-haired actor who hugged Beth's shoulders.

"Oh, you thief of love," he addressed Gordon in a booming voice. "Have you come by night and stolen my lover's heart?"

Thief of love? Gordon recognized them as words from the play, but were they aimed as a challenge or mere banter?

"That's my line," crowed a voice across the room. Beth rolled her eyes toward the ceiling as she escaped the embrace.

A joke, then. He didn't wait for Beth to take his arm. He took hers. It felt firm and narrow beneath the slippery black garment. He guided her toward a painting. Wall decorations were meant to be praised. With this one, he needn't feign admiration.

Rippling curtains in shades of tan and beige framed a rectangle of azure ocean. Both realistic and improbable, cool and welcoming, it reminded him of Grey Gallows beach.

Gordon loved it, but he curbed his joy. Humans didn't celebrate each discovery. It was one of their saddest shortcomings. "Tell me about this," he encouraged her.

"Do you like it?" As with the play, she assumed he did and rushed on, a little breathless. "I bought it on Union Square from a street vendor. An illegal street vendor, unfortunately, or I'd have more of his work."

Gordon leaned forward to study the painting's lower corners. "Unsigned original, but have you searched other tourist-packed areas? Those sorts seem to get around."

"So do I." When she shook her head the herbal fragrance of her hair drew him nearer. "No, I wouldn't be surprised if he'd left the city."

"Just how do you fit into your father's artistic empire? Your playbill biography only listed a degree in Communications and the title 'producer.'"

"You can read that as glorified 'gofer.' Truly," she answered his unspoken skepticism. "I live rent-free above the theater and do everything Phoebe can't bear."

"The creative side of the business, correct? Like writing press releases, angling for publicity, and scheduling *Midsummer Night's Dream* near the solstice?"

"Like that." Beth seemed pleased he'd noticed the play's timing.

"And throwing this party together at a moment's notice."

He watched her draw breath, perhaps trying to spare his feelings and flatter, without resorting to a lie.

With that effort, their eyes met and held. He watched Beth's eyes turn as misty green and unfocused as they had when she lay on the beach, dazed and half-drowned, ten years ago.

"Where do we go from here, Beth?" The next mystical step must be hers, but the words had scarcely left Gordon's lips when he felt watched.

He saw Phoebe beyond Beth's shoulder, but she was pre-occupied with a truffle. Brisk steps clicked an approach, while Beth stood mesmerized by his question.

Since he was the one who'd spoken too soon, he must save her from an intemperate remark. He stopped her in the only way that came to mind. "I meant financial affairs, I'm afraid."

Beth's sun-brushed skin turned deep pink. She cleared her throat in embarrassment. "Well, from here, I go home for a vacation, Mr. Gordon."

Still, the spy hadn't shown herself. He couldn't turn away from Beth and search the room.

"Home?" he coaxed, and though Beth's eyes feinted toward the painting, she remained intent on snubbing him.

"Yes, I've decided the druids had the right idea about mid-summer. Get out of town, dance a little, chant a little . . ."

". . . sacrifice a few virgins." Pointedly tapping Beth's shoulder from behind, Phoebe interrupted. "You sound positively poisonous, Beth. Have some chocolate to sweeten your tongue." She popped a truffle into Beth's unresisting mouth. "Oh, and here comes Carol."

Phoebe might never have spoken, for the effect it had on Beth. "After I return, Mr. Gordon, perhaps we can have lunch and discuss your interest in the play."

A pungent floral scent surrounded them. Beth flinched as the woman planted a kiss on her cheek.

"Beth, dear, sorry I'm so tardy." The indigo business suit flattered the woman's delicate blond features, but Gordon felt an instinctive backing away. Then he recognized her.

"Mr. Gordon, I'm Carol Caxton." By introducing herself, she chided Beth's manners. "I hear you're an admirer of my husband's work."

Damned harpy. She'd split them up once before. At least this time she wasn't screaming. Gordon nodded.

"I find the idea of a television superhero who's none too super in real life fascinating," she recited. "Just the kind of high-concept script that would translate well to television, don't you agree?''

Bearing a champagne flute which she forced into the woman's hand, Phoebe grimaced at Carol Caxton's hard sell. Beth seemed impervious and stiff, as if her skin actually hurt from blushing.

A cold wind, salt heavy and moaning, blasted through from the balcony. Beth grabbed the excuse to move away and close the sliding-glass doors.

He wanted to see her that way on the beach, wind-tossed hair, clothes clinging. This was why he hadn't forgotten her. This was why he remained solitary, unable to find a mate in the sea. Ancient magic had decreed it and he must obey: the female he needed lived on land.

"Mr. Gordon, I feel certain we've met." Carol Caxton ignored Phoebe and sharpened her regard.

"Mrs. Caxton—" Gordon laughed. He shook his head, unable to look away from Beth, unable to smother the joy vaulting up inside his chest. "Anything's possible."

Two

Wet by mist off Grey Gallows Bay, then baked in the afternoon sun, the ruins of the only house Gordon had ever lived in smoked as if they still burned.

Black and broken to ragged lengths, a few boards still framed the home's outline. The foundation edged a lake of cold powdered ash and wood chunks scored by fire, shattered by their crash to the floor. Except there no longer was a floor.

Junior and Al must have escaped. Gordon's eyes closed. He focused his perceptions on this spot. He heard a car sigh past on the street behind him and a gull's wheeling call. Still weary from transformation, he found no magic, only memories.

He squatted, looking for something charred but recognizable. Nothing could burn this completely without warning, could it?

Gordon glanced toward the neighboring houses, sitting untouched. No curtains twitched, hiding watchers. This was a working neighborhood. Fishermen would be afloat, hauling in the day's catch. Their wives would be in the cannery up the coast, coming off shift.

Next door, a Nintendo game blared disharmony. Summer vacation had begun. He could ask the kids what had happened, but he might make some bizarre blunder.

Gordon studied the charcoal skeleton of walls, trying to make out individual rooms. His experience with such disasters was slight. He'd felt loss, of course. The sea abounded with danger and he'd begun learning the perils found on land twenty years ago. But fire confounded him. He found its fierce beauty overwhelming.

The refrigerator! Scorched brown and streaked like marble, it still stood upright. The freezer compartment had rarely closed completely. At any time, he and Junior could expect an avalanche of TV dinners. Now the freezer door hung open, finally empty.

The appliance gave Gordon the landmark he needed. He strode to the front door's threshold and set his jaw, battling a wave of melancholy. The last time he'd entered this house was the day Beth nearly drowned, the day Al kicked him out for saving her.

Gordon faced the ravaged kitchen, as if he still heard the voice that had greeted him as he stood shivering at the front door. No magic, only memories. . . .

"Hey, man, want a burrito?" Junior's head had been in the freezer, but his hand waggled a plastic-wrapped packet.

Gordon slammed the door and leaned against it as if keeping out sharks. How could it be a bad thing he'd saved the girl?

"No burrito, thanks."

Whenever he came ashore, he thought *this time* he'd learn it all. He was always wrong. The first time, he'd discovered a ragged boy named Junior. They'd become friends and Gordon thought that proved he knew how to live among shore-dwellers.

"You been runnin'? You sound like it." Junior leaned his back against the microwave oven while it hummed and beamed light.

"Tell you about it when I catch my breath."

"Whatever." Junior stared into the machine, hurrying it.

Gordon didn't know how to explain the encounter with the girl, but Junior would understand.

Like many of Gordon's family, Junior's mother had died after a shark attack. They'd discovered that bond the first time they prowled the beach together. Humans had frowned at the two footloose boys as they pocketed trinkets careless folk left behind.

He and Junior formed a team, saving bracelets, books, and wallets from washing out to sea. Later, Gordon learned this was wrong. Stealing, it was called, and against human law.

The next time they met, in autumn, Gordon wore seal form and Junior threw a rock, shouting at him to quit scaring off the damn fish.

After that, Gordon approached only during summer, in his human skin. Those times, Junior took him home, fed him, let him sleep in the yard, and taught him human-speech.

Junior hid from his sire, Al, and made Gordon do the same. Gordon hid, though Al was no different from any other bull. They were all reckless and violent with youngsters.

Gordon crossed to the kitchen table, where Junior used yesterday's newspaper as a placemat.

"I'm going to get a Ford 5250. See if I don't." Junior read the classified ads, trying not to drip cheese. He gave an encouraging grunt when Gordon nudged his chair. "What, man?"

Gordon knew he should confess. They were adolescents, old enough that Junior could help him. After all, Junior had taught him with television. Junior had dismissed Gordon's origin as imagination, and laughed at his seal name, saying it sounded like a stepped-on Chihuahua, then encouraged him to pick a name from *Sesame Street*.

Gordon stared at the kitchen window. He couldn't see outside and that made him uneasy. The glass reflected his image. Was he a misfit or a magician? Even his mother couldn't explain his ability to change, at will, from seal to human. In the old times, transformation only took place on Midsummer Eve.

In the reflection, Gordon saw stacks of bills and magazines, a heap of orange fishing floats, paper plates and soda cans, but when he considered his image, he saw what most others missed.

They saw an underfed teenager with gleaming black hair and quick movements. "There's something about his eyes," humans admitted, defending their suspicions. Gordon understood. He knew why his eyes made people uneasy.

His were selkie's eyes and they glittered with magic a thousand years old.

"I have no clue what you're starin' at, Gordy, but knock it off. You're givin' me the creeps."

Gordon settled across the table from Junior.

"Something weird happened." He rushed the words, but now it was too late.

Al's boots crunched on the gravel drive. The front door rebounded against the wall.

"I'll say something weird happened! Pretty damned weird!" Al dropped his lunch pail and flung a slicker across the kitchen. "Sheriff Reynold's got every black-and-white in the county cruising town, looking for you."

Gordon stood. If Al stayed on the other side of the table, things would be fine. Gordon only worried for Junior.

"Why? What happened?" Junior turned in his chair, trying to stay cool, but these fights wrung his feelings in a way Gordon couldn't comprehend.

"Your freakin' friend jumped a half-drowned girl, is what!" Spittle came from Al's tongue, and Gordon smelled beer. Not a lot, this time, but enough to make Al difficult.

"No way." Junior's bored sigh was calculated to inflame Al, to divert his anger from Gordon.

"Shut up! Hell, you wouldn't know trouble if it bit you on the ass!"

"Gordon's my friend." Junior lifted a scrap of cheese from the newspaper. "Kick him out if you like, but don't yell at him."

Gordon moved past Al, bumping shoulders with the man, taunting him, but Al wouldn't be distracted.

"Little girly-boy, hangin' around the house, reading, hiding. What're you going to do about it?"

Junior didn't answer. He waited for the first blow to fall. There came a time when old bulls drove out the young ones. Junior couldn't recognize that time had come.

"Hey, Al!" Gordon shoved the man between the shoulder

blades. Al's white T-shirt was thin, pecked with tiny holes from years of bleach.

Al rounded on him and Gordon slipped aside. Human movements were no match for seal deftness, even ashore.

"Al, I saved a drowning girl, then gave her CPR. That's it." Gordon leaned his weight forward, daring Al to hit him. That was what young males did, no matter how foolhardy.

Al covered his face with widespread fingers, then he forced them through red-gray hair.

Gordon caught Junior's embarrassed shrug before Al scrubbed both palms over the beard he shaved in the predawn darkness. "Damn." With bloodshot eyes he stared at Gordon. "I know that. They don't. And I don't need any cops pawing around in here."

King of the Salvagers, Al MacDonald called himself, claiming it was a fisherman's right, handed down from his Scottish father, going back centuries. Al riffled through the wallets Junior found and kept the credit cards for riotous trips to San Francisco. Once he'd even taken Junior and Gordon. For such a large village, San Francisco bloomed with the smells of fresh fish. Gordon loved it.

"This is a small town, and you picked the wrong girl. Not summer trash, but Beth Caxton."

Al sneered at Junior's reaction. Gordon wondered why he hadn't recognized her. Junior had pointed out the girl on the rusty bike and admitted he was half in love with her.

"Yeah. Her dad's a hermit playwriter, not a bad guy, but he's gone and married some hotshot hotel owner from S.F. She was down there screaming bloody murder about catching the naked kid—"

Gordon remained still. Clothing was another human obsession he didn't understand. Sometimes, when he made the transition quickly, he forgot.

"—she saw hunkered over Beth." Al picked up his slicker, shook it out. The smell of diesel filled the kitchen anew as he folded it over a chair back. He stopped to study his wrinkled hands.

"Y'know what my old man says? He says the sea's a jealous mistress and you shouldn't never save a drowning woman. The sea'll get back at ya." Al shot a glance at his son. "One way or another."

"I don't believe that." Gordon recalled seals who wouldn't leave dying companions. Seals would not, selkies *could not* leave a swimmer in distress. Unless the swimmer had harmed seal folk. Gordon hadn't thought humans were so different.

"Believe what you like, but do it out of my house." Al reached for the wall telephone. "Kid, I don't care if you're a runaway or what the hell your story is, turned loose on the beach all summer, but get out. I'm calling the sheriff just to show what an upstanding citizen I am."

Gordon took a step toward the door. As Al dialed, Gordon met Junior's eyes. With a nod, he promised he'd be back.

"You know where that leaky dinghy is." Al moved his lips away from the phone's mouthpiece and nodded toward the beach. "I'm telling Reynolds' dispatcher I saw you running toward the highway."

Sometimes memory was magic enough.

Gordon flattened his hand on the burned refrigerator. Al was too cantankerous to die, and Junior would have saved his raging father at any cost.

Gordon turned from the unhappy house and walked down the alleyway. That last night he'd avoided streetlights, letting night air, heavy with kelp and the smell of wet rocks, guide him.

Even now, the muscles in Gordon's thighs tightened, driving him on faster, toward the sea, toward home. But—Beth.

All those summers she'd lived in Grey Gallows. Last night in San Francisco, he should have asked her where. Why had he never seen her as he did that last day, cutting through the waters, lithe as a dolphin?

Now he could smile about the way she'd battled drowning. She'd fought back last night, too, when she thought he mocked her attraction. Beth covered her weakness well. If he'd never seen her lying on her tangled reddish hair, still and pale, he might have judged her indestructible. If she allowed it, he'd guard her against any danger.

The licorice scent of wild anise rose from a dry yard as Gordon stopped at the end of a block. A sheriff's car cruised past.

Except for that one night, he'd never had cause to fear them. Still, he did. The car's taillights brightened, letting a child cross the street. Gordon waited, wishing the car's stealthy prowling didn't remind him of a black-and-white killer whale.

Now, at the human age of twenty-seven, he puzzled over the fear that had frustrated his magic and kept him in seal form. He'd ached for his friendship with Junior and curiosity about Beth.

Looking back, he'd known he'd been safer at sea. Grey Gallows' residents numbered in hundreds, not thousands. Someone would surely have recognized him. If they had locked him in jail, it would have killed him.

That feeling, that wild desperation against enclosed spaces, kept him away. No matter that the shore had beckoned stronger than the sea, he could not transform when he was fearful.

Years later he'd returned, hoping to explain, but Junior, his face expressionless and as hard as Al's, pretended not to recognize him.

Surf Street. Gordon remembered crouching behind a boulder, here, at the edge of the last pavement he'd had to cross before walking on sand.

To his left soared Grey Gallows. The rocky spires, visible far out to sea, still jutted into the air from the end of a hooked peninsula with a high bluff and solitary house. To his right, the village had bustled with men eager to become vigilante avengers. Across Surf Street, waves had crested lacy white, offering to hide him, to rock him to sleep where he belonged.

Here he stood again. A dog barked from the bed of a blue truck speeding past. This time Gordon walked toward town.

Beth had forgotten cat food. Nothing else, not anti-venin for a rattlesnake bite, could have forced her into the Village Store. But Peaches was hungry.

Beth reduced her speed as she passed Gimp's, a seedy tavern on the outskirts of town.

Damn. She'd remembered canned goods, milk, a Styrofoam cooler packed with diet drinks, cheese, milk, and ten leftover truffles. She'd brought loaves of Carol's fresh sourdough bread, enough cheap burgundy wine to last the summer, and even a metal tape measure for taking the dimensions of her roof. Because it was now her roof, she'd do the patching it had needed for years. She'd remembered to have the power turned on, too. That sort of self-sufficiency would normally have made her feel pretty cocky. If only she could forget last night.

She'd made an utter fool of herself over the handsomest man in North America.

Beth pulled into the randomly paved parking lot. The small grocery and general store was run by a man she emphatically did not want to see.

Beth turned off the ignition, looked at her image in the rearview mirror, and flicked her fingers through her bangs. She looked windblown, as if she'd just driven two hundred miles with the top down. She had, and enjoyed every mile, until Peaches' complaints started.

The cat butted his face against the plastic of his carrier.

"Couldn't you kill something to eat?"

Peaches yowled a reproach as Beth flopped the Fiat's convertible top forward to shade her black leather seats. She left her sunglasses on, hoping to remain incognito.

Inside the cool cave of a store, Beth pretended fascination with a display of boxed cat food.

He stood at the checkout counter, rotund and caramel-colored from his thinning hair on down. *Meow Mix, Cat Chow, Alley Cat.* Of course, Karl hadn't seen her in two years and only briefly then. But that wasn't the encounter she wanted him to forget. *Salmon flavor, liver, and farm-fresh poultry.* She'd grown a foot taller than the fifteen-year-old he'd loaded into the volunteer fire department's ambulance, ten years ago. *Crude protein not less than 30%.* And she'd certainly gained a certain amount of social polish in San Francisco.

"Hey, hon! They're all the same. Don't take one from the bottom of the display or they'll—"

Crash to the floor, attracting the attention of every single human being within hearing range.

Beth hurried to gather the boxes. By then, Karl stood beside her, helping.

"Happens all the time." He reconstructed the pyramid of merchandise. "Maybe if you took those dark glasses off, inside, it'd help. Hey, aren't you Beth Ann Caxton?"

"Hi, Karl. I thought that might be you." She fumbled with her purse. "I'm hurrying out to the cottage. Hungry cat, you know?" She'd forgotten to bring small bills, but twenty dollars would be a bargain if it ransomed her out of here.

"I think I can hear him yowling, at that." Karl cocked an ear toward the parking lot, but his eyes never left her face. "Charmaine, come on over here." He motioned to a bored woman lounging near the cash register. "Remember Beth Caxton?

Beth remembered Charmaine by the quick flash of resentment that crossed her face, but the eggplant-colored hair was new.

"Hi." Beth had her money out. She moved toward the suddenly serpentine line at the checkout stand.

As he recited prices, Karl recounted that whole awful evening, ten years ago.

"Most excitement this town ever saw. We had the chance to use the ambulance and call out the sheriff. There was walkie-talkies crackling—"

Beth fought off the wash of clamminess as she recalled a voice describing her. *White teenaged female, possible drowning victim, possible assault victim, breathing, but disoriented.*

"I was trying to get a blood-pressure cuff Velcroed on Beth—what are those tomatoes a pound, Charmaine, do you remember?—while her stepmother was screaming, 'I saw him, crouched over her like a vampire!' Remember that, Beth Ann?"

A half dozen customers turned to catch Beth's weak smile. "Carol's still pretty melodramatic."

The customer in line behind her, an old man with a clipped white beard, leaning on a cane, made a soothing sound, but Karl wasn't ready to let her off.

"Turns out no one actually attacked Beth. When she got to tell her side of the story, it was a lot more interesting." All eyes pinned her, once more.

Beth shrugged. "I was swimming, ran into some rough waves, and started taking on water. A stranger hauled me out and gave me CPR." Only one man, smelling of sardines, stood between her and the cash register. "Just a dumb kid, lucky to survive."

"And . . ." Karl's voice dared her to fill in the blanks.

"*And* we all lived happily ever after. Charmaine, you know, maybe I better take three boxes, instead of just one. Could you snag a couple more for me?" The longer she stayed out of town, the better.

"Beth told the paramedics she was swimming and dived under to escape the lightning." Karl's voice underlined Beth's foolishness. "Never did quite understand why you went out in that storm. Anyway, she said her leg got caught in the kelp, and by time she got loose, she was outta breath, sinking, and a seal, a big old black sea lion, jammed her in the back with his snout and pushed her to the beach.

"All this time, Beth's babbling that the seal turned into a *boy* and that boy was the one who gave her CPR! And she's sneezing and coughing up salt water. We were sure she was hysterical, out of her head."

"Could've seen a ghost." The sardine-scented man paused with his change in his hand. He raised his voice against the mutters of derision. "With all the pirate hangings they did there at Gallows Point, it could've been a ghost."

Beth had reached the register, at last. *A ghost.* She'd forgotten the popularity of that notion. Beth bumped the stack of cat food boxes against Karl's hand.

"All I know, is Junior said—"

"You hush about Junior, Charmaine." Karl's voice lowered. "It's all over between the two of you, and I won't hear another word."

"What'd the young fellow look like? I forget." The white-bearded man Beth had taken for an ally piped up behind her.

It took that little to dispel Karl's ire with Charmaine.

"Said he looked like a dark-skinned gypsy boy. *Naked*, said her stepmom. 'Bout that time, Beth Ann—she was only fifteen!—bolts upright from where we had her laid out on the sand and says, 'He was *naked*?' And I said, to the ambulance paramedic, there, 'I think you can upgrade her level of consciousness, Sport. She don't sound disoriented. She sounds like a healthy teenage girl to me!' "

The laughter swelled and broke around her. Beth scooped up her brown paper sack as she headed for the door.

"He saved my life." Beth joined in with the laughter, but she heard her own conviction. "See you later, Karl, Charmaine."

Beth climbed back into the Fiat. She slung the sack onto the passenger's side floor. "I hope you're satisfied, cat."

Actually, Beth felt satisfied with herself. Loyalty was important. Who would you support if not the seal-man who breathed life into you?

The white-bearded guy limped from the store, empty-handed. He paused at her open car window.

"Miss, you're the one lives at Gull Cott, am I right?"

Gull Cott. Beth hadn't heard the name for years.

"Yes, you're right." Only the old-timers knew the gray-and-white cottage had ever had a name.

"I always did believe in your apparition." He continued walking toward the edge of town. Beth couldn't quite remember who he was, until he called out again, over his suspendered shoulder.

"He weren't no ghost, dearie." The old man was Gimp MacDonald, Junior's crazy Scots grandfather. "He was a selkie, sure as spit."

Beth supposed she should feel comforted to have a partner in lunacy.

Three

At the end of the dirt road, Beth found her beach.

She shucked off her shoes, left them in the car, then walked barefoot to the water's edge. Waves rustled like blue petticoats, crisscrossing with contrary tides which kept most tourists up shore, toward town. Solitary and serene, a dark bird paddled in a calm amid the currents.

My beach. Beth dug her toes into the wet sand and stared toward the horizon, filling her eyes with sky and sea. Gladness so sharp it almost brought tears cut through her. She loved San Francisco, but Grey Gallows was home.

"C'mon, cat." Beth snagged Peaches' carrier from the car and grabbed her keys. It was only three o'clock. She'd have plenty of beach time after she'd unpacked.

Beth picked across the gravel parking area and up the rough steps cut into the cliff.

"Ow." While Peaches yowled criticism over his unsteady transportation, Beth consoled herself. Her feet would be summer-tough in a few weeks, ready to take her secret seaward path to the seals' cove.

The weathered cottage was the highest thing for miles, except for the rock spires that jutted up at the end of the football field-sized bluff. Though surrounded by head-high dandelions and thistles, the proud cottage turned its back on the bluff to stare over the ocean.

Beth inserted the new gold key, but the door swung inward, unlocked. Shuttered against the day's heat, the cottage's main room swam aquarium-green. Beth left the cat carrier on the floor and the door open.

Peaches protested. He'd been counting on escape. Frankly, Beth didn't want to close herself inside until she figured out why the unlocked door made her so uneasy.

A faint scent of smoke, more like barbecue than tobacco, hung in the room. She unlatched the shutters, folded them back, and noticed a man's T-shirt slung over the back of the leather couch.

Beth drew a breath, then let it out in a sustained, "Okay." She walked to the doorway of her room. The rainbow spread lay folded across the foot of the bed. She always tucked it up over the pillow.

She'd last been in the cottage in April. She'd driven Phoebe here for a weekend vacation, but the sky had turned gloomy and the water turbulent. Unwilling to sip espresso and doze, Phoebe had fidgeted with cross-stitch, peering up to ask questions. Did the roof always leak? Could waves cover the narrow peninsula road, cutting them off from civilization? Didn't the isolation make Beth anxious?

Not until now. Beth made sure the door stood open, then moved into the kitchen. She flicked the light switch. The power was on, but what she really needed was a telephone. *Hi, Karl, who's been sleeping in my bed?*

He'd probably have a hunch. The curse and blessing of small towns was everyone knowing everyone's business. She'd failed to slip through town unnoticed. Her burglar wouldn't fare better.

He was a very neat burglar. A can of cleanser sat out and the kitchen was cleaner than she'd left it. He'd stacked a pile of paperback books on the kitchen table. They reeked of woodsmoke. Hemingway, *The Best Short Science Fiction of 1987*, a few tattered novels, and a new book. Beth slipped it from the bottom of the stack. *How to Make a Killing at Sea*.

A mound of black and red fish, apparently in their death throes, decorated the cover.

The door creaked. Beth started, dropping the book. No one was there.

Wait a minute. Why should she feel guilty? She wasn't the intruder.

Ignoring Peaches' cry, Beth stormed back to the car for her supplies. She jammed everything in the refrigerator or onto shelves, then snapped open a sack and stacked the books inside. Next, she collected a comb and an electric shaver from her bathroom. Little bits of whisker littered the sink, reaffirming her decision to live alone. Finally she folded the T-shirt, put it with the other things, and set the bag at the head of the path down to the gravel. He had to arrive from that direction. When he did, she'd be perched on her roof, ready to explain she didn't extend hospitality to burglars.

The sun-cooked roof needed more than a few patches.

Squatting on her heels, Beth turned down her radio, peeled off the khaki shirt she'd tossed over her red bikini, and tried to deny the destruction done by years of wet wind. There wasn't an undamaged shingle on the entire roof and some places felt distinctly spongy. Chapter One of her fix-it book said ''spongy'' was a bad sign.

Beth weighed the tape measure in her palm. What should she measure? She'd probably be safer inside the cottage, facing her burglar, than scuttling around on this weak roof. Besides, she wanted to climb down to the cove.

Bobbing black heads showed seals swimming toward shore. If she judged by other seasons, the bull seals would be gone, surging south in search of food. The pups would be about three weeks old, old enough to be left ashore while their moms went out for lunch.

A barking-honking cacophony verified her guess. Mothers and pups exchanged their private calls, pairing up for the evening.

Beth calculated that she could stash the ladder, lock the cottage, and clamber down the path in time to watch the pups nurse. She'd leave the burglar to interpret her message for himself.

Then she saw him.

A blue pickup truck bucked down the gravel road leading to Beth's beach. She stayed crouched on the roof, focusing the niggling memory the truck stirred.

"Oh, hell." Beth snatched up her shirt and buttoned it to her throat. Couldn't a woman make one youthful mistake? Why wasn't there an expression which went "Girls will be girls"?

Junior MacDonald was her burglar.

He slammed the truck door, hushed the big dog tied in the back, and ruffled a hand over his hair before squinting toward the bluff. He climbed the rough-cut steps, kicked the sack out of his path, and headed for the cottage.

"Hey!" Beth stood and walked toward the roof's edge. She hung her hands on her hips. "I guess it's true what they say."

"What's that?" Junior shaded his eyes against the sun at her back.

" 'Only the good die young.' "

"Seems kind of harsh, Beth Ann."

"You scared the heck out of me. I thought I had a burglar." Beth raised her sunglasses to stare at him. That night on the beach, she'd told herself Junior looked like a young, feral Robert Redford. "Besides"—she gestured to the radio—"I'm not responsible. Doesn't this town play anything but oldies?"

"If you're done acting like the lady of the manor, why don't you come down so I can explain?"

"Can't." Beth flourished the tape with professional flare. That stopped him.

"I'll come up, then."

He was still thin and blond with a wispy mustache. He'd apparently graduated from shoplifting to breaking and entering, and she'd bet his father was still the meanest drunk in town.

As he came up the ladder, Beth noticed Junior had filled out a little. It made her nervous.

"My house burned down two nights ago."

Only the good die young. "Junior, I'm sorry! I didn't know. You must think I'm the most heartless—" She grabbed his arm to steady herself.

"Careful. Sit back down. Sheriff'll think I broke your neck to get hold of the house."

She settled into a squat, so the hot shingles wouldn't burn her legs. His remark was a little graphic, but she deserved it. "What started it?"

"Me and Al fought, he drank and I left, but the state arson guys Reynolds brought in say Al passed out on the couch, smoking." He frowned at her sympathetic sound. "Hey, it's a pretty familiar story in my neighborhood."

Her face must have betrayed the questions she was afraid to ask.

"He's going to be all right. Smoke inhalation, mostly, and some second-degree burns on his arms."

"How bad's the house?"

"Burned *down*, isn't that what I said? Since you weren't using the cottage, I helped myself. Now, I'll take my things and stay on the boat.

"I thought about calling you," Junior added, before Beth could ponder the paltriness of his possessions.

Junior and his father, like most fisherman, lived from catch to catch. The size of their checks matched the weight of their catch. Anything left over after food had probably gone to beer, not medical insurance.

"Don't worry about it." Beth managed to keep her voice cordial. "You can stay."

"Yeah? Maybe after you go home." He glanced toward the steps. Was he considering sleeping in his truck? "How long are you gonna be here?"

"I'm not sure." Unwilling to admit she had two places to live, Beth stalled. Finally Junior's blue stare made her blurt the truth. "Dad gave it to me."

"Gave it—but you're not planning to live here, not after San Francisco?"

"You don't know anyone who'd buy it, do you?" She'd

meant it as a joke. The rage that flashed into his eyes reminded
Beth she barely knew Junior.

Home-schooled by her dad, Beth had known few children
until the day Junior laughed at her clumsy bike-riding, then
patched the flat tire her father was too preoccupied to fix.

For years they'd watched each other, but rarely spoken, until
the night of her rescue. While everyone else gossiped, Junior
slipped into her hospital room to say he believed her. Before
he explained, Carol shooed him out and subjected Beth to an
hour-long harangue against bad boys.

The lecture backfired one night when Beth was nineteen.

"Sell it? You're not one of those Sable Bay-ers, are you?"
Junior's smirk jarred her worse than his glare.

"I don't know what you're talking about. Let's get down
from here." Beth backed toward the ladder.

"Sorry. Just—some folks, like Karl—want to rename the
town—"

"Rename Grey Gallows? Sable Bay sounds like an upscale
subdivision! They can't be serious."

"Pretty serious." Junior's face turned as grim as it had
when speaking of the fire. "They think it'll attract outsiders.
Karl wants this to be a 'bedroom community' for San Francisco. I guess it's possible. I had an offer—more than Al and
I make in two years—on our lot before the fire department
quit watching for hot spots."

"Will you take it?" The idea of yuppies infiltrating her
refuge horrified Beth, but it might be a way out for Junior.

"And do what? It's not enough to quit, and we can't do
nothing but fish. That's what the Sable Bay-ers are counting
on." He frowned toward the water as the seals' barking carried
on the wind. "Damn pests are drivin' us out. Get rid of them
and a man might make a decent living."

California sea lions were protected by law. She needn't fight
with him over that, too. Junior turned back to study her legs.

"What're you tryin' to do here?" His hand brushed her
knee as he picked up the tape measure.

Beth rearranged the hem of her khaki shirt. "I'm reroofing
my house."

"The hell you say!" Junior laughed outright.

Beth did not shove him off the roof. "It's been leaking for
a long time. I thought I could just patch it, but once I got up
here, I decided just to measure the whole thing."

"I'll help you."

In fact, Junior directed and Beth obeyed, and though his
skill saved her hours of study and labor, she resented it. It was
her roof, her house, her tape measure, and she craved the satisfaction of fixing it herself.

Junior even remembered the dimensions until they reached
the ground. "Write them down, but you can't shingle over
what's up there, you know."

Beth kept the incredulity to herself.

"There's at least forty years and a thousand pounds of roofing up there. Add another layer and it's gonna collapse."

There must be a tool for removing old shingles before adding new ones. She'd bet Karl knew what it was called.

"You need a roofing shovel," Junior mused. "And probably a Dumpster to pitch all that in." His face lit. "You know,
I could do it for you. It'd be a good deal for both of us!"

Junior's house had burned to the ground. His father lay in
the hospital. She was banishing him to quarters on a fishing
boat. He needed the money. And though all that made her feel
heartless, she wanted to do this herself.

Junior misread her hesitation.

"Look, Beth, if it's about that night on the beach—forget
it." He sank his thumbs so far into his pockets Beth heard his
boots creak. "I have."

"It's not that—"

"Forget it." He made a wide dismissing motion, then
scooped up his sack, moving away through the twilight. Beth
trailed after with half-uttered offers of dinner. "Really, forget
everything. I'm sorry if I messed anything up."

As Junior stamped down the steps to his truck, he looked
like the boy everybody's mother warned them about, only sad-
der.

"Hey, Junior!"

Past her Fiat, he stopped, but he didn't turn back.

"I just want to do my own roof. It wasn't the beach." Beth saw him climb into his truck. At first she thought the wind had snatched away her words.

His tires bit gravel in a reckless turn away from the shore. As he sped toward the highway, Junior's huge fisherman's hand appeared out the window, gesturing thumbs-up.

He'd drive off the other male and hope he could stop short of murder. Jealousy was one human emotion which turned bestial in a hurry.

Gordon placed his seal skin back into the water-proof ammunition box. He fastened the lid, then dived into the cave beneath Lyre Rock. There, he cached his most valuable possession.

In the old tales, selkies basked on the rocks in gloriously naked human form, leaving their skins strewn anywhere. Men always arrived on the scene and enslaved them, for a selkie without his sealskin must remain human.

Oh, they called it love, those men who took selkie wives and hid their skins. Or they called it rescue. Selkies were fallen angels, said some storytellers, so they couldn't be left as poor dumb animals.

Gordon surfaced to a night sky studded with stars. The black waves were low and calm, perfect for sleep, but he forced himself to walk ashore.

Gordon shook the water from his hair. *Poor dumb animals.* A lesser creature would sneer at the arrogance of human beings, and though Gordon considered himself more than a man, he'd tame his selkie nature to claim Beth.

A growl rumbled in his throat. He disliked the smell of the truck's exhaust, still hanging on the air.

He stepped into blue jeans. Wet from his last-minute change of plan, they clung to his legs, an uncomfortable substitute for his sleek, furred skin.

The selkies of old had been careless. The night Al MacDonald had shown him the ammunition box he used to stash lost credit cards, Gordon had resolved to use such a box for his skin.

No man knew where he hid it. Even if one had, he'd lack the lung power to dive beneath the rock and find the cave.

Earlier, elated by his return to Grey Gallows—by the new things discovered and old things remembered—Gordon had joined the throng of people who crowded into the Village Store, searching out food as evening deepened. There, he'd learned where Beth lived. Everyone was talking about her, and they hadn't forgotten him.

Ten years! After all this time their simple-minded preoccupation annoyed him. His was a casual magic. It needn't disturb anyone. Their interest alone would have made it difficult to court Beth. And now he had a rival.

Soon she'd come down to the shore. Gordon recalled the yearning in her face, as they'd lingered before the painting in her flat. Beth couldn't resist the call of the sea, so she'd surely understand his plight.

Since the day he'd left her on the shore, Gordon had felt alone. Seal folk watched him uncertainly, but with reverence, granting him a title which translated, roughly, as Dark Prince, Solitary. On land, rather than expose his pleasure in ordinary things, he stayed apart.

But Beth, who collected odd friends, could help. She could accept their bond and gather his two worlds into one.

A stone rattled loose from the bluff. Beth might come down on the cove side, but the overgrown path would offer bad footing at night, and she'd disturb the slumbering cows and pups. He thought Beth would be sensible, and come down this side, where steps led to the gravel, then to the beach.

Gordon lay back in the shadow of Lyre Rock. The night sky looked as deep as the ocean, mysterious as his choice. In human terms, mating meant marriage, but that custom made him uneasy. If he followed his seal nature, he'd mate once each year. Bulls drove off rivals and copulated with such all-consuming lust, they often didn't eat for weeks. Then they left, and returned the next summer.

With that urge sated, could he leave Beth?

Up on the bluff a screen door creaked open, tapped shut.

He heard ice cubes tinkle in a glass. Was Beth, too, looking into the night sky?

Neither mating mode suited Gordon. Once again, he'd make his own way. Damn Nature, for singling him out! Once each hundred generations, selkie magic fell on some hapless seal pup. From his mother, he learned to swim, to hide and hunt, but no one taught him how to merge his two lives.

He'd listened to old stories, human and seal, alike. They gave some comfort, because he wanted Beth as his mate, and the ancients said selkies and humans could come together. Gordon heard her footsteps. Light and sure on the cliff steps, crunching across the gravel, reaching the soft, welcoming sand. *His Beth*.

If only one of those stories had a happy ending.

Stupid, stupid, stupid. Beth wondered if she was doomed to repeat the same error, over and over again. How could she find a husband if she wasn't willing to accept a boyfriend?

At twenty-five years old, Beth had spent a lifetime resisting romance. All right, it only felt like a lifetime. Besides, early on, Carol had applauded her right to be particular. Then "particular" became "choosy," followed by "fussy," and finally "impossible."

She'd tried, but every time she dipped her toe into the lake of love, something bit her. Just when intimacy escalated and men turned enthusiastic, she stopped. It was as if she heard the rising chorus of "Someday My Prince Will Come" and choked up.

There was a name for girls like her. It wasn't a nice name, and she'd heard it plenty. Maria's tea leaf reading had been a curse. Beth's left brain might not believe in fortune-telling, selkies, or magic, but her right brain was in league with her heart.

The night with Junior had begun as a vigil. As a college freshman, she'd decided to lure her selkie back. She'd waited for Midsummer Eve, then, armed with a tape player and cassettes of bagpipe music, she'd driven to Grey Gallows.

Hers wasn't the only midsummer bonfire along the shore,

but it had the power to conjure up Junior and two of his drunken friends. Junior hadn't been drunk, but he carried a bottle of wine and the scent of marijuana on his shirt. When Junior sent his friends away, Beth had sipped herself far past tipsy.

Actually, Junior was in very elite company. He'd gotten a hand under her blouse and he hadn't called her names. When she stopped him, Junior's breath was coming fast and she braced herself for his anger. It was worse than that. In the firelight, he'd looked at her as if she were a goddess.

Then she threw up.

Beth woke up in Gull Cott the next morning, thoroughly sick, and completely disgusted with the way she'd debased herself and Junior.

Today she hadn't even allowed him to leave mad. Anger was more dignified than falling for her wretched teasing. Walking away was better than false hope. Junior could never be more than a friend, never be her—

Damn those tea leaves and Maria Rosetti!

The moon peeked from behind a veil of cloud, and Beth watched the waves search the shore.

"Soul mates" didn't exist in the nineties, but Mr. Gordon had shimmered with potential.

Not that he seemed suited for anything as tame as a boyfriend. As a lover—Her stomach dipped away in enthusiastic response. Oh, yes, right up to the moment he turned into an arrogant jerk. "Where do we go from here, Beth? . . . I mean *financial* affairs, I'm afraid."

Her face had still ached from blushing when Maria, seeing Mr. Gordon depart, drew Beth aside.

"I read your cup after you left." Maria had held her breath as Carol passed by. Then she'd bent forward, confronting Beth nose-to-nose. "It was the same cup."

"As—?"

"As I read for you ten years ago. Same heart, same shield, same urgency." Maria had drawn a shawl threaded with gold up over her shoulders. "I thought you should know."

As she'd evicted her remaining guests, Beth felt excitement

pound in the pulse at her wrists, in her throat. As she put away food and swept, Beth told herself if she'd been touched by magic, she'd never have to do such chores. But as she polished silver dishes and slipped them into their flannels, Beth had hoped.

Tonight, a rainbow reflection ringed the moon. Beth leaned back against her palms, trying to recall what that meant.

Her only warning was the sight of a dark figure, blacker against the blackness, a few yards away. Moonlight picked out a silhouette. He approached silently and he wore no shirt.

Danger sluiced adrenalin down her arms and legs, readying her to run. But it was too late. If she sat very still, maybe he wouldn't see her.

He had. The contrary moon shone illumination bright as noon, casting his shadow before him, spotlighting Beth on the blanket she'd spread over the sand. He moved closer.

Black hair dripped over his shoulders, and its dark curve against his cheek stirred faint remembrance.

Too late for running. Beth stood up and confronted him. Standing with her hands on her hips, she lifted her chin and stared where his face would be if the moon hadn't tricked her again.

And then he extended his hand, going for hers as if they were friends. She felt a trembling recognition at his touch.

"Remember me?" he asked.

And she did.

Four

Moonlight spilled over Beth's hair as it streamed back on the breeze. With her feet braced wide and chin jerked up, she looked as firm as a ship's figurehead.

In that first instant she'd tried to snatch her hand away, but he'd held tight. Last night he'd surrendered it all too quickly. Now they were alone in darkness, with no one to note his manners or their lack. He didn't let go.

"Mr. Gordon. Of course I remember you." With prudish grace, Beth's right shoulder dipped, trying to shrug the gaping neck of her sweatshirt back up her arm. "It's only been twenty-four hours."

Her fingers rippled in his, then tugged loose. Had he frightened her? Humans so often reacted with irritation when they were afraid.

Gordon ignored her words' reproach. Instead, he smelled the sea salt on her skin. He resisted the inclination to taste it. The courtship of Beth Caxton called for human charm, not the skin-slapping enthusiasm of a seal.

"I will admit I'm surprised to see you. Here, I mean."

As Beth waited for him to speak, she used an index finger to edge the sweatshirt hem down over her shorts. As she crossed her arms at her waist, Gordon realized the woman was virtually tying herself in knots to hide from him.

The waves' murmuring told him he'd stood silent too long. He must quit staring and answer her.

"And I'm surprised to see you. I'm used to swimming here, alone." Not only was it the truth, it explained his wet hair and bare torso.

"Really? The undertow's tricky and the cove is so rocky, most people stay closer to town." She sounded faintly bothered.

"I know the waters and I use Lyre Rock to keep my place." The rock rose black and jagged toward the stars, and it came to him, as calmly as the waves sought the shore, that Lyre Rock would watch him come together with Beth for the first time.

Beth retreated a step toward the gravel parking area, toward the path up the bluff. Instinctively Gordon moved to cut her off and Beth's breath caught on a gasp.

She'd fled; he'd followed. Predators had no choice, and now he'd frightened her.

"That's my cottage." Beth sounded stiff, as though a bone had caught in her throat. She waved a hand toward the cottage on the bluff, then cinched her arms together at her waist once more.

He should have found a shirt. And her territoriality surprised him. She didn't fish the waves or prowl the beach for food. He'd never learn human ways if he lived ashore forever.

But this was Beth and this was her beach. He could apologize. "I hope I haven't trespassed."

"Don't be silly, Mr. Gordon. You're welcome, though revealing your first name might go a ways toward dispelling some of our awkwardness."

"Is that all it is?" As he blurted the words, Beth laughed and shook her head and he almost read her mind.

His touch, darkness, and lonely beach stretching away around them. Those elements fused and formed this brittle conversation.

"Just call me Gordon." Beth's way of balancing on one leg was fascinating, the trick of a gull, not a human being.

"Gordon, then." She nodded, satisfied. "Even if I set out to guard this beach, I couldn't. Every teenager for miles comes down to our parking lot to watch the submarine races."

"*Really!*" Gordon couldn't imagine such a thing. In all the years he'd haunted Grey Gallows' coast, he'd never seen underwater craft.

"Are you British?" Laughter laced through her voice.

"Do I *sound* British?" Another cursed thing to worry over.

"Every now and then, but 'watching the submarine races' is sort of a colloquialism, slang for something else."

"For what?"

"Kids come down here and park." She hesitated. "You see, boys tell girls they're bringing them down here to see the submarine races, then they sit in their cars and make out. Kiss, you know, while they stare out at the ocean."

"Ohhh!" In the instant he understood, Beth's leg wobbled. "How on earth do you do that?" He probably saw better in the dark than she did. "*That*," he said, pointing at her leg.

Beth looked down, then collapsed backward onto her blanket.

He sat beside her, ignoring her fall. Humans could flash into anger if one mentioned their ungainliness. Besides, another image demanded his attention.

"Were you ever lured down here, in a car, under such pretenses?" If he'd worn a shirt, he might let his shoulder graze hers. It was peeping out again, her bare shoulder, though she'd hidden her legs by pulling her knees inside the sweatshirt.

"Never. I lived here, remember?" A flicker of longing crossed Beth's face.

"Smart girl," he said, but his mind saw a teenage Beth, alone on the bluff, looking down as muffled radio music rose from parked cars with steamy windows. Her "never" stung, until he resolved to give Beth every *first* she craved. He hated the boxed confinement of cars, but he'd brave even cars to teach her "submarine races."

"Are you staying in town?"

"Offshore," he answered, then chided himself. Lies might

be unavoidable, but he'd already used that one, and Beth knew it.

"Well." She stood and brushed sand from the back of her thighs. The instant he stood, she swung the blanket over her shoulders like a cape. "I better go on up. Maybe we can talk while you're in town."

Dismissing him quickly as that, Beth apparently expected him to move along. How dare she show such human arrogance? He could not condone it.

She shifted her weight to one leg. "I'd ask you up, but it's late." She glanced toward the cottage, but he knew no one waited for her.

With the requirements of manners fulfilled, she strode away. Gordon matched her steps until they reached the edge of the gravel parking area. "You're on vacation, aren't you?"

She made a stalling hum in her throat. "I've barely unpacked."

"I could help you."

"No, thanks." Her words were as cold as they'd been last night when he'd hurt her feelings by mixing business and flirtation. "Besides, I've brought some work along with me."

What had he done this time? Did he simply fear him as a male? But no, he'd heard this excuse before, most recently in a San Francisco elevator. One of his bankers had tried to coax an attractive woman to dine with them. She'd used "work" as a shield to shove back the affection and fun she clearly craved.

He'd thought then, and he believed now, that such an excuse might be easily pushed aside. He watched Beth's hair rise on the sea breeze. She was only half set against him. Should he force her to remember?

Since that evening she'd lay beneath him, half-drowned, she still hadn't truly looked into his eyes.

Now he stepped close enough that she had no choice.

Come on, Beth. Where she gripped the blanket, Beth's fingers twitched. *Let me, Beth.*

It was too dark. He couldn't force her to take him to her cottage, to truly look at him, to remember. He'd have to be satisfied that her fingers touched his wrist in a glancing caress before she bolted across the gravel lot, toward the dirt staircase. His calf muscles tightened, demanding he follow, but Gordon forced himself to remain.

With one bare foot poised on the lowest step, she looked back. "It's a small town. I'm sure we'll see each other."

Beth had eaten all the chocolate. She poured a glass of wine, huddled into her father's cozy old chair, and propped the clipboard on her knees.

She'd come here to write poetry.

The refrigerator hummed. Peaches padded across sea grass, woven into patchwork mats covering the kitchen floor. She followed him and stared from the window. Outside, a tiny boat glowed with hidden light, a night bug chirred and the waves shushed it. Midnight.

She returned to the chair, feeling full, giddy, ready to burst out of her skin. She wouldn't allow herself to leave this chair. Pacing was pointless, though she knew, as clearly as if she could see through the white plastered wall, she knew Gordon paced along the sea's margin, below on Lyre Beach.

Last night he'd proven himself a boor. No, a *tease*! She recognized the symptoms well enough. He'd flattered her vanity, saying how much he'd admired her portrait in the lobby and in the playbill. He'd pleased her with praise for her work, and ingratiated himself by displaying interest in her dad's work.

He'd walked beside her, lithe and silent, admiring her beach painting, luring her to like him, then he'd slammed the door in her face.

Now he showed up here. On a road map, Grey Gallows earned no more than ant-track lettering next to a faint scoop in the California coastline. Could he have followed her from San Francisco? Even if that notion were paranoid, she couldn't swallow the coincidence that he'd ended up swimming on her beach. And what about that furtive move to cut her off when she'd started back to the cottage?

Sea water had dripped past his collarbone and onto his

chest. And his shoulders! Last night's suede blazer had hung loose over his linen shirt, barely hinting at his strength. Except for that handshake, he hadn't touched her, but she wouldn't test his power. It was obvious.

Speaking purely as an observer—a *writer,* she reminded herself, scribbling a tangled knot on the paper before her— Gordon's shoulders, arms, and chest were magnificent. Not that he swaggered under the python-thick muscles of a weight lifter. No, his were the long, smooth sinews of a splendid—

She *never* noticed such details about men. Beth took a long sip of wine, then swirled it in careful circles, squinting at the burgundy shadow left within the glass. Gordon Whoeverhewas had cast a spell on her last night, and tonight he'd cruised by to make sure it took.

Beth flicked her pencil eraser against the clipboard. Peaches leaped into her lap to feint at it with his paw.

"What kind of man swims out there, this late, when he was just high-rollering around in San Francisco last night? Huh?"

Peaches mewed and arched his back beneath her chin.

"With shark warnings posted, water like ink, and an undertow that could suck him down to Mexico, his motive would have to be pretty extreme."

Peaches tapped her cheek: twice without claws, once with.

"Get down!" Beth stood, dumping cat, blanket, and clipboard to the floor. She'd walked as far as the front door before good sense reasserted itself.

She was *not* going down there. She wouldn't even touch the doorknob. The man already carried himself like a king. He didn't need more brass on his ego.

And yet, Beth knew that if she crept to the bluff's edge and looked down, she'd see him pacing, too, black against the moon-white sands, not haughty at all.

Why had Gordon followed her?

A scratching like cat's claws grated against her bedroom screen in the other room and a board creaked on the deck. Peaches started sideways and glared his reproach.

"It's only the wind." But Beth couldn't be sure, because of her shell curtain.

During her twelfth summer, no shell was safe. In place of boys or rock and roll, shells became her obsession. At dawn she had prowled the shore, bending and snatching until her back ached. With a hand drill, she'd bored tiny holes, then threaded her booty, like wampum, onto clear fishing line. By summer's end, she'd had almost thirty feet of delicately strung shells.

Finally she'd cut them into lengths, tied them to a curtain rod, and divided her room from the rest of the cottage. They lent her vague privacy and she loved their subdued rattle, a musical talisman from the sea.

Just now they blocked her view of whatever brushed against her bedroom window. From the deck which ran the length of the cottage's windward side, she could see the seal cove, below. She and Jack had vowed never to block that view with curtains.

Suppressing a shiver, Beth closed the living room shutters and chafed her hands together. No telephone. No television. No bedroom curtains. She curled back into her father's sagging yellow chair and told herself she'd longed for such poetic isolation.

Gordon, she wrote.

Gordon.

Dark magic

Beckoning, summoning, whispering

. . . a finger down my spine.

Drivel! She tossed the pencil and watched it ricochet off the coffee table. Clearly she wasn't suited to the artistic life. Tomorrow she'd ask Karl to order shingles and a roofing shovel. In the meantime, she'd pry the old shingles up with a butter knife. She couldn't be any worse at roofing than she was at poetry.

She clicked off every light, locked the front door, and rattled the knob to make sure it had caught. A city habit, but ten years in San Francisco had made her a city girl.

Undressing in her room's darkness, Beth heard the skittering again. She remembered the gold Jerusalem artichoke flowers and purple thistles she'd seen pushing up from beneath the deck. They needed trimming. That was all.

She turned her back to the windows, then pulled on a flower-sprigged flannel nightgown and climbed into bed.

"Kitty kitty." Beth pulled the sheets up to her lips and sighed. "Oh Peaches, don't pout. C'mere kitty."

Peaches curled up at the end of the bed, a discreet two inches beyond reach.

Wind-driven waves and soft purring had lulled Beth half asleep when the scratching turned to a distinct tap.

"Beth?"

Gordon? A burglar. In her room? Her brain fumbled, then stopped. The whisper came from outside and it held no threat.

Wriggling on her belly to the foot of her bed, Beth looked out. Window screen cross-hatched his face into a million tiny squares, but it couldn't hide Gordon's sheepish smile.

"I had to come."

"That's all right." *Had* to?

"I forget why, exactly," he confessed.

"I'll be here when you remember." Until daybreak, probably. His voice had provoked such a flood of adrenaline, she felt limp and keyed-up, at once. Beth cupped a hand over her lips, hoping he wouldn't mistake her yawn for a lovelorn sigh.

"This is sort of a teenage thing to do, too, isn't it?"

"Yes, it is."

"I didn't think you'd let me in. Would you have?"

"Probably not." Their chuckles tumbled over each other, and then there was only the creaking of a loose shingle in the wind.

"I'll go. But, Beth?" His low voice made her shiver. "Don't ever think I leave because I want to."

Before she could ask him to explain, Gordon's face vanished. His tread crossed the deck. His shoes scuffed the dirt stairs to the beach.

Beth's bangs crinkled against the old metal screen and she breathed the tang of rust as she tried to watch him go. What kind of man slipped up like Romeo beneath Juliet's balcony, said he didn't want to leave—ever—then did it?

Beth flopped down in bed. A man with a girlfriend? She stroked Peaches and stared at the ceiling. A married man?

As a child, she'd imagined dolphins, starfish, and mermaids sculpted into the plaster. Even now, she could pick out Neptune's steeds cavorting overhead.

A member of the Mafia might duck through dark waters, braving sharks, hoping spotlights wouldn't catch him smuggling narcotics through sleepy Grey Gallows.

No, Gordon was an innocent, more sheltered than she. "This is sort of a teenaged thing to do, isn't it?" he'd asked. Eyes closed, Beth sighed, smiled, and let her fingers stir Peaches' fur. Gordon had clearly never heard of parking, either.

But what had forced him to go?

Silvery pink and pearl green, the dawn sky shimmered like the interior of an abalone shell. Two dozen seals lounged on the beach, heckling the human above. Calm waves reached for the shore, reflecting the sky's hues on their glossy necks.

Beth had maneuvered through thorns, which made her wish she'd worn jeans. Her fingernail beds stung from clinging to salt-slick rocks, and now that she'd reached the switchback, the only part her girlhood self had deemed "tricky" on this inches-wide track to the seal cove, Beth had no place to step. A clump of moss burrowed in the crevice where she should wedge the rubber edge of her tennis shoe. She'd slip for sure.

The rock face grazed Beth's lips as she peered back up the way she'd come. High as a two-story house, it made her roof look level. She hazarded a glance over her shoulder, down toward the cove.

During her entire childhood, she'd scampered up and down this trail as nimbly as a goat. And she'd dived from the cliff edge to the cove. Another two-story house, at least. Unbelievable! Had Beth-the-teenager possessed absolutely no imagination?

"Oh, get a grip." Beth clung to a ledge before her and swung one leg into space before she touched the path below. She avoided a red rock that looked as slick as ice. Olympic divers plummeted from ninety meters or something. This was her secret path and she'd descend it.

She did, and when she finally rested, clammy and proud, the view was worth it. Female seal lions in coats of dark chestnut velvet lolled between jagged boulders, suckling brown-black pups. The mothers regarded her with wide, trusting eyes.

Beth had read that human IQ scales ranked seal lions just below chimpanzees. Still, these creatures didn't know her. Why did they believe her harmless?

One female, larger than the others, swiveled her head toward the waves. The others looked, too. Beth saw nothing, but the mothers barked, wriggling closer together, squeezing pups against boulders and each other.

Then, though memory told her it was far too late for him to be here, she saw the bull. The male sea lion ripped through the glassy waves. White spume mantled his shoulders as he thrust upward, forward, then dove again, vanishing from view.

Beth shifted on the boulder, which was more pointed than it had appeared. She scanned the waves, waiting for the bull to surface.

Nothing. She hoped he kept swimming.

Bulls meant bellowing and battles. Too often, females couldn't shield their pups, and they were crushed during bloody combat. From a survival standpoint, it probably didn't matter, since the bulls had dozens of mates in their harems.

The cows shifted. One, lighter than the others, bawled a warning, and Beth saw a dark shadow slicing through the water, gathering speed, before he broke the surface. Thick-shouldered and sleek, he rained silver drops as he arced across the mouth of the cove.

''Wow.'' Beth waited, only realizing her fingers had clamped over her knees when her knuckles creaked in protest.

The blond cow rolled her pup onto his back. She licked his fuzzy throat, and Beth knew the bull had gone.

''Wow,'' she said again.

Unmarked by battle, he must be a bachelor who'd lagged behind, trolling for an unprotected rookery to call his own.

Beth waited until her cheeks stiffened with the beginnings

of sunburn. The bull wouldn't return. Besides, she needed to get to town. She needed a garbage can, the biggest one she could fit into the Fiat's excuse for a backseat, if she intended to fill it full of her cast-off shingles. She needed Karl to order new roofing, too, but Beth hated to leave.

This secret cove hid milky tranquility alongside explosive power. This was the Grey Gallows she remembered, and this was the stuff of poetry.

The Fiat selected Monday as a day of rest. Once Beth had washed her face and slicked on lip gloss, braided her hair, and found her supplies list, the sports car refused to start. Although Jack claimed the Fiat's faulty solenoid was to blame, Beth believed the vehicle threw fits of pique.

"Turin is the center of the earth." Beth cranked the key again, hoping this was one of the days the green sports car would respond to glorification of its birthplace.

When flattery didn't work, she tried force. Beth left the car door open as she surveyed the slight slant from the gravel parking area to the highway.

Slight, and she'd need to get the Fiat rolling fast before she jumped back in and started the engine by popping the clutch.

Beth admitted she was finally paying for her sloth. In San Francisco parking on a hill was no challenge, and Jack loved muttering and prodding under the Fiat's hood, so she'd put off repairs. And Grey Gallows' terrain was nearly flat.

Still, this wasn't a new stunt. Beth left the keys in the ignition, made sure the gear shift sat in neutral, then set both hands against the Fiat's frame. She jogged in short, sluggish steps until the car rolled. Then she trotted faster, almost running before she leaped into the driver's seat to mesh ignition, clutch, and gear shift in the voodoo shuffle Jack had taught her years ago.

The Fiat shuddered, sputtered, and sped off toward town.

Inside the sawdust-floored market, the aroma of fish hung so heavy, Gordon might have chewed it. One counter advertised "fresh fish," though the flesh smelled old. Behind him, people

lined up for another sort of food, but the haze of cooking oil
made his throat close, so he didn't investigate. He'd eaten well
enough, this day. Still, the shop and its people attracted him.

As fishermen exchanged small catches for quick cash, Gordon looked for Junior. Most humans would label his aching
need for his friend "childish." The last time they'd met, Junior had spurned him, but Junior had also taught him how to
walk and talk like a man, how to eat human foods, how to
sleep within sight of structures. Gordon couldn't slough off
the memories.

Gordon eavesdropped on a knot of men cursing tourists for
clogging local waters with recreational craft. Another group
grumbled of state game wardens on the lookout for abalone
poachers who sold their illegal take to high-toned restaurants.
Thing was, poachers were smart. That left wardens with plenty
of time to harass honest fishermen. But no one mentioned
Junior.

Inside one glass-fronted refrigerator case, a large ling cod
gaped at Gordon. He touched the glass with the back of his
fingers before he felt the watcher.

Gordon rounded on the old man. "Hello." Humans, except
for adolescents, didn't respect proper distance between males.
As they grew older, their lack of deference increased. Still, he
greeted this one civilly.

Ruddy with overindulgence and years of sun, his face edged
with white whiskers, the elder stared at Gordon's hand.

"Hello. Name's Gimp MacDonald." Ridged and calloused,
the palm which clasped Gordon's had known work and hard-
ship. "I run Gimp's, the pub down the road."

"Next to the video store." Gordon nodded, recalling ropes
and weathered timbers arranged to look like a dock. Unlike
the clutter of movie posters and neon lights next door, Gimp's
suited Grey Gallows.

"Y'wouldn't be Irish, would you?" Though casual, the
cagey question made Gordon smile and instinct helped him
understand.

Gimp MacDonald knew the selkie stories. That explained
his study of Gordon's hands. In the old country, selkies were

known by their webbed fingers, dark hair, fathomless eyes. And Grey Gallows had superstitions of its own.

Gordon rose to the old man's game. "My heritage is rather murky, Mr. McDonald."

"Murky, is it? Not black Irish, then. You have the look."

"I lost my mother years ago, sir. And my father before that." He shrugged as if that explained his ignorance, and the old man commiserated.

"I'll stand you a wee pony of ale, if you come down for a talk."

"Drink doesn't hold much appeal, but perhaps for a talk, sometime."

"For a talk, then, if you're around past Midsummer Eve?" Gimp MacDonald angled like an old fisherman, reminding Gordon that selkies of old only sang on the rocks, in human form, on Midsummer Eve.

"Longer, I hope." If Beth would have him, much longer.

Gimp chuckled and his blue eyes misted. He rubbed ragged knuckles over his lips. "Come after our Minny, have you?"

Streams of warning ran through Gordon's veins. If Gimp had said *Beth*, the remark might have made sense, but *Minny*? What mischief had been blamed on him? Or had another selkie trespassed here? He'd kill any impostor who tried to pass himself off as Beth's selkie.

Rage pumped him full of so much hot blood, Gordon thought his neck would burst with it. Human imagination paired badly with a sea lion's fiery instinct. But they shared patience. Gordon drew a deep breath and pretended to feel patient.

Gimp settled his blue captain's cap. "No sense to what I'm saying, man." He shuffled toward the other counter as a clutter of people parted to show a woman frying fish in vile oil before she wrapped it in sheets of newspaper. "Pay me no mind."

Five

Contrary to good sense and propriety, Beth Caxton felt ill with jealousy.

The Village Store offered an air-conditioned, canned-music escape from the blue and gold day outside. Patchworked with commercial displays, and produce on one side, with tools, plants, and hardware on the other, it represented the sort of normalcy Beth needed to maintain her sanity.

Last night a millionaire had stalked her to the water's edge, then mooned around her bedroom window like a lovesick boy.

This morning she'd traversed a cliff-face in time to watch a rogue seal's courting display. While she'd sat there, sun-burning, she'd wished he were her selkie, wished he'd wade ashore on human legs and embrace her with a man's arms.

She needed a concrete explanation for what had happened to her. So far, Grey Gallows had offered dreams and fancy, but not one chance to convince the village she'd grown sen-sible.

The store shook as a logging truck passed on the street outside, and Karl covered the telephone mouthpiece with one hand, whispering loud to be heard above the rumble.

"You sure you don't want to go for shakes? With redwood siding your place could be a little gem. Besides—"

Beth shook her head.

"—spotted-owl crap's going to blow over soon. Already got men doing 'salvage logging'—"

Huge as a high-rise on wheels, one of the double-trailered rigs had rushed past Beth on her way in today. It had left the Fiat shuddering.

"Fire danger." Beth reminded him of the MacDonald's house fire.

Karl paused, tapping the receiver with a gaudy topaz ring, then returned to his telephone conversation. "Yeah. Got it. Wednesday." He hung up and turned back to her.

"Okay, Beth Ann, those shingles'll arrive in a couple days, the shovel with 'em." Karl ripped off an order form and gave Beth the yellow copy. "Locally, I can't think who I'd trust to do the work. Probably have to hire someone from Parish."

"That won't be a problem." Beth let him think she'd already made arrangements. He'd hear of her folly minutes after she banged her first nail. Just now, she'd try distraction. "By the way, who does night fishing off Lyre Rock? Last night—"

"No one I know of." Karl closed his receipt book with emphasis. When Karl looked up, his was a salesman's smile. "For any work you might want on your place in the future, don't forget this town is changing. You'll have the opportunity to employ skilled contractors, not local yokels who'd rather be throwing out fishing line."

The sigh of bus brakes made Karl frown.

"Charmaine." Karl snapped his fingers in the direction of the magazine stand, and wisps of Charmaine's purple-black hair appeared above *Family Circle* and *Diver*. "I'll be in back. I can't stand the racket of those schoolkids," he explained to Beth.

Charmaine's shorts exposed winter-pale legs as she wheeled toward the cash register. "They spend a lot of quarters."

"Candy bars and soda," Karl snorted. "I should put up a sign. Make a minimum purchase of two bucks."

Beth calculated the cost of her brown paper sack of mushrooms and the diet cola in her right hand as small feet stamped down the bus steps outside.

"Mama! Kids coming?" The child who dodged past Karl to snag Charmaine's thigh and spin around it was about three years old.

"Yes, they are. Stay back here with me." Charmaine hoisted the child onto a stool behind the counter. Her dark face was elfin above a shirt printed with pink kittens. A tulip-shaped birthmark marred one of her cheeks.

"Is this your daughter?" Beth longed to touch the child's silken hair.

Charmaine nodded. Beth might have turned to see who'd brought a current of warm air inside, except that Charmaine, with lips set, stood ready to note any slight.

"I have a cat," Beth said, pointing to the little girl's shirt. "His name is Peaches."

The little girl bounced, trying to reclaim her mother's attention from the doorway. The child looked back at Beth. "Peaches," she explained softly, "is food."

"I know." Beth matched the child's solemnity. "But his fur is the color of peaches."

"Oh," the child answered, then kicked her legs in excitement as a troupe of adolescent girls, high schoolers or a bit younger, flocked to a meager cosmetics display.

Beth glanced at them, then turned back to her open wallet. Charmaine was mouthing silent words her way.

"What?" Again, Beth looked at the teenagers. Was Charmaine prepared to impart some nugget of village gossip?

No. Charmaine was watching Gordon.

Beth shouldn't have recognized him. Not from the back, not before he spoke a word or moved a muscle. She should have noticed the tall man wore a royal blue polo shirt. Set on showing her prim conventionality, she might have frowned at his longish black hair, brushed back, curling slightly at the ends, wet enough to leave a damp crescent on his shirt. Instead, she knew him.

As he turned, Gordon's idle smile mesmerized Charmaine. His sun-tanned face radiated clean vitality, and his teeth shone so white, he might have been auditioning for a toothpaste com-

mercial. But Beth had spent years around actors and she knew
better. Gordon's grin was genuine.

Charmaine's index finger pecked at Beth's hand.

"Cuuute!" Charmaine whispered, as if shared awe had
made them friends. "Is he one of Larry Cloudcap's boys,
d'you think?"

Beth shook her head. She'd bet her cottage that Gordon
wasn't a Miwok. Then her suppressed vaunt of pride turned
to anxiety. Why hadn't Gordon recognized her?

"You're right." Charmaine mused. "Probably a tourist, but
doesn't he look like those Genghis Khan guys? You know,
Tartars?"

Beth hazarded another peep at Gordon, but she needn't have
sneaked. Fluttery as gulls, the teenagers pressed around him,
claiming his attention.

A Tartar? She pictured his warrior-slim torso, flying braids,
and then her imagination balked. Atop a Mongolian pony,
Gordon's feet would drag. And she couldn't imagine his teeth
bared in a fearsome battle cry.

Gordon was no menace. She watched him preen for the
girls. His smile turned him benign and gentle. Last night on
the beach, darkness had fooled her into believing he posed a
threat.

A little hussy in too much mascara and a green crop-top
leaned across Gordon for a can of hair spray. Her shoulder
grazed his and she jumped back. Then she apologized, displaying her pierced naval and flat abdomen with the skill of a
belly dancer.

"It's quite all right." Gordon nodded. His faint accent set
the girls twittering. Beth waited for Gordon to meet her eyes
in droll adult understanding.

His gaze washed over Beth with such disregard, she felt
queasy. Was this the same man who'd lingered at her window
or did he have a clone? What color were those eyes, anyway?
In San Francisco, candlelight had lit them toffee-brown. Here,
they glittered like shards of a broken beer bottle.

What if he *were* an outlaw? Suppose he found her irresistible, and though he felt compelled to follow her, he couldn't

risk attracting attention to his secret identity. Now, there's a sensible explanation.

"Charmaine, when do they bring their catches in, down—" Beth gestured toward the fish market up the street, unable to remember its name as Gordon glanced her way. She'd drown her confusion in fresh salmon, rice pilaf, and Carol's beaujolais.

Karl emerged from the back of the store to scoop up a Styrofoam tray from the meat case. "We have fish. Sprinkled with pepper and brandy, this'd be great."

The twin trout had eyes like dull gray rivets. They were no fresher than the plastic covering them.

"Thanks, but I'm going to spread my money around town." Beth had toasted him with her cola can and headed for the door, when Charmaine's daughter, darted by, set on an escape.

"Hey! You don't want to go." Gordon dodged past Beth and blocked the child. He squatted in the doorway, jeans pulled tight over muscular thighs fit for an athlete. "Big trucks are just roaring past, out there."

The child shifted from foot to foot, as if considering her chances of dodging past him. She looked down at Gordon's feet, tanned and smooth in his thick-strapped sandals.

Beth thought of a sand lion's trap, of innocent bugs sliding down a sandy funnel into the lion's jaws, and she felt herself falling. Her heart didn't stand a chance against a man who even had beautiful feet.

"*Big* trucks." Gordon extended his arms far as they reached. Their undersides looked almost tender, and the child stepped closer, leaning into the half-circle of his open arms.

A truck horn blared so loud Beth felt her intestines vibrate. Tires skidded, brakes screeched, car horns bleated just outside the store's front door. Metal slammed, crumpled, then the impact faded, followed by tinkling glass.

"Minny!" Charmaine's cry was more dreadful than any reprimand, and the child darted back.

The teenage girls stood silent. Gordon, still crouching, looked neither surprised nor relieved.

As Minny tolerated her mother's tight hug, Karl sidestepped

past Gordon. He went outside and stood with hands on hips, blocking the window, casting greenish shadows over Gordon.

"Don't you ever go out there without an adult." Charmaine paled as she gave Minny's shoulders a slight shake. "Do you hear me?" Charmaine buried her face in her daughter's dark hair.

As if Charmaine's horror thawed them, the teenagers rushed toward the door.

"Wow, man, she would've been right there!"

They streamed out, allowing sunlight and shouts inside. "Lookit that, *look!* That car is totally trashed!"

The blonde hovered in the doorway, reporting over her shoulder. "It looks like Roo tried to turn in here, and he slowed down, yeah, I bet he tried to miss one of those loggers and that other car, a Saturn, I guess, punched him in the tail-pipe and sent him spinning into the parking lot."

The girl's eyes widened and Beth noticed her pierced eyebrow. "Poor Minny would've been squished like a—"

Beth moved close enough to give the girl a gentle push. "Hush."

"No, really. Check out the angle. If he hadn't kept her in here—" The blonde's face turned solemn. "Whoa, poor Minny."

The door closed and the Muzak played on as Charmaine wept.

"Thank you, so much." Charmaine looked up. "How did you know?"

"Lucky guess." Gordon shrugged. "I've had my eye on those trucks ever since I came to town."

"They drive too fast and they don't—" Charmaine let Minny cling like a baby monkey, arms and legs clamped tight.

"Are you going to be okay?" Beth touched Charmaine's shoulder, but Karl, reentering with a stride too brisk for his egg-shaped body, interrupted.

"Roo got a little sheet metal damage, is all," he scoffed. "That truck didn't touch him. Charmaine, those are last week's *Enquirers*. Get back to stocking, huh?"

"Karl, you need to do something about those trucks," Charmaine insisted.

Karl's eyes rolled toward Beth as he groaned in exasperation. "Roo's a burnt-out surfer, brain fried on drugs, but Junior and Sloan—you remember Sloan?"

Beth shook her head. Except for Junior, she knew none of the men he'd mentioned.

"They toss a little work his way when they can. Roo was probably drinking. When isn't he?" he asked Charmaine.

"I don't care. Those damned loggers have to keep their speed down till they reach the highway. You know they do."

"Charmaine, do you know what those 'damned loggers' spend in this store between runs? What they're contributing to this town's economy? Which, by the way, sure ain't supporting itself on fishing." Karl waggled his eyebrows in such ill-timed merriment, Beth withdrew a step. "Charmaine's having a little trouble moving into the nineties. When you have time," Karl said, tracing her retreat, "we should talk about Sable Bay."

With a packet of gum in her ringed fingers, the blond teenager approached the counter and released her words like a well-aimed cue ball. "My dad says Sable Bay and Sable Bay-ers suck."

Karl rolled back a step. "Stefanie Morris, you'll watch your mouth, if you know what's good for you."

"You ain't my daddy." Stefanie's taunt was as conspicuous as the wiggling of her trim backside as she sidled out the door.

Beth felt a prick of unwilling admiration for the teenager. Karl needed someone to take him down a peg.

Beth waited a moment for Gordon to approach. When he didn't, she followed Stefanie outside, then froze. The spinning cars had stopped inches from the Fiat, which glittered green in the sun. One driver leaned both elbows on his hood, while the other stood in the Village Store's phone booth, shouting and gesticulating.

Still, Beth didn't move. Finally he'd followed. The air stopped circulating behind her. Sound altered, turning flat. Like harsh sun, Gordon's presence pulsed heat into her back.

He'd known. And there was something weird in the knowing. There'd been no squeal of brakes before the horn, no squalling tires, no hint anything was about to go wrong. Yet he'd intercepted Minny, making a barrier of his body. Was he psychic or, as he'd said, just lucky?

Anyone in town could have guessed why she didn't pursue that thought. Beth had turned into a solid young woman with common sense. She deliberately recalled his wintry manners and dug her car keys from her purse, afraid that if she turned and met Gordon's eyes, she'd forgive him on a wish.

Blood still steeped the sea red, spreading like smoke, swirling around Gordon so cloying and thick, it clouded any sign of shark.

Gordon surged through the water, patrolling. He could do no more, now. He'd arrived too late. Standing behind Beth as she stared at the wrecked vehicles, he'd sensed the seals' tumult. As clearly as if he'd basked in Beth's cove, he'd heard them call. He'd run, shedding clothes and human form—too slowly.

These cows, russet and wide-eyed, turned to him with a mixture of reverence and anxiety which couldn't be translated to human syllables.

They adored him and feared him, worshipped and distrusted him. Most of all, they stayed remote.

He'd plowed through the sea, power jutting him above wave crests at each fin stroke. The pup was dead before it fell down the gullet of a Great White who'd tipped its snout skyward to gulp.

Too early, too soon, the pup had braved the waves, the cows told him. The shark had been so near, its belly grated as it rushed through the shallows to grab the youngster.

Hit hard and destroy. Human trucks were no different. Sea sharks, shore sharks, both overpowered prey before destroying it. This pup had been very small. Even the scarlet tendrils of blood had vanished. Nothing remained to mark its life or death.

Gordon swam around the rocky point between the cove and

Lyre Beach, which bordered Beth's parking area. He didn't look for her. He marked his place by Lyre Rock and nosed through the unworldly stillness Bringer of Crimson had left behind.

Flickers of fish returned. Sated for a time, the shark had deserted the shallows. Unwilling to meet a bull seal's challenge, it had likely drifted to a fathoms-deep refuge. Still, something had driven it to attack here. Old age, injury, laziness, or caprice? Gordon followed the watery path, hunting the hunter.

Too early, too soon, the mothers lamented. And all the other males had gone, gone. Each time he surfaced, the cows' dirge hung on the wind. Gordon accepted the burden. The Dark Prince, alone, could stop Bringer of Crimson from making it happen again, too early and too soon.

When Beth strolled past Lyre Rock, dusk had crept in over the ocean, dragging with it a pall of fog.

Gordon felt a surge of relief. Though the shark lay someplace, waiting, Beth had worn the baggy red sweatshirt and cutoff jeans. Her hair lay in plaits on her shoulders, and she carried a child's painted tin pail. She had not dressed for swimming.

Her steps slowed as she shaded her eyes and stared into the fiery horizon. She gazed past sandpipers which flicked thin black legs over silver swathes of beach, probing for worms and crabs.

Gordon floated, sleek fur crowned with fading sun. Beth, he knew, saw nothing but satin-gilt waters and dark bumps, which could be seal lions or rocks, kelp or shadows.

A gnawing ache beneath his breastbone made him want to thrust through the water, bowl her flat with his weight, and hold her hands pinned with his. He'd force her to remember.

In the Village Store he'd waited patiently for her greeting. It had never come, though she'd certainly recognized him. He, after all, had the more difficult task of picking her out from the pale, amorphous shapes of her kind. And he'd done it without difficulty, because she was Beth.

Gordon sniffed and shook sea water from his whiskers. Beth

didn't notice the sound. She stepped along the shore, stopping to inspect the waves' offerings, hurdling a channel, picking her way through black boulders and tide pools before she turned to scan the waves once more.

A full city block out, indigo waves crashed white-veined in warning. Even as he felt a flicker of faintly warm currents, Gordon knew what Beth searched for.

Built by years of erratic waves, the sandbar ran parallel to the beach. Outsiders rarely noticed it, except when low tide exposed lacy skeletons and abandoned homes of snails, mussels, limpets and other creatures. Humans valued the pretty leavings called shells. Sometimes, in their fixed downward staring, they stranded themselves on the sandbar. For a time they'd be surrounded by water, waist-deep on the shoreward side, over their heads on the seaward side. Finally the tide would rise and cover the sandbar altogether.

Beth might be a villager, but she still knew the shore better than the sea. Though the two moved together in ceaseless longing, shore and sea only tested each other's borders. Beth was of the shore, and though she was neither arrogant nor oblivious, she underestimated the secrets in the sea.

The shark had come again. It advanced toward the shallows with smooth, head-swinging sureness. If Beth waded between beach and sandbar, if she reached the sand bar but ventured too low on the seaward side—

Warning blared in his head like trumpets. His heart's thud must vibrate through the ocean like a drum's pounding. How simply the Bringer of Crimson's jaws could snatch Beth's delicate ankle, before sinking low to vanish.

Humans were rare, unsought prey, and yet, to be safe, he must warn her.

One bark and any cow seal would obey him and flee. But this was Beth, ignorant of his first language and too independent to obey without an explanation.

Gordon rose up in the water, catching her attention with a dolphin-style smack of his flippers. She trotted to the water's edge to investigate. Shading her eyes against the setting sun, pail dangling from her fingers, she went on until soft wavelets lapped her bare legs.

Currents telegraphed the shark's snapping movements of excitement. *No, Beth, go back.*

Gordon ducked beneath the surface, surveying. There. The shark's eyes might have been expressionless scraps of black paper as it swung wide in an arc which allowed it to avoid Gordon, avoid risk. The shark skirted the end of the sandbar. His swimming accelerated. His route would dead-end at Beth.

Gordon heard Beth's coo of delight and knew she mistook the ripples for the surging of more seals. He had no choice and perhaps no chance. Sharks were dumber than kelp, so their behavior was impossible to predict. Gordon only hoped this one was touchy enough to charge a bull seal lion.

He dove in an underwater somersault, slapping his back flippers against the shark's belly, rocking it so hard the water swayed crazily around them. Gordon recovered first, darting past the shark's snout and shuttered eyes.

It had taken television to teach Gordon why that dulling ocular film signaled serious attacks. The membranes served a simple purpose; they kept sharks' food out of their eyes.

Gordon sped upshore, away from Beth, toward Lyre Rock. There, he knew every dip and fall of underwater terrain.

Bringer of Crimson was fast, but Gordon was nimble and lust for survival had crushed all human pity. As Gordon swept close to each jagged boulder and darted beneath sudden rock shelves, he wanted the shark to die. He skimmed by sharp barnacles, willing the shark to scrape its thick hide, willing it to bleed.

Shore! In a leap which sent him rolling, Gordon threw himself onto Lyre Beach. Breathless and blinking, he watched the shark drift away.

Beth was probably safe, but he'd take no chances. *You need a nap, do you, seal man? And if that detached killer takes Beth before she can scream and struggle, will you ever rest again?*

Using shame as a goad against weariness, Gordon endured a change exhausting as birth. He shed his hide for the second time that day, stashed it, and swam back along the shoreline, toward the sandbar and Beth.

The terror pulsed far away now. Must he tell Beth how he'd watched over her and protected her from danger?

Salt stung the shin he'd abraded on the shark's hide. Should he say he'd spied on her? Beth, who valued freedom over friendship and love? She must, mustn't she? She'd left Phoebe and Eddie and Jack.

Gordon hesitated. Sometimes he misjudged humans. A long history of lies and silence allowed misunderstandings to flourish among them. Even after years ashore, Gordon could only guess at the wild profusion of assumptions that grew beneath human words and deeds.

Would she resent his intrusion or appreciate his consideration?

Truly, he had no idea, but there she was now, kneeling at the seaward slope of the sandbar, face wet from fog and the tossing waves, the tassel tip of one braid brushing the sand as she pushed up both red sleeves and reached for a shell.

Off balance and alone, she made perfect prey. No matter her response, he'd return Beth to Lyre Beach and her home.

Gordon gathered his legs beneath him to touch bottom. As he shook back his hair and waded toward her, Beth saw him and her knees wobbled. Then sandy fingers flew up to cover the wide O of her lips.

Gordon rehearsed his words. Nothing worthy of a San Francisco millionaire presented itself. Without the sea's floating support, he felt heavy. Chill water dripped from his chest and thighs. He rolled the muscles in his shoulders, fighting fatigue.

Beth scuttled backward, tipped her pail, righted it, then stood, holding the tin bucket before her like a shield.

"Sorry to disturb your beachcombing, but I thought you should know." He might have touched Beth, if she hadn't backed down the other side of the sandbar. "There was a shark hereabouts. A Great White." Gordon kept his face still, concerned that Beth stared and gaped like a cod. He tried to soothe her. "It's probably gone now."

"I—thank you." She splashed into the water between the

bar and the shore. "I'll be going home to dinner now. Thanks, really."

He couldn't allow this haughty dismissal to become a habit. Gordon matched her step for step, pressing through the wispy fog. He set his bare feet alongside hers, but Beth didn't speak. Now that she'd pried her startled eyes away, she refused to look at him. He studied the sweetly straight part in her hair. She studied watertracks, scored feathery on the sand.

"A grateful woman might reward me for the warning by offering dinner." Gordon thought of the salmon she'd mentioned. Even seared on her hibachi, it might satisfy his hunger.

"Um." The sound came from her as if it were a word like *no* or *help* or *vinegar*, but he knew Beth was stalling. "Um," she repeated, "Mr. Gordon? I make it a rule never to share dinner with a naked man."

Six

When Gordon blushed, stammered, and stood rooted in the sand, Beth didn't have the heart to desert him. He struggled with speech so thick he might have been a pagan deity brought to life from hewn stone.

"I only thought of the shark. And y-your safety." His right hand, rather than dropping to cover himself, rose in appeal.

"Well, then." Shamed by her pettiness, Beth cleared her throat. If he'd shared her preoccupation with propriety, she might be bleeding into the bay.

Fog swirled between them. Beth dashed the back of her hand across her eyelashes to banish the dew starring her vision and spangling the fog with iridescence.

Far behind him, a boat floated. She tried to blink it into focus. Had he swum in all that distance?

"I apologize." Beth confined her gaze to his face while she gathered her run-amuck thoughts. "If you'll give me an hour, I'd be pleased to have you over for dinner."

The invitation transformed his hang-dog expression to the brashness of the man who'd strode from the sea.

"After you've dressed." Beth spoke with the force of a schoolmarm.

"I will." His boyish delight told Beth he'd knock early at her door. "Shall I bring anything?"

"Just—"

"Clothes, I know." His laugh broke over her, then buoyed her up.

When Gordon turned to go, Beth watched. She'd never before seen a naked man. Grappling with optimistic suitors, watching R-rated movies, reading lively romances—nothing had prepared her for Gordon. The pale vee of his Achilles tendons led up to tanned, bunching muscles in his calves. His flanks were lean, entirely different from her own, and his shoulders fanned above his rib cage, spreading upward with the power of raptor's wings.

A sinew in those shoulders signaled his turn, and Beth pretended she'd just turned back as well. "If you bring an armload of driftwood, I'll make a fire in the hearth."

He waved an arm in agreement. Beth congratulated herself on her quick thinking and hoped no one had seen them together.

Beth turned her unlocked doorknob, stepped inside, and sighed. With Gordon on his way, her cottage no longer felt cold.

Earlier, she'd almost choked on homesickness. Gordon's disinterest, the accident, and Karl's oily insistence on moving Grey Gallows into the nineties, had prompted her to crush into a phone booth and call San Francisco.

The throaty nonchalance of Phoebe's answering machine made Beth hang up before the message ended and when she called to announce her safe arrival, her father said, "Never figured any different. Write your heart out. Have a good time."

As if the two were the same. Even Peaches had greeted her with an unblinking stare.

What had she expected? She'd always been alone in the cottage. Growing up, she'd done her lessons at the table while Jack hunkered in the corner, pounding his typewriter, two-fingered and fast, his back to the room. And her.

Jack had treated Carol just the same. Their marriage taught Beth what she did not want. *Hers* would be a match of total devotion: sleeping together, rising together, working side-by-side, eating meals on opposite sides of the same table, every morning and night. Like two pitchers of cream poured into one huge bucket, their lives would blend.

Beth switched on a light, banishing the gloom. Gordon had followed her to Grey Gallows. He'd rescued her, too, sort of. Those things and his astounding good looks overshadowed his coolness in the store.

The sun's glare had fired the sky to hammered copper behind him, but it had been Gordon who'd singed her retinas until her vision was fractured with streaks of violet light.

She should sit down and write what she'd seen. If visions of Gordon's body couldn't jump-start her muse, the wench was dead.

As her attention wandered, Peaches feinted with soft paws, mewing and arching his back in a manner calculated to trip her. "Sure, now you love me."

She should ask herself why he'd been swimming nude and what had compelled him to come plunging to her "rescue" when she was in no danger. Gordon was an unusual man. She wished that disturbed her more.

Beth scooped up the cat and slung him over her shoulder.

"How's it look to you, Peachy?" Beth surveyed the cottage's main room. "It hasn't had time to get cluttered."

In fact, Gull Cott's gray stone mantel, weathered board walls, and hardwood floors were bare. A year ago she'd painted the kitchen cupboards turquoise and laid down seagrass mats, but in the living room, except for a braided terra cotta-colored rug and adobe jug lamps, the room remained sand and white.

Peaches hauled his body upward and launched himself over her shoulder to the floor, flipping his tail as he negotiated past the shell curtain into her bedroom.

The curtain, in fact, had sent Beth down the beach with a plan to bring nature's bounty indoors. *Thank you, curtain.*

In the days B.C.—Before Carol—she and Jack had beach-combed during his rare recesses from the typewriter. They'd displayed shells, rocks, and driftwood in ever-changing displays on windowsills, tables, every horizontal surface.

Now, night wind brought the smell of smoldering charcoal in from the hibachi she'd filled before entering Gull Cott. She'd start dinner right after she spread the treasures of her pail over the coffee table.

She'd never found so many perfect sand dollars. One covered her palm in a moon-pale circle. In its center a finely etched five-petaled sea flower lay on a backdrop mottled like a storm cloud. Another was backed with branching like a Christmas tree inked with indigo. The next one rattled with internal fragments and sand sifted onto her bare knees. It must have broken when the pail tipped.

Beth set it aside, still embarrassed by her mind's manic ricochets—off Gordon's resplendent body, down to her hands, back to Gordon.

She would not make too much of this. She'd bathe, change into fresh jeans, and forget his peculiar actions.

Beth turned two brass handles full on. The claw-footed tub took forever to fill. She darted back to the kitchen, where she set rice water to boil, located a bag of almonds, checked the sliced apples she'd thrown into cinnamon syrup, and returned in time to ease into the tub. The steaming water rose high enough to lap at her lips.

If Gordon's odd behavior continued, she might be eating alone. In San Francisco he'd hurdled all the usual steps of flirtation in a single bound, then turned away with crossed-arm smugness. Last night he'd whispered at her window. Today in the store he'd stared right through her.

The soap bobbing around her knees had turned mushy by the time Beth stepped out of the bath and unraveled her braids. She'd brush out the crimps later. She had to hurry. She just knew he'd arrive early.

Beth jerked open a drawer and considered her clothes. At the Foghorn, Gordon had looked elegant in jeans, a trendy linen shirt, and a worn suede blazer which surely cost more than the Fiat. She would never look elegant.

Beth tugged on one leg of her white jeans and stood hesitating over a top when a knock sounded and Peaches catapulted through the shell curtain.

Way early. Suddenly Beth couldn't remember what she'd planned for dinner, what she'd meant to say, why she'd lured a millionaire to this tumbledown cottage.

"Just a minute!" Her muffled shout came through a T-shirt, once emerald, now faded to misty green. She sacrificed footwear for speed, shouldered through the shell curtain, tripped over the cat and into the living room.

Although her childhood vocabulary had been the envy of many, only one word remained on her tongue. "Hi."

Gordon stood inside the front door. He shrugged, making his armload of driftwood rise and fall. "I let myself in," he said.

"I see that." She couldn't let him think his audacity didn't matter. Tinging and dancing on a cushion of steam, the lid to the rice pot reminded Beth she had a meal to prepare, but she didn't move.

"I'm a little early," he added.

"No problem, but you'll have to amuse yourself while I get dinner going. *I'm* a little late."

At that they exchanged places, bumping arms in passing. Beth lingered in the kitchen doorway and Gordon released the wood beside the hearth, then stood on the terra cotta–colored rug, arms spread as if he'd embrace the living room.

"Do you mind if I look around? I admire old cottages. I imagine that if I ever got to Scotland, I'd buy a croft overlooking a loch. Peat burning hearth and all, you know?"

The pensive tilt of his head seemed at odds with the gunpowder-gray shirt and onyx cuff links. She could more easily envision him as laird of an ancient castle.

"I've always wanted to go to Scotland, too."

His face lit with such eagerness, she felt he might flag down a Learjet.

"And why is that?" He walked toward Jack's yellow chair and the bookcase.

"Because of the fairy folk, of course."

"There aren't enough superstitions to keep you busy in Grey Gallows?" He reached toward the spine of her black poetry notebook, then glanced over his shoulder, awaiting her answer.

Beth's breath caught as if her throat had stiffened with starch. "Superstitions?"

His index finger tipped the volume back, probably seeking a title. "Midsummer and pirates' ghosts and—" His sidelong glance hinted he'd heard about her selkie, too.

"Kids' stuff." Beth exiled herself to the kitchen. She opened the refrigerator and stared at the apples soaking up rosy cinnamon syrup.

"That's not what I hear."

She ignored his taunt, took the fish from the refrigerator, loosened the paper tape, and unwrapped it. A better hostess would have offered appetizers and drinks. "Would you like some wine?"

"No, thanks."

Beth wished for a CD player, a tape recorder, even a radio, not to entertain the man, but to cover the plank floor's creaking beneath his feet.

When his footsteps stopped, she imagined he'd settled in Jack's chair with her poetry. She couldn't resist peeking around the doorframe.

He squatted next to the coffee table. His hands hovered over the mounds of shells with the reverence of a man at worship.

She tucked back into a corner of the kitchen and closed her eyes. "I hope you like fish!" she yelled, a little too loudly.

He chuckled. "I eat very little else."

With flat-footed human steps, Gordon followed Beth onto the deck. He wouldn't let his stealth frighten her again.

Beth balanced a platter in one hand and a cooking implement in the other as she bent toward the grill. The ends of her hair floated too near the ashy embers, and his fingers itched to brush them back. Before he could, Beth tossed her mane back over her shoulders.

"I brought you something." Gordon slipped the necklace from his pocket and studied her reaction.

The platter wobbled as if her wrist had gone weak, but a heartbeat later, Beth uttered a murmur of protest.

"Is it ugly to you, then?" He squinted at the inch-wide collar of gold, at the rectangular emerald that would have glinted near the hollow of her throat, and sighed.

"Gordon, no. No!" Beth shook her head with such vehemence, he thought she might have touched him, if her hands had been empty. "It's beautiful." She licked her lips and considered. "It's just a wildly inappropriate gift. We hardly know each other."

Inappropriate. Flowers, candy, and wine were appropriate. He knew that, but none had seemed right for Beth. Still, he was used to such failure.

"Come on." Beth spoke patiently, as if she expected him to lag behind. She pointed the way with rippling hair which still smelled of sea mist, then stepped gingerly over the deck's weathered boards, avoiding splinters to her bare feet.

The tight kitchen was aromatic with almonds she'd sliced over steaming rice. He could swallow a bit of that. The fish, crisscrossed with grill marks, looked edible, too.

Beth's hands perched on her hips. She expected something from him. He shoved the jewelry back into his pocket.

"It's too expensive, Gordon." When Beth whispered his name, her lips moved into a kiss. Gordon liked her lectures exceedingly well.

She opened a dish cabinet above her head, and he fingered the necklace inside his pocket, considering the bauble's cost. "I could have spent that much on a bottle of wine, and that would have been fine."

Her hand hesitated over a pair of white candlesticks. Instead, she grabbed two turquoise tin plates, two forks, and a pair of linen napkins.

"You're absolutely right, Gordon," she said. "But I still can't accept it, no matter how much I'd like to."

"I wouldn't tell anyone."

"No, I won't even look again. It's too beautiful." She

forked salmon steaks onto both plates. "Now, which will it be: the kitchen counter or the living room coffee table? I'm afraid the dining room table moved to San Francisco."

He chose the living room, where shells lay scattered before them. Beth handed him their plates while she kindled a fire.

Reluctant to disturb the shells and unwilling to miss the spectacle of Beth kindling fire, Gordon fit the plates on six inches of bare wood at the table's end and grabbed up the upholstered yellow chair which held the old scent of male.

When he turned back, Beth still sorted sticks into rough sizes. Keeping his eyes on her, Gordon hoisted the chair and plopped it down, canted toward the end of the couch. He'd seat Beth on the couch while he took the chair.

Beth placed two sticks about the size of his human wrist parallel to each other.

Hastily, before she progressed further, he glanced at the dinner arrangement. It would serve. They'd balance plates on their laps and gaze down the length of shell-covered coffee table to the fire.

Gordon settled into the yellow chair and watched Beth. She'd taken a red-handled pocketknife from the mantel before she sank, cross-legged to the edge of the brick-colored rug.

"It's a crime to jam that necklace in your pocket." Beth made slices into a short thick stick. "You'll ruin it."

Gordon leaned back and fished the trinket out of his pocket. She watched with unwilling fascination, then displayed her handiwork for his approval.

"It's a fuzz stick." She twirled the stick's base between thumb and forefingers and Gordon saw she'd carved it to resemble a loose-petaled pine cone. "Since I always wanted a fire in the hearth and Jack didn't have time to build one or teach me how, I got a copy of the *Boy Scout Handbook* and taught myself.

"This is what they recommended for wood that might be wet on the outside . . ."

Beth continued her explanation and though he found it fascinating as the orderly movements of her fingers, leaning smaller pieces of wood against the fuzz stick, a chant had taken up all his attention: Who is Jack?

"You're sitting in his chair, by the way."

"Whose?" He was only half successful in suppressing his snarl.

"Jack's. Jack is my dad." With one brow quirked high enough to disappear beneath her bangs, Beth reached for a box of matches.

Gordon remembered the man on the beach before he thought of Jack Caxton, playwright. That man had seen Gordon crouching above Beth, and he'd uttered a roar protective as any bull seal's.

"I didn't meet Jack."

Beth blushed. "No, but you've seen his work and that's the heart of him. He's sort of reclusive. Carol—his wife—does enough socializing for both of them."

A ribbon of orange twisted through the sticks. Smoke whirled and Beth leaned near, pursed her lips, blew. The fire caught with a rush, but she continued to encourage it. Tonight, just being near Beth wouldn't appease him. Tonight, he wouldn't leave until he'd kissed her.

"You could have shoved these aside, so we had more room to eat." Beth dusted her palms against the front of her white jeans, without noticing the gray marks she left.

"This is room enough." Gordon offered her the other plate, luring her to sit at the very end of the couch. "I didn't want to disturb them."

"They're not arranged or anything. Oh, dinner got cold while I was fiddling with the fire." She half-rose, reaching for his plate.

"Sit down, if you're doing it for me. I prefer it this way. I can taste fish instead of charcoal."

"Great. I'm starving. I suppose you think it looks pretty touristy, all these unremarkable shells dumped on the coffee table."

"I think it looks beautiful."

She smiled. "You know, it really does." She snagged the shell nearest her. "I mean, take this one: a common mussel shell, but it's this great inky blue, smudged with mother of pearl.''

As she laid the shell on the flat of her knee, Gordon's heart vaulted up. She loved the sea as he did. They would blend their two worlds into one.

But he must be careful. As a young selkie, he dived into sex with a fury to match any bull, claiming a dozen young females as his harem. But human females expected more than physical frenzy. They wanted him to stay. When he'd tried to leave, their reproachful tears were too painful to bear. Finally he'd weaned himself from need, living solitary, thinking of Beth.

"—and these curves engraved into the shell, these striations and *inside*"—she flipped the shell onto its curved back, moving her knee so that it grazed his—"there's this wash of iridescent honey color over the silver—"

She set it aside, before turning back to her dinner. They still sat knee-to-knee. Gordon barely managed to eat.

"I'd never mock the sea's riches." He kept his empty plate balanced on his knees, afraid she'd move back if he didn't. "It made my fortune, after all."

Though some humans found it crass to talk of money, Gordon had learned tales of treasure hunting transcended bragging.

"Really? Not undersea oil drilling or something like that, I hope." She pushed a lock of hair behind one ear, spearing him with an expression that said she'd contest his right to do such a thing.

"Nothing like that. I found a pearl."

"*One* pearl?" She waited for him to nod.

"Titania Pacifica."

"It must have been a beauty." She set her plate aside. "They don't often name pearls, do they? Where did you find it?"

"In the Philippines, in a warm, sheltered bay much like your seal cove."

"How did you know where to look? Are you a professional?"

"No, I just found it." In fact, he'd planned to make dinner of the huge oyster, but he didn't think Beth was ready to hear that. "I'm not a professional at much of anything, except swimming and diving and having a good time."

"A beach bum." An envious smile touched her lips. "A surfer, too, I bet."

Beth's hand curved in a cresting dive through the air and Gordon wanted to catch her wrist. He wanted to show her they could slip through the waves, side-by-side, but he only answered.

"Sometimes, but I knew there was more." Gordon interlaced his fingers. Tightly. "Something lured me to San Francisco." *Not the theater, Beth. Not museums, art galleries, nor fine restaurants.* "Selling that pearl gave me the means to go."

She took a gull feather from the clutter of shells. "So you live however you want." She stoked the feather against the dip of flesh between her thumb and forefinger, watching him.

"Not extravagantly."

She used the feather to point out his onyx cuff link, then arched a brow toward the gold necklace on the table. For some reason, her unspoken criticism pinched.

"What does it look like—Titania Pacifica?"

"White, stunning white, with a rainbow glitter. And big." Gordon unlocked the stem of each cuff link and set the onyx ovals aside before rolling his cuffs. "The Philippine pearl buyers—before they knew I'd sell it there, at auction—told me any pearl over 100 grams is classified as 'treasure.' " He saw Beth drop the feather, saw her breath fill her chest. All humans reacted the same to this revelation. As he had. "Titania was almost 200 grams."

"I'm not very cosmopolitan. I've never learned the metric system," she admitted. "Is that big as an orange? A volley-ball?"

He caught her left hand and formed it into a loose fist. Beth watched as he surrounded her hand with both of his.

"About this big." *Big as my heart, which you must hear thudding to escape my chest. . . .*

"Wow. I—I've heard they grind pearls up—uh, in the Orient for medicine, for—a lot of um, calcium, I bet—" She fumbled for words, but at last she stared into his eyes and a shiver of recognition took her.

"Beth." He'd never spoken her name. Now he allowed it. And more.

Once, long ago, his lips had touched hers. That time he'd rescued her. Now it was Beth's turn.

"I *know* you." Awe touched her voice and her face.

"Yes." He didn't pretend to mean that mundane cocktail party introduction. He released her fist, cupped his hand against the silky curve of her hair, and drew her close.

Beth's lips moved before he settled her, before he breathed of sun and sea and cinnamon, and knew her. As if a wave broke softly on his nape, he knew, with Beth, there'd be no rutting, only magic. No quick slaking of appetite, but gentle, careful joining. She'd understand who he was, and love him for his difference. He felt absolutely capable of crushing the red urgency of sex, for this warm, binding current which would end his apartness forever.

Seven

"I *know* you."

Gordon's eyes, deep brown and curiously familiar, compelled the words from Beth. They came unwilling as a secret she'd sworn never to tell.

"Yes." Gordon's voice matched the sure movements of his hands, as if he'd always known.

It wasn't sudden, this kiss which had built all night, all week—Lord, forever. Meeting his eyes, fully, for the first time, she imagined the impossible. Impossible, because only one boy's eyes had ever looked rollicking as a gypsy's, yet wise. Impossible because Gordon was not a fantasy, he was a flesh and blood man.

He pressed her to meet his lips, then pulled her to stand, while the fingertips of his other hand brushed the small of her back. He might have slammed her against him for the impact she felt from his slight touch.

"Gordon?" She said it against his mouth.

"Yes?"

She'd never done such a thing before, spoken while a man was kissing her, breathed his breath. Such intimacy obliterated her ability to form words. She could only kiss back.

Wind gusted around the cottage, squealed under a doorsill

and through an age-sagged windowframe. She felt as if she'd sat outside all day, facing bitter weather, only to come home to this fire-crackling warmth and Gordon.

Her arms clasped him. Warm and solid, he loomed above her. Chin tilted upward, she refused to break the kiss, though she only reached the level of his breastbone. Without flirtation or force, Gordon was seducing her. Had seduced, because she wanted nothing more than him.

His muscles all snapped taut at once, as the shell curtain's clack heralded Peaches' arrival. She felt weak at the sudden absence of his body, but she sidled away, between the coffee table and couch, toward the kitchen.

Safely separated by walls, she called to him. "Would you like coffee?"

"No."

Did he sound angry? Annoyed that he hadn't pounced quickly enough?

"Tea?"

"No." This time she couldn't mistake Gordon's curtness. What had come over her? Beth put the kettle on and reached for a tin of chamomile tea. If Gordon had swept her into the bedroom, she would have rejoiced, not resisted. So why, in the instant his attention veered to Peaches, why had she plummeted from passion to fear, as if he'd kicked her feet from under her?

She spooned the cinnamon apples into clear glass bowls, then considered the carton of heavy cream. She rubbed the back of her neck and felt the echo of his touch. Drat, she didn't have the enthusiasm to whip this cream or to face the man in the other room.

Before she could escape, Peaches' thunderous purr announced them.

"This is a friendly cat." Peaches pressed his face hard against Gordon's bicep, reclining along the length of his expensively shirted forearm.

"Rarely." Beth stared as the teabag leaked chamomile leaves into the bottom of her china cup.

Two nights ago Maria had sashayed down the staircase,

giddy with champagne as she whispered, 'It was the same cup. Same heart, same shield, same urgency.'

But not the same man. The true love Maria had promised long ago had never arrived.

Gordon slung Peaches over his shoulder with the same casual affection she used. His slicked-back hair had dried and fallen forward to brush his brow. He lounged against the doorframe, jaw set, watching her.

Maria had been wrong then and now. Gordon was mysterious, undependable. His eyes harbored some harsh knowledge he couldn't hide. He represented a negative of the cozy, familiar man she'd marry. Beth Caxton had lived with uncertainty too long. She wanted a puppy dog, not a panther.

So, why had she let him kiss her? Perhaps, her reaction had been a mirror image of what her heart demanded. Its frantic beating had urged her to flee. She'd mistaken its warning for excitement.

Beth slapped spoons into the bowls of rosy apples. She took a step toward Gordon, but he didn't move from her path. And he wouldn't look away from her, as if he'd cast his trance once again.

Finally he stepped aside, then followed so close Beth felt his eyes study her backside. She plopped into Jack's gold chair, forcing Gordon to sit alone on the couch. But he didn't.

Peaches leaped from his arms and Gordon squatted next to the coffee table. He cradled a single piece of driftwood in his hand.

"Now I know what I should have gotten you." Gordon's smile banished the menace she'd imagined. He sat cross-legged. Absently he brushed a bit of cat hair from his charcoal shirt.

"A lint brush?"

He ignored her, studying the driftwood's shape with such intensity, Beth felt abashed by her sarcasm. With her emotions somersaulting, she settled on the rug beside Gordon, trying to see what he saw.

"If I'd gotten you something like this, you would have accepted. And it's just as beautiful, isn't it?"

The mottled wood formed a rough, horizontal *S*. Gordon's thumb stroked the form, already smoothed by years of pounding surf. On its short top curve, a dark indentation, perhaps a knothole, gave the impression of an eye.

"A seal pup!" Beth cried, as if she'd solved a puzzle. "Of course. But they don't come that color, do they?"

"Rarely."

Beth heard the echo of her earlier, snappish reply. Though Gordon softened it, she took the word as a rebuke.

"I'm sorry—" Beth's throat tightened. How had things come so far, so fast, that she wanted to fling herself into his arms?

"For being frightened?" Gordon frowned. "Of this stranger who barges into your house and—"

"I wasn't frightened."

"I came on pretty strong, and suddenly." He stared at the driftwood in his hands as his self-mockery turned darker, and all wrong.

"It wasn't sudden." Beth rose up on her knees and touched his crisp shirt collar, urging him to meet her eyes. "Those—things—have been brewing between us—" Beth couldn't finish, because the word she'd almost said was *forever*.

When he did look up, Beth felt disoriented, as if she were falling forward, forehead drawn toward his by a silken thread. She thought he whispered her name, but his lips stayed still. One of his arms stole around her waist as she knelt, and then she *was* falling forward, to kiss him.

Because she'd initiated it, because it was the second time or maybe because that dark demand in his eyes broke free for a few minutes, this kiss was different. All over again.

When he stood to leave, his smile had returned. And when the door closed behind him, Gordon's presence remained in the cottage, all night long.

At dawn Peaches' loud insistence on freedom roused Beth. Through sleep-blurred eyes, she watched the cat sidle among the blackberry bushes, until a watery huff drew her attention to a sleek black form in the cove. Sparse grass chilled her toes as she jogged to the edge of the bluff and stared at waves

which purled like gray satin. Nothing. And now Peaches had
vanished.

There! Slicing through the waves, a ridge of blackness rose
and dived again. Peaches could take care of himself. Beth
tugged the hem of her striped nightshirt lower and started
down her path. She stepped over the slippery reddish rock
she'd noticed before and scolded herself for not putting on
shoes and jeans. Still, the nightshirt was long enough to pass
for a bathing suit cover-up. Besides, she'd be alone.

Descending, she couldn't see the cove, and guilt grabbed at
her conscience.

"Peaches?" Beth called, but of course the cat had gone the
other way. Could she trust him to stay away from the highway
and stalk in weeds bordering their dirt road?

Splashing sounded, but the seals had deserted the cove.
They did, sometimes, swimming over to Moon Isle, but usually that was after the pups were half-grown.

An inner tube, lashed with yellow nylon rope, floated not
far out. Divers used such markers to keep oriented along unfamiliar coasts. She heard splashing again, and hissing.

Beth stopped, telling herself it was to rest her rock-stabbed
feet. So, a diver had disturbed the seal mothers and sent them
swimming off with their pups. The diver must not know he
was trespassing. The thought of confronting an intruder and
telling him he'd invaded private property, made Beth uneasy.
But that was exactly what she'd do.

Negotiating the last turn before the beach, she saw the diver
rise and clear his mask. A second one, surfacing right in front
of her, made Beth stumble back a step.

"Hi, gorgeous."

For an instant she thought he was Gordon. Tall and wide-
shouldered, he had Gordon's build, but he also had buzz-cut
hair, a sulky mouth, and stony eyes fixed a good foot south
of her eyes.

With sleep-tangled hair and unbrushed teeth, she looked
anything but gorgeous, and this lewd creep looked nothing like
Gordon.

"Hope you don't mind, we're taking a few abalone."

So he *knew* he was trespassing. He sloshed closer, unzipped the neck of his wet suit, then signed an "OK" to his friend.

"No. It's all right." It was *not*. Beth tried to summon the confidence to order them out of her cove. She didn't want them here, scaring her seals, but she was dressed in a *nightgown*, for crying out loud, and this guy was taking an eyeful. "Isn't it illegal to use any kind of air assist?" She indicated his diving tanks with a nod. If she'd moved her arm to point, he would have marked the movement of her breasts.

"You're right." He sawed his fingers along the chain hung around his neck, and his expression turned boyish. "If you tell Sheriff Reynolds, we're in deep shit."

"Well, don't take too many."

But he'd already turned his neoprened back and something about his wet suit bothered her. What was it?

"Limit's four abs a day, right?" She called, stalling, but he only waved a hand, not even turning.

Lord, she felt stupid. Beth picked her way back up the path. She hadn't asked their names. Or gotten a look at the second diver. On the other hand, her uneasiness was probably only a result of being perused so boldly.

Maybe they needed the food. She thought of the two homeless men who regularly raided the Dumpster behind the Bronze Iris. Sometimes Jack left them a six-pack of beer. Carol called him incorrigible. Beth called him kind. Maybe these divers were taking abalone in place of food stamps.

Inside Gull Cott she concocted a huge pan of breakfast. Its aroma should have lured the cat—or Gordon—to her door.

She'd hoped Gordon would be taking a sunrise stroll. After all, he claimed to be nothing but a beach bum in rich man's clothing, and she wanted to tell him about her intruders. What would he have done?

But she hadn't asked Gordon when she'd see him again. She knew how to sour a romance, even if she couldn't tell how to kindle one.

When he didn't appear, Beth decided to eat later, after earning brunch by clearing old shingles off the roof.

•   •   •

Sweat burned into the second blister to break. Feet set wide apart for balance, Beth leaned against the handle of her improvised roofing shovel and yelped.

"Ow, ow, ow!" She used the back of her hand to smooth her hair back, then waved the stinging hand in the air again.

The driver of the blue pickup sluing down her gravel road probably thought she'd greeted him. Junior. She'd feed him breakfast, but she wouldn't allow him on her roof.

Beth had splashed water on her face, pulled a shirt over her sadly askew ponytail, and started reheating coffee when Peaches' mew and Junior's knock sounded together.

"Well, look what the cat dragged in." The door creaked as Beth admitted them both.

"Are you always so polite to visitors?" Junior scrubbed his fingers through hair that already rose in a tawny coxcomb.

His swollen face and puffy eyelids over blue eyes swimming in red-streaked whites convinced her Junior was hungover.

"It's a beautiful morning without a cloud in the sky." Beth gestured with her spatula. "Any reason you're not fishing?"

"Geez, woman, you want something to mother or are you looking for a fight?" He yawned and considered the pan. "What is that?"

"It's kedgeree, made from leftover rice and fish, hard-boiled eggs, curry powder, cream—"

Junior extended a stifling hand as if her description sickened him. "Never heard of it."

"My dad used to make it. It's an Anglo-Indian dish." She paused at the sound of barking outside. "Is your dog tied in the back of your truck?" Junior nodded. "Why do you do that? Tied dogs get mean."

"You're right," he said. "Cash could bite your hand off."

Beth rescued slices of sourdough bread from the toaster as Junior mumbled.

"Indians had curry powder?"

"Oh, Junior, not American Indians—" Frustrated, she whirled on him, only to see he was shading his eyes against the glare from her kitchen window, and smiling.

"Give me a little credit, Beth Ann. And some coffee." He paused while she poked at the kedgeree. "Pretty please."

Junior had managed two helpings of kedgeree and a half loaf of sourdough toast when he pushed away from the counter, rocking his chair back on its hind legs.

"Actually, I was sent to kidnap you. That's why I'm not fishin'."

"Yeah? The condition you're in, I think I can whip you."

The front legs of Junior's chair slammed down. "You don't want to go too far with smart-mouthing me, honey."

Beth's head snapped around. Junior's sandy-blond hair was tousled like a child's, but her mockery had honed an edge on his lowered voice.

"Okay, sorry." Beth picked up both their plates. Before she stepped beyond reach, his grip on her elbow turned her back.

"That night on the beach, I didn't have to stop. I—"

"Okay!" She shouted and her mind scrabbled to dilute his anger. "Sleeping on the boat must be tough. I think it's made you a little cranky."

Laughter sputtered from him as he leaned back and stretched. "I swear, you haven't learned any city manners."

He'd lost his house and almost lost his father. He needed money—which she'd denied him—and self-respect. Besides, she was probably acting tough with him because she'd been such a wuss to the diver in her cove.

"Is there still plenty of abalone along here?" Beth changed the subject, gesturing a sponge toward the window.

"Enough," he snapped. "Why d'you want to know?"

Beth cautioned herself to be a bit more considerate of Junior's feelings. Especially when they were alone.

"Some guys were diving in my cove." She swished off a dish. Junior would laugh if she mentioned her uneasiness.

"Who? Were they taking any?"

"We didn't perform introductions." Beth scoured the skillet with false diligence. Considering Junior's second question, she suddenly knew what had bothered her about the diver's wet suit. He'd had no bag at his waist. If you were taking abalone, you needed a place to carry them.

"Doesn't it bother you, being out here with no phone?"

"I find it relaxing," she said, though a rill of shivers trickled down her neck.

"And being on this peninsula when the tide's up? How many times a year d'you suppose you get cut off from the highway?"

"Almost never." She dried her hands on a dish towel. "So, who sent you to kidnap me?"

"Karl."

"Karl." Beth's tension flushed away at the thought of the round-bellied shopkeeper. "Karl?"

"Yeah, actually I'm staying in the trailer behind the store. Nice of him, considering . . ."

"Considering what?"

Junior watched her face carefully, as if he were about to confide a secret. "A few weeks ago he invited me over for a drink, to share his plans to help 'Sable Bay' prosper." Junior cracked his knuckles. "Being the farsighted sort, I said, 'Hell, no. I work alone, man.' Then my house burned down, and instead of gloating over my rugged individualism, he offered me the trailer. He's been driving into Parish to see Al in the hospital, too."

No way. Beth folded the dish towel in half, then thirds. Far be it from her to squelch Junior's idealism, but she'd seen Karl's disregard of Minny's danger. Karl Malcom didn't have an altruistic bone in his body.

"Anyhow, he's having this little meeting about the town's Midsummer festival. He'll be there with Charmaine, Lucinda—"

"The librarian?"

"Yeah, and Gimp and a bunch of other 'local merchants.' " Junior tightened the strap on his wristwatch and tapped the crystal. "Karl wants your 'input,' you being a San Francisco barracuda of a businesswoman."

Beth thought of the struggling Foghorn Theater and smiled

as she poured more coffee for each of them. "I don't like this," she admitted. "Not in Grey Gallows."

Junior rubbed both hands across his face. "Better get used to saying 'Sable Bay.' " Junior recited the name in a fussy fashion, then gulped more coffee.

"My dad can't stand Karl." Beth remembered Jack's anger the day she'd almost drowned. He'd called Karl's jokes "exceedingly tasteless."

"He's talking *money*. Money has a way of making folks listen," Junior said.

"Jack heard that when Karl was parks director in Idaho, he got run out of town for forcing city ways on the country folks."

"Yeah? What'd he do?"

"Paved acres of green grass, chopped down trees, then landscaped to look 'up-to-date.' Jack heard Karl was taking kickbacks from the guys pouring concrete and wielding chain-saws."

Junior stared toward Beth's ceiling, stroking his throat. His huge fisherman's hands contradicted his lean form.

Beth wondered how many villagers, besides Karl, would actually profit from Sable Bay. "Why are you running Karl's errands?"

"I wanted to, all right?" Junior's boot beat a nervous rhythm on the floor. "Look, Al had a bad night. When I stopped by the store after leaving the hospital—"

To get a couple six-packs of beer ...

Beth didn't say it, but Junior's hesitation and the glare he sent, said she might just as well have.

"—Karl said if I wanted to sleep in, I could do some stuff for him."

"Is he paying you?" She drained the last of her coffee and set the cup in the sink.

"Jesus Christ!" Junior slammed both palms flat on the counter.

Beth knew she should hush, should leave him some dignity, but her ire against Karl, who'd prey on Junior's weakness, wouldn't let her. "Is he?"

"Yeah, so what?" Junior sat up straight and smoothed his mustache. "Maybe I can't afford to keep my morals as rigid as yours. Maybe I have bills *my* daddy can't pay for me— hospital bills, diesel bills, docking fees—"

"Fine." Beth rocked Junior with a buddy-boy sock in the shoulder. "Let's give the man his money's worth."

"What?"

"I'll go to the meeting, keep an eye on Karl, and tell you what he's up to. Give me fifteen minutes to change."

"You look great."

Beth considered her cutoff jeans and T-shirt. She sniffed the sweat earned from manual labor.

"I look like I just came down off the roof." Midway through the shell curtain, she stopped to explain. "I brought a dress, just in case I had to rush back to the city on business. Give me a few minutes to change into it."

The black Picone dress wasn't her costliest business uniform, but it was her favorite. Snatched off a Macy's sale rack, it had a mock turtle neck, a snug waist, and a faintly-flared skirt which brushed her knees. Entirely plain, it fit like a dream. That, and a matching bolero jacket piped with red, kept it from looking ordinary. The jacket hid the ensemble's only flaw.

No matter how warm and stuffy the meeting, she couldn't remove the jacket. From the neck band to the base of her shoulder blades, the dress opened in a revealing teardrop.

Beth hung the dress on the bathroom door and arranged her lingerie and stockings nearby. Then she heard Junior climbing her ladder.

"Stay off my roof," she hollered toward the ceiling.

"Doin' great." His voice came muffled, but there was no mistaking his amazement. "Better hope it doesn't rain, though."

"It won't." She heard the shovel's scuff. "Leave it, Junior."

She yelled from the tub and he didn't answer, but a sunbeam which had wavered overhead vanished as he shouted through her ceiling.

"Did I see you on Lyre Beach with a naked guy last night?"

Beth bit her lip and concentrated. Gordon's reputation and the tatters of her own rested on her answer.

"Sure you did," she answered. "Actually I like to keep a string of them, like some people keep polo ponies, you know?"

She slammed open the drawer containing her makeup and applied a stripe of eyeliner with a surprisingly steady hand. "I'm about ready to go. Want to take the Fiat or your truck?"

No answer, which was just as well, since she'd failed to pack a vital piece of her favorite outfit. Her black heels sat in her San Francisco closet. Instead, she'd grabbed the red. Black dress, jet-tinted stockings and red spike heels.

"Bimbo." She stepped into them, since it was that or running shoes. Grey Gallows was not the fashion capital of the West.

By the time she grabbed her black bag and jacket, Junior stood in the living room.

"Let me help you with your coat." He snatched the bolero.

"I'm fine." She tried to dip away, but Junior moved quickly.

"Whoo-ee!" Junior tilted his head back to howl like a coyote, then guided her arms into the sleeves. "I wish I could be there to see you take off your coat and get down to business."

"I'm not going to do that." Beth tugged the jacket straight. "Karl just wants a consultant, right?"

"Uh-huh." He grinned. "That is some kick-ass outfit."

"Thanks."

"You want to be my lawyer or something?"

"Hush. Are we taking your car or mine?"

"I got other things to do." He jerked his head toward the beach. "You better take yours, and hurry." Junior consulted his watch and whistled. "You've only got about ten minutes to get there."

Water diviners worked magic by yielding to invisible, irresistible tugs. So Gordon had heard. Now he believed it.

He stood outside Gimp's tavern. Two blocks away, dressed in black, Beth slipped between parked cars. Her presence had lured him out of the darkness, into the sunny street, and though he tried interfering with her thoughts, as he had before, she defied him.

Beth, come to me.

Communing with denizens of the sea was simpler. Most had fewer layers of thought to repel his instructions.

As she clattered across Grey Gallows' main street in those amazing red high heels, Beth didn't even glance his way.

"Is it the wee one, then, or Beth Ann?" Gimp limped up to stand behind Gordon. Surely his weak eyes couldn't see so far.

"Hard to tell, from here." Gordon closed his eyelids to keep from going blind on reentering the tavern, which smelled of yeasty beer and the sourness of spilled wine. It took greater powers than his to make the dark den a haven, but Gimp MacDonald did it.

"Aye? So what had you startin' to your feet, heading for the door in the midst of Domingo's complaints?"

"It's Beth." Her name fell like a prayer from his lips. If he'd been reared to religion, he'd draw his faith around Beth and her goodness.

Gimp clapped Gordon's shoulder and steered him back inside.

Gordon settled at the bar. He despised the throat-stinging cigarette smoke and spindly-legged bar stools, but he could study the antique coins sealed under plastic atop Gimp's bar, enjoy the aimless society of fishermen, and hum along with scratchy jukebox wailings of cowboys, trucks, and poolroom disasters.

Just such a pool table sat in the corner, and Gimp shouted toward a muscled, copper-skinned man poised over it.

"Domingo, are you off pouting, then? Me 'n' Gordon"— Gimp rolled the name with a burr—"would hear of your fishin' troubles if you'd recommence."

Domingo answered with a spate of Spanish that made his companion laugh.

"My Junior, now, he might make some sense of that."
Gimp indicated the melodious language with a shrug. "You
know my grandson Junior, you said." Gimp slid a green pot-
tery bowl of peanuts toward Gordon.

"No, I didn't." Gordon cracked a peanut shell between his
teeth. He relished eating them whole, but it attracted stares.
Carefully he extracted the nut and gulped it. "But I came
ashore here, when I was a boy. We crossed paths, then."

"He was too rough a sort for you. Is that what you're saying?" Gimp polished the bar with a damp towel.

"No, we were a fine match for rough." Gordon remembered spraying sand as they ran rag-tag down the beach, collecting abandoned buckets of fried chicken and frowns,
stock-piling forgotten valuables and oddities bumping against
mossy pilings under the pier.

". . . arrested for those funny cigarettes, though he says he's
given them up . . ."

If things had ended differently, Gordon might share their
boyhood days with Junior's grandfather. Now Gordon needed
to study the old man.

". . . Minny, and she bein' my Junior's child—"

"Is she?" As the little girl clung to him, Gordon had
thought her more pleasing than a seal pup. "Junior's married
to the purple-haired woman? The one who works in the Village Store?"

"No." Gimp shook his head, shifting one bottle in an already orderly row. "A shameful thing, but no." Gimp's voice
lowered to a belittling croak. "Junior says Minny's not his.
He'd see different if he remembered Jimmy."

Melancholy made the old man's face droop like melting
wax. "It could be Minny looks as she does because she's
destined to go with Bridget. Al's wife."

Gordon recalled the child's elfin darkness and her birthmark, but he felt the mark wouldn't harm her. "But Junior's
mother—"

"Aye, killed by a shark, was Al's story. Poor Bridget always yearned for something. Maybe she swam out to find it
and it found her first." Gimp snorted. "Most likely she

yearned to leave Al. The man's my own seed, but a more fearsome sot you'll never find.

"She seemed resigned to life, did Bridget, till Junior was three. That's when she bore Jimmy and lost him. Ever after, she walked the shore, mourning, with Junior hip-hopping behind, dragging his little stick and singing nursery songs, unconcerned for Bridget's misery."

Gordon felt a twinge at Gimp's unfairness, but he let the old man ramble.

"She was a good mother, Bridget. The day the shark took her, she left Junior locked in his room, a chair wedged beneath his doorknob, so he might not follow."

Automatically Gimp drew two beers, for Domingo and another who'd drifted back to listen.

"She might have run off." Gimp nodded, bottom lip protruding. "But 'shark' is what Al told the boy."

Gordon remembered how that tale had tormented Junior, who ached for every torn seal and sea bird washed ashore, half-eaten. One rainy night, unable to identify even the species of some ripped remains, Junior had drawn his pocketknife and stabbed the wet sand over and over, rather than weep.

The ballad of a serving wench, her sea captain, and a gift of Spanish silver drifted through the bar. In a glance, Gordon saw he wasn't the only one caught by the sentimental refrain about a sailor's devotion to the sea.

As that song gave way to another, which bellowed of friends in low places, Gimp slapped his bar rag over his shoulder.

"In faith, I think she swam off with a selkie-man." Gimp might have issued a dare.

"Gimp, you're crazy as a coot on that subject." A man named Horatio yanked off his watch cap, baring white hair cut so close it exposed pink scalp. "Don't go telling visitors such nonsense, gettin' them soft on seals. It's a bad time for it. An awful bad time."

A threat chilled the fisherman's words and Gordon would have pursued his meaning, if Gimp hadn't pressed on about selkies.

"Ungodly handsome and bright-minded, they can lure a woman out to sea. And Bridget always had a yen for the waves."

"*Seguramente*," began the dark-skinned man who wasn't Domingo. As he continued, Domingo translated the words of the man he introduced as Juan Comacho.

"Juan knows a myth telling why women love the sea."

"Will he tell it?" Gordon's blood hurried through his veins. Beth's craving for Grey Gallows had been clear the night she'd shown him the painting in her flat. If he understood, he might make the ocean's magic his own.

Domingo and Juan laughed with such enjoyment, Gordon had to join them, before he even knew why.

"He's saving it for a bigger audience." Domingo pounded his friend's back, his grin bright beneath a black mustache.

"Selkies, now," Gimp halted the conversation's detour with a throat-clearing rasp. "It's during Midsummer they come back for their own. And isn't that a night of enchantment?" Gimp leaned forward, whispering, and Horatio moved closer, agreeing with a nod. "You'll need to see some o'that, young Gordon, not just the tawdry nonsense on Sunday. Saturday night, man, you'll not get to sleep before dawn. The bonfires are bonnier than a wench's wild locks, the legends—" Gimp waggled his brows toward Juan.

The old man was encouraging Juan to weave his tale beside the bonfires. Gordon knew he'd be there to hear it.

"—and the Wheel. Oh, y'must see the Wheel." Gimp had turned his attention back to Gordon.

"Juan, he wants to know what *la fogata*, the bonfire, means to your poor daughter-in-law." Domingo wiped beer foam from his lips.

"During the solstice, on Midsummer Eve, selkies—the seal folk—shed their seal skins and cavort on the beach. You can lure them to you with a bit o' music and kindness, then steal their hides and keep them as wives."

"Good wives and mothers." Horatio slapped down the price of one of Gimp's famous "bottomless" tankards of ale, as if to cover his grudging fascination with the legend. "But always pining for salt water. Let them find their skins and you're one splash away from being a widower.''

"And never," Domingo added, "never should a man shed a selkie's blood, for fear of raising a storm which will smite Grey Gallows like, eh, *el mano del Dio*." He drained his remaining beer and added. "The fist of God."

"It may be Bridget'll come for little Minny," Gimp said. "Even selkies have need of human company. Isn't that so, Gordon?"

Why did Gimp probe so? Gordon's few confessions—to Junior, to a nun in San Francisco, and to a bespectacled girl he'd admired in a seaside amusement park—had been laughed off as fantastic. Selkie magic was deemed a fairy tale, less credible than Bigfoot. Was Gimp determined to steal his seal skin and keep him captive?

"You know the stories better than I, Gimp." Gordon winked at the fishermen.

But what if Gimp's fables were possible? What if he could transform Beth and take her to the sea, to swim and dive and hunt with him, to make love in the sunshine, in white sandy coves?

"Midsummer Eve I'll be watching for Bridget," Gimp promised. "Basking on the moonlit rocks."

A coiling warmth moved in Gordon's belly. On Midsummer Eve, mischief and magic would be afoot.

He'd have Beth, one way or another.

Eight

Because the Neptune coffee shop boasted good food and a phone booth, Beth gave in to temptation after the Midsummer Fishermen's Faire meeting in Karl's back room.

Karl had apparently never heard of a business lunch. He'd kept twelve artisans, merchants, and others hunched around an aluminum table in his storage room for two hours.

"Without offering so much as a Ding-Dong," Lucinda Wright, former schoolteacher and current librarian, had sniffed as she'd opened the Village Store's door to let Beth pass. "He is the stingiest soul in town, but I'm not. Ms. Caxton, may I treat you to a bowl of chowder? Sy can't get as much abalone as he used to, but it's still the best meal in town."

Lucinda had no trouble commandeering a red-leatherette corner booth with a view. Her lime-green sweatsuit and racoonish spectacles, her wit and curiosity made Beth wish she—like most of Grey Gallows' residents—had spent her school days in Mrs. Wright's class.

Beth fidgeted with a plastic-covered menu, but her mind wasn't on lunch. To make good on a promise she'd made to the committee, she needed to act fast.

"You go on and call your partner." Lucinda snatched Beth's menu and shooed her toward the phone. "I'll see to lunch."

Beth passed a counter cluttered with paper napkins, french fries, and catsup bottles and turned right. Afternoon sun and archaic air-conditioning made the café stifling hot. If she closed the door on this coffin-sized phone booth, she'd suffocate. Besides, the hiss of grease and lunchtime bustle would cover her conversation.

Beth waited through the recording of the Foghorn's end-of-season ticket bargains. She removed her red high heels and hid them beneath her purse. Finally Phoebe picked up.

"Hey, Madam Beachcomber, how's it going?" Phoebe crowed. Beth heard the squeak of her friend's antique chair as Phoebe leaned back to talk. "Latch on to Seal Man yet?"

"Not yet." Beth swallowed, recalling Gordon rising naked from the ocean. "Maybe someone even better." She immediately felt disloyal.

"Who? The old boyfriend?"

"No, not Junior. Nothing. That's not why I called."

"If you want to spill your guts, girlfriend, I've got nothing better to do." There came a tapping sound.

Beth wondered what color Phoebe's fingernails were today. "Maybe later."

"I know you want time for poetry and stuff, but we really should do summer stock." When Beth didn't rise to the bait of their old disagreement, Phoebe sighed. "So, what's happening?"

"I called because I need your professional advice. That does *not* mean money." Beth spoke over Phoebe's moan. "I just went to what passes for a business meeting in Grey Gallows."

"Damn it, Beth." True irritation crackled through Phoebe's voice. "You went there to vacation."

"Hush. This will be fun. I'm going to—*we*'re going to—revitalize the town's economy. It's not a job for Wonder Woman. We can do it in an afternoon."

Phoebe chuckled. "Some people take in stray dogs, Beth, but a stray economy?"

"There's going to be a Midsummer Fisherman's Faire this weekend—" Beth snagged a small notebook from her purse.

"And today is only Wednesday. Piece of cake." Phoebe paused.

Beth imagined Phoebe closing her false Betty Boop eyelashes, mulling over a challenge she wouldn't resist.

"Are we talking artsy?" Phoebe asked. "Or cotton candy and carnival rides?"

"Sort of both. Shakespearean and nautical. Folklore, handcrafts, game booths, food—" Beth read.

"And you need—what? Give me a list."

"Only if you promise to come, too." Homesickness surfaced from nowhere, and Beth deluged Phoebe with pleas. "*A Midsummer Night's Dream* closes, the weather's great, and it's only for the day. No excuses."

"You are so pushy."

"And if you're a good little manager," Beth wheedled, "I'll let you gaze upon the handsomest man in the hemisphere."

"Hallelujah, the girl's in love!"

"Just—interested." Beth hated the voice quiver that contradicted her words. "Bring all the actors you can bribe to stay on at"—Beth sucked in a breath, Karl had offered no compensation but for the good of Grey Gallows—"seventy-five dollars for the day?"

"There goes my budget for summer refurbishing." Phoebe sighed dramatically. "No more important than breaking a nail, dear. I'll let you explain to Carol. Now, you'll want them costumed and delivered in my van by noon, I suppose?"

Two children stampeded past the phone booth, fighting for first entrance into the bathroom before Beth answered. "Actually, Sunday morning about ten—"

"No problem." Phoebe's complaints were punctuated with more tapping. Fingertips assaulting a keyboard. "Actors never party after the last show. What about press passes?"

"You don't have to—" Beth fanned herself with her note pad, wondering if Phoebe had stumbled onto her Rolodex.

"Like you can't use free publicity to revitalize your pet economy? Just give me the who, what, when and I'll make a few phone calls," Phoebe insisted. "I'm not as good at this as you are, but I'm learning. I'll convince them Midsummer at Grey Gallows Bay is the hot press preview of the decade.''

Jealousy gnawed at Beth, but faintly. ''Good idea, because I'm trying to undermine—'' Beth blew her cheeks full of air, then exhaled. Could she put a better face on her interference? ''You won't believe what they want to do, Phoeb. Change the name—''

''Grey Gallows is a great name! Gothic, misty—''

''They want to call it Sable Bay and build cheek-to-cheek condos.''

''Who's 'they'? A city council? While I believe you're demented to enjoy living in such a—''

''Provincial backwater?'' Beth supplied.

''—it seems a shame to cram it down the garbage disposal of urban blight.''

''That's why I called *you*,'' Beth rejoiced. ''Actually it's only one man, the jerk I mentioned from my childhood? Who got excited over the prospect of me hallucinating a naked—''

''I remember.''

''Him, and a few others who've fallen for his slogans and seal logo for Sable Bay.''

''Which brings us back to Seal Man.''

Beth leaned her forehead against the booth's cool glass. She tried not to compare Gordon's broad shoulders and hungry arms with the gypsy boy who'd rescued her, long ago. Even if it was like giving up a teddy bear for a boyfriend, she couldn't do it.

''He's a selkie, not a seal man. If all goes well, I'll lure him out of the lagoon and have him give you a fishy kiss Sunday morning.'' It was a weak joke and Phoebe, who knew how devoutly Beth believed, didn't laugh. ''Gotta go. My chowder's cooling.''

''Where can I call you? Get a phone, Beth. You're not the hermit type.''

''I'm thinking about it.''

''How about a fax?'' Phoebe insisted.

''Call the Grey Gallows library. They have the only machine in town." Beth stood. She shouldn't have left Lucinda so long.

"This is a far cry from writing poetry and relaxing." Phoebe waited. "Tell me you're screwing yourself silly."

"Phoebe!" Beth clamped her eyes shut against a vision so vivid it shamed her. "I'm trying to live down my reputation as a madwoman, then I'll relax. See you Sunday."

Oddly dissatisfied, Beth stepped into her shoes, left the booth, and girded herself for conversation with Lucinda.

Beth tugged her jacket closer and sidestepped a waitress trotting toward the ladies' room. She turned out to be Stefanie, the multiply-pierced teenager who'd so delighted in baiting Karl.

"Hey, Beth, right?" Stefanie smoothed her frumpy uniform and grimaced. "Before you say anything, I'm doing this job to explore the pink collar ghetto. I, of course, will be an attorney like my parents. Gotta run." Stefanie turned back once more and gave Beth's black-stockinged legs a thumbs-up sign. "Love the retro-hooker look."

Beth's eyes skimmed over the heads of diners. She'd just located her booth when she heard a throat cleared, near at hand.

Charmaine sat on the counter stool nearest the phone booth, clearly eavesdropping.

"She gots a cat!" Minny waved the remains of a grilled-cheese sandwich.

"And a big city attitude," Charmaine snapped.

Beth's cheeks heated with embarrassment as she reviewed her conversation with Phoebe. Besides scoffing at the seal logo and Karl, what had she said?

Beth rushed by, excusing her haste with a nod toward the table where Lucinda sat waiting. Charmaine's slit-eyed glare told Beth that whatever she'd said, it had been far too much.

Outsiders didn't roof their own cottages, didn't bask in the sporadic sunshine of their own seal coves, didn't stroll their own beaches, Beth reminded herself. Just now, though, she walked away from her beach.

"Peaches, here kitty." Beth scanned the weeds bordering the unpaved road. Wind rubbed grasses together, as if the cat stalked alongside her, smirking.

"Peaches!" Beth stood still. Silence absorbed her call.

At least the thunder had stopped. For two days and most of last night it had grumbled impotently.

She walked on, worried, because Karl claimed to have seen an orange cat way out by the highway.

Exile—self-imposed, to be fair—had followed yesterday's lunch with Lucinda Wright. The tense encounter with Charmaine had magnified Beth's enjoyment of Lucinda's plan for a faire booth she'd christened Sea Serpent Press. She'd offer reasonably priced books, sheets of handmade parchment, and calligraphy pens. Even better than her plan for the faire was Lucinda's store of good-natured gossip.

Halfway through lunch, Charmaine had stormed past their table. When Beth confessed her guilt, Lucinda explained Charmaine had taken a correspondence class to become a "real-tor," so, of course Charmaine favored Karl's plans. She wanted to sell her parents' harborside home and bait shop before destitute fishermen flooded the market with rustic dwellings.

Lucinda opposed all Karl's schemes except the faire. Grey Gallows, she reasoned, might benefit from an infusion of culture.

With an ally sitting before her, Beth had worked hard not to stare out the diner's front window. She'd felt a feverish awareness, as if Gordon stood just outside, whispering her name. Of course, she'd been wrong.

He hadn't come last night. He hadn't come today and it was past three o'clock. He'd probably sailed down the coast, where summer wasn't so sullen. With storm clouds gathering and the seals huddling together after playing hide-and-seek with the sun all day, Gordon would be foolish to return, even though he'd left his onyx cuff links behind.

Beth sprinkled cat food on the path and waited. All those months in San Francisco, the hollow beneath her breastbone had ached. For Grey Gallows, she'd thought.

Beth brushed the last crumbs from her palms and placed her hands on her hips. Damn it, she loved Grey Gallows. And she didn't mind solitude. But she did mind Gordon's disappearing acts.

"Okay, Peaches, last chance!" Beth shouted. "No food, no shelter from the storm, no cuddling."

Beth strode toward home. Peaches would come slinking back when he was hungry, and Gordon . . . She couldn't comprehend his hunger.

Beth stamped up the steps to the bluff and slammed into the cottage. Lois Lane might shrug and smile at her hero's odd disappearances, but Beth Caxton would not.

She fished out running shoes and shorts. She pulled them on, yanked her red sweatshirt over her head, and headed for Lyre Beach.

Storm clouds glowed, underlit by the sun. An autumnal tang floated on the wind. Some old-timers burned their garden plots each spring, and Beth fancied she smelled green shoots pushing up through black earth.

Staring at cliffs that might have been gouged with a giant's thumb, eons past when the clay ran wet and gooey, Beth stretched out her hamstrings. She flexed her Achilles tendons and considered a flock of turkey vultures circling overhead.

"Not tonight, guys." Forget jogging. She'd run hard and sweat out every pitiful drop of melancholy. If it meant she'd run five miles down the beach by the time Gordon came sailing back, that was just dandy.

His masquerade couldn't work while the cows called him Prince and protector. Why, when their matriarchy functioned so smoothly, must they turn to him? Now that Bringer of Crimson had vanished, a new threat had arisen and they called upon him for help.

Gordon torpedoed up from the depths. Darkness faded as he shot higher, past kelp outspread to catch the sun's energy, past fish dancing in a random glimmer of emerald. With each flipper stroke Gordon moved closer to the warmth and light, nearer Beth.

Two cows had died. One, ensnared in a fishing net, had drowned. The other, by her companion's description, had been bludgeoned to death by men.

Gordon had found only the first cow. Drifting open-eyed, she trailed clumps of strangling-tight mesh. After taking her out to sea for burial, Gordon floated through the timbers of an ancient shipwreck, exploring, relaxing, until he felt ready to sleep on an unfamiliar outcropping of rock. At dawn he began diving again, surfacing to pelting showers, to whipping curtains of rain, to thunder. Still, he couldn't find the other.

Radiance warmed his muscles and dappled the waters of Beth's cove. Here, he'd face the cows' and pups' fear. Should he give in to their worry and move them to a basking spot where they felt safer?

One last thrust sent him above the surface. He arced into oxygen-rich air, and a breeze warm with land smells combed his fur. The sea ran bright as liquid gold and pelicans came gliding.

Once more he dived, skimming the sandy shallows, shaking off weariness. After he calmed the cows, he must go to Beth.

Men often raised their shoulders to roll out stiffness, but Gordon found it of little help, especially within the confines of his black T-shirt and jeans. He'd even put on the white leather shoes to go looking for Beth.

She hadn't been at her cottage. It figured. He'd found nothing else he'd looked for all day.

He had encountered her miserable cat, shivering amid ear-splitting cries. Gordon had tried the door, found it unlocked and let the animal in, but a single breath told him Beth had gone.

He followed her patterned tread down the beach until he heard her returning. He leaned against a black rock, and waited.

Cloud-strained sunlight shimmered on Beth's reddish hair as it swung side-to-side behind her shoulders. In the cooling air, her labored breath spun a halo around her face.

Beth's grating, trotting steps slowed to a walk as she saw him.

"I should have known I'd find you here," he greeted her. He *had* known, but something in his slight ability to sift Beth's thoughts frightened her.

Her hair, beaded with moisture, fell in loose waves from her temples. It sparkled as she nodded in agreement. Her chest heaved beneath the red shirt. For a moment, she breathed too hard to speak.

"Hi," she said, finally, brushing her lips with her sleeve.

Gordon fell into step beside her. Their feet moved in a gentle pace which soothed away his weariness.

"That night in your flat, by your painting—" Gordon paused as she looked sidelong at him. "I saw how you longed for the beach."

Beth frowned. "I'm beginning to think it wasn't the beach."

It is. He coaxed her mind to accept the truth, but Beth hid, bending to find a nugget of blue glass polished by time and waves. *The sea and shore, you and I. You knew, Beth. You remembered.*

Beth flinched as if he'd whipped her. She rolled the glass between her palms, fighting his invasion, but the connection with Beth's mind echoed loud as a hand-clap.

When she looked up, her green eyes met his. A breeze plucked at her hair, fluttering tendrils before her eyes, almost masking her hesitation.

Gordon took her hand. Hot and small, it clung to him at once. Her face flushed with such naked expectancy, Gordon knew she wanted his kiss.

His weariness was good. He linked their hands and lips, but Beth closed the distance between their bodies. Her lips, a little dry from sunburn, sought after his when he slowed to take a breath. And when she finally faltered, her breath sounded a tremor of want.

He didn't release her hands as she leaned back, swinging their arms, confident his grip wouldn't let her fall. Beth's trust tasted as sweet as her kiss.

"What's in the bag?" She stared like a child peering at a Christmas gift.

"A surprise." Gordon glanced down at the white canvas bag he'd dropped next to the rock. "Two surprises, actually."

"Mmm." Beth slipped free, but Gordon snatched the bag up from the sand.

"For later," he said, and followed her home.

Gordon sorted through papers Beth had left piled like rubbish on her kitchen counter.

> "A shark crossed the bar before me
> seeking sun, seeking salmon, seeking life . . ."

Below those lines, Beth had scrawled "frivolous, petty, trivial." Were the words criticism or the seeds of her next stanza? Gordon looked up as rain plopped on the roof overhead, then glanced toward the bedroom, where Beth had gone to change her clothes.

She'd left the work next to a hammer, a screwdriver, and an unopened tin of roofing cement. He understood the use of such tools, but the meaning of poetry, like religion, often eluded him. He understood the first part, recognized and rejoiced in his role in it, but the last bit was nonsense.

A second poem lay beneath the first. It spoke of a puppet show. He tried reading it in a whisper. "Who pulls the strings as we dance . . . ?"

The shell curtain rattled. Beth, in faded jeans and a loose shirt cut from midnight blue velvet, moved toward him with raised eyebrows.

"You left it out." Gordon replaced the poem, not sure if he should apologize.

"It's all right." Beth gathered the sheets and folded them together. "It sounded better when you read it than it did in my head."

"How can that be?" Gordon asked. "If you don't like the words, if their meaning doesn't suit you, where does it come from?"

"You're serious?" Beth regarded him with suspicion and pleasure, then slid the papers into her back pocket.

"Of course I'm serious. I could learn to roof a house." He weighed the hammer in one hand. "Or cook, or dance, but I could never make poetry. Is it work or is it a gift you're born with?"

"Both, I guess." Beth regarded the seamed ceiling as she listened to the quickening tempo of the rain. "Some of it blows in on the breeze and some of it is pulled up out of me, screaming like a mandrake root."

His horror must have shown. Laughing, Beth steadied his arm with her hand. For that, he'd let her mock him all night long.

"I only meant it as a figure of speech." Beth's laughter tumbled over itself as her fingers stroked back and forth, consoling him. "Your face—Gordon, I just meant—" Beth blinked as a wet drop slid down her cheek.

Her hand left him to touch the drop, just as another plopped between her eyes.

"Oh, no. The roof." Beth stared, aghast, toward her white ceiling. "I've stripped off all the shingles in—"

She paced to the kitchen, then to her bedroom.

"Gordon, come here."

Although it was a summons he'd longed for, Gordon doubted Beth was considering lovemaking.

"Does it look to you like—" She darted through the shell curtain to glance at the living room ceiling.

Gordon had time to smell lemon furniture polish and see silver earrings cast upon her dresser-top, then she returned, pulled him toward the middle of the room, and pointed.

"There." Her index finger grazed his cheek. "Is the ceiling bulging? Could it possibly be filling up with rain?"

"I think it could." The charred skeleton of Junior's house came to mind. The structure of Beth's cottage couldn't be too different. "What's between the rafters and the ceiling?"

"A little sawdust, for insulation." Her voice pleaded against her own good sense, as if Beth, too, turned to him as a male, hoping he could change reality.

"Ohhh." Beth vaulted onto her bed. She kicked at a pile of clothing, muttering, "Bucket, bucket." A pair of black stockings fluttered to the floor as she balanced on the rainbow-hued quilt, bit her lip, and stared prayerfully at a bulge rather like the bottom of a shallow bowl.

She jumped down, almost into his arms, then halted his embrace with a flat-palmed gesture. "Stay here. I'm going to need your help. I've never tried this, but I think it will work."

That, at least was promising.

An avalanche of pans and cookie sheets sounded from the kitchen before Beth returned, juggling a huge soup tureen and a screwdriver. Gordon lost hope. These were not the tools of seduction.

"Stick it in there." Beth slapped the screwdriver into his palm. Then, using her hip as a battering ram, Beth scooted her bed across the rug.

"I'm sorry," he said. "I'm not sure I understand."

Beth uttered a frustrated groan as pattering increased in the living room. She ran back through the shell curtains, shouting.

"Stick the screwdriver in that swelling and *maybe* all the rainwater will drain into my tureen, instead of collapsing my ceiling."

She'd placed a cooking pot under the leak in the living room. Now she stood, arms folded, waiting for him to puncture her house.

He extended the screwdriver to within a half-inch of the bulging plaster. "Wouldn't a champagne toast or something be in order?" He heard Beth's impatient shifting and a sound awfully like a growl. "Right," he said, then jammed the tool home.

He jumped back from a shower of plaster chips and a stream of rainwater which fell, as thin and straight as a silver pencil, right into Beth's tureen.

Gordon stared until his eyes stung with it. He thought the bulge flattened as he watched. "What do you think?"

She took his hand and kissed the knuckles of the fingers still gripping the screwdriver. "Not bad," she said with a satisfied chuckle. "Not bad for a couple amateurs. I assume this *is* the first ceiling you've perforated, Mr. Gordon?''

He wanted her. He wanted to tackle her down to her bed with its rumpled quilt and mattress askew from her shoving. But the moment spun out a heartbeat too long and Beth grew nervous.

''Now for the toast.'' Beth padded out of the bedroom.

There was nothing for it but to coax her full of drink and hope she'd catapult back into his arms—this time, for all the right reasons.

Nine

A border of daisies decorated the snifters Beth used for brandy. She poured slowly, completing the simple, celebratory gesture. It wasn't as if she'd concocted a love potion. Why did she feel foolhardy?

She heard his steps stop in the doorway behind her. Even without entering, Gordon made the kitchen feel crowded.

Beth handed him the snifter, snatching her hand away so quickly, the glass wobbled between them.

"I've got it." Gordon steadied the snifter, but his brown eyes fixed on her and a feral smile haunted the corners of his mouth.

Anyone could see he was bad news, the kind of man cautious girls didn't trifle with.

"To unwitting expertise." Beth clinked her glass to his and wished for an interruption. Futily. No outside interference would block whatever Gordon planned. At Gull Cott, no visitor clattered up the steps for a cup of tea. No television blared distracting commercials. No telephone rang.

"Listen." Beth tilted her head toward the living room. "The pinging's stopped. In my spaghetti pot." As her calves collided with the stove door, Beth realized she'd backed away from him. As far as she could. "By relieving the pressure in the bedroom, we've solved the problem. At least temporarily.''

Her diversion worked; Gordon looked as bored as a bench.

Beth sipped the brandy and felt it burn. The dusty bottle had presided on that top shelf for as long as she remembered. ''It's not very good brandy,'' she apologized.

''It's fine.'' He set the glass on the kitchen counter. ''Sounds as if the rain's slackened.''

Wind hunted among the rafters overhead and Beth shivered. She needed something—not a blanket, not a tablecloth—to cover the roof. ''I don't suppose you have a canvas tarp on your boat?''

Confusion clouded Gordon's face before he answered. ''Sorry.''

With folded arms, he leaned against the kitchen windowsill and gazed out at Grey Gallows' namesake spires. Raindrops slipped down the glass, and fading afternoon light cast drips on his face like tears.

Beth rolled a roofing nail she'd left on the counter. ''D'you think I'd be smart to tack something over that, in case this is only a lull?''

Without looking at her, Gordon shrugged. She shouldn't feel irritated because he watched the stone spires instead of her.

''They're the remains of a ghost forest.''

His brooding ceased as he turned from the window. ''A ghost forest,'' he echoed.

''Once, a grove of trees stood there and a lot of little sea creatures blew inland. I'm not sure who told me. Maybe, Jack. Anyway, living and dead, the creatures stuck to the mossy bark.''

With unquestioning raptness Gordon leaned back against the kitchen counter. His bronzed arms crossed above the intersection of his black shirt and jeans.

''I don't know if the trees died because the weather changed, or they couldn't send roots deep enough into the bluff.'' She warmed the snifter between her palms. ''I'm not a biologist or botanist, but apparently, after the trees died, their bark softened and their interiors rotted away, but those millions of little skeletons formed casts of the trees.''

Though she knew them by heart, Beth turned to the window. "Only those two were strong enough to stay."

Gordon took her under his arm as wind sent a scattered shiver through the house. "Not a bad way to end."

This stranger mirrored her thoughts as no one else. Soon she must ask him who he was, where he'd come from, why he courted and confused her. Beth settled her head against his shoulder. Soon.

A cascade of raindrops from under the eaves splattered against the glass.

"Hey!" With a boyish shout, his arm fell from her shoulders. "Let's go outside and play with your present." He swept up her running shoes and chucked them toward her. "Put on some shoes."

"You got me a toy?" Beth slipped her feet into the damp leather. Gordon had already lifted his canvas sack.

"You don't mind getting wet, do you?" He looked, for an instant, as if he'd committed another faux pas.

"Of course not." She tied her laces and crowded after him, eager to see her gift. "I'll dry. I spent nine-tenths of my childhood in the water and rain. Jack always said I was half seal, anyway."

"Did he, now?" Gordon's chuckle warmed her more than the brandy. She couldn't see his face as he slid a cardboard square from the bag.

"What do you think?" He shoved the package into her hands. "Is it more suitable than the necklace?" He fidgeted as she examined the Frisbee. He gave her no time to answer. "I saw children playing with one on the school lawn, but I didn't join in."

Beth imagined his broad-shouldered form loping amid a flock of first-graders. He'd given her an emerald and a hot-pink Frisbee. He loved the sea so much, he wanted to gaze out at it forever, like she did. Maybe she hadn't questioned his past because she didn't want the answers.

Stronger than curiosity and caution was the fact that she liked Gordon. Nothing must change that.

"The package does warn that it's not an indoor toy." He frowned, misinterpreting her silence.

"Gordon, I love it. Thank you." Beth stood on tiptoe to kiss his cheek. "No one's given me a toy in a long time."

"Why not?"

"Maybe they think I'm too old and serious to play—"

In one sinuous movement Gordon swept her outdoors. Although he'd never played the game before, in seconds he learned to curve his fingers under the lip of the plastic disk. In minutes he could send it spinning over Beth's head, sailing a quarter-inch beyond her reach or homing right to her. He snagged Beth's clumsiest tosses from the air and accused her of attempting to bully "the rookie."

Only when Junior's blue truck bumped down the unpaved road did their laughing and leaping stop.

"Damn him," Gordon growled. He rarely swore, considering it a symptom of impotent human rage, but now he paced Beth's living room rug of twisted wool, unable to tamp down his fury with huge strides. He clenched his fists while Beth chatted with Junior and his recuperating father, Al.

Gone was Gordon's craving for friendship. For an instant he'd longed to hug the boy who'd called him "Gordy," but then he'd seen Beth's reluctant face, saw her body stiffen, and felt anxiety crackle through her mind.

"I'll battle him for you." Tension had risen like a snarl in his throat and Beth had seen it.

"Don't be ridiculous." She'd glanced toward the truck again before turning cool and polite. "Gordon, why don't you wait inside?"

And he had. He'd allowed himself to be banished like an unruly dog.

Junior's jabbering indicated he'd stopped by Gull Cott on his way home from the hospital in Parish. Al, mere hours out of a hospital bed, had puffed up the rough-cut steps to the bluff before collapsing into a chair on Beth's deck. Watching Al shuffle across the yard, Gordon imagined the stiffness of burned flesh, the jets of pain accompanying each skin-crinkling step. Stubborn old bull.

Peaches meandered into the living room and sprang onto the couch. The cat licked his shoulder fur, pretending nonchalance as he kept vigil over the intruder.

Gordon ignored the cat, concentrating on Beth's sweet commiseration with the two fishermen, once his family.

"Told you so, Beth Ann." Junior's singsong tone carried quite well. "We were on our way home from the hospital and I said to Al I'd best bring you my tarp—knew you wouldn't have one—so you didn't flood yourself out of house and home."

Gordon wondered when Junior had grown so small-minded and boastful. Was he denigrating a female to earn his father's approval? Why hadn't he outgrown such foolery?

"Damn him to hell." Gordon bent the Frisbee in half and relished the cursing.

She was thanking Junior, declining his hammer and nails, his help with the unwieldy ladder.

"You can't leave your tools out in the rain, Beth Ann. Ladder hinges'll rust, you know."

They clambered about overhead. Gordon set the resilient Frisbee on Beth's coffee table and stared up. What if the beams were too weak to hold them both? What if she fell and he were helpless to save her? Mixed with fear came the image of Beth's midnight-blue shirt, wet and clinging as she moved side-by-side with Junior. Gordon wanted to roar.

Peaches arched his back and narrowed his eyes. He puffed his fur in primitive reprimand, then stalked from the room.

He'd been scolded by an animal, a mere cat. Gordon interlaced his fingers, trying to armor himself against such a nuisance emotion as jealousy.

Voices moved down the ladder, away from the cottage, growing distant as they discussed the fair, berry cream cakes, garlands and games. Perhaps the men were leaving.

". . . kissing booth?" The voice was Junior's. He'd spoken of kissing Beth.

Damn. To keep from bolting through the door or diving

through the window to smash Junior's face, Gordon glared at the rafters. *Damn*.

"I hardly think so. The high school girls are saving that duty for themselves and they're welcome to it." Cool San Francisco Beth was the female who answered Junior. Though he took her hint, Al didn't.

". . . tight-assed do-gooders. It's a tradition." Coughs riddled Al's voice. "If they can't stand the sight of good-natured swapping of—"

Junior apparently had the good sense to hustle the old man away before he collapsed. Just as Junior glanced back to flash Beth an apologetic smile, he stopped. He bristled, staring toward the living room window where the shutters were open wide and Gordon stood watching.

Gordon stepped aside. If Beth wanted him hidden, he'd hide. If Junior challenged him, the paltry boy would be sorry.

Caught by wind and not a little ire, the kitchen door crashed open against the wall as Beth stormed inside. She closed the door and leaned against it, clearly angry.

"What in the world—"

Gordon caught her cold, wind-red cheeks between his hands and kissed her.

Beth's head jerked aside and her arms shoved against his shirt front. *You're mine*. The breath she took in protest made her mouth vulnerable and jealousy made him a beast. Gordon's tongue thrust between her lips.

It wasn't enough. With a groan he should have suppressed, would have suppressed if he could, Gordon lowered the arms Beth used to push him away. He locked his fingers through hers and pressed her arms against the door, prolonging the kiss with every secret he knew.

The wet warmth of her mouth welcomed him, tempering his rage until he remembered. She was not just his female, vivid and lively. Beneath that, she was Beth, unutterably sweet Beth.

While his mouth tempted her, his mind chanted her name, glorified her beauty, her warmth, and their need for each other. She heard him. Her hands fell weak in his. Her arms drooped as if her elbows had turned to heavy stones she couldn't support.

Human willpower. He needed it. It would not be a waste of time, no matter the rush in his veins. Once Beth accepted his difference, his common magic, he wanted her to fall in love with him. That was an enchantment even ancient sorcery couldn't weave.

When Beth's chest heaved a heavy sigh and she spoke against his mouth, Gordon stopped. He could translate the language of Beth's body, but not her utterance. He waited as Beth's head eased back against the door. She stared up at him and her eyes shone dragon green. Finally she gathered enough words to speak.

"I am not like this." Incredulity blurred the guilt in her voice. "And, as I was about to say when I came through that door, what in the world was that"—she gestured to the bluff—"all about?"

Beth hardened her resistance. Gordon had looked absolutely vicious, ready to jump Junior and beat him bloody. Such men were dangerous, not to be trusted, and certainly not her type.

"I told you I used to come here as a child—"

"No, you didn't." She blinked, certain she would have remembered.

Gordon shrugged. "I recognized Junior as a ruffian and I could tell he made you uneasy."

That was believable, but he was keeping the full truth submerged.

"I wouldn't have hurt him." Gordon's bravado fell away. He kicked at a loose strand in her braided rug. "I was sort of a ruffian, too." He looked up. "But I don't want him kissing you."

"I don't think there's much danger of that." Beth made herself joke it off. No matter how primitive and possessive that kiss had felt, Gordon wasn't claiming her. He was being a guy. It had been so long since her last boyfriend that she'd forgotten how territorial males could act.

Rain pounded the roof with renewed intensity. They both glanced toward the spaghetti pot, then laughed.

"It's turning into what my girlfriend from the Gulf Coast would call a frog-strangler." Beth watched Gordon blink twice before the weak joke evoked a smile.

Wind butted against the side of the cottage and she felt glad *she* wasn't sleeping out on the water, harbor or not. "If this keeps up, you won't get much sleep tonight."

"Just where is it you think I'm staying?" Gordon asked slowly, as if he spoke to a child.

With someone else. The answer ricocheted inside her skull.

"You always have wet hair, so I thought, probably, you stayed on a yacht moored at the harbor, then swam down the coast. For exercise." Beth forced herself to stretch and yawn, then caught her reflection in the night-dark window and tugged down the hem of her shirt. "I hadn't given it a lot of thought."

"You're pretty close." Gordon smoothed a hand over his hair, as if checking for wetness. "I don't mean to be secretive. It's just—I told you, this, uh, wealth and stuff was sudden. I—"

"You deserve your privacy." Beth nodded and glanced toward the sheaf of notes she'd compiled since the meeting in Karl's office. She'd promised to negotiate the cooperation of Horatio and Jewel Clark early tomorrow, at their bait shop. "And I deserve to get to bed, myself.

"Before opening your second present?" As Gordon retrieved the canvas bag, Peaches sidled against him, hampering Gordon's removal of a tightly rolled poster. He unrolled it like a scroll.

In the full-color photograph a herd of seals raced across a rippling sea. They swam in graceful formation, except for one sleek animal. He executed a midair somersault. Beth couldn't quite make out the blue script printed on the poster's lower margin.

" 'If you . . . ' " she began.

" 'If you obey all the rules, you miss all the fun.' " Gordon let the poster curl back into a spiral, then handed it to her. "It's an invitation."

The living room window shuddered under assault from both wind and rain.

"I wouldn't even walk up the beach in this weather."

"It's coming up from the south," he said. "At least it's warm."

"You could stay here." Her heartbeat drowned out the hammering raindrops.

"I'd never stay where I'm not wanted."

The words came with such velvet slowness, Beth knew he wasn't questioning her hospitality. There was no safe way to answer.

"On the couch," she blurted.

"No." He seized a belt loop on her jeans and tugged her forward a step. "What about my invitation?"

Invitation? If he'd issued a summons to the White House, she might have missed it. She only knew Gordon's index finger stayed hooked through her belt loop.

"I was in Gimp's pub." He released her. "The men told me I should take in Midsummer *Eve* as well as the daytime festivities."

What else had the men in the pub told him? About her teenage hallucinations? About Beth's "bonny selkie"?

"Beth, I only want a local guide to the bonfires and storytelling and ceremonies. Would you go with me?"

"Like a date?"

"A lot like a date, except the fellows say merrymaking goes on till dawn."

Which was exactly why Jack forbade her to go. He'd refused to subject her to rites evoking Grey Gallow's primitive roots.

"I'm not sure."

Beth wavered, remembering another night of dark gaiety. On Chinese New Year in San Francisco, she'd strolled alone, exalting in clanging chimes and clashing cymbals, in the stately frolic of a dragon draped in red and gold. Then a boy tossed a string of firecrackers. It soared, plummeted, and exploded close enough to singe her shoes.

If you obey all the rules, you miss all the fun.

Beth tossed the rolled poster toward the couch. And missed.

"Did Gimp tell you things can get sort of rough?" Beth

watched Gordon's chin lift a notch. "Midsummer Day has good food and games for the children," she explained. "The night before is sort of the dark sister of the real festival."

"Gimp told me it *is* the real festival."

Beth imagined druids swaying in moonlight, flowers fed to flames, wine drizzled on shrines of oceanic deities—offerings from fisherfolk who relied on Nature's bounty.

The storm hushed, listening for Beth's answer.

"I've never been before," she admitted. "It's mainly for adults."

His rogue's smile warned her before his arms circled her ribs. "I would be willing..." His thumbs traced down each side of her spine. "... to vouch for the fact..." His hands reached her waist. "... that while all of Grey Gallows had its head turned, you've ripened into a grown-up."

His hands flattened over her back pockets, and Beth twisted away, covering one rustling pocket, herself.

"You're trying to steal my poetry, that's all."

"Miss Caxton," Gordon said, moving toward the door. "Whyever should I steal what I know you'll give freely?"

He'd twisted the doorknob. *Was* he talking about the miserable scraps of doggerel she'd managed to write in the past days or was it another double entendre?

Beth's breath clogged in her throat. If so, Gordon's insufferable, intolerable, unendurable arrogance was right on target.

He waited, with the door opened, but not enough to allow Peaches' escape.

Gordon needed his arrogance jerked right out from under him, but he'd have to find someone else to do it. "What time?" Beth rocked back on her heels.

"At moonrise." As he pulled the door shut behind him, Gordon made a swift gesture. He might have blown her a kiss.

Ten

Waves lapped gentle and rose-gold in Beth's cove and so far, there'd been no divers. Perhaps she'd frightened them off.

She tied her sweatshirt hood, poured coffee steaming from her thermos, and settled cross-legged to share sunrise with the sea lions. The cows and pups' gabbling came with such frequency, it seemed as if she should understand it.

The storm had caused rocks to tumble from Grey Gallows Point. Now, a few yards out from shore, waves funneled between two mossy boulders, forming a white-foam waterfall. Several pups, motley as they shed their woolly birth coats, played in the cascade while their mothers supervised with watery snorts.

The only other sign of last night's storm was a fog bank curled along the horizon like a ghost wave. Perhaps tonight's Midsummer Eve bonfires wouldn't be rained out, after all.

Beth slipped a peanut butter and jelly sandwich from her sweatshirt pocket. *"Bon appetit."* She took a bite and looked for the acrobatic bull. Plush chestnut animals caught sunlight on their basking sides and the curves of surfacing heads, but the black bull had apparently followed his fellows south.

She, too, should quit dawdling. It was time to seek out Horatio and Jewel Clark. Charmaine, whose parents they were, had washed her hands of the cantankerous couple.

"Try all you like," Charmaine had told Beth. "They're impossible."

The Clarks' feud was so long-standing, villagers had come to regard it with amusement. Years ago Horatio had stood at the counter of Clark's Dock and Bait and swapped a pound of mussels for an equal amount of mushrooms harvested by a now-infamous "hippie from Washington State," then gone home to fix Jewel a midmorning omelet.

Instead of the promised morels, the mushrooms turned out to be "death angels." Only a hundred-miles-per-hour freeway dash to the hospital in Parish had saved Jewel's life.

Shortly thereafter, Jewel served Horatio a nicely sautéed sea bass infested with intestinal worms. She swore the mishap was coincidental; Horatio swore he'd get even. Since then, including the months during which Charmaine was conceived, born, and raised, the two had cooked separately and come down on opposite sides of every social, political, and economic issue anyone could remember. Now Jewel wanted to use their picturesque fishing boat to give rides to tourists who attended the Fisherman's Faire tomorrow. Horatio refused, and he was the boat's captain.

Beth sighed, poured her cooled coffee on a parched purple thistle, and stood in time to see a curve like polished obsidian flow past Grey Gallows Point.

With loud barks and swishing flippers, the cows announced him. The bull glided into the cove, skimmed above the sand, then came ashore. Beth stood still, marveling at the male's grace. Unlike true seals, which scooted along on their bellies, seal lions moved nimbly as dogs. This one made his majestic way among the females.

Beth crept down the path. She held her breath when scree drizzled from under her shoe. Unafraid, the bull shook his head and lunged forward, flashing white incisors.

Beth froze as the bull's stare turned aloof. He barked a single challenge, then returned to the cove. Every pup and cow swam in his wake.

"Come back." The boulders and crags absorbed her voice,

without an echo. Not a flipper faltered as they surged after him.

They'd be back. Years of observation had taught Beth the animals stayed loyal to their rookeries. Still, the disturbance left Beth troubled.

"Go ahead and sample his scrambled eggs, Miss—"

"Beth, please." Beth pulled a ladder-back chair up to a kitchen table cluttered with fishing magazines and catalogs.

"Beth, then." Jewel Clark's white ponytail flared like a whale's spout from the crown of her head. She used a forearm to clear Beth a place at the table. "I don't think he's a danger to anyone but me." She lifted one shoulder toward her husband. "Or wait and I'll fix some for you, soon as he finishes scouring that skillet. Better do a good job, Clark."

"Pay her no mind, Miss Caxton." Horatio Clark's military-cut white hair showed patches of pink scalp as he bobbed his head in apology.

"She *wants* to be called Beth."

"Beth." Horatio accepted the correction. "Jewel's crazy as a coot on the subject of eggs, but I'd be glad to fix you a plate."

"Just coffee would be fine." Beth raised her voice over Jewel's snort.

With most commercial fisherman long at sea and most rec-reational anglers still abed, the Clarks enjoyed a leisurely breakfast. During three cups of coffee, Beth explained all she knew of the plans for Grey Gallows' Midsummer Fisherman's Faire.

"I don't want to hear any more economic diversity crap." Horatio scraped a few eggy scraps to the center of his plate, then pointed his fork toward Jewel. "And we're not selling out and moving."

"Then again, we might." Jewel smiled at Beth.

"Jeez, Jewel, it'd kill you to leave here." Horatio used a crust to mop his plate.

"Charmaine—"

"Has had no use for this town since Junior MacDonald

dumped her and Minny." Horatio slapped the table hard enough to make it rock. "Sorry, Beth. Family matters."

Beth nodded.

"I'm surprised you're backing this Sable Bay"—Jewel fumbled for a word which would rob Horatio of ammunition— "—project. Seems to me Jack Caxton always road-blocked anything that'd 'spoil' Grey Gallows."

"Still don't have a telephone, do ya?" Horatio asked. "Or a paved road out to your place?"

"Still don't." Beth felt a surge of stubborn pride. "I am putting on a new roof though."

Horatio chuckled, then sobered. "Gonna sell?"

"I can't imagine anything that'd drive me away from here."

"Charmaine would. Guess she hasn't got to you, yet," Jewel said. When Horatio agreed with a short laugh, Jewel snapped, "Shut up." She raised one eyebrow toward Beth. "Why are you doing this, then?"

Beth ran a finger around the lip of her coffee mug. "I want to live here." . . . *without having people stop talking when I enter a room, or make hushed explanations to friends as I pass by on the street* . . . "And I think visit-on-the-weekend tourism is better than stringing motels and fast-food places up the coast from here to Parish."

While both Clarks nodded, Beth added, "And I've heard it's a bad fishing year. I thought this might help supplement—"

Horatio's snarl intruded. "F—"

Jewel rapped her husband's knuckles with a spoon.

"*Friggin*' seals're like a pack of swimmin' rats, chewin' through nets, gobbling fish. And then we've got Gimp serving up his Scots foolishness as side-dish to a man's beer."

"As if we've extra cash to plunk down at Gimp's."

Beth nearly thanked Jewel for the diversion. Gimp's "Scots' foolishness" meant selkies.

"Craziness is in the air, I tell you." Horatio studied Beth as if she stirred a hazy memory. "Rampant. Some young fellow from out of town, with odd sort of eyes, blank one minute, sifting your soul or looking for a fight the next—"

" 'Sifting your soul.' " Jewel laughed.

Horatio stopped, eyes fixed on Beth. In the uneasy silence Jewel watched as a spider lowered from the brass lamp overhead.

"I tell you, he's too old to be reading that new-age junk. 'Sifting your soul.' Poor young man probably has an astigmatism."

"Jeez, honey." Horatio despaired over Jewel's reasoning, then his memory clicked. "Hey! Beth Ann Caxton. Now, I remember. 'Beth's selkie.' "

Beth raised both hands as a shield. "I was fifteen years old and half drowned. Show some mercy, Mr. Clark."

"But you saw one. She said she saw a selkie. Right, Jewel?"

"I bumped into a herd of seals in the kelp and some stranger dragged me ashore and gave me CPR." Beth stood up, intending to carry her mug to the sink, but Jewel motioned her to sit.

"The rest is Karl's imagination, is what you're saying." Jewel met Horatio's eyes. Both cleared their throats, then looked toward the doorway leading to the bait shop.

"Well, we've got serious seal problems, is the truth," Horatio said. "And if you hear any different, talk to Junior MacDonald. His dad, Al, is leading a move to wipe out the pests."

"I've always been partial to seals." Beth refused to think of the contented cows basking in her cove as pests. "I always heard seals helped fishermen. You know, predators follow predators. Fishermen follow the seals, seals follow big fish, the big fish follow little ones . . ."

"So it mighta been in the old days, but Al claims we've got a rogue bull seal. Stayed behind after the rest left. This bull's leading the others astray." Horatio scratched behind one ear.

Alarm burned like acid in her wrists, under her arms, at the base of her skull, but Beth didn't give in. "I know they're smart—" she began.

"Smarter than dogs." Jewel gathered the plates. "The warm-blooded lords of the sea."

"Says who?" Horatio dropped his forehead against his hands.

"Jacques Cousteau, is all." Jewel shot him a withering look.

"Jacques freakin' Cousteau is not in Grey Gallows. He hasn't seen this bull." Horatio turned to Beth. "Black as sin and twelve feet long, if you believe Al."

"That's an *if* the size of an anchor," Jewel whispered as she retrieved Beth's coffee cup.

Should she tell them the bull had led his harem away or pretend Al had invented him? Beth tried a distraction, instead. "About local fishing . . . some abalone divers were in my cove—"

"I hope you saw 'em off," Jewel sniffed. "Sy's chowder's turned into slop, 'cause of outsiders snatching so many."

"Sort of, but these guys weren't having much luck. They weren't even carrying game bags."

"Probably throwing them in a boat. You take yourself a nice damp gunnysack, stuff it full of kelp, and abs will keep. . . ."

But there'd been no boat. Beth was about to say so, when Horatio, undaunted by her interruption, cut in.

"I tell you, it's not right, having a bull here in summer." He ignored Jewel's exasperation. "No telling how he'll turn things upside down. I'm not so ignorant about your stinkin' balance of nature, now am I, Jewel? Admit it."

Jewel ran hot water into a dishpan. Steam clouded up around her, and she pretended not to hear. Horatio jerked a thumb in her direction and winked at Beth.

"Come to think of it, maybe I'll take *Paloma* out and take Charmaine's *turistas* for a spin, after all." Horatio leaned back and ran his tongue over his teeth when Jewel squinted in his direction.

Beth folded her hands together. It would be great to tell Lucinda she'd won over the odd couple.

"I'll keep my eyes open for that rogue, while I'm out."

"Don't you go bringin' a gun, Horatio Clark." Dishwater showered off the spatula Jewel waved in his direction.

Beth's hands knotted into fists as Horatio taunted them with maniacal laughter.

"Who said I'd shoot 'im? Hell, ladies, that's against the law."

Cat's eyes.

That night Beth half-believed Gordon could see in the dark. Nothing else explained his ease navigating her secret trail to the cove. Citing the fat gold doubloon of a moon as light enough, Gordon climbed as if he knew the narrow ledges by heart.

Now they'd reached the cove, silent, deserted, and oddly bare as low tide retreated from Grey Gallows. Gordon leaped from boulder to boulder. With each landing, he reached back to clasp Beth's hand.

Moonlight glazed rippling tide pools and inlets, but with Gordon's guidance, Beth hadn't once wet her feet.

A good thing, too, since her flat ballet slippers were just inches below the hem of her borrowed skirt.

After leaving Clark's Bait Shop this morning, Beth had left Lucinda a note, assuring her *Paloma* would ferry visitors around the harbor during tomorrow's faire. She hadn't expected Lucinda to pay her a visit.

"I wanted to bring you these, for tonight." The librarian had sidled through Beth's screen door bearing clothes covered with dry cleaners' plastic. "I'm past cavorting by bonfires."

Lucinda had brushed Beth's protests aside, insisting the costume was indestructible. And appropriate. Midsummer Eve at Grey Gallows had grown into a sort of darkling ball.

"It'll be bright as day, with dozens of fires. Jeans and a turtleneck simply will not do," Lucinda said.

As Beth modeled the black skirt and laced-up kirtle, Lucinda had stroked the underblouse with a wistful sigh. " 'Ashes of roses.' That's what we called this color. Lovely, isn't it?"

Now, walking the black beach beside him, Beth smiled. Gordon's approval had confirmed Lucinda's praise. On arrival he'd walked around her, then bowed as if she were a princess.

"Do I need a disguise?" he'd asked, while his eyes traced the crisscross meshing of the braid she'd woven like a head-band from temple to temple. "Is it like Mardi Gras or some-thing?" He'd seemed mesmerized by the thin black ribbon Lucinda had tied around Beth's neck.

Taking in his full-sleeved shirt and long hair, Beth decided he already had the look of a pirate. She'd stood him before her bedroom mirror, folded the skirt's black sash into a rough scarf, and tied it off, over one ear.

"Well done." Gordon had watched Beth's reflection as she hovered on tiptoe, adjusting the scarf, but when she offered to add an earring, he stopped her. "Don't push your luck. Isn't that what they say?"

"All the time," she'd conceded, taking a step back from him.

"But if this scarf is yours, your *favor*, after a fashion, doesn't that make me your—" In his faintly foreign way, Gordon sought a word. Beth's heart hammered as she waited. "Sweetheart?"

"No one will ever guess it wasn't part of your original ensemble," she said and wondered how she'd introduce a "sweetheart" whose full name she still didn't know.

For two miles they walked on packed wet sand toward lights that sprinkled the darkness to their right. Utter darkness, ex-cept for the moon-touched waves, stretched off, left. Ahead, squawking kazoos and whining harmonicas mixed with off-key voices and the crackling of bonfires reaching for the stars.

Several girls, including sassy blond Stefanie, clustered around the nearest fires.

"Hey, Beth Ann Caxton." Stefanie lurched over to shake Beth's hand. "My mom and dad told me all about you after I mentioned what happened at the store the other day."

Though Stefanie's multiply-pierced brows lifted, insinuating something scandalous in the stories she'd heard, Beth couldn't help liking her.

"My hero!" Gauzy swathes of fabric draped Charmaine like a harem girl as she elbowed through the teenagers, toward

Gordon. "I'd treat you to a cup of grog." Charmaine lifted one bare foot. "But the cauldron's way down there." The bells around her ankle jingled as she pointed her toes up the beach. She leered as if she'd consumed entirely too much grog already.

"No hero, Miss Clark." Gordon snagged Beth's hand as he spoke. "Is Minny here?" He peered down the beach.

"Yeah, somewhere. Probably with my dad or Gimp. My dad—that's Horatio," she confided to Beth, "thinks she should see this"—Charmaine gestured vaguely, then righted her silver cardboard crown—"before it disappears. He and Gimp think it's part of Minny's 'heritage.'"

While Charmaine flirted, Stefanie tugged Beth aside. "Your cove is private, right?" Beth nodded and Stefanie went on. "Remind me to tell you what I saw the other night."

Beth thought of the divers. She wanted Stefanie's news now, but the blonde brushed her insistence aside and turned back to her friends.

"She's a nice little girl," Gordon was saying of Minny. "I'd like to tell her hello." Gordon started to sidle past, toward the next fire.

"It's way past her bedtime, so you'll probably hear her fussing."

"Then I shall have to try and cheer her up."

"That's cool." Stefanie nodded and jutted her lower lip in an approving pout. "A guy who really likes kids." Her friends agreed. "But don't forget to do some of the mystical stuff— like gazing through the flames at your lover to see her true face and jumping over the flames." Stefanie darted an appreciative look at Gordon's long legs.

Rowdy merrymakers in hats—cowboy hats, towering red-and-white striped Cat-in-the-Hat caps, and one topped with a winged gargoyle—swept past with flashlights.

"The only charm I know is dancing around nine bonfires before dawn." Charmaine yawned. "It guarantees you'll be married by year's end." Her laughter stirred stiff smiles from the girls. "Which explains why I don't set much store by this hocus-pocus."

A shower of orange sparks drifted toward the sky as Stefanie loosed an armload of driftwood into the bonfire.

"Come back later!" Stefanie shouted as Beth and Gordon started away. "Junior promised to bring some special brownies."

Beth tugged Gordon's hand, leading him toward the next fire. Woodsmoke swirling from every direction rekindled her memory of the other Midsummer Eve she'd spent on this beach. With luck, Junior's brownies would keep him from remembering.

"What is grog?" Gordon asked.

Clean-shaven and smiling with boyish eagerness, he made an unlikely pirate, here on the dark beach. What had she seen smoldering in him, before, to make her think him a buccaneer?

"Some kind of drink, alcoholic, certainly. I'm not sure."

"We should try it, shouldn't we?"

"I never have," Beth began.

"We'll let this be a night of firsts, shall we?"

And then, as if the import of what he'd said didn't rock him at all, he led her toward the most crowded bonfire on the beach.

Skirling bagpipes and a flute's soaring notes played "Greensleeves" over the waves' melancholy rush.

Gimp wore a tartan kilt and a plaid fastened at his left shoulder, and for all that his white beard was patchy and sparse and his were knobby old-man knees above his stockings, his eyes were sharp. While the villagers looked on dreamily, faces turned amber by the flames, Gimp performed with a piper's hard esteem for his instrument.

Lucinda Wright, in a dress patchworked from autumn-colored velvets, played the flute. She ended the piece with a long note which faltered on the air, even after her lips parted from the flute and the villagers began to clap.

"That one was for you, Lucy," Gimp snorted, then his head jerked up like he'd heard something amiss. "We'll have a proper Scots air, in a moment, and that'll please you, won't it, young Gordon?"

Gimp jostled up close and Beth dropped Gordon's hand so

he could greet the old man. "Greensleeves" was probably English. That explained Gimp's snort at Lucinda, but was Gordon a Scot? Could be, but why should Gimp know, when she didn't?

"That was great." Gordon pumped Gimp's hand, awkwardly, since Gimp still cradled the leather bag as if it were a child. "I've never heard them like this—outside, in person. Gimp, it was wonderful."

Gimp shook his head, making a deep growl of embarrassed delight. "Yes? And what have you got yourself up like? A pirate?"

Gordon shrugged and grinned sheepishly as he touched the silk folded over his head. But he didn't remove it. "I was led astray by a beautiful female."

"And that's what the night's all about." Gimp shifted the chanter away from his lips as Lucinda, flute tucked under her arm, offered a tray full of steaming cups.

"It's *not* what the night's all about, you old lecher." Lucinda's laugh held the same tattletale sarcasm it had in Neptune's coffee shop.

"I thought you weren't coming." Beth lifted one side of her skirt, as if Lucinda should be wearing it herself.

"I said I was too old to be cavorting. I said nothing about playing with this old codger."

As Lucinda joked with Gimp, Beth saw Gordon sip his grog. His eyes opened wide, as before, when he'd had some of her brandy. Beth sipped some of the hot brew. It hit her throat with a harsh sweetness that made her face tingle, but it really didn't seem that strong.

"—only brings out his pipes a few times a year. I couldn't miss a chance—"

"To make me play that English drivel." Gimp drained his cup and looked pointedly at Gordon. "The pipes, d'they make you weep?"

Gordon wiped his eyes with his sleeve, smiling at Gimp's matter-of-fact question. "No, I think it's this." He held up his tin cup. "What's in it?"

"Rum, tea, sugar," Lucinda said. "And lemon, I think."

"Y'said you weren't much of a drinker." Gimp stayed watchful.

"And I'm not." Gordon turned expectantly to the librarian.

"I'm Lucinda Wright." She extended her hand. "I've seen you in the stacks, but we haven't met."

"I'm sorry." Beth stepped forward. "I should have introduced you. This is my friend Gordon." Beth rushed, trying to block Lucinda's curiosity with details she *did* know. "We met in San Francisco. He's an admirer of my father's work."

"Jack's a gifted writer." Lucinda still clasped Gordon's hand.

"I agree." Gordon shook her hand, then reclaimed Beth's. One of his fingers drew circles on the thin skin at her wrist. Beth caught her breath. It was an innocent and, to judge by his expression, unconscious gesture, but it reminded her of last night's kissing.

"Aye, and when Lucy and Jack were pups—"

"Ancient history, Gimp. Have you noticed how his brogue thickens as he drinks?" Lucinda's remark was directed at Gordon.

In fact, the librarian seemed fascinated by him. A pulse of worry started up in Beth's throat. No matter how she denied his dark side, Gordon was obviously a man with a past. Did Lucinda remember the days Gordon had run wild with Junior?

"Lucinda, if this celebration isn't about romance"—in the darkness, Gordon's fingers burrowed beneath the elastic cuff of Beth's blouse—"what is its purpose? What brought it to Grey Gallows?"

"The early settlers, no doubt." Lucinda's head cocked to one side. "Our records are sketchy, but in the earliest days, solstice fires were lit to warm the sun and give it energy as it moved down, toward the horizon."

Gordon's feather-light touch was driving Beth crazy. He traced the curve of her wrist bone, over and over.

"—some thought the height of the flames would bode well for the growth of crops and here—according to some poking around I did at Stanford, when I was finishing my master's—

fisherman thought tall flames would tell the sea gods the size of the catch they expected.''

"Not enough attention paid to that lately, I'd say." Jewel Clark, wearing denim overalls and a shimmering magenta blouse, hugged Lucinda with the warmth of old friendship. "Throw more wood on that fire, boys. Better yet, some of those wooden pallets of Karl's. We want a catch that stacks as high as Grey Gallows' spires."

Under cover of a dozen "amens," Beth scolded Gordon. "I can't concentrate when you do that." She twisted her wrist, dislodging his fingers from inside her sleeve.

"Is this a frequent problem?" Gordon's eyes were warm, concerned, even. The gold flames reflected in his pupils were extinguished when he leaned close to hear her answer.

"No, I—" *I don't usually have men's hands inside my blouse?* Beth took a breath to start again. She was over-reacting. For crying out loud, Caxton, he's touching your wrist! "No, I rarely have trouble concentrating, Gordon. It's just—"

"A night for firsts, as I said." With that, Gordon's fingers forked firmly between hers. Beth's stomach dropped away as if she'd stepped off the top of a beach dune, into thin air.

"—burning cartwheel at midnight, any minute now." Lucinda pointed to the dark hills in whose rainshadow the village lay.

"Could you explain that?" Gordon asked. "Gimp mentioned it before."

"It's one of the really old traditions," Lucinda said.

"And y'defer to me as one of the ancients, is that it?" As Gimp repositioned his bagpipes, his kilt hiked up and Beth noticed the healed gash above his knee. "If you look sharp, you'll see my Junior and his lot hauling it up the hill, through the canyon, along the old creek bed."

Beth stared at the black hillside. Old-timers remembered the Great Depression and the leaden days when Grey Gallows was battered by water from both sides. The lazy trickle down the canyon had turned to a deluge, and only sandbags had kept it from destroying the homes below. Beth didn't know whose

homes. Before her birth, whoever lived at the foot of Sandbag
Creek had heeded Nature's warning and moved. Probably regretted it, too, since Sandbag Creek had stayed dry and empty
for at least twenty years.

"You haven't seen Horatio and Minny, have you?" Jewel
broke in. "I was supposed to meet them, here."

After a brief, fruitless search, they all stared back at the
dark hillside. Spots swarmed before Beth's eyes, but she saw
no movement, no sign of Junior. She was glad. Gordon's reaction yesterday had gone beyond jealousy, and the two had
barely glimpsed each other. Add drink and darkness . . .

"Shall we hike that canyon?" Gordon's voice was pitched
low and his fingers pressed harder than before, enveloping her
inner wrist in heat that reminded her of last night. "I'd like
to trace the creek to its source and see how it finds its way
home."

Before Beth answered, Gimp continued. "Used to be a real
cartwheel. Now it's a wire frame stuffed with weeds and straw
and such. They'll set it alight." As Gimp spoke, yellow flared
on the hillside, "ahs" bloomed around them as if fireworks
streaked the sky, and Gordon put his arm around her shoulders. "Some say the wheel carries the sins of the whole village
along with it, burning 'em up for a fresh start. Look, they've
got it rolling."

The fiery *O* spun like a pinwheel, smoothly at first, then
somersaulting, bucking into the air, showering sparks as it
struck rocks and ravines.

Completely out of control, Beth thought. What if it starts
spot fires on its way down? What if it careens into a bunch of
mindless revelers? She glanced up at Gordon.

He stared, enraptured by the blazing glory of a sight he'd
probably see nowhere else on earth. His arm tightened around
her.

The wheel bounded surely toward the sea with no need of
direction. From all along the beach, people came, cheering the
wheel's fiery progress.

"Go! Roll on, roll on," they chanted.

"Yeah! Keep going!" Stefanie and her entourage screamed

as if urging a running back toward a touchdown. A madman with an accordion played encouragement.

"If it reaches the sea before it burns out," Gimp explained, "it means good luck for the entire year."

Gordon slipped his hand into her skirt pocket and Beth felt something drop. A pebble? A bead? He caught her wrist before she could investigate. "For luck," he said, then kissed her fingers.

An instant later his warm hand vanished.

Eleven

The flaming Wheel slammed against a boulder a half mile above them. It launched into the night and came sizzling down. Beth backed away as burning straw rained around her. The wheel wobbled, jerked upright, and whirled across the sand, chasing the low tide. Finally it caught the waves. Hissing like a sea monster, it fell.

Not until men moved into the waves, hooking the wheel out with gaffs, did Beth look around for Gordon.

The crowd broke up. Knots of friends drifted back to favorite bonfires. A few pushed boats into the waves, determined to view the fires from the sea.

For a moment Beth didn't recognize him. Silhouetted black against Gimp's fire, the man stood with feet planted apart, looming taller than any male on the beach. His shoulders spread to an almost menacing width. On them, Gordon carried Minny.

"I see the—I see big fire coming!" Minny jabbered, bouncing up and down, tapping the top of Gordon's head with flat-palmed pats. "Big fire!"

"Come down, Minny girl." Gimp held his arms up toward his grandchild.

"Go fast!" Minny's finger pointed toward Sandbag Creek.

"Where was she?" Jewel reached up as well. Even in the uncertain light Jewel looked pale.

"No!" Minny wrapped her arms around Gordon's brow.

"Can't see to walk if you do that." Gordon laughed. "Minny? Can you loosen your grip a bit?"

"No!" She bounced for emphasis and flattened her chin against Gordon's hair.

"Jeez, Minny!" Horatio Clark stumbled into the circle of firelight. "She gave me the slip when the wheel started down."

Hands outspread, he appealed to Jewel, his dismay so intense, Beth wondered if Grey Gallows had a physician. Was the nearest medical care still in Parish? Twenty-five miles would be too far to take Horatio if he collapsed.

"She's all right, Horatio."

His windy sigh said he took Jewel's words as merciful. "Bless you, young man," he added.

As Gordon shrugged, Minny giggled. Lucinda appeared with another round of grog, swearing by its medicinal properties. Only Gordon refused.

He'd done it again. Beth formed her hands to the warm cup, breathing the pungent fumes as Minny kicked her feet and directed Gordon's head, pretending to rein him around the fire like a horse. Gordon had looked away from the fiery wheel, into the darkness, in time to keep Minny from harm.

Where the hell is Charmaine? No one asked, and Beth tried to believe the question irrelevant. Charmaine thought Minny was safe with her grandfather. Still, shouldn't maternal instinct have warned her to check on Minny when conflagration came hurtling out of the sky?

"Let's go listen to the storytellers." Gordon moved to stand behind her. Caring radiated from him, surrounding Beth like a cocoon. Vigilant and protective, Gordon was always on guard.

Beth leaned her head back against his breastbone, knowing she couldn't blame her unsteadiness on grog.

A tiny tennis shoe kicked the back of her skull.

"Careful, lass." Gimp talked to Minny, but he was chewing

his lip, studying Gordon. "Want to come to me, now?" He
held his arms up once more. Heavy-lidded, thumb drooping
from her mouth, Minny squirmed out of Gordon's steadying
grip and plummeted down to her grandfather.

Lucinda tugged at Beth's elbow. Here it came: the revelation of some juvenile delinquency she couldn't ignore. But she
couldn't stop looking at him, helping Gimp off with his pipes,
disentangling the old man so he could cuddle Minny.

"I like your friend," the librarian whispered.

"Yes?" Gladness warmed Beth. She couldn't suppress the
giddy smile tugging at her lips. "So do I."

"It's an old-fashioned concept, but I think he's trustworthy,
Beth, in a world where so many men—and women—aren't."
Lucinda watched Gordon arrange Minny in Gimp's arms, ut-
tering a soothing sound at the child's cranky whimper. "Handsome enough to knock you breathless, too, but there's a
brightness there that's—deeper."

"I know."

"Mercy, that's a chill breeze blowing in, isn't it?" Lucinda
patted Beth's arm. "Well, it's nearly one o'clock, and I'm for
bed."

Shifting Minny to his shoulder, Gimp turned around, tsking.
"You know as well as I, you should stay."

"Oh, Gimp." Lucinda sounded indulgent as she pawed
through a tumble of coats beside the fire and finally drew out
a rectangular box.

"All magic, good and evil, is afoot tonight. You need to
stay awake, Lucy, guard against the bad and gather in the
good." He watched as Lucinda nestled her flute inside the
box's blue velvet lining. "You have to dance around nine
bonfires—just nine, Lucy—to guarantee yourself a marriage
in this new year."

"You old goat." Lucinda snapped the case latches in place,
stood, and straightened her patchwork skirt. "I'm off."

"All right, then, Minny and I'll see you up to your car."

"Horatio and I'll come, too," Jewel added.

Beth and Gordon waved, then stood alone beside the fire.

Beth loosened the shawl she'd tied around her waist and raised it to cover her shoulders.

Wordless, Gordon slid his hand around Beth's nape, lifting her hair to lay outside the shawl.

Villagers clustered close to the warmth of the largest bonfire. Stepping among those seated on coats and blankets, Beth and Gordon finally found a spot to listen while Juan Comacho, newcomer to Grey Gallows, told tales as Domingo translated.

Gordon sat, knees canted up, feet flat on the sand. When Beth gathered her skirts to settle beside him, he drew her down between his knees, offering his chest as a backrest.

Juan was a fine storyteller. Beth knew she'd recall the myth later, but now, as his fluid voice set the scene in the faraway Straits of Magellan, Beth only felt Gordon's denimed legs, supporting her on each side.

Juan and Domingo described a tribe of women who ruled over men by the grace of their goddess Tanuwe. Dancing with masks and painted bodies, the women worshipped Tanuwe in a secret shrine hidden from men. Beth pictured it all, until Gordon leaned forward and circled her with his arms.

Juan's hands bent like claws in the firelight as he told of the awful day the men discovered Tanuwe's temple. Armed with lances and harpoons, the men tried to steal the goddess's power. Set on murder, they charged down on the dancing women. Beth's dismay vanished as Gordon's lips brushed the back of her hair, then nuzzled through to her neck.

Tanuwe saved her fleeing, faithful subjects, Juan said, by transforming them into sea animals, then sending a giant wave to carry them to safety.

"And that is why, though men take from the sea—reaping always, never sowing—women turn to their sea mother—"

Beth remembered how recordings of the humpback whales' song had made her weep, how dolphins' chittering made her sure she understood and her selkie . . .

"—women are longing to go down to the ocean, in times of need, even if they've never heard of the goddess Tanuwe."

Domingo's words combined with the elation of Gordon clasping her nearer for a gentle kiss.

Before the kiss ended, dancing began. Tin whistles and kazoos, accordions, ocarinas, even Celtic harps played by two
women from Parish, incited the villagers to wild contortions
that faintly resembled dance steps. They circled flames that
stretched tall, trying to span the dark between earth and
heaven.

Those who came in off the sea claimed seventeen bonfires
lit the shoreline. Holding hands and clasping forearms with
Domingo and Juan, Charmaine and Stefanie and strangers,
Beth sang until her throat ached and danced the stumbling,
vining step until her ballet slippers filled with sand.

Always, she peered through the flames, watching Gordon
as he watched her. Always, she felt his mind pulling so might-
ily, she might have walked through the flames if he'd asked
it. Never did either let on that they were counting the fires
around which they danced. It was certainly coincidence that
made them leave the noise and carousing when they reached
the number nine.

He'd tell her tonight. Mist spangled with light draped the sky
above and the rocks all around, just as it had the day of their
first meeting.

Gordon drew the chill night into his lungs. Magic, dazzling
and irresistible, hung in the air. He knew how to wield it.

Beth seemed uneasy. She looked over her shoulder at the
footprints they'd left behind. Burnished copper by fog and
bonfire smoke, the moon cast shadows on rippled sand usually
hidden by water.

Arms linked, hips bumping as they walked close together,
he and Beth moved like courting dolphins. Still, she wouldn't
meet his eyes, so he didn't embrace her. Not yet. Tonight,
he'd ask her to believe in magic, to believe in him and trust
him for a lifetime.

"Is 'truth or dare' a boys' game?" He stopped and Beth
continued a few steps more before facing him. That night in
San Francisco, he'd wished for this. Beth on the beach, with
wind-tossed hair. "Is it? Junior and I used to play, but he said
we couldn't include girls."

"That's because Junior was a little sexist piggy. Still is." Beth's hands perched on her hips and silver hoops sparkled in her ears. "I'll play."

He looked skyward, pretending to consider. "Think you're man enough?"

"Ohhhh." Beth moved toward him with a chuckle. "You'll be sorry for that." Beth dodged left, as if she'd trip him down to the sand, then right, then darted behind. He blocked each attempt and she stood tapping her foot. "Maybe I'll let you fret over it for a while," she threatened. "You never know when I'll strike."

He loved her this way, playful, aggressive, unconcerned with appearances. "I go first." Gordon folded his arms. "Truth: Last night, when I was kissing you, you said, 'I'm not like this.' What did you mean?"

In the moonlight he couldn't tell if Beth's sun-brushed skin grew red, but she cleared her throat and made several false starts before she spoke. "Okay, what's the dare?"

"That's not the way we played it."

"Well, I didn't get to choose 'truth' or 'dare.' We'll do it this way, Gordon. Like a penalty."

Laughing, since he'd felt the pulse-pounding kiss replay through her mind, Gordon surveyed the beach and pointed out a cairn of rock mounded by the sea. "Climb that and jump into my arms."

Without hesitation, she scrambled up, altering her route for loose rocks, scuffing her shoes on sandy surfaces. Once, she slipped and dangled by her arms.

"Kick off your slippers." Gordon swallowed as Beth chinned herself, planted a shoe beside one hand, and continued climbing. "Your feet will grip better."

"And get slashed by barnacles?" She huffed with effort. "No, thanks."

The rocks reached no higher than ten feet, a trifling height compared to her dives into the seal cove. Still, Beth hesitated at the top.

"Come on. I'll catch you," Gordon called.

"I'll bowl you over. What if I hurt you?"

"Hurt me?" he taunted. What fun it was, acting like the rough boy he'd been years ago! "Give it your best shot, Blondie."

Beth jumped. He might easily have sidestepped, but he'd promised to catch her. As he did, Gordon realized she'd been right. Her small weight overbalanced them. Gordon staggered a few steps holding her, then fell.

With a ladylike grunt, Beth extricated herself, rolled clear of him, and stood, breathing hard. "My turn."

Gordon brushed the sand from his hands. "Okay." He tried not to sound grudging, but she might have let him hold her a minute.

"Truth," Beth said and he nodded, tucking his shirt more tightly into his jeans. "What's your last name?"

He hadn't anticipated that. "Last name?" he stalled.

"You know. Beth . . . Caxton." She walked backward down the beach, mocking him with her smile. "Gordon . . ."

"Otariidae." It wasn't quite a lie. The scientific name for sea lions was close enough for a child's game.

"No way," Beth whined. "You made that up."

"I didn't."

"Prove it."

Quicker than she could dodge, Gordon kissed the side of her neck. "Now, how can I do that?" He stepped back before he succumbed to the warm scent of her.

Beth brushed her hair forward to surround her neck. "I want a peek at your driver's license."

"I don't drive." That, too, was true. Relinquishing control—*daily*—over one's own movement was one of the truly insane habits of human beings.

Beth turned her attention to the rocky trail, but she hadn't abandoned the inquisition. "*Otariidae,* huh?" They'd reached the bottom of her secret path up to the bluff. Beth linked her hands behind herself and gazed up at him. When he remained silent, she started to go. "Here we are."

He couldn't bear the thought of following Beth indoors, and he would not leave her. "One last dare?" he baited. "Unless you're afraid."

"Afraid?" Like a youngster trying to provoke a fight, Beth pushed Gordon's shoulder. "I'm never afraid."

"Yeah?"

"Yeah!" Beth jutted her jaw and preened in an entirely unconvincing male parody.

He wanted to trip her down and undress her right here on the beach. In fact, he could think of no reason he shouldn't.

Except that there'd be no second chance at seducing her once he'd fallen on her like an animal.

"Dare." He'd lure her onto the last decent stretch of beach before six miles of rocky shore and entice her into his arms. "Run around the point to Lyre Beach."

"Mmm, I don't know." Beth shook her head. "The tide's started coming back in."

"Look at it." He pointed toward the far glimmer of waves. "I'll take care of you."

"I'll take care of myself, thank you, but these skirts—"

Before finishing, Beth grabbed the skirt with both hands. She pulled it up past her knees and, spraying wet clods of sand, Beth ran.

A small fire burned on Lyre Beach. Gordon recognized the scent of the one who'd kindled it, but surprise couldn't overshadow his craving.

He felt Beth's longing, though she stared at the bluff, at the glowing yellow windows of Gull Cott and safety. He would not harm her. What could she possibly fear?

"Help me build it up," he asked Beth as the wind freshened.

She contributed to the revival, but her face stayed pensive. While he walked around the fire, rearranging brands, adding sticks, Beth positioned her black shawl on the sand and reclined upon it.

More than breath caught in Gordon's throat. An obstruction the size of a sun-perch, perhaps. Even a seal-witted simpleton couldn't mistake her invitation.

Gordon walked to the end of the shawl and stood at her feet. Beth watched him, her face luminous. Firelight picked out her eyelashes' gold and left her eyes shadowed. Wind brought the tinkling carnival music of Midsummer Eve. The melody of magic.

"Beth." For the third time in his life, Gordon allowed her name past his lips. It lit his world like lightning.

He knelt on the shawl, his back turned to the darkness, then lowered himself so Beth would be warmed on both sides. His arms surrounded her and wind rushed wild around them as he burrowed into her neck, breathing past tiers of scent—salt on her hair, rum and sugar on her lips, violet soap and powder on her skin—to Beth.

Slowly he touched his lips to hers, prolonging the simple kiss an instant past the time her mouth opened.

Her mind stayed closed to him, misty as the night. That was not acceptable. He must understand Beth's fear before binding her to him.

To curb his eagerness, Gordon delayed, pillowing Beth's head on one of his arms as the other hand searched under her hair for the softness of her neck and fluttering end of the black velvet ribbon. Beth's lips never left his, until he pulled loose the tiny bow, and trailed the ribbon across the delicate channel below her ear.

Beth shivered, tossed her head back, and in the moment she offered her throat for kissing, her mind opened.

Confusion—red and black, slashed with heat, riddled with amazement and splintered thoughts. She'd never given so much, so soon. Didn't want to. Couldn't help it.

He slowed his kisses, confined them to her face, stroked her back in soothing moves meant to calm her. And then she sabotaged his tenderness. Beth's hands thrust under his shirt. Her nails skittered over his ribs, reaching as high as his shoulder blades.

Passion, overdue and obsessive, made him tug her blouse free of her skirt. He jerked loose the laces on her kirtle. His torso slanted across the bared warmth of her, shielding her from the night and from himself. One glimpse of creamy skin and he'd be lost. If he saw the softness that radiated warmth through his shirt, he would delay no longer.

He must bring her closer. Beth's body could be his in one

thrust, but he must convince her mind and win her heart if he wanted her as his mate, forever.

This is all that matters. She nodded. He took her with him, rolling on his side. *I'll come to you, out of the sea, every night.* His toes shucked the ballet slippers from her feet. *Wait for me on the shore. I'll always come.* He matched them, lips to lips, chest to breast. *This is all that matters. Our minds, our spirits, our bodies . . .*

Beth surged against him. As her bare leg lapped between his, he reached down, forming his hand to her thigh. *Nothing else is real. Nothing else lasts. Your past and future lie here, with me.*

He rose above her. Was the time right? If he teamed the sea's magic with his could he make her trust what her heart had known from the beginning?

Astride her on his knees, he lifted Beth's shoulders and her garments fell away. In the moonlight, Beth's green eyes shone as clear as crystal, the eyes of a maiden seer who knew and accepted. And so he told her.

"Beth. I am your selkie." He didn't touch her breasts. Only, with one hand, lifted her chin. When she'd been drowning, he'd done the same.

Warm acceptance trickled through her mind, a single tear-drop in the ocean of human logic. Then it vanished.

Her mind plunged into dark breakers of distrust, drifting out of reach. Beth stared over his shoulder into the bleak darkness. She thought him a liar.

He rolled beside her, sheltering her flesh, trying to call her mind back to safety. Gordon's chest echoed the betrayal threatening to split Beth's breastbone in two.

"Believe me." He held her closer, though her hands fought free of his entangling shirt and shoved at his shoulders. "Beth, wait."

He'd done it all wrong, trusting her cursed human brain to see the simple truth. Beth must quit fighting. She remembered. Why couldn't she accept?

She slid from beneath him and sat up. Hands trembling, she

buttoned her shirt. "I really am crazy." Her voice ran cold with self-loathing.

"I know it's hard for you to believe," he spoke softly, but her head jerked up as if he'd struck her. "But you felt it, Beth, we both—"

"Don't talk." She stuffed the shirt back into her waistband and laced her kirtle so tight the fabric puckered.

"Listen to your heart." He might as well have flung orders at the sky. Now her loathing turned on him.

"I might be crazy, but I'm not stupid. What you're suggesting is impossible. I believed it"—Tears gripped her for a moment, but she refused them—"when I was a kid."

"Let me prove it—"

"I'm sure you heard all those stories—" Her lips pressed together as his voice reached her. "Go ahead." She tugged her cuffs down, past her wrists, nearly to her knuckles. "Prove it."

Gordon sat up straighter, eyes closed, evoking the moments so vividly Beth must see them. He tried to take her hand, to bind her to him physically, but she jerked away, all but snarling her revulsion. Unfair.

"What have I done to earn your hatred? *What*?"

Both hands in fists, Beth faced him, but she couldn't answer. "Prove it," she whispered.

"Thunder and lightning ranged above us. My people rocketed past you on all sides, through the kelp, and you tried to follow. Disoriented, you swam downward. You were running out of air. I—" Gordon stopped, his trance cut jagged by her mind's rejection. "I lifted you by the chin, remember? Too hard. You went spinning backward, bubbles streaming from your mouth—"

"Who else is in on this? Karl? God knows why he'd leak all these juicy details."

Gordon's teeth ground together. Fighting anger, he pointed an index finger at her. "No. Here's something he doesn't know, you don't even know. On the shore I had to leave you. For minutes, too many minutes, so I could change back. I couldn't give you CPR in seal form, and I feared—" Against his will, Gordon felt the panic, the cold and exhaustion, the bone-white terror he'd be too late. "That you'd die while I was—"

"Oh, *please*." Beth's sarcasm ripped like a gaff, but he kept talking.

"And then your stepmother called out, and your father—"

She stood and pushed him away. "Shut up!" she shouted.

Fury blinded him. She'd shoved him and shouted at him. She'd ordered him to shut up, as if he were the basest of her kind. Gordon opened his eyes, trying to remember this was Beth's dear face, not the face of an enemy. He was more than a man. He must act like it.

"You have the most uncanny ability to look truth in the face and deny it," he began, but his anger made Beth more comfortable, as if his harsh words confirmed her suspicions.

Gordon sifted through his own memories, meticulously searching out one irrefutable detail. And then he knew.

"Shall I tell you the last thing I said to you?"

Reflexively Beth clapped her hand over his lips. Just as quickly she recoiled, covering her ears. Her palms trapped long glossy strands of hair. She looked so childlike, adrift on her own fear, shaking her head, refusing rescue. Gordon hardened his heart.

He grabbed Beth's wrists and held them at her sides. He heard his own panting and drew two long breaths before making her listen. "I told you to remember me. *You do*. Beth, you can't change that any more than I can change what I am."

She'd bit her lower lip so hard, a drop of blood emerged. Beth shook her head, her eyes begging him to stop. As if he tortured her.

"You remember me in every cell of your being. Why can't you admit it?" He released her wrists and let her back away.

Selkie memories, black remembrances, roiled through his mind. Selkies expected the best of men and fell prey to their mystical misrule on Midsummer Eve. In that dream state between seal and human they were enslaved. Captured. Confined.

"I'll give you a chance, then." Beth's voice came in a

whisper. "Show me. Transform *here*, where I can see you."

Even Beth was not to be trusted.

"I am not"—he fisted his hands, lest he shove her as she had him—"a godforsaken circus animal."

The sea's far-off thunder and the glimmering of false dawn signaled the tide's return. The enchantment had ended.

Beth looked suddenly haggard. Everything about her was raw and bare, so easy to read. She despised herself, because she loved him. *Oh, Beth.*

Torrents of wind ripped the last vestiges of mist.

"Meet me at dawn, in your cove. I'll be there in my seal form. I promise."

She shook her head, red-gold hair whipping around her face, and then she was half-running from him, leaving her slippers behind.

Twelve

Summer had arrived and Sunday promised to be hot. By nine on Midsummer Day, Beth had buried a broken-necked bird who'd mistaken her window for thin air. She'd jogged a half-mile, then broken off, unable to fight the dry gasps left behind by last night's tears. She'd begun reroofing, and quit after nailing six shingles and her thumb. More times than she could count, she'd started down to the seal cove and forced herself to stop.

Gordon had deceived her, played her for a fool, but she didn't know *how*—or what to do about it.

Beth leaned both elbows on the Fiat's hood and stared toward the heat snakes already squiggling up from the highway. The days of rain and thunder might have passed in a dream, but last night's disgrace was no nightmare. Here in the gravel parking lot, on the driver's seat of her car, she'd found her slippers and the black velvet ribbon. Sniffing like a lovesick teenager, she'd held them on her lap and downed a carton of orange juice.

The yellow VW bus wailed off the highway, turned left on Surf Street, and left again on Beth's dirt road. As the vehicle stuttered to a stop, Beth pushed off the Fiat's sun-warmed hood. Phoebe's arrival felt like homecoming.

Phoebe rolled down the driver's window and peered over the tops of her sunglasses. Beth's eyelids had swollen so puffy, they blurred her vision. Phoebe frowned.

"As my Baptist mama from Shallow Water, Florida, would say, 'you look like the wrath of God,' girlfriend."

The driver's door creaked open, revealing several actors slumped snoring in the backseats. Phoebe hopped down. With her face bare of makeup and her arms open, Phoebe looked like what she was—Beth's best friend in the world.

The thought carried her into Phoebe's hug.

"Thanks for your professional evaluation." Beth gave Phoebe a hearty smack on the back. "Can you do anything about it?"

"Claim a cold and cover you with cold cream before Carol and Jack arrive."

"What?" Beth pressed her hands to her temples, though she was relatively certain it wouldn't really explode. "Tell me you're joking."

"Jack wanted to come along for old time's sake."

"How did he even—" Beth stopped when Phoebe fluffed crimson fingernails through her shiny black ringlets.

"I had nothing to look forward to except reupholstering Rows L through O." Phoebe rolled her eyes skyward. "So, I might have done too good a job publicizing l'event." Phoebe reached into the van for the pink entertainment section of the *San Francisco Chronicle.*

"Wow, Phoeb." Beth skimmed the small item. "Good job." Her friend glared at the electric blue sea, repositioned her sunglasses, then grabbed a handful of garments on hangers. "You take these." She shoved two powder-smudged gym bags toward Beth. then slammed the van door.

Beth stood on tiptoe, surveying Phoebe's cargo. "Your passengers look like corpses," she said, before leading Phoebe up the rough-cut stairs.

"Let 'em sleep until we've had time to repair the damage." Phoebe elbowed into the cottage, flung the costumes on Beth's couch, and returned Peaches' lavish greeting before towing Beth toward the kitchen. "I want to work in natural light if we're going to be outside all day. How old is that coffee?" Phoebe sniffed the carafe.

"This morning's, but be careful of that glass." Beth tried to sound casual over the superstitious experiment poised on her windowsill.

"Looks like a science project." Phoebe splattered coffee into a cup before leaning against the counter. "Am I safe in assuming Mr. Wonderful won't be putting in an appearance today?"

"Who knows?" Beth perched on a kitchen stool. "Everything I can say would be a cliché." *Except for the part about being a seal.* Beth gulped back a grim laugh and shook her head.

The screen door slammed open and the Foghorn Theater's consistent leading man, Spencer Churchill, staggered into the kitchen under the burden of more costumes. His red hair spiked in all directions. His eyes were bleary and perplexed.

"Spencer?" Beth slid off the stool, arms extended. For a minute, he watched her, frowning.

"Pardon me for saying so, ma'am, but I doubt it." A cowboy swagger replaced Spencer's concern. "Y'all are looking limp as a neck-wrung rooster and worthless as a bucket of hot spit."

"*Fisherman's* faire, Spencer." Beth reminded him, then pulled her hair back with a rubber band and presented her face for Phoebe's rescue while Spencer continued his attempt to amuse her.

"I'm auditioning for a *nouveau* Western on Tuesday and I'm getting into character, Miz Caxton." Spencer tugged the brim of an imaginary Stetson.

"Sweatshirt off," Phoebe ordered as she consulted her tote of makeup.

"That's what I always say," Spencer agreed.

Beth fought free of the bulky garment, fretting over the skin bared by her bikini top.

"Aw, shucks, ma'am." Spencer's brows waggled in melodramatic appreciation. "Y'all don't have to——"

"Spencer Churchill, the man who won the West," Beth

muttered as Phoebe assaulted her with lotions. She heard footsteps crossing the bluff. Where would she put them all?

"I'm considering changing my name to Bubba." Spencer
moved behind Beth's stool to knead the back of her neck.
"Bubba Churchill. What'd you think?"

"I think you'd better remember she's the boss' daughter
and keep your hands in your pockets." Jack Caxton entered
growling, and Spencer fled, claiming the bathroom as his
dressing room. Banishment accomplished, Jack turned to his
daughter. "How's the Fiat running, Bethie?" His hug nearly
slid her off the stool.

"Daddy." Beth closed her eyes so the tears wouldn't start
all over again.

The sooner Jack asked after the Fiat, the more he'd missed
her. Their long-standing emotional shorthand had developed
during years of muttered, shoulder-brushing conversations
conducted under the sports car's hood.

"I pushed it down the driveway the other day, then had to
pop the clutch to get it started." Beth kept her eyes shut,
giving in to Phoebe's ministrations, listening to Jack move
around the cottage.

"Were Misty, Ian, and Lex stirring when you came by the
van, Jack?" Phoebe shouted after him.

Jack answered with a noncommittal grunt, and Phoebe
leaned closer to Beth, holding a brush dabbed in pearly pink.

"Go like this." Phoebe shaped her own mouth. "Do it, or
I'll paint on a clown smile."

"Where on earth did you get this?" Jack's voice rumbled
with such surprise, Beth had to look. He stood in her bedroom
doorway holding the black skirt and kirtle.

"I borrowed it from Lucinda Wright."

Jack stared at the gown, as Phoebe cut in. "Wear that, Beth.
It's perfect."

"No. I—I wore it last night." Sand drizzled from the garment as she watched. "Dad, Lucinda said to tell you hello."

"Did she?" Amazement touched Jack's voice as the scent
of Carol's perfume clouded the room.

"Hi, Carol." Phoebe joined Beth in the perfunctory greeting.

In raw silk trousers and a champagne tunic matched to her hair, Carol glanced around the cottage. "It didn't take them long to muss your house, Elizabeth." Carol's arms stayed close to her body, as if she'd get soiled. "But then you're a much better sport than I am, dear."

"You were down on the beach last night?" Jack barked as if Beth's words had finally soaked in.

"Yes." Beth scrambled for an excuse. "I'm helping organize the Fishermen's Faire, today, and part of—"

"In this?" Jack shook the kirtle in Beth's direction.

"It looks modest enough, Jack," Carol said. "Heavens, she's twenty-five years old."

"You don't know what it's like down there on Midsummer Eve." Jack concentrated on Beth's face, vigilant for guilt. "Did Sy cook up a cauldron of grog?"

"Someone did." Time might sour the memory of rum and sugar, but not yet. "It wasn't wild, Dad. Loud, but pretty harmless."

"All the old renegades moved away." Carol took the costume from Jack and whisked it back into Beth's room. "The festival gets underway around noon, right?" Carol consulted her watch. "Jack, you promised me breakfast."

Her father clapped his hands as if breaking a spell. "Right. The Neptune coffee shop makes the kind of artery-jammer Hangtown fry you can't get anywhere else."

"The man's incorrigible, but I think I'll keep him," Carol said as Jack opened the door to admit the remaining actors. "Oh, Beth," Carol lingered, "Check the pockets of that gown, before you return it. And try getting a little more rest, dear. Cosmetics can't cover fatigue."

As the door shut, Phoebe stepped back to examine Beth's face. "You look great. Put on that little spring green number and braid your hair while I pull myself together. Then we'll give the common folk a thrill they won't forget."

Beth searched for a dressing room of her own, but Spencer

still claimed the bathroom and Ian, Misty, and Lex had collapsed in a slumbering tangle on her bed.

"Just what are your duties?"

Beth moved back toward Phoebe's voice, closed the shutters, and joined Phoebe in changing clothes in the living room.

"Unclear." Beth stepped into a green dress which fell far short of her knees. "No manual labor, since the booths and stands were hammered together last night." As she tied the drawstring neck, her fingers remembered the black bow. Had that little scrap of velvet held the sorcery to make her lose her mind? "I think I handle emergencies as they come up."

"How hard can that be?" Phoebe wriggled into a bloodred gypsy dress and glanced up at Beth's dubious silence. "Don't be silly, Beth. It'll be like shooting fish in a barrel. The Foghorn's offered us one calamity after another."

Phoebe moved back to the kitchen and set up a makeup mirror. "Now. Did this *other* disaster happen last night?" Phoebe seemed to address her reflection as she pitched her voice low enough that Spencer wouldn't hear as he vacated the bathroom and left via the sliding-glass door to Beth's deck.

"Yes."

"How bad was it?" Phoebe daubed her lips a glossy crimson to match her nails.

"The worst day of my life"—Beth despised exaggeration—"on which no one died."

Phoebe spun away from the mirror, eyes full of pity.

"Stay back," Beth said, half-laughing. "One step closer and I might cry and ruin this terrific face."

Phoebe penciled on a black beauty mark and touched up her brows. "Bastard." She exhaled a snarl or a sigh. "It's that damned Mr. Gordon, isn't it? He followed you up here."

"How did you—?"

"I knew he was weird." Phoebe groped for a paper napkin. "Damn! How long before I quit sticking mascara wands into my eyes?"

In the quiet, the refrigerator hummed and Phoebe repaired her makeup. Beth knew what Phoebe wanted to know. It was the same detail Phoebe *always* wanted to know. This time it had been a near thing.

Phoebe pinned her skirt up on one side, flaunting a dagger tied to her thigh. "What?" Phoebe peered up through extravagant false eye lashes, awaiting reproach.

"That might be a little kinky for Grey Gallows."

"Fishing faire it may be, but I won't wear a slicker and rubber boots in this heat." She repositioned the pin to expose less flesh. "*That* really would be kinky."

Phoebe gazed out the kitchen window, giving Beth silence enough to confess. Outside, a gull cackled three descending cries like scornful laughter.

"No. I did not sleep with him," Beth admitted.

Phoebe turned as slow as a mechanical doll, eyes just as wide and fixed. Agog, apparently, that a woman would forego such an adventure. "Beth, I don't know how you do it."

The screen door ricocheted open once more.

"Does no one knock?" Phoebe affected Carol's voice. Beth laughed as if a string bound tight around her chest had snapped.

Wearing Huck Finn overalls and a battered straw hat, Spencer blared a fanfare and displayed a brown paper bag.

"Bagels," he announced. "And cream cheese and strawberry jam." He wafted the sack beneath Beth's nose. " 'Now comes the wanton blood up in your cheeks—' " He smiled and added, "*Romeo and Juliet,* Act—I don't know."

The aroma of food roused the others. Ian, Misty, and Lex stalked in like hungry zombies, crowding Beth out of the kitchen.

"Eat up, kids." Phoebe tidied the countertop as she spoke. "Then get dressed. You're on in about thirty minutes."

Although the combination of food and confession lifted Beth's spirits, she was jarred by Junior's arrival.

Red-eyed but energetic, he burst into the room and flashed a new gray T-shirt reading: TODAY'S SUSHI—TOMORROW'S BAIT. Beneath that swam a cartoon fish with Xs for eyes and the legend: CLARK'S BAIT SHOP, GREY GALLOWS, CA.

Junior shoved a bag of daisies Beth's way and explained

that both Sheriff Reynolds and Karl had asked him to check
on her. Then Junior noticed the others. He gave them a cursory
glance before focusing on Phoebe.

"Hel-lo." Junior dashed untidy blond hair from his eyes.

With deliberate care, Phoebe set aside the sponge and fixed
Junior with the full force of her *femme fatale* gaze.

Junior straightened three inches taller. "I think I just found
the best hangover cure known to mankind."

Phoebe left the actors squabbling over bagels and sauntered
closer, hiding her interest behind sarcasm. "These fishermen
are pretty darn suave."

Though the remark was apparently addressed to her, Beth
kept quiet and watched the two size each other up.

"Hey now." Junior inspected Phoebe with exaggerated
scrutiny. "You look like you might have a little fisherman in
you."

Phoebe regarded him with disdain. "Not hardly."

"Well, would you like to have?" Junior asked.

"Why, Beth, you told me the men here lacked polish."
Phoebe's smile contradicted her scorn. "You didn't say they
were absolute Neanderthals."

"You're playing with a master, honey. Don't hurt yourself." Junior turned from Phoebe. "Beth Ann."

"Yes?" Beth hefted the bag of daisies, questioning.

As if he were reluctant to turn his back on Phoebe's continued stare, Junior stalled. "Beth," he said again. Smoothing
his straw-colored mustache seemed to put him back on track.
"Karl needs to see you, soon as possible. He wants you to
troubleshoot while he and Charmaine run their booth. Okay?"

"Sure. What about these flowers?"

"They're from Gustine's Garlands. I don't know what the
hell you're supposed to do with them." He shifted, trying to
ignore Phoebe's chuckles. He jerked a thumb over his shoulder. "Who's your friend?"

"Phoebe Dahlberg helps run the Foghorn Theater, and she
brought a few actors down to add—I don't know why I'm
babbling. Neither of you is listening. Phoebe"—she nodded
to Junior—"This is Junior MacDonald."

"Your old boyfriend?"

"Not really." Beth and Junior spoke together.

Wordless, Phoebe matched her fingertips and tapped her long red fingernails against one another.

"Gotta go." Junior turned abruptly. "So long."

Beth's sleepless night had turned her cross. Junior's wave and Phoebe's laughter made Beth want to strangle them both.

" 'Fish in a barrel,' huh?" Beth rotated Phoebe's arm to see her friend's wrist watch. 12:01 and they stood between the ranks of embattled churchwomen.

The Midsummer Fisherman's Faire boasted a dozen booths ranged side-by-side around the grassy village square in front of the school and library. The first trouble erupted at the northwest corner of the square.

Polite but resolute, the Holy Cross Ladies' Auxiliary insisted they'd pack up their Peg o' My Heart ring-toss booth and leave if the Methodist women didn't alter their sign. Although the red and white lettered plywood announcing BERRIES AND CREAM, BY GOD seemed innocent to Beth, the Holy Cross ladies deemed it sacrilege. Beth couldn't afford to lose them.

Barbie's Babes, a rag-doll crafter, had left after declaring her booth "too rustic," and the proprietors of Heart's Ease Massage had departed over artistic differences, maintaining both male and female masseuses must perform bare-chested.

Perspiring from the roots of his caramel-colored hair because he'd already lost Barbie's Babes, Karl was clearly unprepared to handle personnel problems outside the Village Store. He'd stood before an audience of outsiders, wheedling with the Heart's Ease manager, when Beth arrived.

In minutes Beth had explained the family nature of the event, promised to work something out for the following year and given each masseuse—for his or her inconvenience—a purple ticket good for a cruise on the *Paloma*.

As the masseuses left, far from disgruntled, Karl marveled over Beth's skill at handling the conflict.

"That was nothing," Phoebe scoffed. "You're witnessing

the calm of a woman who placated a lawyer over the destruction of his Armani suit on a nail in his fifty-dollar theater seat.

"This is a woman who keeps a supply of pillows for patrons who complain they can't see the stage, a woman who sweet-talked Big Harley—of Harley's Hot Jazz and Beer—into timing band breaks to coincide with Hamlet's soliloquies."

"I'm impressed." Karl's nervous laugh signalled his eagerness to escape. "And I'll bow out by returning to my booth and telling anyone with a crisis to find the redhead with flowers in her hair."

The battle of the church ladies was trickier, and complicated by Beth's feeling Gordon stood somewhere nearby, just out of sight.

Holy Cross Ladies' Auxiliary's ring-toss booth was already crowded with children. Since dozens of out-of-town visitors had parked along side-streets and alleys, every booth must stay open.

"How about changing it to 'Berries and Cream, by Golly'?" Phoebe suggested.

The Methodist women balked, saying the day was too hot, the time and trouble too great to right an imaginary transgression. Then Beth suggested obliterating the sign's comma with one slap of white paint.

"That'd make it 'Berries and Cream by God.' Does that convey the right thought?"

While all eyes examined the sign and weighed the suggestion, Beth considered the booth's wares. Midsummer Cake appeared to be white cake layered with strawberries and blackberries, iced with whipped cream and decorated with gumdrops. Junior's assault on Gull Cott had kept Beth from the bagels and she was famished.

Famished and fully recovered from Gordon's scheme. Some dreams didn't deserve to come true.

Beth's hand fell into the clasp of a stranger. In fact, ladies shook hands all around and a call went up for a ladder. Her proposal was a success.

"The queen of compromise," Phoebe praised Beth as they

passed Magic Mirrors, a maze built and staffed by Grey Gallows' elementary school teachers.

Not to mention compromising positions. Beth scanned the thickening crowd for a dark man taller than the rest. Of course Gordon wasn't here. Unpredictability was his forte, his bait for luring dumb females to disgrace.

Beth and Phoebe dodged around Horatio's Headgear, where Charmaine and Karl sold caps while the real Horatio piloted *Paloma* in the bay, then lingered at Seascript. There, shaded by a blue umbrella, Domingo and his father sold scrimshaw etched on bone, plastic, on a tropical nut resembling ivory.

One piece, small enough to fit the hollow of her hand, depicted a harbor seal. Its body looked soft and babyish compared to a seal lion's.

"Are you okay? Do I need to hunt down Mr. Gordon and sue him for brain damage? You look kind of dazed."

"I'm fine." Beth reached for the work, feeling it nestle in her palm before she even touched it.

Though a tourist snatched it away, Beth's imagination pursued it.

That black male sea lion . . . Beth envisioned him as if he swam before her. She smelled fish frying. Pollen-heavy flowers mixed their scent with the hot tar odor of asphalt. Gimp woke his bagpipes for a skirl. Somewhere a clarinet honked and children shrieked over a contest won, but the scene before her blurred. If she'd gone to the cove this morning, would he have met her? Would his black-brown eyes have shone with a man's intelligence?

"I've got to have one of these," Phoebe's voice yanked Beth to the next booth.

Gustine's Garlands boasted the most ornate sign and the biggest crowd on the square. The proprietress's frazzled white ponytail made her look just like Jewel Clark.

Phoebe balanced a wreath of crimson roses, baby's breath, and purple streamers on her curls and asked for Beth's opinion. Around them, others purchased garlands for telling fortunes.

One of the browsers was Stefanie Morris. She looked up

from one of the smaller wreaths, to greet Beth.

"Look, Beth, no rings!" Stefanie thrust her face forward for inspection. "My parents said if we're going to spend the summer together in Santa Cruz, I had to let them grow back." She looked around with great drama and patted her tummy. "Still got my belly button stud, though." Then Stefanie took in Phoebe's city-vamp chic and smiled. "I bet your friend's from San Francisco."

During introductions, Beth admired Stefanie's modest blue gown and her ballerina-tight bun.

"We're just taking a quick break from the booth," Stefanie explained. The Fleurettes, a high-school service group, staffed the controversial Kiss-a-Lass booth and Hearts and Tarts, where they sold heart-shaped cookies and lemonade. "Where's your hunky—"

Beth held up her index finger, "Just a minute, Stefanie. I need to be official for a minute." It was only a small lie. "Jewel? Why does the sign say—"

"It always has. I don't know who Gustine was, but I'm peddling garlands this year. Now, Stefanie, go down to the water and cast it out on the waves, far as you can throw. If it drifts back to shore, you'll never marry."

The teenager sighed. "No great loss."

Then a tiny voice intruded. "Steffie—want one, want one."

"Minny, is that you, darlin'?" Jewel peered over the counter at her granddaughter, clinging to Stefanie's hand.

"Her mom's really busy. And Minny likes hanging out with me. Don't ya, Minny Mouse? Go ahead, Mrs. Clark."

"If your garland floats out of sight, you'll wed."

"What if it sinks?" Stefanie fumbled in a leather pouch slung shoulder to shoulder across her bodice.

"That doesn't bear thinking about." Jewel made change from a pocket in her apron. "There you are. And here's a magic wand, for sweet Minny." She handed the child a stick wrapped with ribbons and topped by a star.

Minny regarded her wand for a moment, then swung it hard. "Make a kitty." She struggled loose from Stefanie and swung the wand again. "Make a *kitty*!"

"It might need a few days to warm up to that one, dear."
Jewel smiled at her granddaughter's vehemence.

While Jewel watched Minny, Stefanie grabbed Beth's elbow
and whispered urgently. "Last night, actually, toward dawn, I
saw guys in wet suits down in your cove."

Beth caught her breath. She could see herself grabbing Stefanie's shoulders and demanding what else she'd seen. The
teenager shrugged and made a guilty primping poke at her
hair.

"I just thought you might want to keep your eyes open, in
case they're, like, burglars or something."

Before Beth asked for more details, Jewel caught Stefanie's
attention. "Now, every year boys 're out there with boats.
They'll snatch your wreath quick as anything and that fortune's not hard to tell. Just male mischief, same as always."

Mischief. No doubt that's how Gordon saw his scuttled seduction. A prank, not the destruction of her dream.

"Still no sign of him?" Phoebe asked as she paid for her
wreath and waved good-bye to Stefanie.

Before Beth answered, Junior sidled up. Looking into a cup
full of icy lemonade, he frowned, regarded Phoebe, and regarded the cup, once more. "That Phoebe's so damn hot, she's
melted my ice cubes," he groused.

"Oh, my." Phoebe pretended to fan away faintness. As
soon as Junior turned away, she grimaced toward Beth, then
knocked her fist against her head as if it had turned wooden.

Even though the two were completely mismatched, Beth let
Phoebe's pleading expression convince her to follow. Junior
led them to Whales and Ales, an outdoor café supplied by
Gimp and the fish market. Junior introduced his friend Sloan.

Sloan wore buzz-cut black hair. His pack of cigarettes was
tucked in a sleeve rolled above a swastika tattoo. Her poacher
looked about thirty, not as young as he'd appeared smiling in
his wet suit, knee-deep in her cove. When he shook Beth's
hand with a paw scarred by rough work, he didn't mention
they'd already met.

Phoebe and Junior were so busy measuring each other with
their eyes, they didn't notice Beth's uneasiness. Still, for fish

that smelled this delicious, she could stand in line beside
Sloan. Maybe she'd even get up the nerve to ask where he
was stashing his purloined abalone.

The gossip eddying around them centered on how Roo had
replaced the car damaged in last week's close call with a logging truck. Roo's new red Dodge Ram had to be pricey, snickered a man behind Beth. How had Roo come up with that kind
of dough?

Sloan stood silently by, as talk turned to the overnight appearance of a billboard by the Village Store. Featuring a smiling cartoon seal with extravagant eyelashes, the sign promised
Progress and Profits from changing Grey Gallows to Sable
Bay. Bewildered profanity dominated both discussions.

"Took a shot at a seal this morning, near your cove." Sloan
blurted the words like a dare. "A big black bull."

Beth gritted her teeth and searched for a civilized response.
"They're a protected species. You can't do that."

Sloan smirked. "I did it, all right. Spear gun." He mimed
the pulling of a trigger. "Just beneath his belly as he was
swimming off."

One explanation for the blood roaring in her ears was that
she'd half-believed Gordon. That wasn't so, she was simply
repulsed by Sloan's cruelty. "Don't do it again," she ordered,
but his only response was a grunt.

"Sit down over there." Sloan's hand squeezed her upper
arm and he pushed her toward a plank table. "I'll bring you
your stuff."

Free of his grip, Beth had decided to just keep walking
when an artisan from Beachlord of the Rings proclaimed an
emergency.

"Hey, you're Beth, right?" He gestured toward Horatio's
Headgear. "Reddish hair with daisies in it, Karl said." Then
he explained his brother needed help with a kayak. "All
y'gotta do is watch my cash box. No one's buying jewelry."

Though her stomach growled a lament as she left Phoebe
to eat and flirt, Beth couldn't wait to escape Sloan, so she took
over. Once, as she stared across the square, she saw Gordon

talking furtively with Karl. Anticipation and melancholy hit her square in the chest.

How dare he come? What on earth could he confide in oily Karl? Then the two men welcomed stiff-legged Al MacDonald. As the fractious fisherman brayed his greetings, the group parted and Beth realized the dark man among them was Sloan, not Gordon.

After the Beachlord's return, Beth moved from booth to booth, spelling other merchants. At last she worked her way to the waterfront. There, a fire boat hosed down every soul on the dock, including Beth.

It was all in fun, she supposed, but it ticked her off. She wrung out the hem of her green dress and plaited her soaked hair into a braid. Actually, she felt much better.

Her relief was short-lived. For no apparent reason, Karl and Charmaine cornered Beth at the dock and insisted on introducing a lackluster couple named Justin and Sarah Darling.

"We just love your little cottage." Justin's face had the unformed softness of a pupa. He blinked at her drenched bodice and used his Sable Bay cap to gesture down the coast.

"Thanks." Beth squinted out toward the *Paloma*.

"It must seem a true retreat from the city." Sarah Darling should have picked a Sable Bay cap of another color. From top to toe she wore gray. Only a playful seal, stitched russet on the cap's logo, broke the monotony.

"It is." Beth watched Horatio and Al stand on the *Paloma*'s deck, swilling bottles of beer as passengers boarded. A lawsuit in the making, Beth mused. When she refocused, the cheerful smiles Charmaine and Karl exchanged warned her. The Darlings and Gull Cott. "Except," Beth searched for a daunting drawback. "The telephone company won't run a line up the bluff."

"We both have cellulars." Justin patted a bulge in his fanny pack, taking the bait.

"Won't work. I've tried it." While that wasn't strictly true, Beth figured ethics had gone by the wayside. Charmaine and Karl, damn their devious hearts, were trying to sell her house out from under her. "Lacking a phone's not bad, unless the tide cuts off the road. Then, the isolation gets a little eerie.''

"Heh, heh.'' Karl's egg-shaped body shifted uneasily. "This *is* the nineties, folks. That rarely happens.'' It was probably optimism that made Beth think Sarah Darling's face wore a green tinge as the unwelcome group moved on.

By four o'clock Beth's dress was merely damp, but her satisfaction had faded. Her eyes felt grainy and she needed a shower. As her father and Carol drove away, Beth's spirits plummeted. When Phoebe and the actors left, she'd excuse herself from volunteer duties and go home.

She missed Gordon. She ached as if she owed him an apology. She felt limp, as if she'd lost life's backbone. Logic said she only needed a nap, time to absorb last night and a piece of Midsummer Cake.

Before she reached Berries and Cream by God, Phoebe and the actors headed for the yellow van. From the counter of Whales and Ales, Junior eyed Phoebe. Her conversation with Spencer included such head-tossing animation, Beth knew Phoebe felt Junior's attention. But love at first sight was probably a myth neither believed, so they avoided a farewell.

Until Phoebe and Beth exchanged hugs next to the yellow van.

"Don't let that S.O.B get you down,'' Phoebe whispered. "And come back for a culture break. Soon.''

"You bet.'' Beth gave Phoebe an extra squeeze. "Watching you reupholster sounds like a thrill.'' Over her friend's shoulder, Beth saw Junior. He approached scowling, as if he couldn't understand this attraction, either.

As she climbed into the driver's seat, Phoebe noticed Junior. She cranked the key in the VW's ignition, then slid her sunglasses up her nose with unnecessary firmness.

The actors chorused good-byes and Phoebe had begun rolling up her window when Junior moved near enough to pose one more irritating question. "Hey, Phoebe.''

"Yeah, fisherboy?'' The VW idled so loudly, it almost covered Phoebe's insult.

"You ever seen the Loch Ness Monster?''

"No, I can't say—''

Junior hefted his belt with a leer. "Would you like to?''

Thirteen

"Just ten minutes, Beth, please?" Stefanie Morris squirmed in Beth's path, blocking her steps past Kiss-a-Lass. "Our club adviser said if she came by and we weren't here, we'd lose credit for the entire day. The guys are taking the boat out *now*."

Stefanie glared toward Karl, hawking hats to departing tourists. "Karl had them handing out Prop Two leaflets half the day, and they think they've earned some fun. You know how guys are, once they get something in their heads. It's like—hello, we're leaving.'"

"It's for a good cause," wheedled another girl.

"Really." Stefanie nodded. "Fleurettes is the school's top service organization. We're donating every penny to the Parish Women's Shelter."

A coffee can full of dollar bills showed the girls' diligence and the line-up of teenage boys had finally dwindled. She'd probably spend the last minutes of business alone. No customers would queue up to kiss loony Beth Caxton.

Most tourists had vanished. Family groups had given way to locals. Among them, only Junior had expressed interest in kissing her. He sat at Whales and Ales' plank tables, throwing sticks for a black dog, swearing and swigging with Al and a half-dozen other fishermen impatient for Gimp's bar to open at sundown.

Before she agreed, Stefanie leaned close to her ear. "About that thing I told you before? If they're taking abalone, it's, like, weird. Because Roo and Sloan—"

"Who's Roo?" Beth asked.

"Holey moley, watch out for him," warned another Fleurette, pointing out a bushy-haired man across the square. "He drools."

"—if it *was* them," Stefanie continued, quietly. "They used to sell their extras to the Neptune."

"You can't resell them, can you?" Beth found herself whispering, too. "I thought it was illegal."

"Beth." Stefanie rolled her eyes. "All I know, is now that I work there, they're not selling them to the cook and the chowder is practically all clams."

"So, are you going to do it, Miss Caxton?" asked a Fleurette.

"It would be a shame if your wicked adviser denied you credit. And you only need me for ten minutes?" Beth confirmed.

"We can close up at five-thirty." Stefanie began edging away.

"That's twenty minutes, so you have to bring me a piece of Midsummer Cake before you go." Beth crossed her arms, driving a hard bargain.

By the time Beth squeezed past the prickly juniper hedge at the back of the booth and stationed herself at its hastily nailed-together counter, cake and summer dusk sat before her.

Sprinklers chirred on nearby lawns and a breeze brought their faint mist. Two flags flapped from the library flagpole, and dusk's chill told Beth her dress wasn't as dry as she'd thought.

"Kiss-a-Lass. Quaint, but an awful health risk, don't you think?" A tourist in latex shorts and Rollerblades skated past on the cement path without giving Beth time to answer.

Beth plucked gumdrops off the whipped cream, saving them for last, then tried a forkful of cake. Somewhere, a cricket urged night to hurry, but Beth hoped the shadows would wait. The cake had probably tasted better this morning. She licked cream off her fingers and set the cake aside. Loneliness rose up strong enough to choke her.

Over at Whales and Ales, men's voices roared as Roo and Sloan swaggered across the village green. Oh, drat.

"Pucker up." Sloan's breath stank of beer and marijuana.

"Sorry, Sloan, the girls have all left." She busied herself with the money can, vowing to stand up to him this time.

Sloan slid his tongue across his lips, then lit a cigarette and stared with an intensity that might have been sexual or violent. Or both.

"The booth's closed." Pessimistically, Beth glanced at Roo. He squinted through the smoke of his own cigarette, seeming amused. Across the way, Lucinda single-mindedly packed up her wares. The church ladies' booths stood empty.

"I'm good for the buck." Sloan slapped his hand atop hers.

He'd only trapped her little finger, but when Beth moved, his weight made her wince.

"Shit, just be a good sport," Roo yawned.

"I will not! That's enough, Sloan. When you sober up you're going to be ashamed.

"What makes you think I'm drunk?"

Any other explanation would be worse, Beth thought. "Let go."

"C'mon, man." Roo sounded bored. "Let's go."

"I'll see you again, Gorgeous." Sloan pointed a wavering finger as he swaggered off. "And you're gonna like it."

Beth cradled her bruised hand inside the other, then both hands began shaking. Nothing had happened.

Besides, what were the odds Sloan had ever heard of sexual harassment? About the same as those of a woman in Kiss-a-Lass launching such a charge against him.

Trying to ignore the guffaws from across the square, Beth counted out the Fleurettes' earnings. *When you sober up, you're going to be ashamed.* Nice, Caxton. Forceful as a sparrow pecking a moose. Her hands grew steadier. She'd tallied the Fleurettes' earnings and written an accounting of the total when the juniper hedge behind her shook the entire booth.

"Gordon!" Her words broke over him, a wave of praise and pleading and then Beth's arms jammed beneath his, before he shook free of the ripping vegetation, before he uttered a word.

Wet, her green dress slapped against him. Her cheek rubbed back and forth against his shirtfront and her cold hands, fingers slim and shaking, drew his head down.

Gordon held Beth, fielding her kisses with confusion. Her lips parted and her tongue darted at the corner of his mouth.

"I missed you." For an instant his thankfulness needed words, but then he rejoined their lips.

Gordon blocked sounds of the dying day—male altercations, children singing, a dog's impatient woof—as Beth drew breath and her eyes clouded. He wouldn't let thought hinder this moment. All day he'd fasted, leeching away anger over her narrow-minded prejudice, trying not to blame her for this morning's injury.

Thought was the genesis of their troubles, but he knew how to slay it. He had magic and he'd use it. Just this once, he'd wipe her mind free of human logic.

Gordon caught Beth's wet braid, wrapped his hand in it, and urged her lips back to his. One heartbeat after their lips met, Beth's hands brushed butterfly-faint along his neck, rising up under his hair, learning the shape of his head as her body surged forward, learning the rest of him. Hot, sweet Beth.

How could they each have been angry? And if they had this, wouldn't love follow?

Joy streaked through him. Even though he hadn't purposely probed her thoughts, he'd heard her answer *yes*.

"Wait." Beth drew back, eyes greener than ever before. "Did you say something?"

Though the neck of her dress dropped enticingly low, he only nuzzled her neck. "Not a word."

"I need to think about—what you said."

"We won't talk about it, now." As he touched kisses along

the violet vein in her neck, Gordon recognized the approach of trouble, but his senses were too full of Beth.

Not until the dark man grabbed Beth's sleeve did Gordon react. The tug brought him alert. He recognized the man who'd shot him. He recognized a male so stupid he'd touched Gordon's female while she was in his arms.

Rage launched Gordon over the booth wall. Backing from the unforeseen attack, the intruder stumbled and fell.

Excitement gushed through men bidding for a better view.

"Get up, Sloan!"

Tethered tightly, even the black dog barked threats and dragged the wooden bench a foot toward the fight.

Sloan stood, pretended to shake his head free of dizziness, then charged. Gordon leaned left, letting the dark man reel past. The second time he came in low and Gordon moved aside once more. Now Sloan fingered a knife sheath at his belt.

Gordon felt his injured leg bleeding beneath his jeans. The dark man had inflicted more harm than he knew, but Gordon reasoned that if he kept dodging Sloan's clumsy charges, he'd tire and humiliate him. That sort of revenge was even finer than split flesh.

Before Sloan pulled his knife, Al MacDonald grabbed him from behind.

"That's enough, Sloan." Others joined Al, trying to hustle Sloan away. The dark man resisted, frowning at Beth.

Gordon caught tangled currents of sex and domination coursing through Sloan's mind. Gordon smothered his own inhuman growl, but his fury burned bright as the Wheel flying downhill, throwing sparks as it spun out of control.

Then Junior grabbed him. Gordon knew Junior's touch, and though he shrugged it off, the instant of contact brought flashes of memory: Junior teaching him to read, polishing his English, schooling him to cooked food and human emotions. Junior, his only friend.

Beth's hand touched Gordon's arm. "It's okay," she said, and where Junior had failed, she succeeded.

Gordon gave a quick nod. He let Sloan be hauled away by

his companions and extended his hand to Junior.

Junior ignored it as his lips twisted into a sneer. "Still coming to Bethie's rescue, huh, Gordon?"

"Someone needed to," Gordon taunted, but it was Beth's gasp that filled Gordon with satisfaction. Would she believe *now*?

"What are you talking about?" Beth demanded, though Junior clearly wanted no females in this dispute. "Junior, tell me what you're talking about."

Their arena was only made up of spectators, and it seemed to tighten around them as Junior's tone lowered. "Christ, Beth. Don't act like you can't believe it. Look at him. He was the one who pulled you out when you were drowning. Not some seal."

"But I saw—"

"He came home all wet to us, and Al kicked him out so your dad wouldn't press charges or something."

"What's that?" Al lurched forward as Beth stepped back.

"Nothing," Beth spoke like a sleepwalker. "Sloan just had too much to drink." Beth moved a little in front of Gordon, facing Junior and Al. "He was acting rowdy and Gordon got him to stop."

A dozen villagers and several strangers smelling of cars and plastic had gathered. Fishermen surrounded Junior, expecting him to take up the fight, but they jostled aside as Lucinda Wright, the librarian, appeared.

"Junior MacDonald, tell your cohorts to go on home." Lucinda waved her index finger and one young man fled on his own. "They've overindulged and lost their good sense. Prove to me you haven't."

"We're just talking, Miss Wright." Junior's voice brimmed with respect. Orders issued, Lucinda left for the library.

"Sloan was being a jackass, Junior." Beth seemed to have regathered her nerve. Her blunt words made a few men smile, but not Junior. He seemed to resent the sudden role of females in this battle. "Ask your friend Roo what happened."

"Didn't see nothin'." The blond narrowed his eyes. " 'Cept Sloan wanted a kiss. *She* wouldn't sell him one."

"Want to see what I refused?" Beth blushed at the need to guard her own honor. "That's where he jerked my sleeve."

Then Gordon noticed the rip. Where the sleeve had joined her dress, Beth's shoulder showed golden and bare. Madness came pounding back, but he controlled it. "When you see him, tell Sloan to keep his hands off her."

"Imagine such a thing." Junior frowned in mock-contemplation. "A man thinking a girl standing in a kissing booth was actually selling kisses." Junior's audience—even Karl and Charmaine, fidgeting on the fringes of the crowd—laughed. "Beth Ann," Junior added, "You've always been a little tease."

When Junior's words made Beth blush deeper, Gordon felt ready for violence, eager for it. But Beth gave a faint shake of head and her fingers meshed through his; somehow he obeyed.

"Small towns have long memories, honey." Al nodded, as if underlining Junior's word *tease* for all to hear. "Personally, I been thinkin' the seals returned to town with you. I know you always admired 'em. Damn things're worse than ever, wreckin' our nets, eatin' our catch—"

As a youngster, Gordon had hoped for a chance to tell humans how to work with seals, not against them. Only a youngster could have been so naive. Humans saw the sea as their private slaughterhouse.

"Gonna be takin' chum and a baseball bat out with me, next time." The bushy-haired man Beth had called Roo cleared his throat and spat.

Though Gordon didn't know this use of *chum*, he knew baseball bats could be used for more than fun. Roo spoke of killing. The cow with net embedded in her plush fur bobbed before his mind's eye. And what of the cow he'd search for? Teaching these men seemed fruitless as that search. Better to wait beyond the shoals, cause an "accident," and leave them to drown.

Beth flinched from his sudden grip. Gordon loosened his hand as a man spoke from the edge of the crowd.

"Forget it, Roo. That's Sloan talking, not you." Bearded,

bespectacled, and dressed in khaki shorts, the man looked more field biologist than sheriff, but Gordon had seen him drinking coffee in Gimp's and heard him identified as Sheriff Bob Reynolds. "We've got a Great White spotted off Lyre Beach. You're not going to bait it with chum and dead seals."

"You—" Shuffling feet and murmurs of surprise attended the female. "You act as if dead seals would be an annoyance." A newcomer to the village, the female spoke over Charmaine's protest. "Don't you people know those animals are federally protected?"

"Sure they do, Mrs. Darling." Karl's tone stirred the fishermen's scorn. "That's what Proposition Two is all about." Karl gestured toward the heart of town, and though the billboard was out of sight, few missed his meaning. "I assure you this village is moving into the nineties with great gusto."

Guffaws rebounded as *"great gusto"* was repeated, passed around the ring of spectators, and only softened when Gimp offered the lure of special entertainment at his bar.

"Being as I got the pipes warmed up last night, I'll give a wee concert." Gimp stroked his bushy white beard. "That is, if any of you lads still has a taste for a pitcher or two of ale."

Though the men obviously warmed to the idea, Gordon could see they weren't distracted from the prospect of another fight.

With Minny on her hip, Charmaine approached the space that opened like an arena between Junior and Gordon. She boosted Minny higher. Minny flapped a beribboned stick toward Gordon and waved to Junior, as her mother spoke.

"Outsiders don't understand how rough you guys joke." Charmaine met Junior's smile, then shepherded the Darlings from the square.

The crowd might have broken up, but again, Gordon felt Junior rebel against such intercession by a woman.

"Listen, *Gordon*." Junior's sarcasm reminded him of the day they'd chosen the name. "You can't return to the scene of—" Junior let the insinuation hang as he took a cigarette from Roo, studiously lit it, drew and expelled a stream of smoke. "Who Beth lets touch her is her business, but let me bring you up to speed on seals in Grey Gallows.''

Who Beth lets touch her. A dozen lurid scenes flashed in Gordon's mind. He couldn't help glancing at her.

"We've got damned few fish because of seals," Junior said. "They rip our nets, eat fish we've already caught, and what they can't eat, they set loose." Junior waited, blue eyes gauging Gordon's reaction. "If the dumb animals get tangled in the nets and drown themselves, we've got that mess to deal with.''

Gordon set his jaw and forced himself to check the onlookers before answering Junior's taunt. Only the tourists and Beth would bolster his stand. The rest looked openly hostile.

All the same, he took up Junior's argument. "Both seals and men are predators, right? With men the more intelligent. So how is it they don't notice the obvious cause and effect between using seals to mark good fishing areas and these financial disasters?''

"Before you get calluses patting yourself on the back for such clever talkin', why don't you inform us poor simple fishermen about this 'cause and effect'?''

"You use seals to mark an area, right?" Gordon waited until the others grew impatient.

"Yeah, so what's your point?" Al interjected.

"Isn't it possible men are trespassing on seals' hunting areas?''

"Yeah, what's your point?" Roo mimicked.

"If they've got such great fishing grounds staked out, how come they come eat our bait?" Junior asked, emboldened by the agreement around him.

"Because they're hungry?" Gordon speculated. "Because you've overfished their feeding spots so they can't even find fish that are too small for a commercial catch?''

As the others turned to Junior, he sucked on the cigarette and struck a menacing pose, thinking. "Even if that's true, there's a natural order here. Higher animals and lower ones. And you don't see us carrying filthy parasites.''

"Parasites like cod worms?" Gordon asked, and the fishermen nodded, grunting. "They are troublesome, but nothing compared to trawling and purse seining and culling.''

The last word burned his throat. He'd never understood how
he came to know of culling. Seal folk told no coherent tales
and he would not watch those atrocities on television. But
some sore, vibrating spot inside Gordon remembered the carnage.

"We don't do that no more," Al said.

"It's illegal," the sheriff confirmed.

"But you remember what it was like, don't you? Cutting
your motors far out, paddling silently toward the breeding
grounds where pups and cows lay sleeping. The fierce males
were long gone, of course.

"You probably used baseball bats"—he nodded toward
Roo—"instead of rifles, so you didn't wreck the fur. I bet
seventy or eighty percent of your kill was pups. Those protective mothers must have barked and charged. Did one ever
try to bite—"

"We don't do that no more," Al repeated.

Junior threw the cigarette down and scuffed his boot over
it time and again, before looking up. "When did you turn into
such a damned bleeding heart?" Junior looked less angry than
he did concerned and Gordon felt a current of hope.

If Junior had shaken his hand, if Al hadn't appeared drained
by the memories, if there'd been no assembled gawkers, they
might have mended their friendship.

"You gave a nice speech and I'm sure they understand,
Mr.—?" Sheriff Reynolds wanted more than a name. The police radio crackled from the patrol car.

Gordon wanted to tell the truth, since Reynolds had the
power of captivity over those who defied him. "Gordon," he
supplied.

"Bob Reynolds." The sheriff shook Gordon's hand with
unstudied pressure.

"I vacationed here as a boy." Gordon needed the sheriff's
regard and it made him nervous. Captivity filled him with fear
enough to paralyze his shifts from seal to man. He'd never
give Bob Reynolds reason to lock him up. "I always wanted

to come back and look up a few friends, see how the village had changed.''

"I did the same thing when I left school and applied to take my dad's job." Reynolds rubbed an index finger behind one ear and settled a hand against his gun belt. Clearly, he didn't admire Gordon's knack at renewing old acquaintances. His belt squeaked a reminder of authority. "I'm going to walk a lap around the green, make sure we've got no lost kids. When I come back, I'd like to see everyone moving toward home."

They moved. Without planning it, Gordon and Beth left together, each shielding the other from accusing looks.

"Beth Ann?" Jewel Clark, her white ponytail bedraggled, jogged to catch up with them. "I thought you hated this Sable Bay plan. And I sure didn't think you were the backstabbing sort."

"I'm not. I hate Karl's idea," Beth all but shouted. When Karl turned to glower, she jerked her chin higher. " 'Progress' doesn't impress me. I'm the one without the phone, remember?"

"That's what we thought." Horatio had followed more slowly. "But you're here summers and weekends. We stay year-round. How're we supposed to live if we can't fight our competitors, even if they are seals? Things've been balanced before, but somehow they're getting out of hand. And once the fishing dies, Grey Gallows'll be nothing but another damned row of T-shirt and popcorn places."

Gordon squeezed Beth's hand. They called her a traitor because he'd spoken out and she'd stood beside him.

A volley of barks made them turn. Junior stood with one boot on the bench to which he'd tied his Rottweiler. He toyed with the dog's rope as he argued with Sloan.

Gordon stiffened. He should have noticed the dark man's reappearance. Now Junior called out as Sloan started their way.

"Tell you something else, asshole." Sloan's voice was low and deadly. Gordon thought he'd derive great pleasure from breaking Sloan's teeth and helping him swallow them, but he waited. "Out there—" Sloan motioned to the sea. "There ain't no nineties, no federal law, no environmental impact bullshit. No one knows what goes on out there, and if he does, he damn sure doesn't tell. So don't get caught in my territory. Got it?''

"Oh, I've got it." Gordon restrained an ironic laugh—*his territory, indeed*—then followed Sloan's glance. Sheriff Reynolds walked toward them with quiet purpose.

As Sloan swaggered away, Gordon breathed deep of the misty wind. He had work to do here, as well as at sea. But he'd ached for this fight half his life. If neither Beth nor his magic deserted him, he might even win.

Fourteen

Sand crab holes bubbled on a shore strewn with the tiny crustaceans' molted shells. Gulls prowled, cocking white heads to listen, but rarely pecked. Their prey lay far below the surface, where they'd dug down to safety.

"Thanks for taking my side, for standing next to me." Gordon's words were the first either had uttered since leaving the village.

Beth squeezed his hand, glad Gordon hadn't guessed half the reason she'd stood so steadfastly beside him was because Junior's words had frozen her in place. *Don't act like you can't believe it. He was the one. . . . He came home all wet to us. . . . He was the one.*

Hands still linked, they stopped at the cove. Gordon's lips pressed together and his dark brows lowered as he stared at the bare curve of sand.

The notes of Gimp's bagpipes floated from the village. "Loch Lomand," played with aching woe.

"What's wrong?" But Beth knew. All the seals had gone.

"Probably nothing." Gordon's head inclined toward the horizon, listening, and a shock of black hair fell over his brow. "All the commotion and kids in boats sent them swimming for Moon Isle, I guess."

Moon Isle. On days Jack had submerged in creative labors, pulling his tweedy cardigan closer each time she spoke, Beth had filled her days with diving and swimming, stroking two miles to the sand spit sprinkled with boulders. If not for a constant plague of sand gnats, Moon Isle would have been perfect for basking. Perhaps gnats didn't bother seals.

Three times Beth swallowed and tried to speak. After each swallow, her throat refused to relinquish the words, afraid she'd sound either naive or sarcastic. Mercifully, Gordon didn't notice her struggle, until she blurted, "Do you have to go after them?"

He shoved the hair off his forehead and smiled. "They're already there, wherever it is." After a few strides he added, "It's my own fault. Last night I didn't go back."

Last night seemed far gone as last summer. Midsummer magic had lashed them to each other and though Beth couldn't be sorry for the molten longing, she wished it hadn't led to his confession. Should she feel guilty for keeping him from his clan?

"I should have brought my car," Beth spoke loudly as they climbed the narrow path up from the cove, trying to mute her mind's argument that no man had family in the sea.

"I don't care for cars."

"How can you not—" Beth didn't finish. If Gordon hadn't been raised to the metallic clatter, sudden starts and swooping turns, if Gordon was what he said, then cars might be unsettling.

Beth's slick-soled slippers slid on a patch of scree. That damned red rock surprised her every time. She clung to the unforgiving stone face to her right as a gravel shower pitched off the track, falling.

Gordon's words would take getting used to, but this precarious trail wasn't the place for it.

When she reached the bluff, Beth looked down. White wave-tips piped the cove like icing on a cake. She'd always measured the plunge from bluff to water as a two-story house, times two. That measurement still seemed about right. She shivered, astonished that she'd taken the dive a hundred times,

and many more from each outcropping starting from the beach
and working her way up.

Gordon tensed as she wavered toward space.

"I used to dive from here." Beth locked her knees, refusing
to let thin air intimidate her. "I can't believe it."

Quick perplexity crossed Gordon's face. And then that
smile.

Beth crouched to pluck beach morning glories blooming
amid the eel grass. "I have a set of tarnished copper flagons.
They're Jack's, though I never saw him drink from them.
Won't they look great sitting on the mantel, stuffed with
these?"

Gordon followed her to the door. Both knew he would, but
now Beth felt the pulse spring giddy in her neck and last night
seemed only minutes ago.

"Maybe it comes from working on my own roof, because
I'm certainly not the domestic type, but I've got some great
ideas for the house." She turned the doorknob, trying to fill
the silence waiting on the other side of the door. "I want a
window seat in the living room." She breathed an unfamiliar
oily scent as she shut the door, but it wasn't nearly as disturbing as the quiet.

Beth made for the living room, letting her hands describe
the dimensions of a cozy, pillow-piled bench built to face the
hearth. She strained not to look back at Gordon's empty arms.

"I want to hang herbs from the kitchen beam." Silence
pressed in behind every word as she fled toward the kitchen.
He followed. She stopped in the doorway. Eluding him was
impossible. "But first . . ." Beth stared at the water glass
poised on her windowsill. Her Midsummer experiment. "I
guess . . . I need to finish the roof."

She didn't have to turn to know. Gordon's gaze traced the
bony ridges of her shoulder blades. Then his hands were there,
warm. Each of his fingers pressed firmly, as if he made hand-
prints on the wet fabric of her dress.

*Freeze tag. We're playing a child's game of freeze tag.
When he touches me, I can't move away.*

"Beth?" Gordon's breath stirred a tendril beside her ear

and Beth shivered. "Do you have peanut butter and jelly?"

Of all the words in the English language, these were a combination she'd least expected. Without looking, Beth flicked on the light switch, then turned. "You want me to make you a peanut butter and jelly sandwich?"

Some merging of dusk and kitchen light turned Gordon's eyes tawny. And predatory.

"If you'd rather, I could mash you against the refrigerator and have my way with you. That's what I really want."

Beth's shocked gasp brought Peaches. He padded out of hiding to twine between their legs. Gordon scooped up the cat. Beth opened the cupboard and stared. Just what had she sought amid the orderless jumble and curl-edged shelf paper?

Once she remembered, once she assembled thick sandwiches using bagels in place of bread, once she sat on the rug, facing the shell-strewn coffee table, Beth couldn't eat.

Instead, she watched Gordon. How was it she'd never noticed the agile elegance of a man's wrist? Or the strong motion of a jaw? How could this be the same male who'd issued regal mandates to Junior's gang of louts? Now, she couldn't imagine him any other way, than pushed back from the table, wide shoulders supported by her couch, boyish and satisfied after finishing his sandwich and half of hers.

Beth licked a smear of peanut butter from her finger and let her tongue sift the flavors. Absolutely nothing marine-like greeted her taste buds. Before, Gordon had joked that he rarely ate anything except fish. That would be natural if he'd been reared in the sea. It wouldn't explain this schoolboy craving.

"How is it you came to like peanut butter sandwiches?"

There. To an eavesdropper, it would seem an innocuous, if boring question, but Beth meant to nudge into his past, a past that must be magical or a lie.

Gordon's lids blinked as if she'd wakened him, but he answered quickly. Only a huskiness in his voice hinted that he'd dozed. "When I first came ashore, I lived with Junior."

I used to come here as a child. . . . I recognized Junior as a ruffian. . . . He came home to us, all wet. . . . The echoes made sense.

She'd sensed something stronger than hormone-charged competition since Junior and Al drove up during the rainstorm. Gordon had been ready to beat his friend bloody. His *friend*, Junior. Today's sparring without fists all added up to the resentful melancholy of a friendship lost.

"Al and Junior didn't keep much food. Al spent his pay before he got home. Lots of nights, Junior had nothing to eat except bread covered with mayonnaise." Gordon swallowed audibly. "Of course, I could always feed in the sea." His brown eyes turned wary. Once more, Beth nodded to encourage him.

"But we always kept a secret stash of food under Junior's bed. Peanut butter, jam and bread, all double-wrapped in foil and plastic to keep it from rats. And we only brought it out for watching *Sesame Street*.

"Al never caught us." Gordon's smile turned smug. "Junior thought we would've gotten a beating for watching—two teenage boys, watching *Sesame Street*?" He said it nostalgically, as if beatings were common in the MacDonald household.

"Al beat you?" she asked.

"No. He swung, but he never touched me." Guilt shone in Gordon's eyes. "He hurt Junior too often, but that's the nature of males."

"That is *not* the nature of males! Jack never even spanked me. How can you say that?"

"Because it's true. I know so many pups, scarred or dead from their sires' wrath." Gordon shrugged, unperturbed. "Have you seen Junior's back? One winter he tried to get credit at the Village Store. He couldn't. He was embarrassed, so he confronted Al over never having money even for milk. Al broke the empty milk bottle over Junior's back. I wasn't there, to draw him off." Gordon turned toward Jack's yellow armchair, sitting in the corner. "You were lucky."

Beth broke off a piece of bagel and nibbled, sobered by the idea that she might have been born to drunken Al MacDonald, saddened that Junior had.

"But we were happy eating peanut butter and jam and

watching *Sesame Street*. That's how I learned to read, and
where I picked my name.''

"*Gordon*?'' This time Beth wasn't speaking to the man before her. She remembered the television *Gordon* as a strong,
congenial man with a sleek black head. "How perfect.'' For
a seal in boy's form, how truly perfect.

"I already had a name, but—''

"What was it? Tell me your real name.''

" 'Gordon' is my real name.'' He began fidgeting with the
tabletop collection of shells. "The other doesn't work in English.''

"Oh, please.''

"No.'' He blushed and lined up the shells according to size.
"I can't. It was a baby name. Most seals are called something
similar, it just means 'pup.' ''

Pup. For no reason she could explain, tears gathered in
Beth's eyes and stung her nose and throat. *Pup.* The word's
tenderness brought back Gordon's description of mother seals'
hopeless defense during culling.

"I really wanted to be 'Elmo,' '' Gordon said. "But Junior
convinced me that was no better than the name I already had.''

Beth giggled, wishing no table sat between them, wishing
she could curl into his arms and believe every word.

"All that time, you were over there?'' It would have taken
about thirty minutes to ride her bike to Junior's house.

"I came each summer, once I knew I was too different to
migrate south with the other males.''

"It's such a small village, though. You'd think—''

"I did see you a few times.'' Gordon's eyes left the arrangement of shells and watched her.

His gaze set up an anxious stirring through each one of her
veins and vessels. "When?'' she managed.

"Out there—'' He gestured to the bluff. "That Midsummer
Eve we met, as the storm was rising, didn't you dive from the
cliff?''

"I used to do it all the time, such a stupid stunt.''

"You were beautiful.''

"I was *crazy*.'' She meddled with Gordon's shell arrange-

ment, scooting a few into concentric circles. "I must have
been nine or ten when Jack took me to a foreign film festival
in San Francisco. One showed cliff divers in Acapulco and I
thought, 'Wow, I could do that!' " Beth chaffed her bare forearms against the chill of remembrance. She'd felt so certain
her daring dive would lure Jack away from his typewriter.

"And you taught yourself?"

"I did. I started by sitting on a rock about six feet above
the cove, leaning over and slipping into the water. I remember
clamping my arms over my ears, like the people in the
movie." She did it now, feeling a jolt of exhilaration that made
her calf muscles long for the launch. "Not until I jumped from
the bluff did I understand that was to protect my eardrums.
When you hit the water—"

Clearly as if he'd spoken, Gordon empathized, knowing
how it felt to make such a dive. Beth stared at the wave-
polished stick marked like a piebald seal pup, then glanced
up.

"I watched the seals a lot," she admitted. "They taught me
the body follows the head. Silly not to notice that before, but
for me, it was a revelation."

Were you one of them? Her hand covered her lips so she
wouldn't ask, but she pictured the sleek creatures whose un-
knowing lessons had kept her from dashing her adolescent
brains out on the rocks cascading down from Grey Gallows'
spires.

"I want you to swim with me." Gordon's hand took Beth's
away from her mouth and carried it to his.

Immersed in his touch, Beth couldn't ask whether he meant
in human or seal form. It didn't matter. Gordon was asking
for far more than a dip in the cove.

"The higher I went, the harder it was to keep my toes
pointed and ankles together. I started hitting rocks on the way
down." Though Gordon nuzzled her hand, his eyes were
raised to watch her and to listen. "Jack noticed the scratches
and bruises and asked if what I was doing was safe, so I ended
up tying my ankles together and springing out from the rocks.
That helped, but I was still coming against the sea bed. Hard."

One dive almost made her quit. Her skull had speared solid sand and pain had zigzagged through every vertebrae as she floated helpless to the surface.

"Again," she said, "I watched the seals, saw how they straightened for entry, then curved back *right away*, heading up for the sunlight and air."

Gordon's thumb stroked the flesh rising at the base of her thumb. *I know, I know.* He said it without speaking and she tried to remember what came next.

Jack. When Jack finally came, it was not to see her perform. One day she'd sneaked out before "school" had ended for the day, leaving an unfinished geometry lesson on the kitchen counter.

For some reason he'd broken away from characters who mesmerized him more than real people, deserting his plays-cript to come striding across the bluff. His hair must have been longer then, since she remembered the wind tearing at it and lifting the back of his ratty cardigan. High grass had grabbed at his khaki trousers, too. Nature had taken her side, since Jack was an alien in her cliff-top world.

"What's made you sad?" Gordon seemed to have watched the memory cross her face.

"Nothing, really. I guess I had some adolescent notion of impressing the heck out of my father. And when he finally came to see what I'd been doing for the last couple hundred days, he wasn't excited. He just wanted to make sure I was safe."

Beth's sarcasm froze between them as Gordon's boyish expression returned. Only this time, it was forlorn.

"Because he loved you," Gordon said.

"Maybe. He stood at the edge of the bluff and said, 'Let's see it, girl.'" Beth remembered how her arms had risen to cover the pounding in her ears. "So I dived. He was on the shore when I swam back in, saying 'Never doubted you for a minute.' He was out of breath and that's all he said." Gordon's stare was a reprimand, but he didn't know Jack. "That's all he ever says."

She'd always wondered if Jack had been out of breath from
running, or scared half to death by her leap.

"But you don't dive anymore."

"I'm afraid I've grown too sensible for that." Beth's cour-
age turned soupy at the thought of committing her body to
wind currents and old expertise, but when she saw disappointment in Gordon's face, she wondered if she couldn't still do
it.

Gordon yawned and apologized. Maybe his expression
hadn't been disappointment at all, just weariness.

"Tired?" She asked.

"Not really." He stared toward the hearth, though the cottage was filled with the day's warmth. "Last night"—his fingers tightened on hers, before she could draw away—"after
you left, I stayed like this." With the back of her hand, he
grazed his shirtfront. "I stayed a man, because I thought you
might come to me."

She didn't tell him how many times she'd touched the doorknob, ready to run down the steps to Lyre Rock. She didn't
say fear and anger had burned hotter than desire, but barely.

"At dawn I saw the night sky turn from black to blue
around your house. And your windows were still gold."

"I left the lights burning all night." Beth offered an explanation, though he didn't ask why. "I was so mad at you."

With a move whose sudden grace shocked her, Gordon released her hand and pounced toward the door. Was he leaving?
He paced back a few steps and looked down on her. She didn't
stand, feeling safer, half-twisted to look up at him. And then
she noticed blood welling through his jeans.

"Gordon, you're hurt." Across his thigh, the denim puckered black and wet.

He glanced down and shook his head.

"You *are*. It's bleeding."

"I did it this morning." He gave a curt sound. "I should
have seen it coming. It's nothing." His frustration simmered
as he dismissed the injury and returned to her admission about
the night before. "You were mad." His jaw bulged with hard
muscle as his teeth gritted together. For a moment his black

lashes closed. He frowned in bewilderment, banishing outward signs of anger. When his eyes reopened, she felt as if he cradled the back of her head in gentle hands. "Were you mad because I told you the truth about me, or because I told you before we mated? Because I stopped?"

Beth wrapped both arms around her ribs and turned away. Star-pricked blackness, his hands transporting her above her own body, and lava-thick heat making her languorous and eager, at once. And then betrayal. Gordon knew it all.

Truth caught in Beth's throat. She held the stick pup and smoothed it, with her back still turned. "Both."

"I'd better go."

"Why?" She still couldn't look his way, but she shamed herself. *Tease. Let him go, before there's another fight.* His silence lasted so long, she had to turn.

"I'm leaving because now you believe me. Or nearly do. And there's only one other thing to settle between us. Our missed mating. But you're not ready."

So wrong. Desire grew with every truth he spoke.

"*Are* you?" Gordon's voice was a plea that he was wrong.

Make love with a man who swam as a seal? A man who personified magic? If he touched her, she'd do it.

"I'd better go," he said again. He locked the door behind him as he went.

Beth didn't move until the room had fallen into darkness and her fingers curled with cold.

Her knees creaked as she rose and turned on the adobe-based lamp. The kitchen light still shone, but her elbow ached as she reached for a cabinet left half open. Curled around the base of the peanut butter jar sat the gold and emerald necklace.

Reverently she held the inch-wide collar so it lapped over each of her hands. The emerald sat centered, winking under her dusty kitchen light.

You're a stubborn one, Gordon, my "bonny selkie." Stubborn and generous. This week he'd given her a neon Frisbee, a suggestive poster, heart-pounding kisses, and enough mystery to last a lifetime. And of course, this double handful of emerald and gold.

What if she wasn't up to the challenge? For advice, she had nothing to consult but the glass she'd left on her windowsill.

An ordinary egg, broken into a glass half full with water on Midsummer morn, was supposed to create a symbol that clearly foretold the coming year.

Beth frowned into the glass, wishing she had Maria's talent for signs. She saw white strands of egg defying gravity. Spangled with air bubbles, they reached the water's surface creating something like a blown-glass fantasy land or a miniature Golden Gate Bridge, complete with fairy-fine spans.

No. That interpretation wouldn't work. It made less sense than a newspaper horoscope, because the egg's golden center—which would have to be the sun—lay on the bottom of the glass instead of bobbing above.

Still staring, Beth draped the necklace around her throat. The catch locked with a quick click and the gold settled into place.

Beth turned off the kitchen light, then clicked it on again. She squinted at the glass and sighed. If one were absolutely determined to make sense of such superstitious nonsense, there was only one truth the glass foretold for the coming year: her world had turned upside down.

Fifteen

Beth crowned herself Queen of Grey Gallows. From her roof, she surveyed her kingdom. Overnight, the seals had returned to her cove. Fishing boats dotted the horizon. Peaches sniffed and sneezed beneath her deck, and Gordon cared for her.

True, an unsightly head-high pile of shingles lay on the palace grounds, but Beth's castle roof was fireproof, water-tight, and she'd driven every nail herself.

She'd dressed for the role of queen.

"Emeralds are such versatile jewels," Beth confided to Peaches. Their green fire complimented cutoffs and a kelly tank top as nicely as they would a ball gown. Peaches ignored her fashion dictates, even when she sailed a miscut shingle off the roof into her discard pile.

Beth considered the smoke-gray symmetry of her shingles and resolved to put off poetry just a little longer. There'd be plenty of rainy days when she could do little else. Today, she'd buy a scraper and remove the chipped and splintered paint from her window frames. Next, she'd sand and repaint them. Would Gull Cott's ghosts protest if she brushed the frames with teal-blue paint instead of the cottage's traditional gray?

It would take most of the day to walk into the village and back, but she had no choice. She'd run short of groceries and the Fiat sat pouting because Jack hadn't inspected its innards yesterday. Even abject obeisance to its place of nativity hadn't persuaded the Fiat to run this morning. It sat twenty yards down her driveway, where it had coasted and refused to start by compression.

Beth squared a small stack of extra shingles she'd leave in the lee of the roof, out of sight and handy, should her novice nailing prove unequal to a storm's fury.

She had retied the laces in her tennis shoes, gathered her tools, and begun arching tension from her back prior to climbing down, when a car crunched the gravel of her private road.

A palomino-colored Cadillac navigated the road as if fearful of land mines. When it paused beside the stranded Fiat, Beth imagined she heard Karl's disgusted sigh. He pulled past, headed for the parking area at the foot of her rough-cut stairs.

He might be bearing roses and praise for her adept handling of yesterday's faire. Beth shucked off her gloves and tucked them into her back pocket. She doubted that, but Karl could at least give her a ride into the village. She'd started toward the ladder when Karl began leaning on the horn.

"Well, kiss my tape measure, Karl." Beth's ire sent Peaches skittering into the blackberry bushes below. "Of all the uppity—"

Karl honked again. Beth waved, shouted a cheery "Hi!" and pretended not to comprehend the summons.

"Waddle on up here if you're so impatient," Beth muttered.

Spite kept her on the roof until Karl had puffed across to the cottage. A week of clambering up to the roof and down, allowed Beth to descend the ladder with careful ease.

"Hey, Karl."

"Well, aren't you a sight?" Karl's disapproval focused on the leather tool belt slung at pocket-level over her cutoffs.

"I take it you don't mean for sore eyes?" Beth unbuckled the tool belt and spread it on her deck.

"I hardly believed Junior when he told me." Karl watched as she inspected a blister.

His stare felt crude and intrusive, but Beth maintained her

calm. He'd forgotten she wasn't crazy Beth Caxton anymore. She'd have to remind him.

"But now, speaking of eyesores, that's the prize-winner." Karl pointed to the mound of spent shingles.

"You're right," Beth admitted. Sweat stung the blister and the beds of fingernails she'd abraded climbing the path last night. "The disposal guys were supposed to deliver the Dumpster yesterday."

"County employees don't work Sundays. They're at the store, now, though, is what I drove out to say." Karl shaded his eyes to consider the geometric order of her roof.

"Why didn't they just follow you out?" Beth asked, wishing for water to flush her wound and stop the stinging.

"They won't move without a deposit." Karl raised his voice to be heard over a logging truck passing on the highway. "Not after I told them about your teeth-crackin' road."

"For crying out loud, Karl. A VW bus loaded with actors, costumes, and props managed it yesterday. There's nothing wrong with my road."

"Well, hell, Beth Ann. That's not the impression you gave the Darlings yesterday." Karl's satisfaction-pinked face said she'd walked into ambush.

"Well, hell, Karl, my house is *not* for sale. I resent you telling them it was!" Beth grabbed her tool belt and stormed toward the door. She'd walk to town. "And another thing—" Beth wheeled so quickly, a hammer escaped its loop and plummeted for Karl's polished loafer.

Her mood improved as Karl danced out of harm's way.

"Calm down, Beth Ann." Karl's tone coaxed Peaches out of the bushes, but the shopkeeper didn't notice. "I didn't tell them it was for sale. That's Charmaine's job." Karl consulted his watch. "With her holding down the fort, we'd better hurry. Grab your checkbook and I'll take you back in, unless you're too proud to save yourself miles of walking?"

Beth decided she wasn't. She washed up, slicked her hair into a ponytail, and located her purse. Phoebe must be right. Elusive Mr. Gordon must have left her brain-damaged, indeed, since she had no memory of stowing the purse in her closet.

Stopping before the bathroom mirror, she repositioned her emerald and decided brains exchanged for beauty made a fair swap.

"Pretty nice jewelry for outdoor work," Karl said as Beth fastened the seat belt closest to the passenger door.

"They're doing incredible things with glass and brass these days." Beth smiled out the window, then shivered. Karl's air-conditioning was apparently stuck on polar and the car reeked of cologne and cigar smoke. Beth tried not to breathe.

"I did not say your place was for sale," Karl repeated. He swung the Cadillac so wide, his tires hissed on beach. "I just figured, with all the work you're doing and the bad memories here, you were getting ready to put your place on the market."

"No." She didn't snap that the memories weren't so bad. She didn't say *he* was the one keeping her tainted youth alive in village history. She'd allowed him to provoke her into one juvenile retort and one was enough. Beth folded her hands in her lap and hummed.

Karl turned left onto Surf Street, darted her a baffled look, and accelerated toward the village. "Sable Bay's success depends on getting dual-income commuting couples to buy here. This town's well-being depends on Prop Two, on changing that god-awful name."

When Sheriff Reynolds's cruiser slid from a side street, Karl jammed on the brakes and the Cadillac wallowed down to the speed limit.

" 'Grey Gallows' is such a downer," Karl added.

Beth grinned. Karl's ineptitude with language would be funnier if he didn't take himself so seriously. "Voting day is months ahead, Karl." As they left the neighborhood behind and village stores came into sight, Beth thought of Horatio and Jewel, of Junior, Al, Lucinda Wright, and even teenage Stefanie. "I think you're in for a fight."

"Oh, yeah?" Karl braked and pointed to the billboard. "You wouldn't know anything about that, would you?"

Overnight, someone had vandalized the Proposition Two billboard. Red paint poured over the words *progress* and *profit,* then dripped down the face of the smiling cartoon seal.

"Of course not." Beth's mind sorted through names of the irritated and physically agile.

Karl pulled into the Village Store parking lot, and Beth looked back at the billboard. Junior or Sloan could have climbed up there. Or any one of the teenage boys who agreed with Stefanie that Sable Bay-ers "sucked."

Before Karl could extend the false courtesy of opening her door, Beth swung her legs out. The police cruiser pulling in swung wide to miss her. *Good, Beth.* She winced an apology, but Sheriff Reynolds's sunglasses obscured his response.

"What about that boyfriend of yours?" Karl asked. "He could've climbed up there. And don't bother telling Sheriff Reynolds he was with you all night"—Karl's voice rose over the Sheriff's slammed door—"because he was seen—"

To stop herself from sputtering an archaic protest over the sullying of her reputation, Beth strode away from Karl and entered the store.

The door's bell jingled and Charmaine looked up from her position in front of the meat case, then went back to spraying glass cleaner.

Tiny tennis shoes tapping her approach, Minny shouted, "Mama? Kids coming?" She careened around the end of the front counter, stopped in front of Beth and sucked a finger.

"Not yet, Minny. After lunch." Charmaine stood, adjusted her blue sailcloth skirt, and handed Minny an aerosol can.

"Go spray," Minny explained, then approached the front door and took aim at a door hinge. A sweet oiliness mixed with the summer scent of the yellow pears Charmaine had begun unpacking.

"It's Monday, every piece of glass gets polished and every hinge gets oiled." Charmaine plucked pears from purple paper pockets and arranged them on a green plastic hump surrounded by local berries and last season's spongy apples. "Where's Gordon?" Charmaine asked, without stopping her work.

"Hard to say." Beth loaded a small basket with bread, milk, eggs.

"He's got neat eyes." Charmaine rolled her own skyward. Beth hefted a jar of peanut butter, remembering Char-

maine's gauzy Midsummer Eve gown, the bells around her
ankles, and the way she'd gushed "my hero" at Gordon.
Creamy or chunky peanut butter? She took both, then watched
Charmaine's purple hair glint under the florescent lights as she
kissed her daughter.

"Minny, I think that's enough." Charmaine stroked
Minny's cheek, and Beth thought Charmaine's hand lingered
on the tulip-shaped birth mark before she gave the child a
gentle swat. "Go squirt the back door awhile."

The back door. Beth scolded herself for not locating her
Dumpster before shopping. But she couldn't. She needed to
hear words about Gordon, even if they were from a rival.

"He has a mean streak, doesn't he?" Charmaine slung
empty fruit boxes toward the rear of the store. "The way he
went after Sloan—" Charmaine patted her bosom. "Makes a
girl's heart flutter."

If you fancy brutes. But maybe she did. Beth remembered
hurling herself into Gordon's sheltering arms after Sloan and
Roo had merely teased her. She was an adult woman who'd
lived singly and safely in San Francisco. She didn't need
shielding in a seaside village.

"I'm pretty sure he's just the protective type," Beth offered, then lowered her voice. "Although Karl thinks he might
have—" Beth gestured toward the billboard outside.

"That's just a shot in the dark." Charmaine's nose wrinkled. "Karl has no clue. My money's on one of these rednecks
who won't believe there's actually a future coming. One without fish." She held up both hands to still Beth's interruption.
"And it *will*, whether they prepare for it or not."

Tires and an air brake signaled the arrival of a school bus.
Charmaine frowned and glanced at the store clock.

"That's right. It's finals week. That means minimum day
for the high school bunch. Minny! Kids coming!" She tucked
in behind the counter, stationing herself at the cash register,
but Charmaine's businesslike manner broke for a smirk. "Personally, I think Gordon's a little sophisticated to go climbing
around with a bucket of paint. I can't see it."

"In spite of the mean streak?" Beth asked.

Minny stampeded toward the door, but stayed inside, peering eagerly for the teenagers.

"I'm not saying I'd trust him." Charmaine stroked her bottom lip. "The guy's hiding something, but that doesn't mean I'd kick him out of bed."

Minny scuttled aside as the door jingled and admitted Karl and Sheriff Reynolds. Trying to hide the blush Charmaine's purr had sent flaming over her face, Beth stared at the huge refrigerator used to store cold drinks. *I could mash you against the refrigerator and have my way with you.* Was there no cure for her runaway fantasies?

"Where in hell's the Dumpster?" Karl snarled.

"I told them to go on out to Gull Cott," Charmaine said. "They had some idea the road to Lyre Beach was like the Alaskan Highway. I told them they were wimps if they couldn't make it."

"Great." Karl sighed. "We didn't pass them on the way in."

Charmaine glanced at the sheriff before lowering her eyelashes and her voice. "I think they stopped by Gimp's."

"Great," Beth echoed Karl's disgust. There was no way she'd hitch a ride home with drunks driving heavy machinery.

"Bet I can raise them on the radio." Without his sunglasses, Sheriff Reynolds looked more outdoor academic than policeman.

"Don't worry about it." Beth dismissed his offer, stacked her groceries on the counter, and snagged a chocolate bar. She'd avoid talking with him, simply because admitting how little she knew of Gordon was humiliating.

Karl fidgeted, watching Reynolds watch Beth.

"Miss Caxton, I don't think we've really met. I saw you yesterday, of course, but I'm Bob Reynolds." Behind his spectacles were friendly gray eyes, but his handshake was a trifle too tight.

"Of course." Beth nodded, extracted her hand, and flipped a second candy bar into her stack. "Nice to meet you."

"Steffie!" Minny's squeal heralded the troupe of high school girls entering the store.

Stefanie waved and lifted Minny for a loud smacking kiss. "When's your mama going to let me babysit you, Minny Mouse?"

"Whenever Mama gets a date," Charmaine said, then held out her hand to Beth. "Twenty-two fifty." She answered Beth's unspoken dismay over the price. "That's a lot of peanut butter, hon."

Beth paid, eager to escape the store for the serene sunshine. Karl put a hand on the cash register drawer, to keep it from ending her transaction.

"Bob, ask Beth about that weirdo. That Gordon. He had opportunity and motive. You heard him yesterday, taking on Junior McDonald. Assaulting Sloan. This isn't just graffiti, this is defacing public property."

Beth saw Bob Reynolds control himself. He did not caution Karl to quit watching television shows in which citizens taught inept deputies a thing or two about crime-solving. Instead, he fiddled with the squelch button on his walkie-talkie and smiled.

"Thanks for the tip." Bob turned to Beth. "I'll probably still be in town, when you're ready to go home, Miss Caxton—"

"Beth," she substituted. She'd be polite, but could she be Gordon's alibi?

"—I'll give you a ride."

"I'd just as soon walk." She balanced her grocery bag on one hip and gave him a firm look, telling him she wouldn't betray a friend.

"Well, then," he said.

A flutter arose from the cosmetic corner as Stefanie called, "Hey, Karl, what happened to your pretty sign?"

"That's what Sheriff Reynolds is about to find out." Karl saw Beth and Bob Reynolds meet each other's eyes. He huffed as if he felt persecuted in his own store. "Don't suppose you know anything about it?"

Stefanie advanced, uncowed by the watching adults. She took a pack of gum, opened it, and popped a piece between lilac pink lips. "I know you're not going to make a big chunk of change off our house. My mom was born here, and we're staying forever.''

''I heard you were moving down the coast, to Santa Cruz or something,'' Karl said.

''Only for the summer.'' Stefanie pretended to sympathize as she paid Charmaine. ''You see, my parents are attorneys. They don't need sleazy logging and real estate deals to keep food on the table.''

Karl's outspread hands appealed to the sheriff. ''Isn't this libel or something, Bob?''

The sheriff shrugged.

''*Slander*,'' Stefanie corrected. ''But only if it's not true.'' She blew a fist-sized bubble. ''You know what else? When I come back, I'll be eighteen. Old enough to vote. Isn't that just super?'' Stefanie batted her eyelashes with melodramatic flare before returning to the magazine rack and her friends.

''Someone ought to teach that little witch some manners.'' Karl's breathing was labored.

''Don't let her get to you,'' Charmaine advised.

''Shut up.'' Karl lit a cigarette and stormed for the back room as Beth headed for the door.

In his hurry to hold the door open, Bob Reynolds bumped against her. He smelled of fresh-pressed uniform and graham crackers. She was sure he was a nice guy, but Beth wanted him to go away.

Of course, he didn't. Young Sheriff Reynolds walked her as far as the fish market, loitered across the street when she stopped into the library to assure Lucinda she *would* return the costume, and he stood holding the door again when Beth decided to step into the Neptune coffee shop.

Since the Foghorn's neighborhood was patrolled on foot, Beth knew a number of San Francisco cops. She liked most of them and admired their efficient masculinity. She didn't date them, of course. A woman couldn't ignore their high alcoholism and divorce rates. No, she wanted a safe, cozy marriage. She smothered a sheepish smile and almost apologized to a bemused Bob Reynolds, who still stood holding the door.

•   •   •

Gordon didn't look both ways before crossing the street. Traffic ran sparse and would stop for a large dark man lunging after his woman.

A logging truck blared a long blast as it rumbled by and the honk made the man at Beth's side turn. The sheriff. The man who wielded keys to a cage. Gordon ignored the painful catch in his thigh muscle and continued across the street. Beth belonged to him. If misfortune had dealt him Reynolds as a rival, so be it.

Jealousy burned in Reynolds, too, but not nearly so hot. Gordon saw the sheriff square his shoulders. If Reynolds tried to dismiss his touch on Beth's shoulder as accidental, Gordon would know it for a lie. He'd seen Reynolds' interest yesterday. Now the sheriff was testing Beth's awareness, and Gordon's possession. If Reynolds did not move away quickly, he'd find Gordon eager for the challenge.

Reynolds let the door sigh closed behind Beth. Although he stood under six feet tall, the sheriff looked resolute. Inside the nest of his brown beard, his lips looked chapped from wind and weather.

"Mr. Gordon." His head jerked a quick acknowledgment before he called inside to Beth. "Your friend's here, Beth. We'll talk later."

Reynolds had used her name. He'd implied a later meeting. Gordon spared Beth's startled eyes only a quick glance before he let his own rove the restaurant, searching out other intruders. Finding none, he turned restless, seeking a place they could sit alone. Not here, but Beth must be hungry.

Gordon drew a deep breath, then another, before looking into her upturned face. Beth's red-blond hair was pulled girlishly high. Tawny freckles stood out on her flushed cheeks. Her green eyes rounded with fear and fascination. The magic that had glimmered between them ten years ago had stopped flickering politely. It was about to burst into flame.

Beth dropped her purse and parcels into a red corner booth studded with silver metal. He didn't let her sit. Salt air flowed from an open back door, somewhere beyond a kitchen's fatty fumes. He nudged her past the booth.

"Just coffee." Smooth city Beth tossed the request over her shoulder, reassuring the waitress who poised with menus.

"Go." He breathed the word at Beth's ear, hurrying her by the counter's rotating stools, around a corner, and past an empty telephone booth, toward the open back door.

Gulls feasting on french fries and bread crumbs beneath a redwood picnic table flew up. They banked around a blue-striped table umbrella, fanning it with their wings. No one stood in the building's shadow. It was just as well, because Gordon couldn't wait.

He took her to the wall, pinning her with his chest and hips and mouth. A shuddering breath rose in Beth, shaking him as she tilted her lips to follow the frantic movement of his. He clasped both her hands, pressing them alongside her thighs, holding them until he felt the delicate bones shift and realized he clung too tight.

As soon as he released her, Beth took a breath and rejoined their lips. Her hands rose against his back, reaching up to touch the dampness from his hair dripping down his fresh shirt. He'd been too impatient. Now, Beth's knee, bare and sun-warmed beyond the tight band of her shorts, grazed the inside of his denimed leg.

Thunder roared in Gordon's skull and he grabbed her hips against him. A riptide of lust carried him out, against his will.

"Oh, excuse me." Aproned and aghast, a waitress carrying her padded white shoes in one hand and a bowl in the other stopped before she crashed into them.

Pale soup slopped onto the cement walk. "Shoot," she said, then sidestepped around them to the table.

Fascinated, Gordon watched her for a moment. The curly-haired girl was not about to miss lunch because of two panting strangers. Gordon kept Beth's shoulder beneath his arm, her face turned to his chest as they walked back into the restaurant. When he glanced back, the waitress was watching, a spoon held halfway to her mouth. Gordon winked.

"I need to stop off in the ladies' room." Beth's lips moved against the front of his black T-shirt, starting another blaze of sensation. He let her go, and returned to the red booth.

He stared sightless at the menu, drank his glass of water, and imagined Beth splashing water on her face, imagined her staring into the mirror over the basin, wondering what kind of sin she'd committed behind the Neptune coffee shop.

No sin, he told her as Beth appeared, walking toward the table. She brushed damp bangs away from her eyelashes. *Or only the sweetest sin, which must be allowed by even a human God.* She gave him a grudging smile, then swallowed. The gold and emerald necklace moved with her throat.

Beth sat, opened the menu, and closed it.

"You found it." He'd wondered how long it would take, but Beth had discovered his retendered present right away. Her fingers rose to touch the jewel. She still struggled against a smile, but she'd accepted his gift.

Beth sipped from her coffee. No steam rose, so it must be cold. She regarded him over the lip of the cup.

"You are not my type, Gordon."

He nodded. Though her kisses had told him different, he didn't contradict her. Her body had accepted their bond, and her spirit almost had. He must be patient with her mind.

Gordon waited while she ordered a carrot muffin from the hovering waitress. "Who is your type?" he asked then. "That's a serious question. Sheriff Reynolds? Junior? Karl? He's a bachelor, isn't he?"

Beth's aggravation fizzled. She set her cup back in its saucer and grabbed her throat as if she were choking.

"Beth," he said. "I'm no one's type, except yours."

She reached across the table and worked her hand under his.

The Neptune's screen door banged open and the few diners snacking between breakfast and lunch looked up at Stefanie with a weeping Minny on her hip.

"Sheriff Reynolds?" she called, scanning the room.

At her alarmed tone, a narrow man wiping his hands on a towel came out from the kitchen. "What is it, Stef?"

"Isn't Sheriff Reynolds here?" Stefanie's glance touched on them, then rushed back to the man before her. She jiggled Minny to quiet her. "I need to find the sheriff. There's something down on the beach he really needs to see."

Sixteen

The cow's jawbone, thick and shiny as old ivory, had been shattered. One ragged end protruded through sealskin nibbled wider by fish and crabs. Her jaw showed only part of the damage. The side of her skull caved in, creating a hollow beneath the dull chestnut fur.

Gordon stood with legs apart, staring down. Beth struggled to read his expression. Nothing. Craven and blank, he seemed alone on the beach.

"Could it have been a shark?" A young mother, sunburned and restraining two children with sand pails, turned to Gordon.

Gimp and Horatio were trotting from the dock, but here, amid the gathered teenagers and a few others, Gordon seemed the obvious expert. Except Gordon didn't hear her human words.

"What's wrong with him?" the woman asked.

Beth shook her head. *Did Gordon know this seal? Had he swum beside her, protected her?* Beth took Gordon's hand. His fingers were stiff as sticks.

As if she could find a culprit, Beth looked down the beach. No weekend patchwork of vivid towels, no picnic lunches kicked full of sand, no blaring boomboxes.

"Make it better," Minny keened. She leaned out from Stefanie's grip, toward Gordon.

Stefanie left to find Charmaine, and the other girls followed, just as Bob Reynolds arrived, clipboard clamped under his arm, a Polaroid camera swaying from his neck.

Gimp squatted beside the seal. "Someone's done a mean bit of bashing for this lassie."

Reynolds dropped the clipboard and settled beside Gimp to take his first photograph. "Think she might have run into a ship's bottom or pier pilings?"

"Naw, she'd never do herself so hard." Gimp resettled his blue captain's cap, squinting down at the animal. "Breaking a jaw that size . . ."

A baseball bat, crashing into the side of her face. Involuntarily Beth's hand cupped over her own jaw.

". . . was probably deliberate." Reynolds lay one photo aside and took another. Warm breezes ruffled the forms attached to his clipboard. He used one hand to keep the finished prints from blowing away. When he started to turn the corpse, its head lolled.

Gordon's hand clinched on Beth's. Was it farewell, or reaction to the cow's grotesque movement? He walked away.

Menace marked Gordon's strides. Both Gimp and Horatio sensed the warning before Reynolds did.

"One moment, Mr. Gordon," Reynolds ordered.

Gimp uttered a sympathetic caution, but Horatio spoke like a man witnessing natural disaster. "I'd just get out of the way, Bob."

All three men backed off. Reynolds moved only a step, but their wariness caused the sunburned mother to drag her toddlers up the slope to the village.

Gordon knelt. His arms scooped under the sea lion. As he lifted her free, sand shimmered, sifting back onto the beach. Gordon shifted his forearm to support her muzzle.

"If you've finished with photographs and conjecture, I'm taking her back." Gordon cradled the broken animal as if she were weightless. Instead of looking down upon the cow, he faced the others with the desecration.

"We all find this upsetting." Bob Reynolds set the camera aside. In sympathy, Beth wondered, or in preparation for a fight? "But that's a federally protected marine mammal. As such, I need to keep it and—"

With priestly reverence Gordon turned away and approached the ocean. As waves lapped his shoes and the hem of his jeans, Beth knew he wouldn't stop until he'd carried the seal out so far, none of them could witness her burial.

"Damn it all," Bob pronounced each word with frustration.

"You've got the pictures," Beth assured him.

"Swell. What I need is the body." He glanced up the slope, toward the Neptune coffee shop, and his voice faded under waves that sounded like ripping paper.

She probably imagined relentless whispers from the figures behind the restaurant window, but if they or Reynolds interrupted the dark dignity of this rite, Beth would stop them. She wasn't sure how.

Wet to the thighs, now, to the level of that purple-red gouge, Gordon didn't appear to feel the salt water's sting.

"What *is* wrong with him?" Horatio asked. "Didn't even take off his shirt. Or shoes."

Reynolds sighed. "Without that body, there's no telling how advanced the state of decomposition."

"Jeez, Bob, who cares?" Horatio kneaded his temples, knocking his watch cap to the beach. "We get dead seals along here all the time."

"But with an autopsy," Reynolds insisted, "we'd know when it was done, who was out when it happened—"

"Like today?" Horatio shook sand from his hat as he gestured at the horizon. "Probably got twenty boats out."

"He's right." Gimp patted the sheriff's shoulder and took no offense when Reynolds shrugged him off. "Give some thought to what Sloan said, yesterday. Even if another fishermen knew, he wouldn't talk."

Glassy waves parted for Gordon's chest and rushed shut behind his shoulders. Finally he leaned forward, easing into the ocean. Did he hold the seal with just one arm and swim with the other? Were his legs so strong he drove through the water without using his arms? Would he return?

Beth touched the front of her shirt as if cold water struck her, as well. *Gordon.* She should have thought before acting, should have let Reynolds stop him. This slaughter might make him go, might spoil his yearning for life ashore. And for her.

Gordon. His name built within her, swelling until she wanted to scream it. It hurt, this unfurling of something too large within her chest.

She didn't scream. She paced down the beach—for a better view, not to follow. She didn't run for the cove, for the bluff, for home. She touched her necklace and found it hot, a fact as dazzling as the white shine overhead, where she'd expected a sepulchre of storm clouds.

Karl's arrival, panting and stumbling, was almost welcome. He stared at the knot of crushed kelp and sandy strings of seaweed where the cow had lain. He glared after Gordon, who moved out from shore, indiscernible now, from black boulders, or, perhaps, sleek-headed escorts.

"You gonna hold him accountable for making off with evidence?" Karl asked.

"I'm sure you'll be the first to know." Bob Reynolds jotted notes without looking up.

"Reynolds, you've gotta do something. This isn't just animal rights crap. There's something unnatural about him."

A short laugh, utterly beyond her control, puffed from Beth's lips. "Mercy, Karl. Maybe you better call the *Enquirer.*"

"Bizarre," Karl insisted.

He slogged back up the sandy slope to Charmaine. She stood watching, holding her fitful daughter. Beth shivered in spite of the noon sun. Only Minny wept as if she understood.

Beth twisted her ponytail into a neat coil as she waited beside the sheriff's car. Bob Reynolds had offered to retrieve her purse and groceries from the Neptune coffee shop and she'd accepted. He must be good at his job, to know she didn't relish facing the diners who'd stood at the restaurant window, watching the latest installment in the life of loony Beth Caxton.

Dangling the brown shoulder bag with sheepish pride, Reynolds approached, unaware she'd been rehearsing lies.

"I don't suppose Grey Gallows has progressed so far that anyone brews a decent cup of espresso?" As if donning high heels, Beth put on the crisp tone that served so well in San Francisco.

"You *have* been away." Reynolds relinquished the purse before she gripped it. "Sorry," he said as she retrieved a rolling tube of lipstick. "Really, Gimp makes the best coffee in the village."

Beth declined. Since her arrival, Gimp had disconcerted her. Now she knew why. His head full of Celtic legends could lead to the truth. Sitting in his dim bar, she'd listen. Even if Reynolds dismissed selkie tales as the meanderings of an old man, Beth's faith was too new to be tested.

The patrol car's door slammed particularly snug. Beth examined the dashboard full of electronic gadgetry. She recognized a couple of radios, a tube-like device which might be radar, binoculars, a palm-sized monocular thing, and, between the two bucket seats, a shotgun. Beth drew a breath.

Had stealing the seal's body really been illegal? Beth girded herself to become an accomplice.

"Enough small talk," Reynolds said as they pulled onto Surf Street. "What's Gordon's last name?"

Beth's breath caught. She wouldn't be good at this. "I really don't know."

"Okay," Reynolds nodded, unperturbed. "Where did you meet him?"

"This is really uncomfortable." Beth crossed and recrossed her legs, though she didn't mean the car seat. "Is this on the record?"

"I'm not taking notes, but I wouldn't mind some help. The guy came in out of nowhere. It's for his protection, too."

Beth felt a simmering skepticism. So far, Gordon didn't need protection. Then she remembered Al's sneer, Sloan's threats, and Karl's suspicion. No matter how strong, someone as trusting as Gordon could walk into ambush.

She explained how they'd met in San Francisco, confessed

she had no idea where he'd come from or where he stayed in or around Grey Gallows.

"I do know he used to come here as a kid," she said as Reynolds turned onto her private road, undirected. She didn't mention Gordon's time living with Junior. If the sheriff knew where she lived, he'd probably figure it all out.

As he braked beside the Fiat, Beth lifted her seat belt buckle. "Thanks," she said.

"You don't leave it all the way down here, do you? This close to the highway." He considered the road's slight incline and answered before she did. "Does it need a push?"

Reynolds climbed from the cruiser and perused the Fiat as if it posed on an auction block.

"No, it's a solenoid problem." Beth sneaked a sideways glance. No matter how often she repeated Jack's diagnosis, it never sounded right.

"Yeah?" Reynolds had popped the hood and begun wiggling wires. "I had an Alfa for about half a summer. Try it now."

The Fiat hummed to life and Reynolds followed as Beth drove to the end of the road and parked. When he leaned against the cruiser, she could tell he hadn't finished probing.

"Is he, in fact, an animal rights activist? An eco-terrorist, a tree-spiker, or spotted owl lover?" He prattled on as if he were joking, but Beth shook her head. "With an exit like the one he just pulled . . ."

"I've never seen him do something like that, but I just met him." Beth would have left, if it hadn't seemed impolite.

As Reynolds rambled about declining incomes and sparse catches, she deduced he lived alone, wondered if he were older than his apparent thirty-something, and plotted her escape.

"Village gossip says you saw some weird lights the first night you were home." His indulgent smile stopped her.

"They weren't weird." Beth racked her mind for the snoop who'd eavesdropped on her conversation with—Who had she told? "It was a dim light in the floorboards of a little boat." His tolerant smirk was about to get on her nerves. "Over there, sort of southwest of Lyre Rock."

"They bother you anymore?"

"They didn't *bother* me the first time." She nearly told him about Sloan and Roo's air tanks. If they hid the abalone underwater, they could return for them by boat, at night. But if Bob staked out her cove, he'd see Gordon. It wasn't worth the risk.

When he removed his glasses and wiped sweat from his nose, Beth shuffled her feet. Then, he was off again, maligning tramp loggers and hitchhikers who assailed village ways.

As he began lecturing on Proposition Two, Beth decided she *could* say she must go to the bathroom.

"The village economy is sick, I'll give him that." Reynolds scratched his beard. "But when it comes to winning supporters, Karl's his own worst enemy."

"Not while I'm in town." Beth slung on her purse and whirled toward the steps. "Thanks again for the ride."

"Hey, want me to come up and look around?" Reynolds called after her.

"For what?" Beth wondered if he'd been watchful all this time, stalling in case Gordon reappeared.

"Uh, coffee?" Reynolds gave an oversized shrug.

"Too hot." Beth fanned her hand in front of her face and managed a smile. She might be a poor accomplice, but in a case like this, Gordon was safe. She could contend with feeble flirtation. It was the kind she knew best.

Inside, Beth's shell curtain tinkled and clacked as if someone had just slipped by.

"Peaches?" Her voice sounded hollow, the curtain still swayed, and the patrol car's tires crunched onto Surf Street, a full mile away.

No mew, no padding paws, nothing but wind sighed from her bedroom. The sliding glass door to her deck stood partway open.

Not Gordon. Logic aside, Beth knew her nerves would vibrate with knowing if his presence lingered. Maybe Junior, sick of his cramped accommodations, had paid her another visit.

Beth slid the door closed, snapped the lock into place, and checked the top of her dresser. Gordon's onyx cuff links still lay with a clutter of earrings and a pair of painted combs.

Beth parted the shell curtain and waited. The refrigerator hummed. One morning glory vine had shifted on the mantel. Nothing was out of place, except the wretched poetry she'd left on Jack's chair. She crossed the room and turned it face-down, again.

The kitchen curtains had been tugged together. Had her burglar applauded her lengthy tête-a-tête with the sheriff? The glass holding her Midsummer egg experiment had spilled, slicking her kitchen sink with goo.

"Peaches, you little goblin." Her voice sounded faint, and though she knew the cat wasn't to blame, she wanted his company.

Beth called again, before locking the front door, then hesitated and sniffed the hinges. Recognition stirred like static. She opened the door and swung it. The door no longer creaked, and it smelled like the sweet oil Minny had sprayed in the Village Store.

Cold comfort, that it had been Karl or Charmaine who'd broken into her house to oil her door hinges and rifle her atrocious poetry. Hardly nefarious, though. The Darlings probably couldn't bear squeaky doors.

Beth mopped up the spilled egg, trying to think sensibly, but she could only think of Gordon.

She shouldn't worry over Peaches. The cat stalked everything that rustled and breathed among the grasses along her road. He'd probably been miffed at the day's intruders, and decided to stay afield longer than usual.

Beth took off her emerald and gold collar, put on sunglasses, locked and yanked each door, to test them, then set off searching.

First, she took her secret path to the cove, knowing Peaches wouldn't be there, but hoping Gordon would. She stopped halfway down. Aquamarine and smooth, waters curled around rocks dusted with salt-white. With a little practice, she could learn to dive again, from here, if not from the bluff-top.

Sand scraped under the soft basking forms of a dozen seals. One cow hailed her, but the black bull lion was absent.

Beth trudged back up the trail. Had Gordon's grisly burden made him a target for the Great White? How far out could he swim in human form? Could he transform as he swam?

Beth shambled down her rough-stairs and glanced at Lyre Beach. In the old legends, selkies only changed by the light of Midsummer's moon, hidden amid solitary rocks such as these.

Her tennis shoes crunched loud on the gravel road, echoing so she kept glancing behind her.

"Here kitty. Peaches." Buck up, Caxton. Find out who's after the seals and set Bob Reynolds on them. That's what civilized people do. Call the police.

She wouldn't need to, if Gordon had been around, to hear of her first ride in a police car, to unravel the mystery of her burglar. Phoebe had given her a T-shirt which read: THE MORE I SEE OF MEN, THE MORE I LOVE MY CAT. Peaches would have to serve, but even he was undependable.

At first she pretended a trick of light had turned old leaves honey orange. Then she begged for it to be a rodent, cast onto the road's shoulder by uncaring tires.

"Peachy? Oh, no."

Karl had seen Peaches by the highway, but she was only halfway down her road. Not far from where the Fiat had stalled.

With quiet hands she separated the grasses. Why hadn't she seen him before? Maybe it had just happened, and he'd pulled himself back toward home, to die.

No. His dusty belly stirred with breath. Beth skimmed her hand over him, and the cat's fur contracted. No grease from a car's undercarriage smeared him. She let her fingers move more purposefully. His ears flicked and he didn't flinch from pressure, but when she stroked his belly—a touch which always provoked his back feet to draw up and scratch—his legs lay slack.

A gull wheeled and hooted derision overhead. Maybe it hadn't been a car.

She couldn't do anything here. She needed a vet. Mimicking the gentle way Gordon had raised the seal, she lifted Peaches. Limp, unbelievably limp, but warm, the cat gave a faint wheeze, as she moved him.

She stowed him in the Fiat, returned to the house for a blanket, and swaddled Peaches against shock. In ten minutes she'd reached the phone booth inside Neptune's coffee shop.

"Lucinda, I need the name of a veterinarian."

"Slow down." Lucinda's voice was perfectly pitched for the front desk of a library. "It is Beth Caxton?"

"Something's really wrong with my cat."

"Oh dear, a car—?"

"Maybe, but I think—" Beth stared toward the front of the restaurant, as if she could see through the walls and car, to Peaches. "I don't know, maybe he ate something."

"For a real vet, you'll have to drive to Parish." Lucinda's voice faded and Beth heard the riffling of pages. "Shall I give you the address and call ahead?"

"I don't know my way around Parish." Beth leaned her head against the glass wall. "I could be almost back to San Francisco, to our vet. I just—"

"Is he breathing normally"

"Not normally, but—"

"I'll tell you, for immediate first aid, Gimp's the best in town." Lucinda's voice cautioned her to be fair. "For all that he runs a tavern, the man has a way with animals."

Beth covered her eyes for a moment. "I don't know what to do." She heard the sound of a pencil flicking against a desktop.

"If you'd found him as he is," Lucinda said, "and he weren't your cat, tell me the first three things you'd have done. Quickly."

"I would have carried him inside, wrapped him warmly and offered him some milk. Or food."

"Well, then?"

"I think he can make it to San Francisco." Beth stood.

"Thanks, Lucinda. Thank you." She hung up and hurried toward her car.

Beth crossed the Golden Gate Bridge at sundown, wended her way through the cavernous quiet of the financial district, gunned the Fiat past two Muni buses, and parked on the sidewalk outside Peaches' vet.

The big orange cat had started muttering and stretching, fixing Beth with bleary-eyed accusations, before they reached the city limits, but she wanted an answer.

Dr. Grady set aside the glass jar from which she'd been nibbling artichoke hearts. She took the cat in her white-coated arms. "Hey, Peaches, feeling a little under the weather, there, kitty boy?" She crooned to the cat and dismissed Beth. "Give us a few minutes."

Beth sat. She pulled her knees up onto the chair and used them as a shelf for her cheek. She should call Jack and Carol. Or Phoebe.

In the vet's infirmary, little dogs barked counterpoint to a few big woofs and a parrot's squawk. Beth pulled her purse onto the magazine table beside her. Her theater keys were there, thank God. And *there* was her gasoline credit card. She'd barely had cash enough to refill the Fiat, fifty miles out of Grey Gallows.

Inside her purse's zippered compartment, there was a bump she didn't recognize. A scrap of blue note paper, the kind Carol kept with her at all times, had been folded into a tiny square. Inside, sat a pearl.

"Elizabeth—For safekeeping. I was afraid it would roll out of the pocket and be lost. Carol."

Not Titania Pacifica, but how had Gordon described his treasure? *Stunning white, with a rainbow glitter.* This beauty must be her miniature. The pearl followed a curving line in Beth's palm, collecting the artificial light, turning it to enchantment.

A telephone rang, something screeched like a monkey, and Dr. Grady's voice, muffled through the walls, said, "I'll be here."

Midsummer Eve, *a night for firsts*, he'd said, and then, as the Wheel crashed toward them in a shower of sparks, he'd slipped this into the skirt pocket, *for luck.*

And nosy Carol had found it. Thank goodness. Beth folded the gem away and retrieved her checkbook as she heard the vet approaching.

"I'd like to keep him overnight, but I know you'll do the job, and besides, I think he's past the worst of it." Dr. Grady slipped a faintly protesting Peaches into a cardboard cat-carrier and closed the top. "You're not leaving town, again? I wouldn't get out of range until, say, noon."

"What's wrong with him?"

"We never really know, in a case like this. Not a car, though. Some kind of toxin. Inadvertent, probably, because of the mild dosage." The vet jotted notes inside a manila folder. "My guess is antifreeze."

"Antifreeze?"

"They lap it up like ice cream and it knocks them out, kills them all too often, but Peaches was lucky." Dr. Grady squinted through one of the box's air holes. "Tell your mom to keep you inside." She fixed Beth with a decided frown. "Got it?"

She got it, all right, but Beth didn't believe it. Peaches didn't roam into town, and the Fiat had a leak in the radiator. Last time she'd filled it up she'd used water, not antifreeze.

Closed, the Foghorn Theater provided a homecoming no other place could approximate. Beth stowed Peaches upstairs and hurried down to the empty theater.

She propped one of the heavy doors opened, touched a switch that made glass sconces glitter with golden light, and entered the stillness. The aisle carpets, long swathes of blue-gray, were freshly shampooed, smelling of wet wool. A staple gun and bolts of plush fabric showed Phoebe's foray into reupholstering.

Waiting. The Foghorn seemed eternally charged with expectancy. Seventy years of perfume and tobacco competed with Carol's honeywax candles and lavender potpourri. Seventy years of anticipation swirled above the chandeliers.

Beth climbed the steps to the stage. Freshly buffed, it still showed the scars of fallen props, of gobs of silver tape pressed over cords or marks. The house lights didn't reach past royal blue curtains, heavy enough to take unwary child actors over backward. Beth crept through the darkness, sidestepping huge flats of Verona castlerock, of wrought iron and brick New Orleans.

Entering the backstage world of makeup, spray paint, and excitement, she flicked on a harsh overhead lightbulb. Empty racks rattled with hangers, since rented costumes had been returned and most others were zipped away until fall. Grease from thousands of fast-food meals lingered and smelled good enough to remind Beth of her hunger. In one corner sat Phoebe's eccentricity, the talk of each new cast member: small, neat cots made up with blue and white gingham sheets. They reminded her of Gordon.

During the headlong drive down the coast, she'd convinced herself to tell him good-bye. If he survived the swim with the ruined cow, if he returned to her, she'd end it. She would *not* be left alone to deal with burglars and poisoned cats. She wanted a man who was dependable. Not to mention human.

Gordon made her forget her standards. Witness the tacky scene behind the Neptune! She closed her eyes against the memory of glaring blue sky, white beach, and the cool, dark shade. Her stomach dropped away with an erotic dip as she remembered his hips against hers. Loving Gordon would be a dark secret . . . irresistible, but quite impossible.

Beth kicked one of the cots. "Damn." It really hurt.

She clicked off the light switch and edged onto the empty stage. The blaze of a struck match blinded her.

"Empty, this place makes me horny as hell."

Seventeen

~

"Eddie, do that again and you're a dead man!" Adrenaline sluiced through every vein in Beth's body.

"You always say that." Eddie Kung smiled in the amber glow of his match, then shook it out and led the way toward the theater's front-row seats.

"I *think* I can walk," Beth complained. Her knees wobbled from surprise. The green tank top she'd worn all day provided no barrier to the theater's deserted chill. "You're quick and quiet as—What are you, our new night watchman?"

"Sort of." Eddie strutted. "Phoebe said to keep an eye on the place. From over in the garage"—he gestured—"I've got a great view. And that job sure as hell don't sap my brain power." He played a quick drum tattoo on the back of one seat. "So, what're you doing home?"

Beth recounted Peaches' mishap and the vet's warning not to leave town until noon Tuesday.

"You're not going out, are you?" Eddie's head-to-toe evaluation of her attire evidently caused him pain.

"No, I thought I'd go upstairs and share a can of cat food with Peaches." Beth yawned.

"You don't want to come over, do you? It's my dinner break." Eddie shrugged three times in succession, underlining the rarity of his invitation. "No fish heads and rice," he joked, "Ma made *haar chee meen*."

"What's that?"

"I don't know," Eddie sounded as if he already regretted his offer. "Shrimp noodle."

Beth thought of her drowsy cat, empty apartment, and the long hours since she'd seen Gordon wade into the sea, maybe forever. Left alone, her resolve would weaken. She'd return to Grey Gallows and stare out to sea, wishing him back.

"Give me two minutes to pull on jeans and a shirt so I don't shock your mother." She'd hide the pearl for safekeeping, too. "I'll do it."

"Yeah?" Eddie slapped Beth a high five which made her wobble all over again. "Cool."

Beth stayed all night in San Francisco. Dinner in a dim corner of Kung Foods helped keep her there.

From the crowded street the grocery appeared to be a produce market with plucked chickens, crates of tail-twitching ducks, and a leathery pig dangling from the ceiling. On arrival, Beth nearly declared herself a vegetarian.

Soon, she was glad she hadn't. Although Eddie's mother refused to dine with her son, she hovered in the shadowy store aromatic with garlic and earthy vegetables, roasting meat over a brazier. The pork, shrimp, and noodles were delicious. The brazier lit the store's red and gold drapes to palace brilliance. Between dishes, Eddie translated and Beth explored.

She recognized persimmons and mandarin oranges, mushrooms, little eggplants, and yard-long green beans, and Mrs. Kung gave enthusiastic advice for using six kinds of cabbage, red dates, white radishes, and lotus root.

By the time she left, Beth had two wind chimes—one shaped like a brass pagoda, the other bamboo—and armloads of Oriental delicacies. Most intriguing were paper-thin rectangles of purplish seaweed called *gee choy*. She was supposed to use it in soup. There might be a man waiting in Grey Gallows who'd appreciate it. One last meal together didn't mean a commitment.

• • •

"A very classic look, Bethie." Phoebe sprawled on Beth's couch, cuddling Peaches. Fully recovered, the cat purred, intent on kneading snags in Phoebe's crocheted jumper.

"It's a get-me-out-of-here-quick, look," Beth insisted, fastening the chunky coral earrings she wore with the straw-colored suit. Carol had once declared Beth could make even this sweet Givenchy look utilitarian. That was exactly what she had in mind. She wanted to be home.

Last night, when Phoebe had called to check her messages on the office phone, Beth had picked up. After applauding Beth's arrival, Peaches' safety, and asking after "her" fisherman, Phoebe had begun begging.

"Please, please, please, help me talk to this reporter, tomorrow. He's just the business editor from some little paper down the peninsula, but I don't want to screw it up."

After a pointed reminder of Phoebe's loyalty during the Fisherman's Faire, Beth had agreed to four P.M. tea with the reporter. But Phoebe had kept their destination secret.

"You saved my life," Phoebe said as they walked to the Bronze Iris.

"I wouldn't have, if you'd told me where we were meeting."

"*That* is not a revelation." Phoebe peered in a shop window to fluff her Betty Boop ringlets. "Still, you're the public relations expert. I know plenty about business, but when it comes to *subtle* . . . I'm still working on it."

Phoebe hadn't worked hard enough, but she chatted so politely over Jack's past and future success and bragged so adroitly of the Foghorn's stability in an arts-weak economy, even Beth was fooled.

Instead of monitoring the conversation, Beth noticed how heavy her chignon weighed on her neck and glanced at the tearoom's rosewood clock, wondering if she'd have time to concoct seaweed soup tonight, wondering if Gordon would be waiting. And then the reporter brought up urban renewal.

"The council wants to redo *this* area in an early 1900s motif?" Beth said, trying to dilute the idea with repetition.

"Gee, sounds great to me." Phoebe dipped a finger in her tea, stuck it in her mouth, and removed it with a pop. "Such happy times. Wasn't 1906 the year of the first friggin' earthquake?"

Beth segued in with jargon, sacrificing another thirty minutes of driving time to talk of neighborhood integrity and historic overlays. The reporter's scribbling slowed. Beth felt satisfied she'd forced the interview back on track, until they stood in the Bronze Iris foyer, waving the reporter on his way.

"The arrogant S.O.B.s will only renovate the Foghorn over our dead bodies!" Phoebe shouted after him, waving.

A grandfather clock's discreet bong notified Beth it was five-thirty. She'd have to drive the last featureless miles of shoreline with only her headlights to show the way.

At least she'd avoided Carol. Pushing her luck, Beth phoned Jack from the lobby, enumerated the Fiat's latest maladies, and ducked out before her stepmother could hustle downstairs to critique her suit and the practice of storing gems in skirt pockets.

"I'm not sure you have a genius for public relations," Beth said as they walked back to her flat.

Beth had changed into tangerine-colored sweats while Phoebe captured the cat and slipped him into his carrier. Together, they fit Oriental groceries into the trunk, like puzzle pieces. Beth was finally ready to leave.

"It's a good thing they won't read that interview in Grey Gallows," Beth said. "The Prop Two battle is heating up." Beth kissed Phoebe's cheek and climbed into the Fiat. "King Karl might take 'over my dead body,' as a dare." The thought of her silent hinges gave her chills. What had he been looking for?

Phoebe walked along beside the convertible for a few steps, then yelled, "Tell the Loch Ness Monster I said 'hi!' "

It was nearly seven o'clock when Beth turned north and started steering toward the moon.

Mist spangled the beams cast by her headlights. Beth had put off stopping to raise her convertible top. Instead, she'd turned

on the heater. Now, she was glad. As she downshifted and
banked right on the exit to Grey Gallows, the night air turned
sultry.

Ten-thirty on Tuesday night, the village drowsed. Village
Video's neon was extinguished for the night. Next door a few
men loitered outside Gimp's. Jukebox music flowed from inside as one of them waved. The library's redwood sign shone
by footlights, and Karl's halogen security lights glared vigi-
lance over a forgotten truck parked behind the Village Store.
Along Surf Street, from Karl's to Beth's dirt road, asphalt
stretched black and empty.

Crickets chirred, hushed at her approach, but still Gordon
didn't move. No streetlights, no house lights, just heaven's
starry vault showed him sitting on her porch step. Forlorn or
maybe hurt? Beth tried to stop her resolve from leaking away.
Gordon was a strong, solitary man. She took a tighter grip
on Peaches' carrier. Gordon didn't need her. Beth hefted the
grocery bag up her hip. So, if he wasn't heartsore or injured,
what had become of the sling-shot eagerness with which he'd
always greeted her before?

The grocery bag rustled and Peaches grumbled in his carrier. In a minute, she'd drop them both and run to Gordon's
arms.

No. His hair glinted wet as he stood. That meant he hadn't
waited long. She set down the bag and carrier with deliberate
slowness. Did she imagine that his weight balanced on one
leg?

Gordon gathered Beth to him. His heartbeat pounded louder
than any sound beyond their embrace.

"Last night you didn't come." His arms crossed her back,
faintly rocking. "Tonight, I left, but I couldn't stay away."

"I'm sorry." Beth hugged him tighter. His gentle reproach
cut deep. *I'm no one's type, except yours.* She'd taken her
troubles to Lucinda, to Phoebe, to Jack. For her, there was a
city full of help. Where could Gordon turn?

His chin moved against her hair and she felt passion simmering beneath the tenderness. "Let's go in," she said.

She'd barely unlocked the door and flicked on the light. She dropped the cat carrier as he kissed her.

"I thought you'd gone back for good." He held her shoulders and looked down with brown eyes disheartened and lost.

"No." This time Beth went to him, feeling the warm swathes of muscle beneath his shirt. *This* was real. The waves' call, salt wind, and this man holding her cheeks, parting her lips for a deeper kiss. Her resolve, her dreams of a secure little husband and tidy house, *those* were make-believe.

Beth tugged him closer, one hand straying under his shirt hem to skim his back.

"Beth." Her name was almost a snarl as he slanted his mouth over hers. "I want you."

"I want you, too." Breathless, she wasn't sure he'd heard. She hoped not. Her voice sounded full of conditions, full of *what ifs* and *whys*. She hated them. She reached up to the dangling leather binding his hair and pulled it loose, overriding her mind's caution.

Casual sex. Beth widened the kiss, inviting plunder. *For everyone but me.* The back of Beth's head brushed the wall as Gordon's kiss grew more forceful. *No soul mates. No questions about love, about what kind of children we could possibly . . .* Beth curled her ankle around his, pulling him nearer still.

His kiss softened and he looked down, reluctantly it seemed, to examine her.

Humiliated by her audible breaths, Beth closed her lips and stared toward the cardboard carrier. Peaches' paws paddled loudly, demanding escape. If only Beth could stop the bellows-like movement of her chest, she'd help him.

Her breath caught at an awful idea. On Midsummer Eve, on Lyre Beach, she'd felt Gordon sifting through her thoughts. It was impossible, and yet, she'd half-accepted he was a selkie, a magical being. Was it unbelievable he could read her mind?

With startling suddenness, Gordon dropped to one knee and released Peaches. "Sometimes," Gordon said. "When we're kissing."

"You know my thoughts?"

"Not words." He stood clear of the fleeing cat and jammed his hands deep into his pockets. "Feelings. Inclinations. Your mind has too many layers and sometimes I misinterpret." His smile admitted defeat. "Just now, for instance, I thought, when I felt your tongue—"

"Let me know if you figure it out." Beth took up the bag of groceries and turned her burning face toward the kitchen. "*I* didn't understand what I was thinking. And I don't want to talk about it," she warned, as he drew breath to continue.

She stole glances at him as she unpacked the food. Gordon's mouth was twisted with boyish puzzlement. Beth reminded herself *this* was the man who'd appeared stark naked to warn her of a shark. Next to that, a lively discussion of sex would no doubt seem trivial.

"Now, I'm going to make you seaweed soup."

"Seaweed soup?" He nuzzled the side of her neck. "For a midnight supper?"

"Yes." Beth gathered garlic in her fist and wondered if she could trust her unsteady hands with a knife.

"But you'll hate it." Gordon breathed in the pungent ingredients as she assembled them.

"I'm not making it for me." She smiled over her shoulder. Gordon, silent and predatory, had struck fear into Bob, Horatio, Gimp. Instinctively the men had backed off, there on the beach. Here, Gordon's eyes were toffee-warm and sweet, amazed at a small kindness. "It's just for you."

"Explain love to me." Gordon unwrapped incense-spiced tissue paper from one of the wind chimes. "Not while you're busy, but sometime."

Beth watched him untangle red threads holding the bamboo chimes together. "I don't know if I can do that."

"But your father loves you. And your mother did." He held the arrangement aloft. "And you love Phoebe, isn't that so?"

And you. I love your trust, the way you risk—Beth slammed the side of her knife blade against a clove of garlic, shattering the thought. If he'd heard, what then?

"I just think it's rather interesting." He turned away, fold-ing the paper sack. The ends of his hair curled loosely. "We each have our own kinds of magic, but yours is stronger."

"Don't bet on it." Beth considered listing a dozen dubious deeds done in the name of love. He wandered into the living room before she administered a dose of fact.

"When was Junior here?" Gordon asked suddenly. "Is he why you left?"

"No, it was Peaches." Beth explained, taking Gordon from that first moment beside the road to her arrival tonight, and though Gordon sympathized and caressed the reluctant cat, he returned to his question.

"But when was Junior here?"

"Not since—" Beth frowned. "Midsummer morning, when he met Phoebe."

"That's not right." Gordon circled the living room, head held high, testing the air.

Beth put the lid on her soup and watched Gordon stop near Jack's chair. "You think he's been here since then?"

"He has," Gordon said. "And someone else." Gordon's expression turned closed-in and dark.

"You know," she said, "*someone* has been creeping around my house. And *someone* poisoned Peaches. That wouldn't be Junior, but if you'd been around to—Since you—"

"Since I—what?"

Beth found herself gesturing toward the wall, where he'd said he wanted her.

"I don't understand." Gordon looked mystified, then angry. "You saw what happened, how they'd murdered her." His eyes narrowed. "I had to take her back, explain to the others. The little that I *could* explain." Gordon retied his damp hair with a jerk. "Beth, when they need me, I have to go."

As if they were his people, his responsibility. As if he were their warrior king . . .

"I'm their—" Gordon shook his head. "As a selkie, I'm their—liaison?" When the word didn't fit, his anger faded.

"Like a counselor?"

"No, more like—" His lips twisted, clearly embarrassed. "More like royalty."

"Really?" Beth considered his strength, his manner and sense of responsibility.

"Really."

"Do you have a title?"

"It doesn't translate." He gave a short laugh when Beth crossed her arms, waiting. Then, with the air of a man who has nothing to lose, he answered. "Dark Prince, Solitary."

The title told Beth all she needed to know. He belonged to them, not her. The knowledge ached. Years spent with Gordon would be like childhood spent with Jack. He wouldn't be there, even when he *was* there.

Gordon took a long step toward her, arms outreached, and stumbled.

"Are you all right?" Beth looked down. He wore ripped jeans, intentionally ripped, it appeared. And he had been favoring one leg as he stood at her porch step. "Are you?"

Delicate and precise, she bent, parted the ripped denim, and tested the flesh with a fingertip.

Gordon drew a quick breath. "I'm fine," he said, but the words were rushed.

Self-centered harpy. Your feelings are hurt, so you ignore his injury. You don't deserve Gordon's devotion.

"Liar." The skin surrounding his wound felt hot, infected. "How did this happen?"

"A spear gun," he said.

She looked up the length of him, to his solemn eyes. "A spear gun," she repeated. Silence vibrated around them.

"That man Sloan," Gordon began.

"I know." Beth's memory revived the sound of the Faire's gaiety and Sloan bragging "... *shot a big black bull in your cove* ..." Gordon had been waiting for her, as he'd promised. God, dear, dear God. It was true.

Beth forced herself to make a mental tally of her first-aid supplies. Pitiful. "Even if the salt water cleansed it," she faltered, "you reopened it, swimming out with a burden."

She steadied him with one hand, then dropped on her knees to open the rent cloth. "For two days—almost three, you ignored this. Did it effect your swimming, even when you were in—seal form?'' She pronounced the words, making them true.

His hand fell on her braided hair. When she looked up, an expression like amusement played over his lips, but then Gordon set his jaw.

Beth believed. Perhaps he could convince her to act on her belief.

"Did it effect my swimming? A little." Gordon knew he wasn't playing fair. Beth didn't guess he'd seen the same television nature specials she had. "Once or twice the pain made me jerk and swim in sort of an erratic manner."

Gordon cast the lure and Beth took it.

"Oh, great! Erratic? Jerky? Like distressed *prey*. Just what every shark is looking for, and that Great White's out there, prowling." Disbelief crowded pity from Beth's eyes. "You are not as smart as you think you are, Mr. Gordon. Take off your pants."

This was precisely the turn he'd hoped for. He released the copper button at his waist and began lowering his jeans.

"Not here." Beth grabbed his elbow and steered him toward her bedroom.

Better still.

She stopped off in the bathroom and made a great tinkling and clatter while she gathered supplies. When she came into the room, he had his back turned.

"Don't you wear underwear?" Beth's voice came out rather strangled.

"When I'm wet, I can't get them up my legs properly and since quickness—"

Although her hands were filled, Beth waved them before him, trying to banish her panic or his unsuitable words. Two days without her had apparently effected his ability to communicate in a seemly manner.

"I assume you're going to treat my injury. What would you have me do? Put the pants back on?" He watched her eyes track around the room and settle on a pair of scissors. "We can forget this, you know. I'm absolutely fine."

"I could make your jeans into cutoffs. Like mine," Beth gestured toward denim shorts cast in a corner.

"Cut high enough to expose this"—He lifted the hem of his shirt, and she turned her back—"they'd look outlandish. I can't leave your cottage that way, can I?" He waited. "You've already seen me naked—"

"I remember."

"—so, I don't understand why it's a big deal." As if conjured, his body told him exactly why. For propriety's sake, Gordon plopped on Beth's bed, swathed himself in blankets, and left the leg out at an awkward angle. "Shall we try this?"

Her fingers pressed gently and she watched him as she prodded. Although the wound was tender, it wasn't infected. Still, he hated for her hands to leave him.

"You might check that part again," he suggested.

"Here?" she asked. Her fingers inched back when he shook his head. "On this edge? No? I don't think I've missed any place, Gordon. It's probably just going to stay sore for a while."

And the girl thought she was the worldly one. He sighed, leaned back, and watched her work. With exacting precision, Beth cut three waisted bandages from adhesive tape.

"Butterfly bandages," she said, and her hands were on him once more, sticking one side down, drawing it tightly over the wound and affixing it. "They should keep the wound closed until it heals." She turned toward the kitchen and sniffed. "I'd better check your soup. Don't move."

He did, though, arranging himself in a nest of Beth's blankets. Feigning injury had worked well enough, but now he had another idea.

She came flouncing back, obviously pleased with her concoction. "I think—" Beth began, but his groan interrupted her. "What's wrong?" She rushed to the bedside, jogging his leg in her hurry. "Sorry." The wince was genuine, but his acting talent was deficient. "Why are you moaning?"

When he opened his eyes, Beth's hands perched on her hips and her head tipped sideways in suspicion. Gordon extended his arms and closed his eyes once more, unwilling to witness rejection.

Keeping the blankets between them, Beth came to him. The scant barrier made her bold. Beth returned every kiss and moved against him, without restraint. Gordon thought of cold northern waters, of squid, of reaching his toes past the bed's footboard. He thought of anything other than their centers yearning together, pulling steadily, waiting for that perfect match.

Now, he'd launch his new idea. To keep Beth near, so that she could fall in love completely, he'd stop this courting dance a full measure before she stopped him.

"How's my soup coming along?" He pulled away while her eyes were still closed. When they opened, drowsy and full of him, he doubted his sanity.

"Fine." Beth's lips shone swollen and glossy. She gave him a quick kiss on the cheek before swinging her legs off the bed.

So much for his plan. She'd dismounted like a wife, when what he'd hoped for was her eager insistence that he continue, that he quit fumbling about on the other side of the blanket and delve beneath that bright orange exercise suit.

"Put your—"

"—pants on to come to the table?" Gordon fastened his jeans as he shambled after her. "I have manners enough for that."

"Quit limping."

"I think your doctoring's made this hurt even more," he grumbled. Then he saw her anxious frown and touched her cheek, smiling, before he sampled the soup.

To set the stage for her creation, Beth had set out two candles, but Gordon didn't notice.

"You really like it?" she asked, picking at her reheated noodles as he spooned up his second bowl of broth.

"It's great. Maybe the best human food I've eaten." He meant it, but even better than the soup was this coziness. Beth's quick kiss for his cheek, the soup she'd cooked just for him, and Beth sitting beside him, talking, after midnight.

Flame from the white candles danced off the curves in

Beth's hair. She'd had it braided, but now it flowed loose. He pushed it away from her face, pretending it had come too near the flame.

"I think you should stay tonight," she said. "Because of your leg. I know how that sounds, but it's really for your own good."

He decided not to tease her. "I can't sleep inside."

She studied him softly. It wasn't his first admission of oddness, but it would probably effect her most. "Can't?"

"Well, I never have. When I stayed with Junior, I slept in their yard. Since then, I just arrange to be outdoors."

"As a seal?" She uttered the words carefully, so unwilling to offend. But he could see she did not relish sleeping with a beast. But she hadn't said "no."

He wouldn't laugh at her sweet consternation.

"Beth." He took her hand and kissed it, on top, down one side and in the center of her palm. "I can sleep as a man. I just can't bear confinement. It's the four walls—not this body."

Her sigh rocked them both. "Oh, wonderful."

"You were willing to be a good sport, though, weren't you?"

"I'm not sure." She laughed nervously as she cleared their dishes. "I don't have a sleeping bag." She moved into her bedroom, rummaged about, and reappeared with an armload of bedding. "Can you make do with some extra blankets?"

"We," he said firmly. "We can make do with blankets." Gordon's arms circled her, quilts and all, then he kissed her in a way which proved he felt quite in control of his lust. "If I promise we won't mate, will you sleep with me?"

A hundred thoughts rained through Beth's mind and swam like sun over the surface of her green eyes. He couldn't catch one of them.

Eighteen

Finally Beth pulled away, walked to her room's sliding-glass door, and slid it open. The breeze blowing back her hair was salt-heavy, warm. It tempted him to rest, but not without her. Unless she was preparing to toss him outdoors like a dog?

"Beth?"

"You have to promise you won't even make me *want* to— mate." She tugged at the front of his shirt to ensure his attention. "Of course that means no kissing, no touching, not a single one of your regal, provocative looks."

"I have that much power?" He lifted his head in what might pass for a regal look.

"Maybe. A girl can't be too careful." Beth left him to sit on the edge of the deck.

"What good is power if you can't abuse it?" he asked.

Beth unlaced her shoes, then hurled them through the sliding door, toward her bedroom closet. "Is it a deal?"

When a woman began undressing, he'd tell her whatever she wanted to hear. Gordon knew that from his days as a man. But with Beth, he must mean it.

"You're a female with a mind of her own, a modern woman," he countered. He settled beside her and ran one finger over the arch of her bare foot. "Perhaps you're giving me

credit for power you're immune to." Her toes curled. "I think
we should test that power, shouldn't we?"

"Nope." Beth slipped her foot from his grip. Still wearing
both parts of the orange sweatsuit, she slid under the blankets.
She wiggled her fingers for him to follow. "It's my house.
We play by my rules."

"All right." He burrowed under the blankets beside her.
His jeans bound in a hundred places, crushing the wound most
painfully. It would be a good reminder. If Beth didn't invite—
no, beg him—to disrobe, he'd wear the damned things as a
chastity belt.

When Beth allowed one "good-night kiss," he took advantage
and gave her a dozen. They were of such a chaste and controlled nature, Beth's wits remained orderly and she displayed
no desire to mate.

When Peaches mewed and butted his face against the glass
door from inside the dark house, Beth turned in Gordon's arms
and sternly refused to let the cat out.

"I don't have the temperament for another close call," she
said.

"Not even one?" Beneath the blankets, he touched the
sweatshirt and covered the mound of her breast with one hand.
Why hadn't he noticed she'd divested herself of her underwear?

Beth pressed into his hand, raised her mouth to the side of
his neck, and nipped. "You call *that* a close call?"

He accepted Beth's dare. Before her mouth finished speaking, he was astride her, pinning her ribs with his knees, holding her hands helpless above her head with one of his.

"No, I call this a close call," he said. Beneath the sweatshirt, he cupped the other, neglected breast, then trailed his
hand toward the elastic waist of her pants. "Are there other
definitions we need to work out?"

"You promised," she croaked.

"I don't think I did." He lay back beside her, trying to
quiet his rapid breaths.

Damn, the teasing had provoked him more than her. He

turned Beth's back to him, then scooted her an inch farther
off. He concentrated on watching, filling his eyes with darkness cut with black grass shadows.

She refused to stay put. "I don't want to face away from
you." Beth curled, face against his chest, allowing him to
stroke her back, beneath the furry lining of her shirt.

Her breathing stayed feathery and quick, tempting his fingers to learn the delicate beading of her spine. What would
he pay for a hundred nights like this?

Patience. That was the price. There were things he must tell
her, now that she was quiet.

"I told you once, I'd never leave you because I wanted to."
Gordon spoke close to Beth's ear and she stiffened. The winning of Beth's mind would be his greatest challenge. He
couldn't hurry her.

"I remember."

Oh, he was a brute, but the edge of panic in Beth's voice
pleased him immeasurably. The top of her head lay beneath
his chin, but one arm reached up to touch his lips. She dotted
her fingertip on the corner of his mouth, to see if he were
smiling.

He did, and kissed her finger. "I meant it as a promise. And
I have an addition to it. If I leave, I will always come back,
unless you ask me not to."

On his cheek, Beth's hand flattened, patting him. Against
his chest, he felt her swallow. "Thank you," she said.

"It's no favor. It's something I can't help, but Beth, you
must accept me for what I am."

She pulled herself up so they were eye-to-eye, and tried to
joke past the tightness in her throat. "I won't expect more
from you than I'd expect from any man."

"I'm more than a man, Beth, and I—" He'd run out of
words. Feelings baffled him. Hadn't he told her enough?

Apparently, he had. After a long silence, Beth slept. On the
beach, waves' white fingers searched endlessly. A buoy belled
cold caution, while a killdeer called a lonely plaint.

Now, uselessly, his words returned. Subconscious learning,
isn't that what they called it? Maybe he could teach Beth's

sleeping brain with thoughts too fragile for speech. He let his lips graze her temple, closed his eyes and told her with his heart. *I asked you about love, because I don't understand it. Beth, you looked so scared. I didn't want your confession. I want a guide. What if I don't recognize love? What if I don't tell you in time, because no one's ever loved me?*

When she rolled, thrashing in her sleep, her elbow struck his eye. Then Beth settled again. "You're wrong," she muttered.

The sound crackled down the channels of his ears. Had she spoken in her sleep? Responding to his thoughts? Or was she dreaming? He waited until the strain grew painful.

And then, as if they weren't the most important words he'd ever heard in his life, Beth Ann Caxton burrowed her cold nose against his shoulder and snored most delicately.

"Will I be the first selkie in all history to ride a bike, do you think?" Gordon straddled the seat of Beth's old pink Schwinn and supported himself with flat-footed ease.

She probably should have raised the seat, but after one uncertain kiss, he'd roared with impatience. Searching out a wrench had seemed a bad idea. Now he gripped the handlebars, sighting down the long dirt road to Surf Street.

Beth stood alongside, holding the back of the seat, trying to remember how Jack had taught her. "I'm not sure this is a good idea." She stifled a yawn with the back of one hand.

She'd slept fitfully, waking to see him watching her, rousing to the touch of his hand on her hair, stirring before dawn to touch the leg he'd tossed across hers.

Poor guy, sleeping trussed in scratchy denim. Her fault, too. Keeping watch between nearly closed lashes, Beth had formed her hand lightly to his thigh, thinking how right, how comforting it felt to have his leg hug hers so possessively.

"Change your mind?" Gordon's voice had sounded octaves lower than usual, as his leg tightened and he'd smiled at the swift withdrawal of her hand.

Yes, yes, yes, her mind had twittered, before she answered, "About what?"

"Your rules." By then Gordon's lashes had opened. He kissed her slowly with eyes warm and expectant.

"It's a new day." She'd slipped from the blankets, beyond his grasp, before she could weaken. He caught at her leg, then stroked the peak of her ankle. Looking down, she could have sworn he looked disappointed. "We'll renegotiate," she promised.

While she took a cold shower, Gordon found her bicycle. He hadn't allowed her a moment's peace, since. Now he mocked her reluctance.

"What's the worst thing that could happen?" He bounced his shoulders, eager to be off. "I can fall off."

"I can promise you, you won't like falling off on this gravel—don't sit on the seat, yet—I've done it—and ended up getting stitches." She raised her chin to show a tiny white scar.

"I'm wearing long pants." He sat on the seat, both feet still on the ground. "But promise not to take me to the doctor, okay?"

And have them try to type his blood? Have them take stitches in—His eager smile changed her alarm to grumbling. "You should be wearing a helmet, anyway." The bike lurched out of her grip, and he hadn't even peddled. "If you fall off, you could be brain-damaged."

They walked a few yards with Beth holding the seat while Gordon walked astraddle the bike's frame. "This isn't getting us anywhere," he said. "Did you learn with a helmet?"

"I don't think they were invented, yet."

"Ah, that explains it." He landed a kiss so quickly, she couldn't dodge. "Get back. I'm just going to do it."

"Keep your weight centered," she called.

Gordon's feet blurred the pedals through three revolutions before he tipped. A quickly extended leg kept the bike from slamming flat. "Hmm." Surprised but undeterred, he dismounted and walked the bike a few yards back up the road. Laughing, he watched her skip after him. "I thought it would be easier."

"Let's try this." She listened to the whiplash cracking of

the waves. The day was clear and the handsomest man in the world wanted her to teach him. It was no time for *what ifs*. "You peddle and I'll hold the back of the seat and run alongside."

Of course it didn't work. Beth's arms were no match for Gordon's weight swaying sideways as the bike lurched earthward. If he were a child, he'd be ready to give up.

"*I'm* not giving up." Gordon wiped bleeding knuckles across his jeans.

Beth's arm trembled and sweat stung her eyes. "How about trying again tonight?"

He rolled his eyes, peddled furiously, and hopped off the bike just before disaster struck for the twentieth time. Beth considered the sweat-darkened back of his shirt and wondered if she could tempt him off for a swim.

"When it's cooler, it might be more fun," she suggested.

"I'm having fun." Gordon snatched the bike from her grip and shoved it back up the incline.

She was not a natural-born teacher. He'd watched her and listened to her advice, but—Then she remembered. "I've got it!" She jogged back up the road to stand beside him. He smiled, willing to believe. "No pedals."

"You told me the pedals make it go."

"They do, but you're going to learn the balance, first. Okay, picture this. You're swimming, when you're a seal—?" Giddy with revelation, she wriggled free of the arm he curled around her waist. "And you're riding the waves, body-surfing, sort of. You glide, right? Just balanced on the water? Well, stick your feet out, don't touch the pedals, and—try that."

Before she could elucidate, he was coasting down the incline faster than she could jog. "When you start slowing, put your feet down!"

She tripped, but he didn't. Gravel dust hid his rattling skid, but the bike stood upright when he stopped, panting, next to him. "Well?"

"Yeah." He nodded, swooped the bike around on its back tire, and trotted up the driveway to try again.

It worked even better the second time. Gordon coasted as

far as Surf Street. For one horrible moment, she feared he'd glide out into traffic. But there was none.

"I've got the balance. This time I'll ride." He strode back past her.

"Try it one more time without the—" Beth clapped both hands over her mouth when his looked begged for a little faith. "Just remember what I said about the brakes, okay?"

"Huh?" He flashed her an abysmally simple look as he coasted past.

"You'd better be kidding!" She ran as fast as she could, because halfway down Gordon was pedaling, powering her bike as if he'd been born to it, riding toward town.

He braked as the front tire touched asphalt. Straddling the pink bike, he watched her run to him. If hearts could sing, they were doing a duet.

Panting, Beth paced a circle around bike and rider, grinning until her lips hurt.

"Want to ride double?" He snagged an arm to reel her in. "You sit on the seat. I'll stand up and peddle. I've seen—"

"Don't get cocky, now."

Gordon draped his arms against the sweaty sides of her neck, and Beth linked her hands around his. A car rushed by on Surf Street, but neither looked away.

"Thanks." Gordon kissed her. "For letting me do this."

"As if I could have stopped you."

"You could have. I don't like making you afraid. But wasn't it worth it?" He made her answer with kisses. "Come swim with me."

"In your—how?" Hazy images of floating beside him, sleek and seal-like, came to her. She'd slip through kelp forests starred with silver bubbles, giving no thought to shoreside problems, like blood-type and babies.

"Either way." His lips flattened in frustration. "It's a dream to think I could turn you into something like me."

"One of you is enough." She wanted to stroke the back of his neck, but he suddenly looked narrow-eyed and hard, as if her words didn't count. She kept her hands away.

"I need a mentor and there is none." Gordon perched the

bike frame on his shoulder as they climbed to the bluff. "I
might have the magic to change you. But could I change you
back?" He propped the bike against the cottage wall. When
he turned, she went to his arms, again.

"I keep doing this." Beth pressed him to the wall, feeling
his body surround hers. "That's spell enough. I really don't
do this—"

"—with every man you—?" He broke off, smoothing his
hands down her arms in a sort of apology. "Transform you
to a seal with no long, tanned arms to hug me?" He trapped
her knees between his. "With no strong legs to tangle with
mine? Without lips? Never."

Beyond the waves' call, the cove lay silent. No muted barks
and pups' squeakings. Gone, again. Soon Gordon would follow. Though the blood started up, stinging her cheeks before
she even spoke, she needed to tell him.

"I haven't slept with other men." She moved to arm's
length, then couldn't meet his gaze. "Or spent the night with
one, like last night, or—anything."

When she finally looked, she almost wished she hadn't.
Gordon's expression held so much dark gloating, she felt
every bit the skittish freak, the compulsive tease, the career
virgin, men had called her.

"Damn." She slipped away from his hands and stormed to
the edge of the bluff. The cove was empty, except that there,
amid jagged black rocks, the water shone deeper turquoise and
foam churned a white garland.

"Beth, say you were waiting for me."

Royalty, and now he commanded her. She thought of a
foggy day ripped with gold lightning, of Midsummer, a tealeaf
fortune, and the fated ease with which he saved her from
drowning. Lord, yes, she'd waited for him. Only him.

"I did," she admitted.

He didn't crow his victory, only took her cold fingertips and
warmed them with his breath. Odd that her fingers had turned
cold on an eighty-degree day. Odder still that she would have
loved him instantly, passionately, with no thought for the future, if he'd stayed when she was fifteen.

Waves rocked the sea foam circle wider, calmer. Right
there, her fingers had touched a hundred times, parting the
waters for her clumsy landbound self to follow.

"Do you want to jump to me?" Gordon peered over. "I'll
go down and wait." Without a word about his clan, he started
down.

"It was just a whim, Gordon. I wouldn't really do it."

"Why? You've done it before. Many times, you said. I'd
love to watch you."

"My actions were not tempered with good sense in those
days." Tendrils of dizziness made her sit, but her feet dangled
over the edge. "I had some weird idea that Life tested you,
and if you proved yourself brave enough, nothing bad could
happen."

"Is that a religion? A philosophy?"

"Nothing that refined. Teenage angst, maybe."

"Did it prove true? You acted bravely"—his hand arched,
like a diver—"and nothing bad happened."

"Well, Carol married Jack."

"That's not as bad as dashing your brains out."

"Not quite," she admitted, giggling.

"She screamed at us."

"Yes, she did." Beth squeezed his hand, remembering Gordon's glare toward the bluff and Carol's tiny, protective shriek.

An abalone shell rocked in the cove's low waves, and Beth
wondered who had left it behind.

"Something's frightening them off at night." Gordon
squinted toward the horizon, expecting her to follow his mental leap. "Every night I'm ashore, they disappear. I'm going
to go find them now, but I'll come back before sunset and go
back to them after dark."

"You don't have to," she said.

"Why do you do that?" Gordon struck his palms hard
against his jean-clad thighs, then winced. Sand showered,
rocks pinged onto the track below, and Beth wondered if the
whole bluff would crumble. "You want me to come back,
don't you?"

His expression was three-quarters conviction, but the re-

maining bit of confusion made Beth confess. "Of course I
do."

"Then, don't pretend. Let me know. Big Bird didn't cover
love. You have to teach me."

Beth peddled her bike toward town. Since she had the Dumpster for only a week, she should be heaping loose shingles into
it. Instead, she headed toward Gimp's, set on learning what
the old man could teach her of selkies. His lore would pad
out her library research and supplement the precious little Gordon had told her.

It would change nothing, but she had to know.

Gordon had heaped her heart full of his trust, and still she
was reluctant. He'd shown her the cleft rock offshore and described the undersea cave which held his skin, his clothes and
money. He'd explained no one could reach it without scuba
gear. No one would brave the eel ray that guarded the cave
or swim in far enough to find his waterproof locker.

Only one issue defeated his trust. Before she'd fully assembled the sentence, he'd sworn—with the same venom he'd
used on Midsummer Eve—that he'd never let her see him
transform. Never.

Surf Street's narrow shoulder left Beth no escape from the
logging truck speeding out of the Village Store parking lot.

"Get over!" Beth yelled. Her blouse sleeves billowed and
she squinted against grit raised by the huge truck as it swerved.

The driver toasted her with a brown bottle and a blast from
his air horn, then steamed on in a pall of diesel fumes.

Except for some men clustered behind the store, she had no
witnesses.

"Not that it would matter if I did," Beth muttered to the
seal smiling from the restored billboard. When a logging truck
had run Roo off the road and nearly hit Minny, Karl had told
Charmaine to hush and consider the almighty buck.

Roo had apparently profited from the encounter. It was Roo
who stood behind the store, next to his new red truck, talking

with Karl while Sloan sat on a cooler, narrow-eyed as a snake in the sun.

As she neared Gimp's, Beth recalled Sheriff Reynolds's comment that Gimp brewed the best coffee in town. Too hot for that, but why hadn't Bob Reynolds ticketed loggers for blasting through town? And where had he been the day of Roo's accident?

Junior's blue pickup and a yellow Buick sat outside Gimp's. As Beth wheeled her bike past, Junior's black dog shot up with a volley of barks. Beth dropped the bike on her toes.

"Cash!" At her shout the Rottweiler's tumult stopped. How on earth had she remembered his name?

Beth trotted up the "dock" leading to Gimp's portholed front door, then she stopped. She'd never been inside. She doubted the bar's regulars would welcome her, so she might as well bring an escort.

Beth considered the length of yellow plastic line tethering Cash to an I-bolt screwed into the pickup's floor. "Here, boy." The dog whimpered, flopped to the truck bed, panting. He rolled soulful eyes her way. "Poor Cash. It's too hot out here, isn't it?" The dog snorted and his loose brown lips flapped.

Fully expecting she'd draw back a stump for her good deed, Beth yanked the loose end of the slip knot and the dog was free.

"C'mon, Cash!" She clapped, the dog leaped, tongue flying and landed at her side. "Humane Society!" She bellowed, straight-arming Gimp's front door.

Her shout was meant to approximate an official reprimand, but her sun-dazed eyes saw no one inside react. Except Cash. He bounded past her to an apparently occupied back booth.

"Damn it all. Get your nose outta my beer! Down!" Junior leaned out of the booth without standing and saw Beth. "Mighta known," he said as Cash grunted and flung himself down under the pool table.

Undaunted, Beth marched back toward the bar, but not before she noticed Bob Reynolds leave Junior's booth and amble toward the bar's back door. A thousand frantic brain cells tried to make sense of Junior and the sheriff in congenial conversation. As the door closed behind Reynolds, Beth gave up.

As rites of passage went, this one was humble, but for the first time ever, Beth returned to the bar, perched on a stool, and asked, "How 'bout a Coke?"

As Gimp drew her drink, Beth smiled down the bar at the only other occupant. "Hi," she said, feeling right at home.

The man, smelling strongly of tar, stood, tugged the brim of his cap, and swaggered out the front door.

"Sorry," she said, shrugging toward Gimp.

"He were about done anyway." Gimp spun a dial behind the bar, and the room brightened to aquarium green.

Overhead, fishing nets hung with cork buoys, sea stars, and plastic fish swung in a gale of air-conditioning. Gimp polished a glass. Behind him the walls were tacked with black-and-white photographs of men grinning beside large fish suspended by their tails, bleeding.

"So, Beth Ann, did ya just drop in for a drink?" Junior's disembodied voice rose from the booth in back.

"I came to talk to your grandfather, but you can come eavesdrop."

"I'll listen from here. Bad enough to feel your disapproval radiatin' back here. I shudder to think what it'd be like sittin' next to you."

Gimp flicked his towel in Junior's direction. Beth had begun wondering how long Gimp would polish the glass, when he put it down, patted his white hair into order, then came around the bar with his coffee and a carton of cream.

"So, is it your young man you've come to talk about?" Gimp drizzled a pattern of cream onto the surface of his coffee.

"No. I didn't know you dispensed advice for the lovelorn." Beth sipped her Coke. "Remember the day I returned to town and you said you believed in my apparition?"

Gimp swirled his mug, watched the cream sink and smiled.

She'd meant to patronize him. Letting a neglected old man tell his tales seemed a kindness, and if he calmed her qualms, so much the better. Gimp's expression said he'd indulge her.

"I said he were a selkie, sure as spit." Gimp took a long drink. "And I stand by that."

"After what happened, I read a lot about selkies," Beth admitted. "But they were always women."

"Selkie wives." Gimp nodded, as if the legends were as common as rumors of Santa Claus.

"Yes. A selkie maid come ashore to dance in the moonlight. Some fisherman steals her skin, then keeps it hidden and her captive. I know how she pines, looking through the window to the sea until one of her children finds the skin and frees her—to leave them." Beth summarized the tales to see if Gimp would contradict her research. He didn't. "All the stories are so sad."

"Not always." Gimp's head tilted. "She may take one of her bairns with her. The dark-skinned misfit, that child. And if he stays, in those secret undersea caves, a seal may breathe for him. If that happens, he's fortunate his whole life long."

Carbonated bubbles rose from the bottom of her drink, but Beth saw her own lost breath, bubbling through the kelp, before Gordon saved her.

"A mortal's never the same after that gift. Some say it makes for song singers or tale tellers. Or madness."

"Jeez, Grandad."

"Pipe down!" Gimp's voice squeaked with vehemence. "Or come out and join the conversation as you were invited."

When Junior stayed quiet, Beth pressed on. "All the stories I've read tell about women. My 'apparition' was a boy."

A gypsy boy with smooth skin and dark eyes ancient with knowing . . . and his eyes had stayed the same.

"The men come among us more easily, with no one guessing, except good women who can't resist them. And then there's the dark ones they leave behind." Gimp poured more cream. "Their children," Gimp clarified.

The dark ones. Their children. Beth's belly sucked in so deep, she thought it grazed her spine.

"Most often the young one's fingers are webbed." Gimp held spraddled fingers before her. "And they're dark, silent, sometimes marked, like our Minny."

Sick. Ludicrous. Pure imagination. Beth tried to force words past the noose of tears and she couldn't.

"I've read that," she said finally. "But it makes more sense that people in remote coastal villages or islands blamed selkies for wandering wives or birth defects caused by centuries of inbreeding."

In the abstract, such solid, intellectual explanations soothed her. Until she thought of Gordon.

Gimp ignored her reasoned argument. "Even if they lay with your woman, they're not the sort you'd take on, an' you had a brain in your head." He twisted his stool to look back toward Junior. "Never heard of a man fighting a selkie, come to that."

Cash raised his head from the barroom floor and gave a gruff bark as Gimp continued. "Not that they're immortal. Lord knows Man kills whatever he takes a mind to. But a man who sheds selkie blood into the sea"—Gimp gulped the last cream from the carton—"the storm that erupts . . ." Gimp stood and wiped his lips, unable to relate such a hellish scene.

Junior walked carefully from the back and leaned both palms on the bartop. "Ol' Poseidon really lets 'er rip. Is that it, Grandad?" A silver watch glimmered on his wrist.

"Older gods than that," Gimp said.

Cash snarled as Sloan entered in a snatch of sunlight. Junior caught the dog's collar and gave it a jerk. The Rottweiler stood rigid, head level, hackles erect.

"Shut up." Junior pulled Cash toward the door and bumped Beth's shoulder. "Let's see the lady out."

Beth applauded Cash's judgment. She was glad to go. Taken feature by feature, Sloan would be considered handsome, but yesterday's threats still chilled her.

Outside, Junior released Cash and picked up the bicycle.

"Long time since I saw this," Junior said. At first, Beth thought he regarded the pink Schwinn with nostalgia. They'd met, after all, when he'd fixed the flat tire Jack had been too busy to patch. "Then, I see it twice in one day."

Up close, Junior's face was puffy and his breath was sour with beer. He leaned toward her, flexing the bike's hand brakes off and on. Beth forced herself not to retreat.

"Yeah, I drove past your road this morning and what did I see? You and Gordon twisted together, neckin' over the top of it." At Junior's chuckle, Cash swung around stiff-legged.

Beth grabbed the bike's handlebars, but Junior didn't relinquish them. She stifled an irritated sigh. Drunk as he was, she could probably knock Junior down. But could she run fast enough if he grabbed for her ankle?

"Gordon's a simple sort." Junior gave a maudlin nod. "He doesn't know about sneaky little teases, who get a man going, then cut him off."

Roo's truck pulled up. Two more cars stopped and disgorged fishermen. If Junior was waiting for her slap, he'd have a huge audience. Now, Horatio came strolling from the dock.

Enough. She'd jerk the bike away and if he fell—tough.

Rasping with labored slowness, Al MacDonald climbed from Roo's Jeep. Roo crowed over sending a four-hundred dollar catch to San Diego as Junior leaned his mouth against Beth's ear.

"And I'll tell you one thing, Beth Ann." He stretched her name out with cloying sweetness. "I'm getting mighty sick of seeing you lead him around, like you were a bitch dog in heat."

Avid for her humiliation, Junior smirked, figuring he'd won. If she kept quiet, he'd get away with it. If she fought back, he had a cheering section on his side.

"Oh, Junior, honey, I hope you're not jealous?" Beth had braced for Junior to shove the bike toward her rib cage. She was ready for his bawl of rage, but she hadn't prepared for anything more. Beth flung her leg over the bicycle, scrambled aboard, and pumped as hard as her legs would push, toward home.

Nineteen

~

Gold-glazed water rippled thick as satin around Dark Prince, Solitary. The sea's mantle slipped from his shoulders to his chest, draped his hips, fluttered around his calves and feet. Gordon sloshed, brown and powerful, into Beth's cove. If earth held a being more beautiful, it would surely strike her blind.

For two hours, she'd perched on a rocky shelf above her cove, waiting. The cows and pups had returned, and their snug barks and yips kept her company. Each dark head rising from the waves might have been his—but wasn't.

Backlit by the setting sun, a seal looked like a man. That's how the legend started, Beth told herself, and for a handful of minutes, she almost believed it. Then Gordon rose from the waves: naked, magnificent, and no myth.

His face stayed in shadow as he raised a hand in greeting. The sun limned it with amber.

A poet searching out symbols for her life's paradox couldn't ask for one more obvious. Gordon stood there clothed in magic, but she demanded denim and buttons.

No wonder that instant of transformation was taboo. Turning from seals to humans, selkies were completely vulnerable.

If she snatched his skin and hid it, she could keep him a man, forever.

Remembering his nakedness, Gordon gestured toward Lyre Beach, dived flat across the sea's surface, submerged, then swam around the point. When she met him, he'd be dressed and ready for human company.

That was wrong. *She* was wrong. Beth swallowed hard, threw a stone toward the water and missed. Then she started down to meet him. Why, when she loved Gordon's power, his whimsy and quick mind, when she admired his dark defense of his clan, why couldn't she welcome him into her life?

Sandpipers raced ahead of the waves, undisturbed. Where was Gordon? Beth's pulse thrummed. Though there was no sign, she felt him there. As she passed Lyre Rock, he tackled her.

A surprised shriek drove the lump from her throat as she rolled in the sand. She glimpsed wet hair, tan shorts, and a dark red shirt. He spun her over and over, until all demons and differences fled and she lay spread-eagled beneath him.

He nuzzled her cheeks, drowning her in his fresh salt scent. She'd spent all afternoon memorizing the hundreds of reasons she shouldn't want him. With Gordon forming his limbs to hers, she couldn't name even one.

"Clothes. I hate clothes," he growled.

"But those are nice shorts." Beth felt his bare legs churn against hers.

"Why do you torment me with these confinements?"

Beth had no idea. Her hands burrowed under his shirt, smoothed from his waist to his shoulders breadth. There were important things to say, but she'd forgotten how to say them.

"Take me to your bed." Gordon rose on his elbows. "I have this fear of sleeping indoors, as you know. No one else can cure my phobia."

"They'd better not try."

His face remained winsome, beseeching as a child's, while his ankles trapped hers and tugged them apart.

"You're shameless." Beth caught enough breath to scold him.

"You have no idea," he said.

His words thrilled her as much as his perfect weight, and the sand slipping beneath them. Then he scrambled to his feet, pulled up, and tugged her toward the bluff. *And bed.*

Was it excitement clogging her throat? Whatever relationship he envisioned could not work out. She must tell him, but her heart's tumult said "later."

When he came upon the bike she'd dropped next to the Fiat, he stopped. "Didn't I carry this back up?"

"Yes, you did." Beth glanced toward the street. "I rode into town after you left."

At least Junior hadn't pursued her. Taunting him hadn't been smart, but she was a novice at bar fights. Until today, she'd deemed them exclusively male. Of course, her male hadn't been around.

Beth crossed her arms. "I was in a hurry to get inside, so I dropped it here. Pretty careless." Before she lifted the bike, Gordon took it.

"What did he do?" Gordon gripped the handlebars. All playful seduction vanished. "How did Junior scare you?"

Had she *said* Junior? "He didn't scare me."

"What did he say?" Gordon's eyes glinted black with menace.

"Look, you can't just demand I tell you things." She hesitated as his face tightened. Even the knife-edge slant of his cheekbones said he'd demand; she'd tell. "It's bad enough you go pawing through my thoughts—"

"This is not about invading your privacy. It's about protecting you. Tell me what happened."

This time, his relentless sense of responsibility claimed her, not his clan. He intended to help her.

Perhaps because Jack had been too busy to stop her from jumping off cliffs or because most men took her independence as armor, Beth barely resisted. If Gordon wanted to shield and shelter her, she'd let him.

She explained what Junior had said.

After a quick frown, he looked relieved. "He won't talk to you like that, again." Gordon climbed onto the bike, wobbled a few yards down the gravel road, then peddled in earnest.

She ran after him. "Where are you going?"

He put one foot down. "To make him stop. That's what you want, isn't it?"

"No," she panted, running faster to reach him.

"Of course it is." He sounded impatient as a parent. "Otherwise you wouldn't tell me."

"I told you because you wormed it out of me."

"Oh—" Gordon's sigh exploded before he set his jaw, climbed back on the bike and rode away.

Afoot, she couldn't keep up, and she would not be responsible for Junior's demise. Beth rubbed her forehead. She looked up again, hoping he'd turned around. Instead, he'd almost reached Surf Street.

"Damn it." Beth ran up the steps, into the cottage, sidestepped Peaches, grabbed her car keys, and returned to the Fiat. Gordon had ridden out of sight when she closed her eyes and cranked the key.

The Fiat purred alive as if it had never done anything else. In seconds, Beth drove beside Gordon, pushing sand-filled hair from her eyes, trying to talk sense as he spun steadily toward Grey Gallows.

"Will you just stop!" she said, finally. He did, but he looked insulted. "I don't want you to beat him up."

"I said nothing about beating him."

Beth glanced both ways down the empty road. "Well, you looked angry enough to do it."

"I'm not angry. *You* were angry because I wasn't here when someone came into your house. And when someone poisoned Peaches. I don't blame you." Gordon looked out to sea.

Shame arced inside her chest. A woman as strong as she shouldn't add to his burdens. "Gordon, no—"

"I won't let you down this time. I'll tell Junior he can't talk to you like that. He'll stop."

Junior, sick with his own troubles of poverty and homelessness, might not tolerate Gordon's guidance. "And if he doesn't obey you?" Beth asked.

"*Then* I'll beat him up."

"It's not funny, Gordon. Junior carries a knife."

"He's also very slow." Gordon's arrogance, no matter how warranted, annoyed her. "Besides, he must learn. You're going to be my mate and he can't treat you that way."

The words simmered between them. Beth let the car idle and they stared through another minute of stalemate.

The windshield before her lit with a picture too vivid for mere imagination. Metal flashed in Junior's hand. Gordon's blood, selkie blood, clouded the undersea world like crimson smoke.

"Forget it," she snapped. "Get off my bike."

"You needn't command me like an animal." He pronounced the words so pleasantly, she was stunned when he dismounted and slung the bike into the Fiat.

She was still wondering how he'd made the bike fit, when Gordon strode away, toward Gull Cott. Beth pulled her car to the roadside and let him walk ahead to cool off.

She shouldn't have ordered him to obey. Twenty minutes ago, their legs had entwined on the beach. Then, gallant as any knight tilting at chainmailed chests, he'd chosen to defend her honor. What was wrong with her?

Need and confusion welled up until she had no choice but to stamp on the accelerator and follow him.

When Beth reached the bluff-top, the dark red shirt lay at her jumping spot. A half mile up the coast, she saw Gordon swimming toward Grey Gallows.

"He's barred the damned door!" Roo yanked, but the stout door sat snug, keeping him outside Gimp's. Roo pounded the door with his fist before giving up.

Beth sat in the Fiat, fingernails buried in the leather-wrapped steering wheel, watching Roo and the others.

It had turned into a soft evening. Gray mist curled around Gimp's pretend planks and pilings and veiled the setting sun.

How on earth had Gordon evicted everyone, even Gimp? Domingo and Juan squatted, marking in the dirt as they talked. Roo had turned patient, now that he'd thought of educating Horatio and Al on the merits of his new truck.

"V-10," he boasted. "Gas mileage is lousy, but this baby really moves."

Karl paced. Charmaine, wearing a chartreuse blouse veeing too low on her bony chest, perched on a rail, wielding an emery board as Gimp played his bagpipes. Beth guessed he'd brought them outside to save them from a brawl.

"—damned *tease*—" Junior's voice, muted but badgering, seeped through the door.

Sitting in the Fiat, Beth blushed. With the convertible top folded back, she heard, but no one looked her way as they mumbled and shrugged.

Glass shattered inside Gimp's at the same time Grey Gallows' solitary police car eased into the parking lot and into the space beside the Fiat.

Surely Junior wouldn't file assault charges for a black eye and split lip. And Gordon wouldn't inflict any injury worse than that, would he? Beth pushed back images of ferocious bull seals scored with scars from a hundred battles.

Beth glanced furtively at Bob. His cruiser door slammed and he ignored her.

"No barbecue or beer, so I guess you aren't having a cook-out." Reynolds pushed his glasses up his nose.

"That freak Gordon threw everybody out," Roo explained.

Reynolds consulted Gimp. The old man nodded confirmation without letting the bagpipe's mouthpiece fall.

A muted ping, like a stein hitting wood, made Bob's eyebrows arch. Beth abandoned the car to fidget nearer the door.

"Threw you all out," Reynolds mused. "How'd he do that?"

Beth counted eight customers and the proprietor gathered in the glimmering fog. How little she knew of Gordon's magic.

"Said he wanted to talk with Junior. My boy'll give him a talkin' to that'll lay him out flat." Al rubbed his hands together, but his anticipation looked forced. "Gordon's had it coming a long time. *Long* time."

Juan commented in mocking Spanish. When Reynolds asked for a translation, Juan shrugged apologetically.

Domingo stood and brushed his palms together. "Gordon

asked for private time with Junior. It looked like a good time not to stick around.''

Domingo should have been a diplomat. Even Beth's spare Spanish indicated Juan had said something about Gordon climbing up and down Junior's backbone as if it were a stepladder.

''What're they fighting about?'' Reynolds glanced her way, but Beth's glare turned him sheepish. Or maybe he was remembering she'd seen him slink out Gimp's back door that afternoon. ''He mention anything to the bunch of you about Karl and Sloan's business?''

''Business?'' Karl's voice squeaked.

Staccato barks erupted inside. Could dogs recognize selkies?

''What business'd that be?'' No one listened to Karl. Cash's growls held them all staring at the door until a roar, more animal than human, silenced the dog.

Gimp relinquished his pipes with a squawk. ''It's a private party, is the way I'm considerin' it, Sheriff.'' Gimp met Beth's eyes and gave a curt shake of his head. ''I don't know what Junior's done this time, but if Gordon beats him, my grandson won't get a lick amiss.'' Gimp's sad frown grazed Charmaine as she crossed her legs and jiggled one foot. ''Since I can't give it to him and his father's not inclined, Gordon's not a bad choice.''

Wood screeched and cracked from within. ''Och, there goes me table,'' Gimp said.

''Hell,'' Al snorted. ''Gordon'll come reelin' outta there with his eyes bugged out on each side like a hammerhead.''

''Speaking of that''—Reynolds turned to Beth—''Miss Caxton, do you ever do any diving?''

His formality warned her the words were a trap, but Beth only counted up the years. ''Not for about a decade.''

''I mean scuba diving, with a tank and all,'' Reynolds clarified.

Before good sense told her to stop, Beth's glance flicked to Roo. Sloan's bushy-haired partner blamed her with a look.

''I never learned.'' Beth felt a second lurch of alarm. What if, transforming, Gordon looked like someone peeling off a wet suit? Could moonlight glitter on hide rising from the sea, turning it sleek as neoprene? Should she have said "yes"?

Maybe not. When Karl and Roo stepped toward Roo's truckbed, all eyes marked the oversized flippers sitting next to a Styrofoam cooler. There was plenty of guilt to go around.

Roo feigned great interest in scratching his neck.

"Got any beer in that cooler, Roo?" Karl's voice squeaked, just as it had before.

"Hell, man." Gimp addressed Karl as Roo scrambled into the truck. "And all these years you've claimed to drink nothin' but Cutty Sark."

Roo lifted the cooler's lid in exaggerated display. "Why, no, Karl, I don't have one bit of beer."

"The thing is"—Reynolds straightened the ballpoint pen clipped to his shirt pocket—"the county issued me starlight binoculars, and I thought since we've had vandals—"

"You're prowling around the cove at night?"

Charmaine laughed at Beth's gasp. "Why, Beth Ann Caxton, you're pale as a ghost. Kind of takes all the fun out of a girl having her own private beach, does it?"

"I'm afraid my fun's been limited to roofing my house until dark—"

"Oh, right!" Charmaine's giggle merged with a chorus of guffaws. Beth supposed her excuse had sounded pretty feeble.

"This isn't actual surveillance." Reynolds studied his work boots. The official term hushed them all. "I just want to know if we've got trouble from inside or out."

"Cat's sake, a little red paint gets spilled and you're bringing out the spy stuff?" Sweat ringed Al's pale lips.

"As far as I know, there's nothing on my beach except seals," Beth spoke calmly, but her stomach cramped.

If Reynolds were watching, he suspected more than romantic trysts. What if he called in neighboring law enforcement for help?

The injustice jarred her. It couldn't end this way. If she and Gordon couldn't meet here, she'd return to San Francisco. Would he?

Beth remembered the smooth black gadgetry inside Bob's police car and the ease with which he'd found Gull Cott. His chatter had distracted her while he "cased" her property. A law-abiding citizen shouldn't be under surveillance. If she said that, he'd know she had something to hide.

"—do anything without them sticking their whiskery noses where they don't belong." Roo glared Beth's way. "And I still say they've wrecked the fishing."

"Curious beasts. That's for sure." Gimp chuckled as if he didn't hear scuffling that sounded like an overturned pool table.

"Careful what you say about our little trademark." Charmaine threw a kiss toward the billboard. "That googly-eyed cutie's going to make us all rich."

"I thought you looked like you were celebrating," Reynolds said.

Charmaine preened as Karl spoke up. "You're right, Bob. Roo's asked Charmaine to put his house on the market."

"You're lyin' to me. Roo, ain't he lyin'?" Al's whiskers rasped as he grated a hand over his jaw.

"Don't figure I'll be living here after October or so." Roo patted his truck's grille.

Bob Reynolds turned so intent, Beth knew he would have investigated further, if something heavy hadn't thumped against Gimp's barred front door.

Silence always worked. Gordon had issued his demand for privacy, let the customers flee, then stood silent. Now he found himself alone in the smoke-spiraled murk of Gimp's. He clicked off the switch to the fan cooling his wet hair and torso, then sorted through a bowl of unshelled peanuts, waiting for Junior to leave the rest room.

His old friend had accused Beth of acting like a wanton dog. The words were crude, vulgar, and untrue. He didn't fault a jealous man for thinking such things; Gordon blamed him for making Beth unhappy.

Junior took only seconds to feel the emptiness. Looking up from his zipper, Junior stared toward Gordon's bar stool. If not for his drunken daze, Junior would make a worthy opponent.

"What in hell's going on? Gimp decide to close up early?"

"Something like that." Gordon approached. He bore down on the male he'd called brother. The stench of cigarettes made the bar foul. Gordon felt eager to end this. "I don't want you talking harshly to Beth anymore."

Junior blinked, genuinely confused. Then his arms floated out from his body and his shoulders squared. Like any male preparing for battle, he instinctively made himself appear larger.

"I'll say whatever I damn well please to whoever I want." Junior tried to thump him in the chest. That had ever been Al's prelude to a fight, when Junior had been his target. "And no pansy rich kid's gonna say different."

Gordon dodged the blow, but Junior wheeled, swinging. His manhood demanded fists, not talk. Gordon's blood sang at the challenge.

"Always real quick on your feet, right? 'Cause of that seal crap you jabber about." Junior lifted his jaw. His blinking signaled trouble focusing. "Is that what all that b.s. was about at the faire?" Junior edged toward the bar. Gordon's search had turned up no bartender's weapon except a thick cudgel. Still, he watched. "You think you're a selkie? Hell, Gimp might believe it, but Beth?"

Junior reeked of beer and sour sweat. Gordon hated the sound of Beth's name on Junior's lips.

"Your little princess has got some surprises in store for you, buddy. She's the biggest damned tease." Junior lunged.

Gordon halted him by the biceps and propelled him back toward the barred door. The shove sent Junior five feet before he collided with a table, knocking glasses and ashtrays to the floor.

"Yeah, let me tell you about your little honey." Junior seemed undaunted by the fall, but his mind leaped elsewhere. "You cocky S.O.B." His voice turned childish. "Never shoulda taken care of you. Leech. Use me, live in my house, then take off."

"You know why I left," Gordon said.

"I know you're a wimp. You could have stood your ground instead of running."

Fear of captivity surged up like a drowning-tall wave. Behind it came shame. Junior denied their brotherhood and slandered Beth because he thought Gordon a coward.

"It's no wonder a ball-breaker like Beth'd keep you around to—" Before Junior drew his arm back to strike, Gordon smashed his fist into Junior's nose.

Blood splattered them both as Junior's back struck the pool table and his dog launched out snarling from underneath.

Black and tan with snapping ivory teeth, the dog bit off each bark of warning.

"Cash." Junior reeled upright, his voice muffled.

The dog came on, stiff-legged. Gordon warned it back with a growl all mammals understood. Cash shook as if drenched, retreated beneath the table, and issued a last growl.

"Shut up, Cash." Junior sounded weary as he wiped blood from his nose and mouth. "Believe it or not, I've had kind of a lot to drink today." Junior's weak smile didn't make his words an apology. "Beth's nothing but a friend to me, but sometimes when I drink—she's so cute, with those little gold freckles and that pout." When Junior rubbed a finger over his bottom lip, Gordon wanted to split it. "I start thinkin' what I'd do with those long legs of hers and how I'd close that sassy—hey, man it's the booze talkin'. Know what I mean?" Junior hefted his pants by his belt loops, then leaned both palms on a table.

Gordon felt his neck swell and imagined the din of bulls roaring. In place of Junior's leer, he saw ripped hide and gouts of blood. All concern for Junior's pride fell under the onslaught of a wicked vision: Junior rutting atop Beth.

Gordon flipped up his side of the table. It slammed Junior's jaw with a meaty clunk, sent him staggering and Gordon tackled him down, knees pinning Junior's shoulders while the smaller man's arms flopped like dying fish.

"Shut up." Gordon's fist cocked back, ready to ram home

his message. "Beth's going to marry me. Know what *I* mean? So, just shut up."

Junior exhaled. Spittle and blood sprayed out with his laugh. "Marry you? Tell me she promised to marry you, and I'll buy you a goddamn Cadillac."

Junior's skepticism was valid. But how could Junior know of Beth's reluctance?

Gordon let Junior quit wheezing, then climbed off. He'd meant to leave Junior groaning on the floor, but he'd have to hit him again to accomplish that. Gordon tightened his weak human hand into a fist. Another blow would only damage it further. The deeds he wanted to perform in Beth's bed required both hands in working order.

Junior got to his feet, creaky as an old man. He scowled at his bloody shirt and jeans. "Looks like I've been gaffed."

Gordon gloried in the carnage. "I hope you feel like it."

"Thanks, old buddy." Junior rounded the bar and stopped behind it, near the hidden cudgel. "Now, I'm going to pour myself something strong. How 'bout I buy you one, just to prove there's no hard feelings?"

Gordon passed his hand over his hair, down the back of his neck. Warning, as strong as a shark's tail snapping through the depths, shivered down his spine. He should leave now, but he couldn't. Curiosity was a seal's curse. Every day they died from it. And yet . . .

"Stay away from that stick," Gordon warned.

Junior scooped the cudgel from beneath the bar, then lay it between them. "I don't plan to need it. What'll you have?"

Drinking cemented bonds between men, especially men like Junior. Gordon surveyed the polished bottles and bright labels. The names were as nondescript as lists in a telephone book. Except one. He thought of sun gilding the sea as he'd swum toward Beth. "Mexicali Gold," he said, pointing.

"Tequila? Straight?" If the drink were hearty enough to make Junior grimace, it was perfect. Gordon nodded. Junior glanced up as he poured. "Why the hell aren't you wearing anything but shorts?"

Gordon touched the bare wall of his chest. He should have

progressed past such errors. Was that why the bar's patrons had left so quickly? They'd judged him a half-naked madman?

" 'No shirt, no shoes, no service,' has never been Gimp's policy," Junior said, when Gordon didn't answer.

The small glass Junior pushed across the bartop didn't carry enough liquid to quench thirst, but Gordon swallowed it. Tequila burned worse than Beth's brandy, but it stirred a not unpleasant tickle, just in front of his ears. Not unpleasant at all.

"You still don't get it, do you?" Junior sighed as if he'd lectured Gordon for an hour. "You never did. You'd be nodding away, but you never understood the unspoken agreement among guys." Junior's fingers drew a wide wet circle on the bartop. "It says guys don't tie themselves to one woman. They don't buy flowers, change plans, or make promises just for sex. The game is to get what you want from women without marrying them."

Beth. Outside, he heard her voice, welcoming as sunwarmed sand to a cold belly.

"Gordon, listen. Even if you're going to throw away your freedom—"

"I'm not." Gordon had the oddest notion Junior's rules would make more sense if he swallowed more tequila.

"You are if you're talking about marriage, but hey, Beth isn't going to come across, anyway."

Jealousy slithered through Gordon's belly. Junior extended one hand to hold it off.

"You're not going to like this, but I'll tell you anyway: She'll never sleep with you."

"You wanna bet?"

"You're on." Junior shook Gordon's hand. "Hell, she won't be here by Fourth of July. All this bleeding-heart crap about seals, fishermen, and Grey Gallows keepin' its name?" Junior waved as if erasing words written on the air. "Let things get hot and she'll be outta here.

"Take men. Phoebe told me—You know Phoebe? Tight little ass, curly black hair—?"

"Beth's friend." Gordon licked a trace of tequila from his fingers.

"Right. Phoebe says every time a guy gets serious with Beth, she moves on. Happens all the time in S.F." He nodded. "Some hotshot TV reporter volunteered to go off to Bosnia when she dumped him. And a couple cops. She likes these action guys who're too busy for commitment." Junior paused as if struck by a great profundity, then shook his head.

"You think you're almost home, but Beth won't have sex. Twenty-five years old and pure as the driven snow. Yeah, look all smug, now, but I know. One night she had me so hot—"

"You weren't the one, so she stopped you."

Outside, Beth's voice mixed with the sheriff's. Gordon felt as if he were swimming to the surface, toward light and oxygen, as if he'd die if he didn't get to her.

"That's probably right, but mark my words, man. She's gonna be long gone by Fourth of July, and she ain't gonna be nobody's sweetheart. Ever."

Twenty

Gordon was drunk. Beth knew only that would explain his swagger and easy lies.

Upon lifting the bar from Gimp's door and emerging into the summer twilight, Gordon smiled with a sensual indolence that made her toes curl. They'd curled tighter as he held her hand, rubbed his wrist against hers, and swore that Junior had "whipped him." Of course he hadn't, but Gordon swiped at the gore on his chest and pretended. For Al.

After that, Gordon made sure he brushed against her as he lied to Bob Reynolds. Back and forth, his hand skimmed the cotton shirt covering small of her back as he swore he and Junior had parted on amicable terms.

Now Gordon sat in the Fiat, right elbow propped on the window ledge, head supported by his hand as they sped toward Gull Cott. Beth's chest filled with salt air and anticipation. A handsomer man did not exist.

With eyes half-closed against the wind tearing at his black hair, Gordon shouted to be heard, confessing he'd made a bet with Junior. The bet concerned her virtue.

Beth glanced away from the road in time to see Gordon's eyes close completely. He held his face up for the moon, accepting its silver glow like a benediction.

She concentrated on the video store slipping past, then the Village store and the billboard.

"Are you wearing your seat belt?" she fussed, but the moon's spell refused to shatter.

As Gordon nodded, the ridge of muscle between the base of his neck and top of shoulder rippled, then sloped toward the strength of his upper arm. All that power, yet his eyelashes meshed like a child's. Beth gripped the steering wheel, afraid her fingers would stretch out to touch him.

A long chute of road opened before her, safe and empty. She glanced at Gordon's chest, then couldn't look away. Flat copper disks hid in his dark chest hair. God. She'd *never* looked at a man's nipples before. How degenerate, depraved. Worse, twin sets of muscles enticed her eyes from the end of his breastbone, down to his navel, to his shorts' waistband.

The road's sigh turned to stuttering, then neck-snapping bumps. "Oh, no." She jerked the steering wheel toward center and cleared her throat.

Gordon's eyes sprang open. "Y'okay?" His lazy smile did not dispel Beth's fear that she'd become Grey Gallows' first traffic fatality attributed to lust.

"I'll be fine," she said, "as soon as you explain your bet."

Heaven knew what he'd say or how she'd react. Sixty, sixty-five, she drove too fast, trying to make it home before she crawled over the gear shift and into his lap. The Fiat slued sideways as she turned onto her gravel road. Before the car could pitch nose-down onto the beach, she stamped on the brake.

For a moment she thought he'd fallen asleep. Waves searched and sighed over the shore. The engine pinged as it cooled. Beth touched the sun-lines around Gordon's eyes.

Sleep, ha. He'd passed out. Selkies probably shouldn't drink. His lips parted and she let his warm breath sweep the back of her hand. She touched one fingertip to the corner of his mouth, and Gordon smiled the most knowing smile she'd ever seen. Then he grabbed for her.

"No way." Beth's spine slammed against the driver's door
before she jiggled the handle and ran.

She hurdled the first two rough-cut steps and barely touched
the third. She flew toward home as his footfalls followed. Gordon's legs were muscular, primed for instant energy. He'd
called on his sinews for survival. Why did she try to outrun
him?

Because she was winning. Beth's breath caught on a laugh
as she reached the bluff and darted around the dropped bicycle.
Her hip joints protested such long strides. She was no sprinter.
Worse, this minute-long dash wouldn't give her the finishing
kick of a longer run. If only she couldn't hear his loping steps
amid her pattering ones.

Beth dropped her keys, hoping to distract him. A jingle told
her he scooped them from the ground, just before he struck
her shoulder with his and caught her as she tripped.

"Cheater." Her chest heaved from exertion. His didn't. It
was warm and hard and steady against her cheek. And it was
bare. "A few more steps and I would have won. Put me
down."

"Oh, we were *racing*?" He hefted Beth higher.

"Besides insulting me"—Beth wriggled to get loose—
"what are you doing?"

"Carrying you across the threshold."

He elbowed past the door, slammed it with a kick, and carried her through the dark house, toward the bedroom.

"No. Gordon, no."

He kept walking.

"You're not listening to me." He tumbled onto the bed
beside her. She heard Peaches' disgruntled mew as the rainbow spread slipped sideways, exposing her yellow pillowcase
and sheets.

Beth turned on her bedside lamp. Oh, Lord. When had her
heartbeat migrated to the pit of her stomach?

"What have you been drinking?"

Gordon stretched so long he overlapped the bed's footboard.
"Tequila," he said.

Junior ought to be shot, but her hands were shaking and

Gordon's were steady as he traced her hairline from brow to temple and behind her ear. "About that bet."

Gordon's face loomed so close. Moonlight passed the sliding-glass door, frosting his brown eyes silver. "I'll explain, but first, put on a nightgown." Gordon sat up as if he'd requested no more than a drink of water.

"This is just an experiment. I want it to be authentic as possible. In fact, set your alarm for an hour from now, could you?" Gordon yawned and the tan shorts slipped low on his hipbones. "If I fall asleep, which I doubt, I want to be roused in time to go back out."

One hour and he'd be gone. Again. Melancholy dampened Beth's resistance until she saw his faint smile. An experiment? If he intended to dispatch her virginity in an hour, he had an ugly shock in store.

"I'll take a shower and be right back." Without answering, he turned to go.

"I don't—"

He looked back. "I *can* use your shower, can't I?"

She nodded, certain she was being tricked, but not exactly sure how.

"A nightgown." He pointed an imperious finger, then clicked on the overhead light, banishing seductive shadows. "The prissiest one you own will do fine." He lounged in the doorway, mocking her. "Look at it as a humanitarian gesture. If this relationship is going anywhere, I'll have to learn to sleep in a bed."

The bathroom door had barely closed before Beth slammed open a drawer. *If this relationship is going anywhere* . . . In a singsong voice, her mind mimicked him. She flipped a flowered nightshirt onto her bed. *Humanitarian gesture,* huh? She drew ivory drapes over the glass door, unstrapped her digital watch, and set its alarm.

One hour and five minutes. She lay it faceup on her bedside table, listened for running water, and stripped off her shirt.

Crammed into her old-fashioned tub, Gordon would be eating his knees. She hoped he enjoyed contortions. Beth brushed her hair until it snapped with electricity and strands danced a

nimbus around her head. She stepped out of her shorts and
kicked them into a corner. The cottage's slow-warming water
ought to provide enlightenment to such a regal personage as
Gordon.

Was she grumpy because he'd picked her up? Or put her
down? Because his superior tone implied that no matter what
she wore, dowdy Beth Caxton couldn't provoke him if he
chose not to let her?

From habit, she unhooked her bra and tossed it on the
dresser. Wind ruffled her curtains, but she couldn't guess its
temperature. Beth felt flushed and freezing all at once. She
started to peel off her bikini panties, then stopped. *The bet.*
She didn't trust Junior. She trusted a tipsy selkie even less.

If he thought he could manipulate her affection, he was
wrong. If he thought he had the skill to turn her body against
her brain, she'd show him different.

Beth folded the nightshirt into a drawer and withdrew a
white flannel gown. Although it left her arms bare, forty-two
buttons—according to the catalog description—marched from
chin to hem. She closed every one of them.

The bathroom door opened. Beth still hadn't found the appropriate position. She'd arranged herself like a corpse, flat on
her back, hands folded over her navel. All wrong. She moved
her hands up. Down. *No.* She lay them at her sides. Palm up
or palm down? It must be eighty degrees in here, but her
fingers were freezing. Beth tucked them beneath her thighs.

He turned off the bedroom's overhead light.

If she looked like a maiden sacrifice, Gordon didn't seem
to notice. He spared her a single, dismissing glance before
opening the sliding doors.

"It's so closed in, I don't think I can—" Gordon didn't
finish, only leaned a knee on the bed and reached across to
open the window wider. He remained there on one knee and
she looked up.

Gordon's red T-shirt had probably blown off the bluff by
now. His glorious chest remained bare. Bronze skin and those
muscles. She imagined his chest crushing her own and shivered.

"You're not too cold?"

Gordon's smile said he knew very well she wasn't, but she shook her head. Since she lay centered on the bed, he fit himself next to her, on his side. Her defiance turned watery, diluted by his presence, shirtless and smelling of soap.

"Good," he said. "Blankets might make me claustrophobic." His eyes darted toward the ceiling, surveying it from corner to corner, as if it were a lid fastened on a box.

Beth's desire to put Gordon in his place vanished. His anxiety was no joke. His lips flinched back and faint perspiration sheened his upper lip.

Beth faced him, mirroring his position. Up on one side, she let her elbow ride in the curve of her waist. "Let's give you something else to think about."

"I was hoping for that." His smile fell just short of convincing.

"The bet," Beth reminded.

"The bet." Gordon swallowed as if his mouth had gone dry. "It's more of a pact between males—are you groaning?"

"No, go ahead."

"Junior says you're a tease."

"*Now* I'm groaning," she told him, but Gordon's head had tilted to one side as he noticed her gown's many buttons.

Gordon touched the top button at her throat and ran his index finger down the line of them as far as her belly. "Junior says you don't love Grey Gallows, you don't love me, and you'll never have sex with anyone."

She kissed him. Concentrating all affection, admiration, and trust into her lips, she tried to make this enough. "Can't I kiss you without—?"

"Oh, yes." Gordon swooped around her, arms crossed behind her back, hands bracketing her hips as he tugged her nearer. Their ribs collided and he took her lips with sudden force, fitting words where he could. "But it—would be far—better if—it were *before* mating. Or during—not instead of."

Pinning one wrist above her head, he kissed her neck, nuzzling the gown's high collar aside. Beth's eyes opened to the black glossiness of his hair. Then Gordon's chin rested on her shoulder. He cocked one eye toward her watch. She almost sniffed that she *had* set the alarm, damn it. Before she spoke, he took her wrist to his lips and kissed it.

"One hundred twelve beats per minute."

"What?"

"I checked your watch. The adult human pulse beats about seventy times per minute. Your pulse is going wild."

"Show-off," she said, but she felt the blood pounding in her wrists, her throat, her breast.

"I'm not arrogant, but I hope to become so." He glanced toward the curtain, rising on a breeze, and he took an uneasy breath.

Beth placed her hand on his chest. "Mmmm." She'd never felt anything like the warm skin overlaying his heart's thunder. He was responding to *her* touch, *her* nearness. Why didn't their combined heat brand him? She cooled the spot with her lips, dusting them back and forth.

"I want . . ." Gordon's eyes showed his battle between maintaining control and making her lose it. Without parting their chests, his ankle caught hers and drew it up. His hand clamped the base of her Achilles tendon, slid up her calf to the inside of her knee. "I want to trace your pulse to the source."

He'd said that before. He wanted to hike Sandbag Creek and trace its path home. To the sea. Didn't he? Why couldn't she think?

Gordon's eyes closed her out as his fingers slipped behind her knee. "I want you to want it."

Involuntary and hard, her stomach muscles grabbed and she moved against him. Gordon shoved her gown up and flattened his palm to the pulse high inside her thigh. She heard herself gasp.

Now. If he did it without her consent, she couldn't weigh the risks. He'd make her his. His hand circled the top of her thigh, brushed the leg of her panties. She wouldn't resist.

Then his hand abandoned her. Fisted, it slammed against the wall behind her. "Beth, what are you so afraid of?"

Passion had been flashing behind her eyelids. It would have been so easy to surrender, but he'd—

"Ruined *what*?"

If only his probing of her thoughts had been reckless and rough, like his fist against the wall. But Gordon caught her trouble, cupped it in his hands, and held it to the light.

Sea wind lifted the drapes and brought the sweetness of sea peas into the room. She heard her bike's freewheel clacking and spinning in the breeze. It needed oil.

"What, exactly, do you mean when you say 'mate'? I know the sex part. I *know*, but what about children?"

He smiled, found the pulse in her ring finger, and brought it to his lips. "Are you afraid they'll have flippers and tails?"

"I can't joke about this. Lots of children aren't perfect. I wouldn't love ours less, but I have to know."

"Let me think." Gordon's voice was solemn. His mouth skimmed her wrist, then the bend in her elbow. Gooseflesh climbed her shoulder and flashed across her chest, though his manner remained contemplative. "Seals don't tell stories, exactly, so you'll have to accept legends and my instinct." He looked at her hard and spoke with steadfast certainty. "Selkie and human matings don't make monsters."

She caught his wrist, though it was too wide for her fingers to span. "Would they be like you?"

"Or like you. There couldn't be a hybrid."

"I feel better." Her words came muffled as her lips burrowed into his half-closed fist.

"You believe me? Just like that?" His eyes widened at her trust or perhaps because she nipped the fullness at the base of his thumb.

"I believe you." *And want you and want you and want you*. Relief slipped through her, igniting every sense to his touch.

"You're a brave girl, Beth, to trust a creature that might exist only in your imagination." His fingers forked through her hair, cupping the base of her skull, and she wanted to purr. "Unnaturally brave—wending your way through the back alleys of San Francisco, coming here to live alone. Even as a child, you leaped off the cliff into thin air."

"Not for years." She felt his hand still. Chagrin trickled down her neck, because she wasn't really so brave at all. "And I jumped that way"—the day came back, all silver mist and jagged gold lightning—"because I thought I heard you calling."

"You did."

"Yes, I know it sounds silly—"

"Beth, that wasn't a question." He caught her chin and forced her to meet his eyes. "You *did*. Something told me you were there. I was waiting for you to come to me."

Without thought, they pressed together, and this time his kiss moved deep. His tongue slid against hers, tasting of tequila. His swollen hands moved up and down her bare arms, his knuckles rough from pummeling Junior. His leg thrust around hers, pulling her closer, and his wound caught on the thin flannel gown. She'd tended that injury, the hurt inflicted as he waited for her.

Her fingers found the channel of his bare spine and the clean winglike spread of his shoulder blades. His hands chaffed her arms, formed to the flannel over her breasts, and she arched against him. She quivered, inside and out, not giddy or fluttery, but eager. Only once had his hand moved beneath her gown, so why did every inch of her flesh ache as if it had been buffed raw?

Her shin grazed the rough jut of his kneecap. Every one of her nerves had been scraped sensitive. She'd scream if he touched her and beg if he didn't.

He pulled her with him into a whirlpool. She spun, swirling toward an irresistible vortex. She wouldn't stop herself from drowning.

His hands covered her ears, concealing the insistent beep of her watch alarm. Beth heard, but she refused to listen. "It has a five-minute warning," she lied, tracing the smooth symmetry of him. "And you have the most beautiful arms and shoulders."

"Stand up against the wall."

Beth's eyelids sprang open. The bed groaned as Gordon shifted away from her. Tender but insistent, he drew her toward the white slab of wall beside the doorway, and she went.

She wouldn't do *anything* he asked, but just now, she could think of nothing she'd refuse him.

He squatted before her, less a supplicant, than a workman, releasing the round buttons closest to her hem. She smothered the whimper in her throat, or perhaps she didn't. Gordon reached up and squeezed her hand.

Forty-two buttons. He could only have opened three or four, and hadn't touched a millimeter of skin, but she felt faint, ready to curl forward and form herself over his head and neck.

The instant she forced her eyes open, he knew. Gordon had opened the buttons to her knees. He rocked back on his heels and looked up at her. "Ten," he said.

She stared toward the window. Black, star-strewn night curved over the moonlit beach. Sea wind made her gown Gordon's accomplice. It trailed against her skin, flaring, stroking.

She looked down and heard them breathe together. Gordon's thigh muscles, bulging in their contracted position, began to quiver. "Twenty." That button released the flannel covering the confluence of her thighs.

He stood, pressing close in a kiss which demanded more. In a minute she'd tell him to stop.

Then Gordon's hands closed at the gown's high neck. In one swift move, he slipped the buttons loose. Like popcorn, first one, then two at a time, then a frantic flurry of buttons, until all forty-two were undone. The gown hung loose over her panties of apricot silk.

She shivered as Gordon lifted the gown from her shoulders, slid it down her arms and dropped it. His gaze roved her bareness, and he uttered a sound both vicious and victorious.

"I can't," she said, but he trapped her wrists and kept her from closing the gown.

"It's all right." Forced through his gritted teeth, the words came rasping and deep, not *all right* at all. "I'm no animal. If I were—" His rueful laugh left no questions. Beth almost felt the impact of her head hitting the floor, as if she'd fallen beneath him.

She blocked the mental pictures with all her might, and she must have kept him out, because when Gordon swayed against her and brushed the hair away from her ear, his whisper was mild.

"Come swim with me. That's all."

Twenty-one

~

He walked in the midst of magic, shifting and glittering like star shards, as he carried Beth down the secret cove trail.

Instinct guided his steps away from the crumbling edge and plunging drops down to the rocks. Their concealing cloak faded to mist only once, when his concentration wandered from sorcery to Beth's hands locked around his neck, her breath brushing his throat, her breasts pressing his chest.

Gordon focused on his ancient core, the source of selkie magic which made invisibility possible. Focus wasn't easy.

"No one else will see you," he'd told Beth as he took her naked from Gull Cott.

Banishing Beth's worry over bare skin, over Sheriff Reynolds's surveillance with binoculars that magnified starlight had been simple compared to wearing these jeans. Cautious not to rip her acquiescence, he'd left them on. Soon enough he would be rid of them. Soon enough he could drop this magic curtain and engulf Beth's beauty.

He loved her. Accidentally, Beth had taught him how to love. A sweetness underlay the blood-hot urge to mate. What else could it be, but love? Three times he'd held off desire because Beth asked it. But tonight her mind had opened to him and no matter how long it took Beth to confess she needed him, he already knew.

Soft sand and level footing curved around a shoreline cluttered with supple, breathing humps.

"Do they mind that I'm with you?" Beth whispered as he picked his way among the seals.

Gordon let the crystal curtain disperse. The cows greeted his human form with groggy barks. The pups yipped in fright.

"They don't intrude on what I do as a man." Gordon held Beth closer. The cows didn't understand him anymore than Peaches understood Beth, but to her, that might sound arrogant. He uttered a hoarse, soothing call to the cows.

At the water's edge, he'd begun easing his arm from beneath Beth's knees when she clamped onto him like a limpet.

"Don't put me down yet." Beth tightened her grip on his neck. "Okay? If I'm not too heavy?"

"Never." Her efforts to hide her flesh were obvious. Why would she even try?

"This sparkly fog—You make it, don't you? I saw it that day I jumped." Beth lifted her chin toward the bluff.

"I was watching you."

"But that wasn't the only time, was it? In San Francisco, that night I ran around gathering truffles and champagne for your party, it was all around me."

"I worry about those stinking alleys," he said, and Beth vibrated against him with low laughter.

"I chalked it up to some atmospheric thing. Ice crystals hanging on mist . . . Were we both invisible or just you?"

Warmth bloomed within his chest. In only minutes she'd accepted his ability to hide substance with a flicker of magic. "Both of us, most of the time. It pleased me, after all those years alone, to wrap us in the same silver shimmer. Just us."

She tugged his head down and kissed him, open-mouthed and slow. Her modesty had faltered and he credited himself—not magic—for that achievement. When would Beth remember she wore nothing but that enticing scrap of silk and lace?

"Time to swim." Beth ruffled his hair, sounding playful until he set her on her feet.

At once her arms raised and her hands formed fans like scallop shells over her nipples.

Though the crystalline mantle eddied around them, magic couldn't make Beth more beautiful. She was a sea goddess. The full moon lit her face burnishing her smooth brow and graceful cheeks just for him. Her hair shimmered in a million threads of copper and gold, flowing behind her shoulders.

"You're sure about this. No one can see us, even the shark?" She shivered against him.

Bringer of Crimson was far away, exiled by the same danger that sent the cows swimming for Moon Isle. "He can't see us or sense us, either. Even like this"—Gordon touched his human chest—"I'll be able to protect you."

"All right." Her tone had everything to do with trust, not surrender. Her legs flexed with runner's muscles as she sprinted four steps through the shallows, then dived low and true into the sea.

He was beside her in an instant. With wordless deference, she followed, swimming behind as he penetrated the darkness surrounding the finger of land which pointed out to sea. Then it happened, just as it had in a thousand longing dreams, Beth swam beside him.

She matched him stroke for stroke. Each time she raised her face, dripping, she turned toward him, glorying in his world. Her small, pale hands parted the waves' star-shined crests. He loved her gentleness with the sea, asking passage, instead of demanding it. Only Beth bridged the break between earth and sea.

As they rounded the point to the weather side of Grey Gallows, the ocean roughened. Gordon stopped, treading until Beth bobbed up beside him.

"We did this once before." Her eyelashes and lips were wet and beaded. Her hair's waviness lay flat and glossy as his hidden seal hide. "Offshore from Playland, that dead amusement park? I got a little scared. I don't remember if it was from the tides or sharks, or just being alone. . . ."

"It should have been all three. That's the only unintelligent thing I've seen you do. That coast is a nightmare. I don't know what you were thinking."

Her peddling legs churned beside him, warming the currents, clouding his ire. She ignored his reprimand.

"And then this came up." She spun one dripping hand above them, casting her own spell. "And I stopped being afraid."

A warm gust of wind rushed around them, whispering a fantasy of Beth's small, warm hands divesting him of these pants.

"You're wonderful in the water," he told her.

"Am I?" She sounded both proud and embarrassed.

Beth's legs grazed his and Gordon hooked his knee through hers. She resisted, then let him win. He towed her nearer, until her flat, bare belly grazed the front of him. Her head fell back as if it were too heavy to hold upright. At the sight of her exposed throat, he took no time for nuzzling, only kissed and nipped the thin skin until Beth fell against him.

"Isn't this dangerous?" Her neck vibrated beneath his lips.

He kept her afloat, pulling her above him as he swam on his back. "No, *this* is dangerous." Accursed human clothes! Beth matched so perfectly, gliding so gracefully, he might have been inside her.

Her hands darted like tiny fish, brushing his shoulders, his back, their touch tentative and light as Beth tried not to sink them.

"Gordon." Her voice trembled, half-beseeching. Only cloth and a thin film of sea water separated Beth's feinting hips from his. If she'd known the mechanics of lovemaking, how to position and direct herself above him—But she didn't and he drifted away each time she advanced.

For all her inexperience, she claimed his lips well enough. "Gordon." With only his name, she asked him to finish what she'd shyly begun.

"Go." Gordon dropped from beneath her, turned her shoulders toward shore, and gave her bottom a push that sent her plowing away from him.

For one blinking moment, she looked back. Then she was

swimming. Beth flashed pink and silver ahead of him, streaking below the sea's surface and her hair was touched with
moonlight.

Tatters of shimmering mist streamed behind her.

Beth's knees shook, but not from cold. She'd stopped swimming too soon, let her feet touch sand too early. Now she
slogged toward Lyre Beach and it wasn't the waves' pull that
made her weak.

Gordon stood naked in the moonlight, waves foaming at his
knees, one hand extended for hers. His magic flashed and
dimmed, crackled bright as lightning, then wafted like silver
smoke as she touched him.

"Come here." Gordon faced her. Only their lips touched,
but the kiss overthrew all her common sense. He stood so very
close.

Beth felt Lyre Beach tip. The indigo night spun in bright,
kaleidoscopic wildness. Beth swallowed her gasp. His hard-
ness, the desire she'd fought to overlook in the cottage, sprang
against her. Nothing but ruined silk kept them apart.

Her fists clenched on the air. Logic said not to touch him,
but her body swore mutiny and her hands led the rebellion.
She reached up to his shoulder blades and his breath sucked
in, even before she scored his skin with light fingernails. Her
hands slid down his body, claiming every muscle and tendon
and rib.

"Beth, go slow."

His warning only fanned her defiance. At the small of his
back, his muscles tensed before he took her down to the sand.

Like magic, she settled against cloth. His soft red tee shirt
had found its way beneath her. A trill of panic vanished as
Gordon's hands washed over her, outlining the edges of her
thighs, hips, waist as he lay over her. His thumbs grazed the
undersides of her breasts, and he rose a few inches, leaving
room for his hands to advance and retreat. Each time they
returned, her excitement sharpened.

Riptides started slowly, logic reminded her. At first they
made swimming smooth and easy, teasing you into believing

your own strength, then they wrapped you in renegade currents which swept you far from shore.

Beth remembered drowning, remembered breath trapped in her chest and the need to scream or escape. This was the same—except for the pleasure.

She opened her eyes to Gordon's face. Half-pagan, half-worshipful, he watched her. Mute with desire, he shook his head.

His mouth closed over her breast with a gentle claiming that made her arch, made her fingers claw into the sand beside her, then set her joyfully adrift.

She had no choice. She never had. Long ago, he'd called her, coaxed her toward the edge, and she'd gone.

He gazed up at her and Beth trembled. Those dark, star-glazed eyes could absorb her and make her disappear.

It's all right, Beth. All life came from the sea. You did, I did. You're only coming back to me.

Though his mind beckoned, kindly asking her to risk, his body commanded her.

She felt no fear when his hand splayed over the silk of her panties, felt no violation when his fingertips moved beneath to touch her. She only thought how sweet drowning could be, how the sea wind failed to cool, how desperately she wanted him closer.

Sea and shore, Beth. We'll put the two halves back together.

Only Gordon could stop this tight winding in the center of her being, but he forced it to coil tighter.

And then, with her own cry in her ears, she was falling up, soaring against the hard wall of his body, trusting her grip on his shoulders to keep her from flying into a million pieces.

A flare of opalescent fire shone through her eyelids. She opened her eyes to Gordon looming muscled and primitive above her, with the full moon over his shoulder.

His black hair rose on the wind and his fingertips drifted over her lips. No matter how she wanted to answer their questioning, wonder had robbed her of speech.

"Beth?"

"Yes." It was all she could manage. She tried to smile, to

prove she was fine and she was, until his knee edged hers apart. As if a wine-dark wave crashed over her, sweetness turned to passion. "*Yes.*"

He craved the finish. She saw it in the hardened set of his jaw and his hooded eyes, but his arms trembled, trying not to hurt her. Beth gasped as he moved against her.

I did pain you. One chance, one possibility of doing it right and I—

She heard herself growl. She had become the animal, the female demanding he complete their mating. Want roared in her ears, not a seashell's sighing, but thundering like breakers, pounding as she reared up against Gordon, scoring his flanks with her fingernails. Only then did he slide into her fully.

I love you, I love you . . . His thoughts pounded her to the edge of madness as his thrusts lifted her off the sand. Finally he closed her against his chest, curving them into one being.

"I love you," Beth whispered. Tenderness pricked her eyes with tears. "I do love you."

Do you know what that's like? Do you know you're the only, only creature on earth who's ever said that to me? Joy flooded from his spirit to hers. Beth held him tighter and refused to think.

It was barely midnight when Gordon left her standing in Gull Cott's doorway, dressed in his red shirt. Emotion rolled her end over end as he walked away. She felt proud and bereft. She felt glorious and hollow. She felt like a fit animal and like a fool.

When he vanished down the cove path, she walked across a room that looked alien, sank down on her couch, and stared at the window reflecting her image in cold detail.

Her hair frizzed around her like a child's frantic scribble in orange crayon. Her cheeks had developed windburn or a permanent blush. Her lips were still swollen, glossy, and shamelessly ready for more.

What have I done? Beth bowed her face into her hands with the most fervent of prayers, hoping for a gentle Deity.

The refrigerator's hum seemed louder. The thing was at

least thirty years old and probably ready to give up the ghost. Now it had an accompanist in mechanical misery. Her kitchen faucet dripped, plopped, dripped.

Magic had clearly departed with Gordon. Quick and painless as a sharp knife, suspicion cut her. Gordon could read her mind, but could he change it? If he could create curtains of light, could he twist affection into desire? A flutter like wings rushed through her. Passion. This magical essence was addictive. She wanted more.

Peaches swayed through her shell curtain. Feline vanity required an audience for the cleaning of paws. With one poised just beyond his nose, he glanced around. Ears flicking as if he'd just noticed the hour, he left off cleanliness for comfort, leaped onto the couch, and insinuated himself onto Beth's lap.

Nose to nose, he meowed a reprimand.

"Of course you wouldn't," Beth answered him. "You're neutered." Peaches awarded her a forgiving lick on the nose and settled down, purring.

Gordon had promised to return at dawn. After a peanut-butter and jelly sandwich at her kitchen counter, he'd claimed he was newly motivated to endure sleeping indoors. He'd come back to Gull Cott and they'd practice.

Beth smiled and rolled her neck toward one shoulder, then the other. She should take a bath and go to bed. Instead, she let herself tip over backward. The discomfited prick of Peaches' claws overrode the concussion of the wooden couch arm with her head. She'd run a bath in a minute, she thought. A minute.

In her dream, Gordon wore seal form. Kingly sable from head to tail, he eluded many hunters. Some wore old-fashioned whaling garb and wielded harpoons. Others wore wetsuits.

Haughty and swift, Gordon slipped through the sun-stabbed waters. He left the men behind, but a killer whale, big and unwieldy as a police cruiser, snapped short teeth inches from his smooth-fanned tail. A shark floated in the distance, awaiting his crimson summons.

Disdainful despite them, Gordon cut jagged paths through stands of strangling kelp, then plowed through a red tide, thick with poisonous plankton.

He dived deeper still, irritated by the inconvenience, because he was showing off, playing the rogue for a mermaid in bridal white. He rocketed through emerald-green depths. There was less light here. The mermaid fell behind as he dodged more rubber-suited divers with silver spear guns, dealing death for fun.

Now, the mermaid rode astride him, ducking her head, urging him to hide beneath a jutting rock shelf. From that dark safety, they gazed into the dizzying depths below to shipwrecks. Gordon left the shadows and swam through a galleon draped with slime and chains rusted bloodred. Pearls and emeralds littered the galleon's decks, but they were guarded by tentacled octopi and vacant-eyed sailors whose pockets leaked gold doubloons.

Laughing at the mermaid, gone ghastly pale with fear, Gordon skimmed a sea bottom pocked with caves. He eluded needle-toothed creatures in league with skindivers who hacked at him with gaffs until blood patterned his black skin like scarlet lace.

Out of the darkness a volcano pulsed, red, molten, and steady. Its rhythm was oddly soothing and lava heated the rocking waters to the napping warmth of childhood. It hardly mattered when they looked up through the cerulean layers to see the entire plate of a continent shift, teeter, and fall.

"No!" Beth snapped upright. She shoved the cat from her face and her feet to the floor before her eyes opened. "No," she muttered again and staggered toward her kitchen.

She set water to boil and took down a packet of tea. "Lapsang Souchong" it said in English. The rest of the writing was a swarm of Chinese characters, but the tea leaves' smoky fragrance was unmistakable and suited to the overcast day.

It was barely that, only four A.M., but adrenalin shook her hands. She'd never return to sleep.

Normal gray fog hung low along the shoreline. She almost expected to see Gordon striding though it, coming for her.

He wanted to marry her. The teakettle screamed and she rescued it, pouring slowly. She didn't need tea leaves to interpret her dream. Gordon would never be safe. A selkie would be pursued by dangers—ancient and modern—forever.

Beth let her thoughts steep along with the tea leaves. Gordon thought her brave, but she hadn't jumped off a cliff in years.

Unless she counted last night. For a thousand nights like that, could she withstand a lifetime of secrets? Shivers rained down her neck, pooled in her belly, and stirred a faint echo of ecstasy. Her answer was "yes."

She could stand anything to be with him, but loving Gordon would mean another child with a sometime-father.

Beth pushed her hair back, shoving aside tears as well. If she had a telephone she'd call Jack and tell him what an awful father he'd been—and how much she missed him.

She finished the tea while soaking in the bath, then pulled on sweatpants, Gordon's T-shirt, and wrote.

Hunched over the kitchen counter, she scrawled page after page. If Beth Caxton had been a tease, as Junior and every-otherdamnbody charged, her Muse had been even worse. But now poetry was flowing. The little trollop was really putting out.

When Gordon hadn't arrived by seven, Beth dressed, left the cottage unlocked, and drove to the village to call Jack.

A potpourri of waffles, bacon, and oven cleaner assailed Beth as she entered the Neptune coffee shop. Customers were few, and since she recognized none of them, Beth darted straight for the phone booth.

The telephone rang through the Bronze Iris's switchboard, into Jack's upstairs flat. Beth smiled as the receiver juggled out of its cradle. He'd still been sleeping.

"Daddy?" Beth imagined the coxcomb of hair rising on Jack's head as he scrubbed his scalp to come awake.

"No, Elizabeth, it's me," Carol answered, as crisp as white linen.

"Good morning. Can I speak with my dad?"

"You could if he weren't working. The man was up at dawn, pounding on that silly little Olivetti—"

A day for early inspiration. She could hardly wait to tell him about her macabre ocean trilogy.

"—convince him he should get a decent computer. . . ."

"Tell him I need to talk with him," Beth interrupted.

"It's your neck, dear."

Beth concentrated, sending her need through the phone cord, down the coast, across the Golden Gate to Jack.

"As expected, he won't talk." Carol's exasperation could have been directed at either of them. "If you don't need medical attention"—this time Jack's annoyance buzzed in the background—"he'll call you back."

Beth drew a breath. "He can't, but that's okay." She blinked back more tears, cleared her throat, and hoped her suddenly stuffy nose wouldn't give her away. "It wasn't important."

"Have you got Phoebe's fax yet?"

"No, the library won't be open until ten—"

"How cute. Well, expect something odious. Our city fathers are running amok, and Phoebe wanted to check with you before she took action."

Beth recalled the disastrous lunch with Phoebe and the reporter and turned queasy. "Tell Phoebe not to do anything, *say* anything, until she talks to me." Beth wondered how hard it would be to jimmy locks on a public library and get to that fax.

"I'll tell her." Carol hesitated and her voice thawed a few degrees. "Your father says to enjoy your vacation, dear."

Beth hung up. "He didn't, either," she said, with her hand still on the receiver.

Beth slipped on her sunglasses before she reached the Neptune's front door. It hadn't closed behind her before Charmaine grabbed her arm.

Charmaine's burgundy hair hung lank and her face was bare of makeup. "You haven't seen Minny, have you?" Charmaine scanned the square, fingers picking flakes of dry skin off her lips. "She must've slipped out before I woke up. I can't believe it."

Beth thought of all the times Charmaine had shunted Minny

aside so she could flirt or dance. "No. I guess I'd check with Stefanie or Horatio."

Charmaine's head already shook as she moved down the walk. "Stef's out of town and my dad's helping me look." Charmaine covered her worry with a shrug. "Karl said not to panic. No one'd take such a little brat."

Twenty-two

Gordon took his title lightly. Dark Prince, Solitary accepted his abilities—aquatic and terrestrial—as commonplace. But just now, swinging head-for-feet out of the tight cave with his waxed-wrapped bundle of clothes and wallet, he felt rather smug.

Last night another cow had been injured, struck across the face for venturing too close to a fisherman. Now he knew why.

Once he'd left Beth and resumed seal form, he'd prowled the cold shoreline twenty miles above Grey Gallows and found nothing. Coming back, he'd blamed his failure on distracting thoughts of Beth. Her slim beach-girl body had disguised surprisingly ripe breasts. Thinking of criminals was far less pleasant.

Although he hated encounters with the man who smelled of metal bars and confinement, Gordon had just resolved to ask Sheriff Reynolds what he sought with his starlight binoculars when he saw his answer.

A small boat rocked at the foot of Horatio Clark's boat ramp. Before he identified the fishermen, an avalanche of abalone shells cascaded past him. Pale-edged and shining in the underwater dimness, one floated just before him, bubbles popping through the air holes as it fell, empty, to the sea floor.

With eyes and muzzle above the waterline, Gordon drifted closer to the boat.

"I know nothin' about it and I want keep it that way. That's why you're not using my dock."

Seal acuity layered the dock's creak, the ragged rasp of rope on metal and the smell of abalone, over the human voices. He took minutes to recognize the speaker as Horatio, Charmaine's father and Minny's grandfather. By then, others whispered and rearranged heavy gunnysacks. Over it all hung the oily stench of the boat's engine.

The man whose car had nearly struck Beth's outside the village store was here. Roo. And the enemy called Sloan. Another male smelled so familiar, Gordon coasted closer to be sure.

"We're talkin' the filet mignon of . . . forty bucks apiece." Coughing covered half Al's words. The man had taken no care with his recovery. "One night's haul for three of us, when *they* ain't nosing around . . ." Al's voice faded under the shifting of metal oxygen tanks.

"I don't care about none of it." It was Horatio again. "Just tell me if Junior's involved."

"Couldn't exactly say—?"

"Hell, no—"

The voices came too fast. Without daylight and faces, the conversation wasn't worth his time. He'd heard enough to know the men were trafficking in something illegal and profitable.

But he hadn't hunted tonight. Appetizing as his peanut-butter sandwich had been, with Beth sitting next to him, licking raspberry jam from a fingertip when she thought he wasn't looking, it was hardly a meal. Although abalone were kelp snails inaccessible to seals, they smelled delicious. He imagined the cows trailing the men as they shucked the mollusks, and Gordon wished Al would spill just one overboard.

Now, buttoning his white shirt behind Lyre Rock, Gordon wondered whether he should share his discovery with Beth. This was why her cove was being watched. He'd rather she had the news from him than feisty Bob Reynolds.

Gordon zipped his jeans and scanned the beach. According to Junior, Gordon had already ruined Beth's reputation, but it wouldn't matter much longer. Without saying the actual words, Beth had pledged herself to him.

Gordon crossed the beach, feeling lucky Beth couldn't read his mind. He could not conceal his pride at winning the bet with Junior just hours after it was made!

Smugness was a nasty human trait, certainly beneath his dignity, but love's taming properties were fleeting. He wanted to blare victory like the randiest bull seal. Instead, he'd take her once again. Maybe twice. This time, without magic.

Gordon drew a cautioning breath as he climbed the rough-cut stairs up the bluff. Any male would have done the same. Beth had clearly been willing. She'd only needed a little nudge to release her passion.

The fog had burned off and he smelled flowers turning into fruit on Beth's blackberry bushes. Her roof shingles were nailed down with military precision and the Dumpster had been hauled away. Beth's scent said she was outside, perhaps on the deck.

Gordon stopped for a minute. Falsehood came hard when he talked with Beth. He pounded his fist against his sore thigh, hardening himself to face her.

He didn't believe in secrets between mates, so he'd told her most of his. He'd explained exactly how to get to his underwater locker, should the need ever arise. He'd told her he feared nothing, except captivity. He couldn't lie. If Beth asked about the magic he'd—distract her.

When he rounded the corner of the cottage, Beth looked up from her writing, startled. She dropped the yellow pad, pushed up from the canvas chair, and smiled. Her hair was confined in a braid that swung in an arc as she took two steps. Then she stopped, restraining her gladness.

She wore pink. It was called a sun-dress, he thought. It scooped low over her breasts, bared her tanned arms and legs, and ended at about the level his T-shirt had.

The blackberry blossoms must be interfering with his inhalations. A selkie prince couldn't be such a romantic that his mate's beauty stopped his very breath.

"I came for my bedding lessons."

Beth's pupils pooled wide before she answered.

"Did you?" She raised an eyebrow. "You must have been misinformed, Mr. Gordon. I don't give bedding lessons."

He celebrated her humor. In spite of his pride, he'd feared that awful human habit: regret.

Beth looked down, touched the back of her hair, and firmed her lips against further amusement.

"Will you at least kiss me?" He touched her palms with his, linked their fingers, and watched her resistance fade.

The first kiss kindled their wanting and Beth pushed him away. "I'm not taking my clothes off."

"Miss Caxton, I'm shocked." He nuzzled her neck, then nipped it, letting her hear his rumbling approval.

"You're an animal!" She clapped a hand over her mouth, backing away as if she'd uttered the forbidden.

"We've already established that." He kept her hand and licked it.

"And abnormal." She giggled.

"That, too." He inched the zipper down her spine as he backed her across the deck to her bedroom.

"No, really." Beth's eyebrows lowered. She looked very stern. "I promised the bedding lessons, but nothing else."

"Why?" The back of Gordon's neck tightened as her mirth drained away.

"We'll talk about it later." She took his hand and opened the sliding door.

"We'll talk about it now." He sat on the deck. Resolute, he searched for a clue, then snagged a handful of yellow pages. "Is it this? Am I distracting you from your work?"

Her shrug was like a dare. "It's not ready to read," she warned, crossing her arms. "You won't like it."

He read it just the same. Sometime later he looked up and Beth still stood in the doorway, arms crossed. Gordon touched his face, as if he could feel what she'd been watching.

"Well?" she asked as if the word tasted bitter on her tongue.

"It's scary—"

"Is it?" Beth looked delighted.

"—but sometimes the sea is like that." He looked down, trying not to think of Beth's tongue. She came to read over his shoulder. "And I have to admit some sentimental nonsense I picked up from television makes me glad you worry over my safety."

Beth's hands rested on both his shoulders. Her soap and tea smell made him wish he'd come ashore earlier. She leaned forward and kissed his hair. "For you there is no safety. That's the point."

It seemed a mundane subject for poetry. Of course there was no safety. For anyone. Why did it cloud her voice with gloom?

"The ending needs a little work," he said.

"It does?"

He should have heard it. Beth's affront clicked stiff as bones, but he was well into his joke before he noticed.

"This—" He ran his finger over the final line. "What is this—tectonic plates?" He laughed and grabbed for hands that had lifted from his shoulders. "If I'm struck by a drifting continent, we have no future at all!"

"You're right," she said. Then she was gone. One taunting edge of the pink skirt flicked around the door, before the latched locked.

"Beth, I'm sorry." Gordon laughed as she drew the curtains in front of his face. "Beth!" He jogged around to the front door in time to hear her turn the dead bolt.

"Stubborn wench." Smiling, he walked to the back of the cottage and levered a stick between the frame and screen on the window above her bed.

He dropped the screen and flung himself over the sill far enough to see her. Beth sat on the edge of the bed, unbuckling her sandals, considering his contortions.

"You know what Brendan Behan said." Beth gave him room to somersault onto the bed.

"Who?" He rubbed the back of his neck. All in all, he preferred acrobatics done in water.

"It's what he said about guys like you that matters. 'Critics are like eunuchs in a harem. They're there every night, they see how it should be done—' "

Beth's eyes widened as he came after her, but human reactions made her too slow to escape. Gordon dumped her onto her back and loomed over her on all fours.

"Go on," he said.

She shook her head, laughing until her green eyes misted with tears and her body shook.

"Afraid I'll take it as a dare? I'll bet it ends with something like 'but they can't do it themselves.' Is that it?"

"Something like that."

"You have an appallingly short memory, love. This time I'll have to see you don't forget."

With one hand he braceleted her wrists above her head, then rolled beneath her, reversing their positions.

Beth straddled him, flushed and panting from resisting. "I'm not taking off my clothes."

"That's entirely up to you." Her dress slanted over one shoulder, loose from where he'd unzipped it.

And then Beth's face went blurry. Gordon blinked. The walls behind her wavered. The ceiling plummeted down to trap him.

"Gordon?" Beth's fingers skimmed his clammy brow.

"This is what should worry you." He swallowed deliberately, keeping his eyes closed against the threat of entrapment. "Not sharks and shifting land masses."

The bed dipped as Beth crawled up beside him.

"Am I going to hear about that one lousy metaphor for the rest of my life?" She curled beneath his arm like a nestling, though she was the one giving comfort.

"I hope so." Dizziness receded as Beth kissed his jaw. He fingered the tiny bump of bone at the top of her shoulder and decided to replace her sighs with gasps of excitement. As soon as the room stopped spinning.

"I've thought of several ways to attack this problem. First, we're going to play camp-out.'' Beth drew the yellow sheet over their heads. ''Hold its edge. Tight. Now, bend your knees.''

The cure sounded tolerable so he obeyed her order. He bent his knees and parted them, imagining Beth betwixt. ''Now what?''

''That's all.''

Dissatisfied, Gordon looked at the sheet suspended over the tent-poles of their legs. Warm sunshine streamed through, but Beth's nearness was enough to turn their jaundiced world sultry. ''It's pleasant enough, but the ambiance would improve if you took off your clothes.''

''Gordon.'' Her stern tone returned. ''Do you feel sick?''

''Not at all.'' Only lecherous, but he stifled the words to let Beth exult.

''Then it's time for step two.'' She edged closer, avoiding his lips. ''Keep looking up at our tent.''

She did something silky to his cheek.

''That's a butterfly kiss.'' Beth's eyelashes brushed at varying speeds, tickling and arousing. ''Now you do it.

He did, and Beth moaned as if she were melting. ''Mmmm . . . Careful. Keep holding the sheet.''

''No.'' He pressed full-length against her. ''I have a theory these butterfly kisses can be applied to better effect somewhere besides your cheek.'' He stretched toward her drooping bodice. ''I mean to test that theory if you'll just settle down.''

''You don't want our tent to fall,'' she cautioned.

''I don't care about the bloody tent.''

''You're feeling all right?'' Beth's voice caught as he butterflied past her collarbone.

''Splendid.'' As his hand slid under her skirt, his belly grabbed, but not with nausea.

''Then it's time for step three.'' Beth's arms curled over his neck and her bare ankles locked around his waist. ''I read about this once,'' she whispered.

''And to think there are humans who believe books are a waste of time.'' More than Beth's arms opened to him. Her mind embraced his, and though her impatience made him rejoice, he caught a knife-glint of desperation. Gordon quelled it with a fierce kiss, crushing any hint she wasn't his. The time for joking had passed.

Possession felt good. Gordon's leg covered hers as if it belonged there. Perspiration sheened his face, and silvery starbursts surrounded black pupils as he tried to pierce her thoughts. "Will you marry me, Beth?"

Why hadn't she covered his lips before he asked?

He tightened his leg over hers as she edged away. "Is it because I'm not human?" That fast, afterglow turned into anger. "Can't you stand the secrecy? Are you still unconvinced our child will be fine? Is it all right to open your body, to make love with me, but not *talk* to me? You're no coward, Beth. What is it?"

"Maybe I am a coward because I won't let you do to our child what Jack did to me."

Gordon frowned, shaking his head as if she made excuses.

"I told you I was always alone. I didn't go to school since Jack didn't want to disappoint me by skipping Christmas pageants because he was hip-deep in a play." She pushed her bangs from her eyes. "This isn't about self-pity. It's about what I *want*."

"And you want a normal housewife-and-mother existence?"

"That's right!"

"Who do you think you're fooling?" As he sat up to face her, his hard-sculpted chest became a barricade. "You slink around San Francisco, write poetry here at the ends of the earth, and even if you don't count me, who are the men in your life? Cops and war correspondents? Have you ever dated an accountant, Beth?"

"I don't want my child lonely, and I don't want to lose her to the sea."

In the other room Peaches rubbed against the front door, mewing. Before her, Gordon looked as if he finally heard. His dread made it real. *Oh, Gordon, don't leave me. Just try to understand.* But he'd quit listening.

"*Her*, Beth?" He took her fingers with old-fashioned courtesy. "Doesn't that *she* makes her so real, you can't resist creating her? I wouldn't take her away. Even with my magic."

Guilt swept his face and Beth knew it had nothing to do with their future. She left the bed, separating herself from him. "Gordon, what was different about today, compared to last night?"

He didn't pretend to misunderstand. He swung his legs from the bed and stood before her. His lips tightened in a flash of male restlessness, that drive to move on rather than face conflict. Whatever he saw on her face made Gordon turn.

"Did you use your magic against me? Did you?"

Sophisticated Mr. Gordon, millionaire patron of the arts, would have lied quite smoothly. "Not against you."

"Damn it, Gordon. You can't just wield your magic because you feel like"—why did she whisper when she should have shouted?—"screwing."

A muscle in his jaw flinched. "You came to me freely. I know you did." He touched her shoulders, not with violence, but pleading. "Beth you gave yourself to me."

"How much of that was magic and how much—"

" 'Was love'? I see, it's all right to wield that sort of magic at *your* whim."

"It's not magic."

"It is to me."

Outside, the sound of footfalls was unmistakable. Someone climbed the rough-cut steps to Gull Cott. Though Gordon's eyes didn't leave her, his tenderness did.

"How ironic." His self-mockery cut as if he carved each word with a knife. "All this time, I thought you'd have to steal my skin to keep me captive. Instead, all you had to do was love me, then change your mind."

"Gordon we've only known each other two weeks. And I love you. I do, but you can't expect me to say 'yes.' Not yet."

"This isn't a choice." His hand spanned her forehead, holding her temples in another kind of possession. "How do I convince that skeptical human brain that with the entire Pacific coast to chose from, I came ashore in Grey Gallows because your soul whispered to mine. With every stroke toward your cove, I heard it. When I walked ashore, your soul rejoiced. I was a child, too, Beth, and I couldn't wait to find you.''

He waited, forcing her to remember those hours alone on the bluff when she'd stared out to sea, searching foam-veined waters until her vision blurred and how she'd leapt from rocky outcroppings, diving with the seals in sunshine and in storms.

''What drew you, Beth? That day, I told you to remember me, but I didn't have to. Your every cell recognized me. You couldn't forget. It's why you waited.''

Knuckles fell tentatively on her front door.

''I have to think. That's the purpose of an engagement. We could—''

''I see. You want to be friends.''

''Of course.'' Beth watched him, suspicious of this sudden rationality. ''Always.''

''Let's do that. We can still go out for lunch, I suppose.''

''Well, yes—''

''And I can telephone you, when I feel lonely?''

''I—''

''And what about Christmas cards, Beth? Between friends who've mated in every way except marriage, who've *loved* each other, are Christmas cards quite appropriate?''

The knocking came more loudly. ''Beth? Hello?'' A woman's voice carried from the front door.

That rainy day Gordon had stared from her kitchen window, reflected rain streaking a face longing for the sea, for his real home, right then, she'd known the truth.

''You'd hate me, Gordon. If I kept making you choose land over sea, you'd come to hate me.''

''Irrelevant.'' His hands gripped her shoulders once more. This time it hurt. ''God, if I could shake some sense into you—''

''Don't force me.''

''I've had enough.''

''That hurts.''

''Decide, now!'' He shook her, all pleading gone. ''The facts will never change!''

"Then, *go!*" Her shout shocked them both. The knocking stopped.

When Gordon took her face in one hand, she winced. But his fingers fanned gently over her cheek. His thumb rested under her chin, framing her face as he sorted through her thoughts to make sure. She believed in his magic, just not enough.

Gordon's eyes wouldn't let her pretend. She'd forged this pain and stabbed him with it.

Beth had read that when a star burned out, its diamond brilliance blazed, consumed its own heart, then collapsed in on itself and dimmed to nothing.

She turned away from Gordon's dark eyes and answered the door.

When Beth returned, the sliding door stood open and Gordon had gone.

She folded the fax Lucinda had delivered. From Phoebe, it listed the city council's grievances against the city's theaters. Parking, panhandlers, and price problems must be resolved before the fall season. At best, it meant the delay of Jack's new play. At worst, the Foghorn would close its doors. Beth tried to care.

Surrendering Gordon had been Right. She thought of Solomon taking a child claimed by two mothers, offering to give each woman *half*. When one said, "No, don't hurt him. I was wrong," Solomon awarded the child to her, since she'd acted out of love.

The ivory curtains rose in fluttering praise, the ghost of what almost was. She'd returned Gordon to his first world, instead of rending his heart in two. How marvelously noble.

At her bedside, Beth found a check made out to Jack Caxton, in support of his work. Beneath the check, she found a note written on her yellow pad. Her first note from Gordon, and her last.

The sun hid behind a cloud, making her room as dark as twilight. And cold. Sitting to read, Beth turned on her lamp.

You mustn't think that because things ended so badly,
our time was wasted. Perhaps sea and shore must stay

separate after all. I only know I would not exchange one hour with you, for an entire lifetime alone.

If this was how nobility felt, she wanted to die a selfish coward.

Twenty-three

Within an hour Beth had joined the search for Minny. As usual, the town at midday seemed almost deserted, except for Charmaine. In jeans and a faded T-shirt, Charmaine motioned Beth to stop in front of Gimp's.

"Turns out she's really lost. Really gone." Charmaine's hands moved relentlessly, right hand over the back of the left, scraping with her nails.

"Charmaine, I'll do—"

"You know, it's weird. I can tell you the first time she rolled over and when she got her first tooth, but I guess there's no telling about last times." Charmaine wiped the back of her hand against her jeans.

"Like, last night, my back hurt from stocking on the low shelves and I had a headache and Minny wanted me to read her a story we've read ten million times. You know what I said?" Charmaine met Beth's eyes for the first time. "I said, 'Can't I have one minute for myself? Go watch TV.'" Charmaine's laugh was black and mirthless. "Mom," she called over her shoulder, "I'm going back to the beach."

"Honey?" Jewel sat at a card table positioned outside Gimp's open from door. Charmaine kept walking.

"Should I go with her?" Beth asked.

"No." Jewel's white whale's-spout ponytail wobbled as she motioned Beth to study the Grey Gallows map taped to the table.

"Lucinda and Junior are walking the beach, too, but no one's gone door-to-door. What if you take this two-block rectangle?"

"Whatever you need, Jewel." Beth wished for Gordon, for his protective instinct and affinity with Minny. The little girl probably sat somewhere, playing with a stray kitten or bugs or colored rocks. Probably.

Jewel had inked the map into sections. Her very organization chilled Beth, but she followed Jewel's fingertip as she explained.

"From Surf Street, turn right on Lanai. Do both sides of the street as far as the dirt road. Down at that end, there's only Sloan's house and what's left of Junior and Al's.

"Keep your wits about you, there." Jewel glanced behind her, into the bar. "Sloan pals around with some motorcycle types—"

As if Jewel's worry called him, Horatio came out of Gimp's tavern. "I'm stayin' near the phone, but maybe we'll send one of the men. I just hate to wait."

"I'll be fine. I live in San Francisco, remember? Besides, I'm wearing my running shoes." Beth's tears had left her with a stuffy nose. "Allergies," she sniffed in answer to Jewel's raised eyebrow, and Horatio moved back inside as Jewel continued.

"Then come down this way, on Whitecap Drive, and back up Surf. I'll send someone after you if Minny comes home first."

They both looked up, hopeful, as a car approached. Karl's palomino Cadillac jerked to a stop. Hands in the pockets of his double-knit slacks, Karl traversed the gangplank toward them.

"You women are wasting your time with schemes and tactics." He waved a hand over the map. "She'll come home when she's hungry."

"Minny's not a dog, Karl." Beth's anger blew like a cool breeze over her grieving. It felt great.

"Of course not, but I know kids. She'll turn up."

Karl's Humpty-Dumpty body and small feet would make him easy to knock over. Beth felt adrenaline fizz in her veins.

"How long's she been missing, anyhow?" Karl turned to Horatio, who'd just moved into the dim doorway behind his wife.

Jewel pulled a tissue from the pocket of her khaki pants and squeezed it as she spoke. "Charmaine got up about eight, so five hours now. Horatio and I rolled out at four, as usual. Oh, why didn't we look in on her?" Jewel took the coffee mug Horatio handed over her shoulder. For an instant their hands met. "We're always quiet, so we won't wake them. What a terrible mistake."

It wouldn't comfort Jewel to say they couldn't have known. Instead, Beth moved closer, leaning against Jewel, just a little.

"They say the first four hours are critical in a kidnapping." Jewel closed her eyes against nightmare images.

"That kidnapping nonsense has got to stop," Karl insisted.

"Don't go ordering my wife." Horatio moved toe-to-toe with the shopkeeper. "I won't have it."

"Sorry." Karl jingled the keys in his pocket. "You haven't gone bothering Bob Reynolds, have you? He's due back from Parish any time, now."

"Bothering him?" Beth's disbelieving laugh burned her throat. "You *are* a piece of work."

"I'm not unsympathetic." Karl tugged his shirt, blousing it over a belt let out to its last notch.

Beth snatched up a stack of flyers photocopied at the library. Filling her hands might keep her from wrapping her fingers around Karl's pudgy throat. The flyers bore a portrait of Minny and Charmaine, heads leaned together, licking over-sized lollipops.

"Pretty soon—" Karl gestured toward the Sable Bay bill-board. "This town'll have its own police station, preschool, maybe even a rec center, and we won't have problems like this."

"*This* has never happened before," Horatio sputtered.

"All those improvements from a name change?" Beth demanded. She turned to walk away, then recoiled, letting Karl go first.

Unruffled, Karl started toward his Cadillac. "Sable Bay's just the beginning. A classy name brings in developers and investors."

If his customers doubled, wouldn't he have to expand the Village Store and bring it up to city standards? Who would loan him that kind of money?

At his car, Karl looked up and down the street. For once, there wasn't a lumber truck in sight. "Hey, Jewel," he said, impulsively. "Have you talked to that Gordon fellow?"

"You're right." Jewel studied Beth. "He'd be a good one to ask. Minny likes him so much."

"Wish I could figure where he's anchored." Horatio rubbed his chin. "Beth, d'you know?"

"It wouldn't matter. He'll be gone for a while." Or maybe forever. There's no telling about last times. Beth swallowed hard. If you really believed it was the last time, you wouldn't let it happen.

Karl already sat in his car, so his muttering was indistinct. "I don't like the sound of that."

Beth thought that was what he said, but he couldn't have. Even from Karl, it made absolutely no sense.

Junior's old stomping ground had changed. Beth skirted a small, unidentifiable roadkill and kept walking. While it would be politically correct to call this a working-class neighborhood, it would not be accurate. Whether you blamed overfishing, ocean pollution or the high school drop-out rate, there were too many young men lounging on rickety porches and under jacked-up cars, out of work and out of luck.

Until she'd climbed the porch, Beth didn't realize the first one, smoking and drinking beer in the shade, wore only jockey shorts.

"Have you seen her?" Beth extended the flyer and examined peeling paint above his head. The guy sized her up and watched her leave, before looking at the flyer.

Beth might have missed the second man. Flat under a truck on what looked like half a skateboard, he was hidden, but his headphones blared Willie Nelson so loudly, Beth could have sung along. She squatted to look underneath, surprising him enough that his head slammed on the car's undercarriage before he rolled out to talk.

He happened to know Junior and Charmaine.

"Oh, man, oh, man." He ran a greasy hand over his head, then yelled to a neighbor slinging rubbish into a trailer and hailed a woman across the street.

She wore white lipstick, a perpetual tan, and a bandanna over peroxided hair. Abandoning a push lawn mower with a broken handle, she stepped gingerly on hot asphalt to join them.

"Charmaine's baby? Oh, no." She kept turning the flyer over to its blank side. "We'll help ya look." She turned from Beth and shouted with hands cupped to her lips. "Kelly! Jason! Nicole! Turn off that damned Nintendo and get your lazy butts out here. Kelly, go back and get your brother. Now! You got something better to do."

By the time Beth reached the end of the block, she felt like the Pied Piper, except her followers had dispersed throughout Grey Gallows, shouting and honking for Minny. She rushed past the charred skeleton of Junior's house, then hesitated before a faded pink bungalow with a sagging gate and a yard spiked with cacti.

Roo's Ram Charger glittered in the oil-spotted driveway. A black and silver Harley Davidson held court a few steps beyond. It must be Sloan's house. She followed male voices and braying talk radio toward the garage.

The door was set in a track. Before she could knock, it rolled open a foot. Heavy-lidded and sullen, Sloan fit himself into the space, pinched the end of a joint of marijuana, and offered it.

"No, thanks," Beth said. Behind Sloan, Roo appeared and

rolled the door open farther. A quick glimpse showed a refrigerator, diving tanks and Al MacDonald. "I just came by
to see if you've heard about Minny. She's missing."

"Aw, no." Al ruffled his hair, frowning. He shouldered past
Sloan in spite of the younger man's bristling.

Al was an older outlaw, if not meaner. Sloan didn't scare
him a bit. Beth couldn't imagine Al hanging out, smoking
dope, so why was he here?

"I'll help look," Al said. "You guys finish up."

Sloan clearly didn't like taking orders, but Roo would obviously follow whoever led.

A helicopter swooped overhead, low enough to inspect
hedges, backyards, and cars.

"The village'll be crawling with cops." Sloan squinted
against the rotor-stirred dust and thumped Roo's chest, when
he flipped off the pilot.

"That for her?" Al shaded his eyes, watching.

"I don't know." Beth shielded her nose and mouth. The
helicopter stirred such manic wind, she nearly choked on the
stench of fish guts.

She saw nothing in the garage now, but once, there'd been
a lot of something. Some guys got lucky, even when fishing
was bad.

"I've got to get going," she said.

"Al." Sloan jerked his head toward the garage.

"I'll be with you in a minute, hon." Al coughed, hand flat
on his chest. "Don't go 'way," He followed Roo into the
garage.

"See you soon." Sloan drew the door shut behind them.

Beth caught bits of talk about careless jackasses, weighing-
in, and Karl. She smelled lingering odors of fast food, diesel
exhaust, and solder. But none of those caused her jittery hands.
A single question did: Why was Sloan wearing a handgun
stuck in the back waistband of his jeans?

Complaining of ravenous hunger, Roo fidgeted alongside Al
and Beth as far as Whitecap Drive. Then he sprinted ahead.

"Out *there*, right?" Roo asked.

Al seemed to understand. "Right. Tell him we think Thursday, not Tuesday!" Al shouted, before turning to Beth. "That kid'd forget his head if it weren't screwed on."

When they reached Surf Street, barricades with flashing lights formed roadblocks. In under two hours the village had filled with volunteers and law enforcement, all searching for Minny Clark.

In snatches, she heard the news. Lucinda told how every inch of the Clark's house had been examined and marked with crime-scene tape. The harbor had been staked out by deputies. One of the Fleurettes bemoaned the fact that Stefanie had left for Santa Cruz, just when they really needed her to help search, today.

"Do you know her number?" Beth couldn't help thinking Stefanie's incisive mind might have something to contribute.

"Of course." The teenager dipped into her shoulder bag and retrieved a leather-bound datebook fit for a diploma. She transcribed Stefanie's number onto a slip of paper. "Tell her Tiffany said 'hi.' "

Beth offered the number to Horatio, but he swore he'd called the parents of each of Minny's playmates and said he'd be double-dog damned if he'd call some teenager a hundred miles off.

Gimp kept vigil at the playground, near Minny's favorite swing, and asked Beth to search the library.

Glad to escape the helicopter's racket, Beth investigated the library's stacks and storeroom, even peering under Lucinda's desk and Bob Reynolds's. It surprised her to find the sheriff's desk in the library, but she supposed Grey Gallows was short on office space.

Sitting at Bob's desk, feeling a little like an interloper, Beth called the number Tiffany had given her.

"Hey, babe, this is Stef—"

"Stefanie, this is Beth Caxton—"

"—settling into my new chateau, so leave a message after the beep and I'll—"

"Damn." Beth wished she had a number to leave, but it probably didn't matter. "This is Beth Caxton . . ." Horatio had been right. No matter how bright, Stefanie couldn't help from Santa Cruz. "Never mind."

Who else? Beth tapped her fingers on the neatly organized desk. In San Francisco, she'd have a dozen contacts.

Feeling childish, she dialed Jack's number. Not that *he* could do anything. She just wanted to tell him what a jerk he'd been this morning, refusing to speak to her when she needed him.

"Bronze Iris." The lovely voice proved Carol still liked to keep an Englishwoman on the switchboard.

"Sorry, wrong number." Beth hung up.

Dusk gripped the village as Beth emerged from the library. The village square had been commandeered by the Methodist women, who served coffee and sandwiches to volunteers by the light of camping lanterns. From the beach, tweeting whistles accompanied calls of "Minny." Boats armed with searchlights moved out to sea.

Beth stood in front of Gimp's, arms crossed, shivering, though it must have been seventy degrees. Her Fiat sat hemmed in on all sides, but she didn't plan to leave.

A million times since noon, she'd thought *Gordon*, but repeating his name hadn't charmed Minny home. The inside of her skull felt gritty and her eyelids stung. She couldn't imagine what she should do next.

"Sure as shit, she's drowned." Junior materialized beside her. Swaying, but cold sober, he draped an arm over her shoulder as if he needed a crutch.

"I don't think so, Junior. Minny was born here. She knows to be careful."

"Kids get busy with their own stuff." Junior sighed. "Charmaine says Minny's little orange basketball is missing. She likes to roll it on the wet sand. I never really thought she was mine, until Charmaine said that. Why's that, do you suppose?"

They stood silent as Bob Reynolds, clipping a pager onto his belt, strode toward them.

"Forgot to tell you, Beth Ann, I'm a suspect. Sorry you were seen with me."

All business, Bob Reynolds ignored Junior's sarcasm. He scrutinized Beth, instead. "I need Gordon's last name."

"I really don't—"

"That's not good enough." Reynolds shook his head. A pair of handcuffs swayed on his utility belt and he wore a gunbelt.

"Why are you looking for him?" Beth asked. *Damn, Karl.*

" 'Cause of our fight." Junior huffed a scornful laugh. "Jeez, it was nothing."

"He's an unknown quantity with a grudge." Reynolds's voice started level, then turned clipped and cold. "He's also disgruntled and gone. Plus, he's shown interest in the little girl."

"He—" Outrage slammed Beth. "He was nice to her, I'll admit that. He kept her from getting hit by one of those damned logging trucks. He kept her out of the path of the Wheel! How can you—That's the worst thing, the *worst* thing you could accuse a man—"

Bob Reynolds made hushing movements. They only inflamed her further, but Beth lowered her voice.

"It's idiotic." She swiveled toward the Village Store. "Karl's the one you better put in protective custody. If he turned up dead, everyone in town'd be on your suspect list."

"That's not a damned bit funny," Reynolds snapped.

"You're right—" Beth stopped at his grim frown.

"I'm putting an APB out on your friend. If you see him, tell him to front up to me. Immediately."

Junior directed Beth as she backed her Fiat through a knot of cars and past a signpost. Next, he'd meet Al and join the coastal search. Beth was going home.

"Gimp's planned a summoning for tomorrow morning at nine." Junior jammed his hands in his pockets and kicked the cement base of the signpost.

Beth faltered, afraid to ask. "What's a 'summoning'?"

"Aw, hell." Junior ruffled his hair as Al had earlier. "I don't know. Some Grey Gallows custom or a Scottish thing. They did it when my mom disappeared." He stared skyward, into the uncaring night. "People sing and Gimp plays his pipes at the edge of the sea. It's supposed—'' Junior's voice cracked. ''The sea's supposed to give her back. God. I wouldn't come if I were you.''

''About nine?'' Beth turned her key in the ignition. If she left, the anger growing out of his helplessness might not erupt.

''I won't be there.'' He kicked the signpost viciously, then slammed his fist into the wood. ''She's so damn little. Thirty-five pounds, *thirty-five!* My oilskins weigh more than that.'' He cradled his bleeding fist with the other hand and blinked down at the damage. ''Christ, that helped a lot.''

''Do you want me—''

''I've got stuff to wrap it.'' He motioned toward the dock, shuffled away from her, then glanced back. ''Thanks, Beth Ann.''

''I'll look down my road, too,'' Beth called as she drove past. ''I'm not giving up.''

Beth's headlights hunted through each tuft of weeds. She called ''Minny!'' letting her wheels bump along on momentum alone, listening. She heard a curlew and a distant grumble of thunder, but nothing more.

She finally stopped, switched off the key, but still sat in the car. She bowed her head, let her fingernails bite into the leather-wrapped steering wheel, and prayed. ''Please God, it's not fair.'' She thought of Minny's pink kitty T-shirt, of Minny riding Gordon's shoulders around the bonfire, of Minny waving her magic wand to make a wish.

Beth pressed her hand against her heart. Like some small animal, it battered against her breastbone, trying to get out and escape the pain. ''It's just not fair.''

Without glancing toward her cove, Beth walked to Gull Cott and went inside. She fed Peaches, poured a glass of red wine, then left it sitting. She turned on the light in her bedroom. His note and the check sat on her bedside table. Her bed sheets lay rumpled from his body. She didn't throw herself into them, didn't breath his scent on her pillow. Beth stood in the door-way with her hands hanging limp.

Finally she walked back to the living room and sat on the

couch. She shifted mussel shells and a sand dollar in her hands. She finished the shepherd's crown she'd woven from weeds, stem through stem through stem, then brushed a few grains of sand into her hand. She let them fall on the rug as she took up the piece of mottled driftwood.

Beth caressed the natural sculpture, remembering Gordon's hands, smoothing this wood already polished by waves. They'd both thought the driftwood looked like a seal pup. Since that day, she'd thought of it as nothing else.

She decided to sleep on the couch, because she couldn't stand any more heartache. Not tonight.

Twenty-four

~~

Gordon left the cows safe at Moon Isle and spent the night looking for trouble. Near Beth's cove he found an abandoned inner tube anchored above yellow plastic ropes, but the ropes only led to gunnysacks. Abalone, again. The big kelp snails lay inside, starving, until the men who'd hunted them returned.

It made no sense to catch prey and leave it, unless their taking was a secret. Were the mollusks out of season? Was there a limit on taking them? He'd ask—*Beth.*

In fact, he'd ask no one. He wouldn't go ashore again in Grey Gallows.

Gordon swam one more turn around the sacks, then wheeled away, unraveling their puzzle for himself. The Neptune coffee shop served abalone meat in its chowder. He'd seen it listed on the menu, and knew Sheriff Reynolds drank coffee there, every day. So harvesting abalone couldn't be illegal. Still, Stefanie had told Beth abalone was in short supply, when just last night he'd counted twenty sets of shells heaped beneath Sloan's boat.

This prey explained the divers and disruption but not the injured cows. He searched on, for something more sinister.

Not that the cows demanded his protection. More than ever, their deference isolated him, reminded him that in the

absence of a selkie, females faced males only two weeks each
year.

Most liked it that way. Gordon banked around a thicket of
kelp, arrowing toward Beth's cove. Despite the danger, some
of the cows returned there out of habit.

Gordon dived deep. Only when his lungs burned did he
burst up with unwavering certainty. He shattered the surface
into a million silver drops, aiming for the sun's flat glimmer,
then crashed nose down between the waves.

In the instant spray turned to water, Gordon saw her. He
returned to the surface, shaking droplets into a haze around
him.

She balanced on the lip of the bluff in a red bathing suit,
one defiant splash of color against the dawn.

Gordon swam back and forth, prowling, anxious. She stood
straight, resolved as if she had nothing to lose.

No. He'd told her she was *not* a coward. He'd said he *admired* her bravery. She couldn't possibly have taken that for
a dare.

Gordon swam closer, chest moving prowlike through the
waves, unable to look away.

Beth's upper arms covered her ears. Her fingers pointed like
the tip of a candle flame. Dull pewter sky crowded close, pushing her toward the tentacles of fog.

Careful, love.

A hundred miles offshore a storm waited and Beth listened.
Her mind reached out, longing—but not for him. She yearned
to know the waves' language, so she wouldn't fail.

This time Beth wouldn't welcome his rescue. She was taking a leap of faith only she understood.

Beth's knees flexed. A rippling pool shone blue amid froth-
ing waters and she aimed for it. The balls of her feet launched
her up, out. An afterimage of scarlet hung on the air as the
ocean swallowed her.

Eyes wide, Gordon dived in time to see her arch away from
the ocean's floor. Her hair fanned mermaid gold. Her tidy kick
propelled her toward the surface.

Beth. Her victorious smile vanished as she searched for him.

Bubbles streamed from her lips, wrapping her neck, spangling her shoulders and clasped-close arms.

Gordon released Beth's mind from his and let her continue rising. It was too late to claim what might have been. Beth was safe, so he left her.

Taking deep triumphant breaths, Beth waded ashore and approached the velvet clump with the zest of a woman whose salvage rights included any rare jetsam washed into her cove. At first, she thought it was crumpled finery, shed during Midsummer revels. Then the bump fixed her with huge liquid eyes. It was a seal pup.

Where was its mother? Seals were good mothers, and though they left to hunt, the pups usually banded together. This one lay all alone.

The pup's panicked cries stopped Beth several yards off. She hunched over, hoping the baby would see her as an oddly-shaped adult seal and be less afraid.

Unlike the animals that usually rested in her cove, this pup wore a mottled cream and silver coat, with a white patch on its chest. It was another kind of seal altogether, maybe a harbor seal, and it was hungry. Its little head cocked back with open mouth and free-flowing tears.

"I'm sorry, baby," Beth crooned. She had nothing for it. The baby was almost certainly too young for solid food. Besides, the canned tuna in her kitchen barely resembled fish.

The pup pushed its sad kitten face against her palm, seeking milk. "You just need your mama, don't you?"

Beth recalled hearing of a seal pup raised on "milkshakes" of whipping cream and fish oil. She had neither at hand. Besides, the pup scooted backward, discouraging her attempts at affection.

Beth went a little way up the path, deserting the beach so the babe's mother might return. That didn't please the pup, either. He complained like a tiny engine trying to start.

Beth watched the pup rock from side to side, clearly distressed. She must get into town and call the aquarium in San

Francisco. They'd know what to do, but she hated to leave.

What about the Great White Shark who'd already killed one pup? And bull seals whose vicious disregard for pups was commonplace? And what about the eerie summoning she must attend before doing anything else?

Gordon would know what to do, but Gordon was gone.

"All right, baby." She spotted a peaceful niche with sun-dappled rocks and a patch of shade, out of the tugging winds. "I'm going to tuck you out of harm's way." Beth approached slowly, refusing to let the pup's cries keep her back. "Your mom will find you. Don't worry."

The pup fought, wagging and wriggling its beagle-sized body from side to side, but Beth hung on.

"Come on, sweetie, come on." Beth almost lost her grip. Risking a bite, she imitated the tenderness she'd seen between mother seals and their young. Beth rubbed her cheek alongside the pup's. It quieted. In that serene moment, she hid the pup and fell in love with it.

"Pretty sad." She backed away, remembering other times she'd felt that soft nuzzling.

Pushed one inadvertent step by the mounting wind, Beth planted her feet against it. She would not give in to sentiment or superstition. Her response to the helpless creature was silly, and entirely Gordon's fault.

"Once in a hundred generations," Gordon had told her, so this waif couldn't possibly be another selkie. And as for that mystic hope that the babe could be Minny . . . She'd really tipped headlong into madness if she believed that.

The pup rebuked her with its putt-putt cry, but Beth kept climbing the path toward home.

If sea gulls dreamed, this was what they saw. White sand, white clouds brushing milky wavecaps, and vague human smears all in white as well, because they couldn't yet mourn for Minny.

Although Beth stood in the midst of it, the scene reeled unsteadily, as if she floated above, looking down on the ancient ritual.

Lucinda, Horatio, and Jewel stood together, straight-spined and determined not to weep. Fingers hidden in his armpits, Junior shivered, though the building winds weren't cold. Al stood close beside his son, staring at the steel-hulled Coast Guard patrol boats. Undeterred by the slapping waves, they swooped in S patterns, crossing each plotted section again and again, searching.

Gimp cradled his pipes and played "Amazing Grace" with imploring sorrow.

Charmaine stood apart. She clung to the silver strands of six Mylar balloons straining to escape. They were the only softness about her. Like a woman who held a knife in her skirts, her grief threatened any who ventured near.

At first, the Neptune coffee shop offered Beth sanctuary. Its gingham curtains and red leather booths seemed festive compared to the beach, and, after yesterday's influx of strangers, even Beth was greeted as a native.

The cook waved from the grill, then came out to stand at the counter. Straightening a stack of menus, he said it was a shame about Minny, and tsked over Charmaine and Karl.

"I saw Junior smack the signpost last night. Now, that's a normal way for a man to handle things, not all shut down like Karl. You'd think he was mulling over accounts rather than worrying over a child. Back to work."

A curly-haired waitress tightened her apron strings as she considered Beth, then broke into a grin.

Probably recalling the frantic back door tryst she'd disrupted a few days ago, Beth thought. She tried to return the speculating smile, but failed. No one had sung at the summoning, and it had ended with Gimp's pipes wailing accompaniment to the wind and the hull-slapping waves.

This morning's elation hadn't lasted. The dive had proved she wasn't a coward, that she *had* let Gordon go for his own good. She felt no pride and only a flicker of gladness that Baby—no, naming it was idiocy—*the* baby needed her.

Beth read the chalkboard. As Stefanie had predicted, the Neptune's perennial special, abalone chowder, had been replaced by fish sticks. She asked the waitress for a cinnamon roll, coffee, and two sandwiches to go. Since professionals had taken over the search for Minny, she'd call the aquarium, then spend the day watching over the pup.

"Just bag it up. I'll be right back." Beth headed toward the phone booth.

The San Francisco Aquarium's line was busy, so she called Monterey Bay and got a rapid-fire list of emergency numbers. She tried a marine mammal rescue hotline.

Beth described the pup and his location to a woman named Kate. After three minutes of conversation, Beth wished she could turn her entire life over to the cheerfully efficient woman.

"I need to feed him."

"If your pup's a harbor seal, which sounds likely, it will be fine without food until we get there. Then we'll do a blood test, check for dehydration—"

"But he really seems hungry."

"Look, even here, we have to physically restrain pups, sometimes use n.g. tubes or run IVs." Kate's adamance softened. "Let's hope you get home, and the pup's mom has come for it. If not, if I don't hear from you by morning, we'll be there. In the meantime, you can help most by keeping people away. And dogs."

Beth thought of Junior's Rottweiler and shuddered. "I'd better get back."

Baby was waiting for her, no happier, but grudgingly glad for company. "We're going to have a slumber party." Beth explained her sleeping bag and yellow blanket to the pup.

Kate the seal woman had advised her not to bundle the pup, no matter how he shivered. She wouldn't, but it was tempting.

"If I weren't supposed to keep your body temperature as close to normal as possible, I'd take you into Gull Cott." Beth shook her head at the pup's bawling response. "I have a friend who doesn't like to sleep inside, either." She swallowed the knot in her throat. "But he was learning."

Beth sang to the pup, serenading it with "Amazing Grace"

until her voice cracked. Liquid streamed from Baby's eyes. At first she told herself it was only that seals had no tear ducts. Next, she imagined the pup protested her captor's voice.

As Baby dozed, Beth focused on her book, but the page kept blurring with tears. Yesterday, she'd been certain she was right. Minny's disappearance made her consider how empty life would be without Gordon.

"What's the worst thing that could happen if we got married?" Without opening his eyes, the pup scooted closer to the sleeping bag. His nearness gave Beth the strength to restate yesterday's conclusion. "He'd grow to hate me."

Beth let the feeling turn over in her chest. It hurt, but no worse than being without him.

Marriage to Gordon would have been a first, a voyage to make Columbus look like a wimp. "We might have sailed off the edge of the world—or home free to a life full of riches."

She sneaked a quick caress down the pup's curved backbone. Baby wiggled, then blatted for Beth to stop such nonsense and go to sleep.

All night Gordon watched Beth drowse with the sniveling gray pup. The dim-witted creature was easy to read. It was hungry and thought the sleeping bag looked like its mother. Beth's touch terrified him and he thought she smelled funny. Stupid little scrap.

A dozen times in the darkness Beth had felt his presence. She'd blinked sleepily toward the cove, trying to separate him from the sea-wet boulders, then curled closer to the pup and dozed. Half-awake, her thoughts were muddled, but each layer Gordon penetrated was streaked with thoughts of him.

After dawn strangers arrived to take the pup. They didn't seem to notice they'd left Beth crying. In jeans and a faded red sweatshirt, she sat forlorn, knees up, face buried in her arms.

Gordon swam nearer, and still she wept. The urge to go to her was always the same. Sweet. Blood-hot. Irresistible.

Beth had banished him, but she loved him. If the door to her heart was open just a little, he'd slam it wide and pin her to the wall. He'd done it before. He'd do it now.

Gordon hated the moment he lost buoyancy. As his hide scraped sand, Beth looked up. Gravity dragged at his seal form. Blinking and incredulous, Beth held sleep-rippled hair back from her eyes.

"Gordon?" The hand she held out trembled. Beth knew to be cautious with a four-hundred pound bull but she knew it could only be him.

He intended to commit a breech of selkie caution.

Gordon, I'm frightened. He felt her words and tasted her metallic fear. *Me too, love*, he answered.

If he transformed in front of her, it would be a pledge, a conformation that their differences were very real, but could be conquered.

He stayed out of reach, arching his head back as if bellowing in silent victory. His hide tightened across his throat, over his chest. Breathless. As if he'd dived into black depths and left no chance of return, his vision shrank to a patchwork— gray sky, blue sea, greeneyesgreeneyesgreen, Beth taking the vow beside him—and then a sound like ripping silk.

He staggered up on unwieldy human legs, reached out to part the heavy fur, then dropped it behind him like a cape. After three heartbeats, four, five, he saw Beth's arms reach for him, felt the impact of her warmth against his suddenly bared skin.

His chin rested on her hair and his arms locked around her.

"I'm selfish." Beth couldn't know his mind still swirled. "I want you now, even if you hate me later."

"I could never hate you." Gordon heard her thoughts ring as loud as words. "The cows are no more your rivals than Peaches is mine." When Beth stayed silent, he added. "He's not, is he?"

"I don't know." Beth's lips moved against his chest, taunting every bit as much as her words. "Peaches never talks back."

"Neither do the cows." Gordon snatched his skin up from the sand, intending to stash it as soon as he stifled Beth's rejoinder. He laughed as he kissed her and when her struggles slowed to languorous stretching, Gordon thought he might wait just a few moment before swimming out to his cache.

"Don't you think it's time we did some work on that bed aversion of yours?" Beth whispered, though only the sea birds could hear. "It's been forty-eight hours."

Gordon scooped her into his arms and started up the path. Stashing his fur could wait for later, this couldn't. "Miss Caxton, you're a hussy."

"Thank you." Beth nuzzled his neck in true seal fashion. "Walk faster."

When Gull Cott came into view, she pointed. "I know, we'll cut a sky light in the roof."

"Your *roof*? You worked so hard on it." He recalled bikinied Beth pounding nails, sucking her fingers and pounding once more. "Why would we do that?"

"So you won't feel so claustrophobic. If you still want to marry me."

"More than anything in the entire world. Anything." In a dozen steps they'd reach the cottage. Another dozen and they'd be in her bed and he'd show her. "And if the neighbors ask about me, just say your husband swims for his health." He turned the door knob and shouldered through. "And he wants to stay *very* healthy."

He'd let Beth down and approved her weak-kneed progress toward the bedroom, when a wailing siren cut short and a police cruiser bumped down her dirt road.

"Sheriff Reynolds seems to be in a hurry." Oh, damn. If ever there'd been a time for cursing, this was it. Alarm froze between his shoulder blades, warning it was time to fight, not mate.

Reynolds slammed a solid car door, below. Then a second vehicle pulled up. "Do you have any idea what he wants?"

"Minny." Beth's green eyes glinted as she faced him. "It's got to be about Minny."

"What about her?"

"I forgot." She drew the living room blinds closed. "I was supposed to tell you to go see Bob Reynolds—"

Beth blinked. The beach girl who loved a selkie vanished.

In a transformation uncanny as his own, the San Francisco businesswoman presided over Beth's fear.

"Go get dressed. And put this"—she touched his fur for the first time. Through it's plush thickness, Gordon felt her hands linger—"under—No. *In* my bed. Then make it up." She rubbed a line between her brows. "Will it be all right there?"

The first fist struck the door.

"Of course it will." Gordon kissed Beth's burgeoning frown and spoke lightly. "You won't lose it?"

"I'll guard it with my life." Her chin lifted and though his pelt provided passage to a world without her, he knew she would.

"Not necessary, love." Gordon sent the shell curtain swaying, looking back as more knocks fell like hammer blows. "I'd rather have you."

Beth stood tall, pretending thin filament connected the crown of her head to the rafters. She squared her shoulders, forked salt-sticky hair back from her temples, and answered the door.

Bob Reynolds's glance darted past her, warily contradicting the somber droop of his mouth. "I'm afraid I have some bad news."

"You found Minny's—?" Beth choked on the word. Karl stood behind the sheriff, his bulk showing on Bob's left and right.

"No." Through his glasses, Bob's gaze locked on hers, as if it alone could hold her upright. "It's your dad."

"Jack?" Beth's hand fumbled at her throat, as if she wore a locket. She didn't.

"It seems he's had a heart attack, but he's alive."

Beth gripped the doorframe. "Jack's had a heart attack?" Decorative lines scored the wooden molding. Three cuts of increasing thickness. Gracefully beveled. Sanded smooth. Beth forced herself to focus on Karl, as if he could explain.

"Carol called the store, Beth Ann. She didn't know another number to try. I guess your girlfriend, uh—"

"Phoebe."

"Right. She faxed Lucinda, too. Bob and I met going out to our cars." Then Karl was saying something about getting a phone, at least an emergency cellular, and something about cesspools in Paris.

"I want you to sit down." Bob backed her into her own living room, toward the couch. Neon orange and yellow lights slashed the air before her. Tiny black dots crowded beneath her eyelids. "Sit." Bob pressed her shoulders.

Beth was certain she'd imagined the growl and the tinkling sound of shells, until both men faced Gordon.

"It's him!" Karl wheeled toward Bob.

Gordon stood in the doorway. At first he appeared to slouch. With jeans unbelted and hanging from lean hips, with bare shoulders slumped to one side, barefooted, he looked lazy. Except for his eyes. Beth had no trouble imagining his charge and the impact with which he'd hit both men.

Bob nodded to Gordon, lifted his hands from Beth's shoulders, and told her what Karl had meant to convey before. "Your stepmother said there'll be a Cessna waiting for you at the Parish airport. It'll fly you into SFO. Someone will drive you to UC Hospital."

"Okay." Beth shot upright. She'd change and find her car keys as soon as the room tilted level.

"Better give yourself just a minute," Bob said. "You're looking a little shocky."

Gordon hated it. His eyes smoldered beyond Bob's shoulder, unwilling to tolerate Bob's protective words and gestures. Beth wet her lips to talk, to draw the sheriff's attention away, but she was too late.

"I know this is a bad time, but I need to talk with you." Bob Reynolds didn't sound apologetic. "In my office, if you don't mind."

Gordon's expression might have been called a sneer. The sharp slant of cheekbones and composed voice marked him an aristocrat. "As you drove up, Beth said something about Minny."

"She's missing." Karl perspired with a scent like overripe fruit. Even Beth smelled it. For Gordon it must be overwhelming. "She went missing the same time you took off. And since you've seemed so sweet on her—" Karl grabbed Gordon's forearm.

Gordon leaned back in uncompromising disdain. Then cool violence centered within him.

"Take your hands off the man." Bob kept his eyes on Gordon, not Karl. "Now," he said when the storekeeper moved too slowly, but Bob wasn't interceding, he was only being sensible.

Beth saw gooseflesh prickle over Gordon's upper arms. The only thing he feared was captivity and Bob kept the keys. Would Bob jail him? On what trumped-up charge? Being kind? Why was Karl convinced Gordon had harmed Minny?

And what about Jack?

Beth stood, refusing to falter. *Run, Gordon.* He flinched as if she'd slapped him. *Run.* Gordon shook his head faintly, but she would not lose them both. "He's been with me."

"Beth, yesterday you said he was gone," Bob interrupted before she lied further.

"I'll give you a lift to Parish." Karl jiggled the car keys in his pocket.

Beth ignored him and turned to Bob. Gordon's disapproval telegraphed through the air between them. She ignored it. "Let him ride in front." Beth thought of the shotgun jammed between the front seats and knew his answer.

"I can't do that."

She thought of the metal mesh, the cage enclosing the backseat. Gordon had vanished for ten years the last time he'd been so threatened. "Please."

Bob shook his head.

"Give me a minute." Gordon withdrew without permission, and she followed.

The hanger still swung from where he'd jerked the white shirt loose. "Don't beg, Beth." Gordon shrugged the shirt over his shoulders and left it unbuttoned. "I can do this."

"But you hate it."

"Yes, I hate it." He flipped black hair from inside his collar. "It scares the shit out of me. But I can't run."

"You could." She watched his long dark fingers fasten the buttons at his cuffs.

"It's Karl, you know." He yanked each cuff down and raised his eyes only slightly to confirm she'd heard. "The bad fishing, the abalone, and Minny. He's mulling over all of it, gloating."

"You're positive?"

"He's as easy to read as a sea slug." Gordon loosed a copper button and unzipped his fly to tuck in his shirttail.

Beth glanced at the curtained sliding-glass door. Bob Reynolds was silhouetted on her deck. "You can take him."

"Of course I can." Gordon's arrogance was laced with irony. "And never come back."

"We could meet in San Francisco—"

He silenced her with a kiss.

No. Beth cried out against his mouth. Fierce and aching, this was a last kiss, a kiss to take the place of a thousand others, in case he died in captivity. Then he held her at arm's length.

"We have secrets enough, don't you think?" His attention switched to the sound of Karl's shoes in her living room. "But if they try to lock me up, I won't yield. I can't." He slid his feet into leather sandals. "Ready?"

"I'm not letting you go alone."

"Fly to your father. I hate airplanes worse than cars." His roguish smile turned melancholy. "Kiss me good-bye once more."

She did, branding him with arms and lips and love, until the clink of keys and handcuffs on Bob's belt pulled them apart.

Gordon gave her a last squeeze. "I'm all right."

Beth let him say it. She pretended to believe his charade even after he slid into the backseat of the police cruiser.

Bob put the cruiser into reverse. She could see him talking, but Gordon didn't respond.

As the car drove past, Gordon looked her way. Behind the glass, his eyes showed as pale as Grey Gallows' limestone spires, hardened into rock, forever.

Twenty-five

~

Branding herself a fatalist, Beth wore her black Picone dress with running shoes and set her red high heels on the Fiat's passenger seat. When the car refused to start, she coaxed it with curses and an all-out shove down the driveway. The engine sputtered and caught.

I'm hurrying, Jack. Had she always held silent conversations or was Gordon to blame? Dressing, she'd imagined Jack grumping that he wouldn't get any sicker if she failed to come stare at him.

Beth coasted into a parking spot in front of the library. Careful not to snag her hose, she shucked her running shoes, donned the red heels, and slid from the sports car.

Surf Street lay deserted. A normal Wednesday afternoon, with no sign of a lynch mob. She and Karl might be the only ones who knew Bob had collared Gordon for questioning.

In passing, Beth touched the police cruiser's cooling hood, glad she hadn't lingered over her appearance. She'd spent thirty seconds splashing with cold water, five minutes winding her hair in a tight French twist, and a couple minutes more finding her hammered gold earrings, cologne, and black stockings.

As Beth's heels echoed across the library, Lucinda glanced

up, returned to her paperwork, then looked up again with raised brows. The assessment made Beth hope she'd appear firm and businesslike during Bob Reynolds's interrogation.

She paused outside the closed office door. If Reynolds wouldn't admit her, she'd insist. In San Francisco, she could have called any one of a half dozen attorney friends, but not in Grey Gallows. Stefanie Morris's parents served as the town's only legal advisers, and they were sunning in Santa Cruz.

She'd defend Gordon alone. Under no circumstances would she leave for San Francisco without him. Beth opened the door without knocking.

"Beth." Reynolds barked her name and kept writing on a grid-marked form.

Gordon's eyes, as expressionless as glass, turned to her.

"I hurried." Beth stood behind Gordon's chair and addressed Reynolds. "Have you finished?" She remembered not to fidget, not to cross her arms defensively, not to care if Reynolds thought her brusque. In turn, Bob ignored her. "I must get to Parish right away."

"I agree." Bob pushed his glasses against the bridge of his nose with a chiding firmness. "And this"—he gestured toward the silent fax machine—"could take awhile. I'm awaiting confirmation that 'Gordon Henson' exists."

Henson. Beth caressed the muscles between Gordon's neck and shoulders. How like him to recognize the man whose creatures had taught him everything good about this arid world. Beth set her molars against each other, refusing to be moved.

"I told him most of my records are in London." With hands like frost, Gordon reached up to grab her fingers.

"Has Karl given you trouble over anything else?" Bob wrote with such diligence, Beth thought he muttered to himself.

"Karl?" Gordon asked. "No."

"I did want to talk with you, of course, but Karl's made it his business to be sure I did." Bob glanced up. "No fights?"

At last, faint color rose in Gordon's cheeks. "You must be joking."

"You haven't commented on his, uh, alternate sources of income?" Bob asked.

"His and Sloan's business." Beth recalled Bob's remark outside Gimp's and his quick getaway from Junior's back booth. Was Bob Reynolds taking bribes to overlook an abalone poaching ring? Should she stay silent or speak out? "Is Karl poaching?"

"Not exactly." He dismissed her words, though he didn't seem a bit surprised by them. "It was a shot in the dark."

"Then . . ." Beth tried to match her puzzle piece thoughts. "Are Karl and Junior working with Sloan and Roo?" Beth asked.

"Junior's helping the good guys. But you didn't hear it from me."

"He broke into Beth's house," Gordon said.

"Yeah, that's a bit troublesome." Bob frowned, stroking his beard. "He was playing private eye, even oiled your hinges so he could come and go quietly." Bob watched Beth nod. "*Not* with my permission. But she did lie about illegal activity in her cove."

Beth met Gordon's eyes. Savvy Bob Reynolds had everything under control. Including her.

The ringing telephone startled them all.

"Reynolds. Yes." He frowned toward Beth. "Here." He jabbed the receiver her way.

"Hello?" Before she heard the voice, Beth noticed the tinkle of childish music coming over the line.

"Hey, Beth, it's Stefanie. Where are you?"

"Where am *I*? In Sheriff Reynolds's office. In Grey Gallows."

"Oh, wow." Stefanie broke away. "You want to turn that *down*?" When she spoke into the receiver again, she sounded concerned. "Beth, are you in trouble?"

"No. Well, sort of." Beth pretended not to see Reynolds signal for her to end the conversation. "How did you find me?"

"Yesterday, when you left that bizarre little message, well, my phone has caller ID. It showed your number on the readout.

It's, like, one of my dad's toys. For identifying thugs and all.''

Over the continued racket in Stefanie's Santa Cruz home, Beth heard Reynolds's curt instructions to "hang the hell up." Instead, she took a breath, crossed her fingers and prayed. "Stefanie, we're looking for Minny—"

"You found her." Stefanie yawned, then her hand muffled the receiver against her shout. "Minny, turn that *down*, can't you?"

"What?" If Gordon hadn't occupied the room's only chair, Beth would have collapsed into it.

"I said she's with me. Has been since night before last. I hope Charmaine's having fun in Palm Springs." Stefanie's nails tapped the receiver. "Even a good kid's a lot of trouble."

"How did she get there?" Beth listened intently, afraid she'd have to wrestle Reynolds for the receiver if she made Stefanie repeat a word. "He told you *what*?" Beth gestured for calm, but Bob was busy poking buttons on another phone. Gordon had picked up her elation and revived enough to hug her.

"Stef—" Beth cleared her throat. "Stefanie, I want you to repeat all that to Sheriff Reynolds. Don't you dare hang up."

Reynolds listened, noting down an address. "Stay put. Don't talk to anyone, until you hear from me. Shall I talk with your parents? Okay. There'll be some officers there in a minute."

"He framed Gordon!" Beth exploded before Reynolds replaced the receiver. "Why would he do that?"

"That's how it looks now." Reynolds made a quelling motion and placed another call. "We'll check it out." He waited on hold. "Santa Cruz County has somebody on the way. You two wait here a few minutes more."

Dialogue completed, Reynolds picked up a pencil and swapped it end for end. "Don't discuss this with anyone. I'm going to let you leave for San Francisco, so it should be easy." Reynolds tapped the pencil on his desk.

"But you've got to tell Charmaine. Right away."

"Of course and I'll mention your part in it—"

"I don't care about that." Beth squirmed at the prospect of

Charmaine's gratitude. Suddenly she needed to reach San Francisco and Jack.

"Karl can tell her whatever he wants," Reynolds explained. "We'll just scratch our heads over the whole mixup."

"Stefanie thought Charmaine was going out of town . . . thought she was doing her a favor . . . and so forth," Gordon recited. "That's our story, correct?"

Beth froze. Heaven help them both if Reynolds took Gordon for more than a perceptive listener. It would be far easier for the sheriff to believe Gordon a kidnapper than a mind reader.

"Right." Animated and upbeat, Reynolds snagged a directory typed in minuscule print, and checked its index.

"You like this cops-and-robbers stuff, don't you?" Beth asked.

"Better than fast cars and rare T-bones. The only thing better than this will be hauling him in." Reynolds cut the phone's first ring in half. "On scene?" He looked at Beth and nodded. "Sure." He smiled as he waited. "Hi, Minny. I know, sweetheart." Beth's eyes filled at the sheriff's tender tone. "I'll make sure she calls you real soon." Reynolds glanced at his office clock. "Before cartoons are over. You can count on it."

Jack Caxton wore a generic hospital gown. He sat upright and crabby against three pillows.

Carol offered him juice garnished with a flex straw. "Your color's much better, Jack. Isn't it better, Beth?"

She and Gordon had arrived only minutes ago, and the flight had so unnerved him, Gordon paced the corridors in long strides, too keyed-up to meet Jack.

"You look fine." Beth kissed Jack's cheek and sent a prayer of thanksgiving skyward.

"What I am is pretty damned pissed off." Jack swigged from the straw Carol kept brushing at his lips, then pushed it away. "Told 'em it wasn't a heart attack. Sometimes heartburn and cold sweats really *are* indigestion."

"And the weakness in your left arm?" Carol moved to retie the neck of Jack's gown, and he shrugged away.

"Racquetball. I told you, Phoebe made me go play rac-quetball with Merrill, that idiot city councilman." Jack looked for Beth's support, as he jerked a thumb toward Carol. "She's unconvinced."

"If you'd stay away from that despicable cantina, we wouldn't have to worry." Forceful footfalls made Carol frown toward the hall. She pushed at cotton-candy hair Beth had never seen so mussed. "Mr. Gordon appears quite anxious, Elizabeth. Bring him in to meet Jack while I go call Phoebe and tell her you've arrived, why don't you?"

As if Carol's absence deflated him, Jack sagged. "I don't know *what* the hell it was, Bethie." Jack's eyelids closed. "Or what they're givin' me to relax."

Beth felt Gordon's hand at her waist and leaned against it. He'd entered so soundlessly, she searched for silver sparkles in the air.

"Jack?" Beth put her hand next to her father's on the crisp sheet and waited for his eyes to open. "This is my friend Gordon Henson. We're getting married."

"Think so?" Even with eyes at half-mast, Jack's stare was meant to intimidate.

Gordon's hair grew longer than Jack liked and his white shirt could use a good pressing, but Beth thought, all in all, her *fiancé* presented the sort of rough-hewn image Jack could tolerate.

"Carol says you like my plays." With eyes closed, Jack addressed Gordon. When he hesitated, Beth didn't.

"Gordon's a big contributor to the Foghorn, Jack."

"But is he a good guy? In it for a lifetime?"

"He's the best." Beth drew breath and held it, allowing only four words to escape. "He's also a selkie."

What on earth had possessed her? Beth pressed her lips together. Of course, she'd planned to tell Jack as soon as she could, but she hadn't planned to give him a second seizure. With luck, Jack wasn't really awake.

"A seal," Jack corrected, scooting up against the pillows and reaching for the cup of water. "I'll tell you, find out what they're giving me to relax, honey, and steer clear of it." Jack bit down on the straw, taking in Gordon's muscular frame and confidence. "You mean like a Navy Seal—special operations, undersea guerilla, that sort of stuff, right?"

Gordon's arm tightened around Beth's waist. Later would be time enough for confessions. "A Navy Seal, of course. What else could I mean?" Beth laughed.

Jack nodded, calling down calamity on the idiot who'd pumped him full of dope and the one who'd designed hospital gowns that didn't cover a man's privates.

As Jack's eyes closed, Beth noticed even his eyelashes had grayed. When he patted the hand she'd left next to his, she could have predicted his words.

"How's the Fiat running, Bethie?" His sigh sounded like a hibernating bear's. "You ever going to get that solenoid fixed?"

As they slipped out, Beth intercepted Jack's doctor. Salt-and-pepper-haired and cranky as his patient, Mitch Smith was an old family friend.

"The blood work's not all in, but my guess is it wasn't a heart attack. Was *not*. Anxiety maybe, over that city council crap." He shook a finger in the general direction of the Civic Center. "The idea of those crooks harassing an artist of Jack's caliber is scandalous." Mitch patted Beth's cheek. "But that's all it was. I'll tell you, if everyone they harassed had a heart attack, we'd have to move the cardiac unit to Candlestick Park."

As they awaited the elevator, Gordon battled a hangover worse than the aftermath of tequila. The remnants of fear and the scents of sickness and antiseptic dizzied him.

Beth was the cure. Staring up at the numbers above the closed elevator doors, Gordon plucked out two of her hairpins. Beth didn't resist.

Heartened, he eased his fingers through the tight hair arrangement and tumbled it down. As it fell slick and soft over his hands, his muscles turned almost liquid with relief.

Beth hummed, pretending not to notice. Her nonchalance electrified him. The public setting intensified the challenge of seducing her. Gordon touched his lips to Beth's neck, breathing the mingled scents of cologne and female.

Beth suppressed a little moan. Oh, yes.

Mating had been delayed too long. How improper would it be to yank Beth down the corridor to the empty room he'd spotted?

With his lips buried beneath Beth's hair, he felt quite himself again. "Tell me, Miss Caxton. Why did you really bring me here?" How quickly might he slip those enticing red high heels from her feet?

"To see my—Those are attached." Beth squeaked as his mouth bumped a gold earring. Smiling shamelessly, she pulled back her lapel, offering her neck.

"Bless this sluggish elevator," he said against her skin.

"I haven't even pushed the button yet." Beth glanced back toward Jack's room at the sound of clattering feet.

"Beth, I caught you." Cursed Carol was half-breathless. "I don't understand why it's so important, but your friend from the village, Charmaine? *Is* she, Beth, the young woman with the unfortunate-colored hair? Rather grape-ish?"

"Yes. What did she want?"

Carol glanced at the unlighted elevator button, jabbed it, then gave Beth a patient smile. "She called into the nurses' station, if you can imagine. When she found you'd gone, she said I needed to catch you because she'd heard there was going to be a seal calling in your cove tonight."

"Seal calling?" Seal. Calling. Pronounced separately, the words still made no sense. Beth darted Gordon a sideways glance.

"Yes. I couldn't quite tell if she wanted to be invited. She said you'd understand." Carol poked the button again. "I don't mean to be critical Elizabeth, but if you're entertaining tonight, you shouldn't keep the pilot waiting. I had to comp him two nights at the Bronze Iris—"

"Culling." The idea hit Gordon like a drenching wave. "Not calling, *culling*."

The elevator bell dinged. *They'll kill them all.* The doors yawned and he regarded the closed metal box with a rush of nausea. *All my pretty cows and their pups, gaffed and bleed-*

ing. He could run down the interior stairway, but Beth would never keep up. He pulled her inside with him.

Beth trusted Bob Reynolds, *only* Reynolds, to be outside the fishermen's vendetta. While she shivered in the drizzle at Parish landing strip, wiggling a wire under her car's hood, Gordon slid into a telephone booth and called Reynolds for help.

"You see, though, Bob"—the sheriff's name felt alien on his tongue—"facing down cullers isn't a one-man job. There's gaffs and spears and guns."

"Stay away from the cove," Reynolds ordered, then realized he'd only fanned Gordon's impatience. "I'll put in a call to Fish and Game, but Charmaine's wrong. There's been no activity in Beth's cove for several nights. Most of the seals have moved on."

"These changes don't happen overnight. Some females just won't listen."

"Tell Beth I'll have her arrested for—I don't know, reckless endangerment—how's that sound?"

Gordon regarded the telephone in confusion. He'd been speaking of the cows.

"Hey, Gordon? I've got federal help here, winding things up. Keep Beth away from that cove and—Shoot, is she driving the Fiat? Her road's about half washed-out." Male voices rose nearby. "... *careful.* Looks like it's building up to be one rough—"

"Deposit fifty-five cents for the next one minute, please." The mechanical voice chirred over Reynolds's. By the time Gordon had gathered enough coins, he was listening to dial tone.

Beth's Fiat drew up at the curb and she leaned across to thrust open the passenger door. She'd gotten the machine started at great cost to her appearance. Her hair hung in wet snakes, her dress was drenched and worst of all, she wore athletic shoes. She'd removed her red high heels without him.

"That's it!" Gordon slammed himself inside the car and cinched the seat belt tight. "I'm buying you a new car, tomorrow."

"I don't want a new car, but I'm going to quit being stubborn about consulting a real mechanic. What did Bob say?" Beth sped around a series of sickening turns, maneuvered the car through a puddle in which the tires lost traction altogether, then accelerated onto the highway.

The cullers would come from the village. In the darkness to his right, whitecaps shone under a sickle moon. He'd tell Beth to drop him here, except he wouldn't survive long in such high seas without seal form and his skin was tucked between Beth's yellow sheets.

Irrational longing seized him. What if Carol hadn't caught them in time? What if the cows were forced to survive alone, as they had over countless centuries?

Rain lashed Beth's windshield and she turned on her wipers.

Rapture of the deep. Wasn't that a sort of drowning? He wanted it. He yearned to give up his crown. Why shouldn't he snug down for the night and let the winds howl outside while he mated with the woman he loved?

"Gordon," Beth repeated. "What did Bob say?"

"He said I'm on my own."

Trusting Beth's love was one thing, trusting her to obey was something else, entirely. Gordon skimmed below the sea's surface, avoiding the harsh weather. He'd appealed to Beth on every grounds imaginable, telling her she threatened his masculinity, peace of mind, even his future children. Still, she remained firm in her desire to save his clan. If he didn't defeat the cullers before they reached Beth's cove, she'd be waiting for them.

A drift of rock fish parted before him. The waters were so turbulent, he'd been upon them before he knew it. Gordon drove forward with renewed concentration. Such stormy tumult made disturbances hard to track. Capsizing a rowboat should be simple, but first he had to find it.

Twenty-six

~

"Swear to God, Sloan, you're a madman."

Beth's cove and Lyre Beach lay behind Gordon. He'd swum thirty feet out from shore when he scented squid and heard Junior's voice. Gordon surfaced and lay silent, smelling smoke on the wind.

"If you're gonna quit bein' an errand boy, and be cut in at such a late date, man, you gotta be risking as much as the rest of us." The orange glow of Sloan's cigarette brightened, showing his position in the bow. "I ain't no cop, but the way I see it, you have knowledge of your dad's poaching and now you're trashing commercial fishing waters. Sounds like San Quentin to me."

Sloan pitched something overboard. With a splash and a glug, it sank. Gordon followed. Head down, he sculled around what looked like a coffee can filled with cement. It plummeted, trailing yards of thin nylon rope.

Gordon finned backward as the rope spilled around him. Hooks were attached every foot and each boasted a hunk of dead squid.

Long line fishing. He knew it as a lazy man's fishing method and one seals applauded. As long as they avoided the hooks, it was like a buffet. That might explain the cows' deaths. Sloan would have no qualms about killing a seal seeking squid hors d'oeuvres. But why set his line in the dead of night?

Gordon surfaced, blowing water from his whiskers.

Even in the waves' upheaval, Junior heard him. "Another damned seal."

"Where?" Sloan paused in paying out line and brandished a revolver. "Roo's taking care of most of them. Don't mind doin' my part."

Gordon sank low, leaving only his eyes above the tipping waves. Roo would lead the culling. Gordon remembered the blond boy speeding in his new truck. He must get back to Beth.

"Where did'ja see him?" Sloan shaded the rain from his eyes.

"Maybe it was nothing. Jeez it's cold." Rough fisherman's hands scoured each other. "Let's get this done."

"Almost there." Sloan hefted a second can. "Okay, so next week, when you do it, get five hundred yards of line. Bait it every foot or so, lay it out in a big circle, then pitch this over and never come back."

"How many do we take in a night?"

"You do the math, schoolboy. And remember, we don't *take* any. We catch 'em and leave 'em. That's the point. Old-timers'll just think Grey Gallows got 'fished out' all of a sudden."

Gordon could imagine hundreds of fish rotting on the ocean floor, benefitting neither man nor beast, but he couldn't imagine *why*.

"When do we get paid?"

"Same time, same place as Al, only our envelopes are a little fatter and we keep our mouths shut about it. Yeah, the rest of 'em will live here on their ab money, but I'll move on.

"See, the day's comin' when everyone'll give up on making a decent living fishing. They'll sell out to the yuppies and leave town. Taking lots of abs and fishing out the area just guarantees 'that day' will come sooner. When it does, I'll be long gone, living in Puerto Vallarta. Ummmhmmm. The only fishing I'll do is off my balcony.''

Sloan's cigarette butt went hissing into the sea. "Yeah, never thought I'd work with him, but Karl's set me up pretty good. He found the ab buyers. He handles the business. I just dive. But this"—Sloan's gesture rocked the boat—"was my idea. For a bonus, he cut me in on the real-estate shit.

"His cut of the profits buys places fishermen sell 'cause they can't make a livin'.'' Sloan gave an admiring laugh. "Next, he'll knock down the shacks and build a new town. Sucker has balls, framin' your old pal.''

"Yeah, helluva great guy, Karl. He could've spilled the plan before tonight." Junior spoke through his teeth.

"Was that hard on you? Worryin' about your kid?" Sloan snickered. "You gotta admit, Reynolds went right where we aimed him." Sloan's pause felt planned, as if his next words were a taunt. "I figure Little Miss Perfect Caxton might be so pissed over her pervert boyfriend, she'll come along with me.''

The thunder overhead faded under the roaring in Gordon's eardrums. His self-control threatened to snap.

"Never in a million years." Junior snorted and Gordon admired him. Anger showed in the shadowed stiffness of Junior's shoulders, but he didn't take Sloan's bait.

"Yeah? She left San Francisco for this sorry place." Sloan spat overboard. "If I wanted to—Who'd know she didn't split because she felt like it, instead of trussed up like a bawling little lamb?''

Gordon exploded out of the water as Junior swung the gaff. Gordon had no time to dodge the metal point intended for Sloan. He should have capsized the boat, but he hungered for the slam of his skin against Sloan's.

The gaff slashed a burning arc above Gordon's eye and he roared with the fury of an insulted bull. It goaded him over the center board of the boat, shoving Sloan before him into the sea.

Sloan blew water from his mouth. He tossed hair from his eyes, shook water from the barrel of his revolver, and aimed. Blood blinded Gordon's left eye and the rain thickened. He should swim away, but he wanted Sloan humbled. Or dead.

Gordon bobbed up behind the poacher and let a back-handed swat from the gun slip off his side. Gordon dived and resurfaced, feinting from side to side as Sloan tried to aim.

Sloan had dreamed of tying Beth, of taking her by force. Would Bringer of Crimson respond to selkie magic? Would he come now and bear Sloan away in his jaws? Then Gordon realized the blood blinding him was his own.

"Hey! Stay back!" Junior floundered in the water, trying to right the rowboat and fend off the maddened bull seal.

Lightning cracked gold overhead. In the heavens' glare, Gordon saw Sloan pull the trigger. No sound followed.

Gordon dived again. He had no time for revenge. Beth would be crouched above the cove by now. Soon she'd be in the thick of it. Although it didn't pain him to think of leaving Sloan stranded in the storm, Junior was still his brother.

Sloan's legs flailed beneath the waves. Just above his boots, white sock showed and even paler flesh. The temptation was too great. Gordon flicked a flipper past Sloan's ankle, then inflicted a shallow bite.

"Shark!" Sloan's screams reverberated down through the water and his legs peddled furiously. Gordon held on, jaws shaking as if he *were* a shark, until the revolver splashed and fell in a cluster of bubbles on its way to the ocean floor.

Gordon met Junior beneath the overturned boat. In such inky darkness, neither could see. In the silent swaying, Gordon detected the unmistakable aroma of peanut butter. Together they shoved the boat upright.

Gordon circled once, watching as Junior stroked out to the panicked Sloan. Junior tried a rescue grip, but Sloan was determined to climb him, to gouge fingers into Junior's face.

"Let go, you dumb son-of-a-bitch." Junior swallowed water and choked. "I swear, I'll let you drown."

Junior's fist smacked Sloan's face, and he gave a grunt of satisfaction as he shoved Sloan over the side of the boat.

Gordon left them, forced himself to patrol for another hour, but saw no sign of the cullers. Weariness weighed him down. He wanted nothing more than Beth, and yes, even her bed.

Beth. Gordon felt a twinge of dizziness as the storm roared overhead. *Beth.* Rain stabbed down in needles, bringing a sick certainty that Beth was cold and wet and waiting to die.

For years Beth had crouched amid the boulders, watching the seals' rookery for fun. Tonight she kept vigil.

Maybe the cullers wouldn't come. Reynolds was a professional, after all, and he thought there were too few seals to provoke fishermen into an illegal act.

Beth's yellow slicker bunched and rubbed around her. It kept her dry, but she should have worn wool underneath. She could be out here all night.

Which men should she prepare to face? Sloan, of course. He wouldn't miss a chance for brutality. Roo, since he would follow anyone into anything. Probably Al, and, though she hated to think it, Junior. He needed the money, and he could fool Bob Reynolds.

Beth played her flashlight along the shoreline. Only two stubborn cows had returned. The wind blew canyons in the waves and snatched foam from the whitecaps, spinning it into spray. What a rotten night for moon-bathing.

The clank of metal on metal brought Beth to her knees. As she shifted position, a boulder slipped from its mud mortar to clack on the rocks below. Beth strained her eyes, trying to separate black from blacker on the far waves.

A motionless hush fell and then the world exploded.

Lightning ripped the sky and rain darted against her cheeks. Wind snatched the slicker's hood and tossed sand in her eyes. She blinked, resisting the urge to rub her eyes and grind the particles in as her mind screamed an explanation over the storm's booming rage.

Selkie's blood. Legend warned that the sea would revolt and destroy—at the shedding of selkie's blood.

The booming wasn't thunder. Yellow-white muzzle flashes lit the horizon. A rifle, perhaps two, shot toward her cove. Beth ducked, but she had no cover. Not here, so near the shoreline. Besides, she hadn't edged down that slippery path in the dark, only to hide from danger.

The two cows hadn't separated the rifles' thunder from the storm's. Neither had taken to the water. If they had, the men could simply shoot them as they swam past. This would be no culling, just simple execution.

Beth skittered down the path. From the crescent of sand, she squinted seaward and turned on her flashlight. It fell immediately on the boat. It was so close.

Roo sat alone. Beth swallowed a relieved laugh. *Roo was alone!* He shaded his eyes and shot again.

"Roo!" She bellowed into the storm. Her loose hair wrapped around her neck in a strangling hold, but she kept her flashlight trained on Roo's eyes. "Stop it!"

Of course, he couldn't hear. Beth snatched a pebble from the beach and slung it toward him. It missed, but she tried again. She'd either drive him away or get herself shot. If Gordon's blood had triggered this tempest, it didn't matter which.

This time the rock struck. Beth shifted her flashlight to her left hand, waded into the shallows, and pitched another.

"Get out of my cove, Roo." Waves crested at Beth's knees and she stumbled. "This is *my* beach." Wet to her waist, she screamed at him. "You're trespassing!" As if he weren't poaching, harassing protected mammals, and trying to blow her brains out!

Moonlight glinted on metal as Roo lowered the rifle. Should she launch another rock or back off? Beth's hands began shaking, then her arms and knees, as she heard the liquid dip of oars.

Still squinting at where he'd been, Beth slogged backward, toward shore. The rustling of her slicker would spook the cows if her shouts hadn't. She stood and waited. Her jeans held the wet against her. If she sat, she'd freeze to the rocks.

Roo had rowed out of sight. The flashlight beam danced so from her shivering, Beth turned it off and slipped her hands up opposite sleeves, hoping her own skin would warm her.

One cow cooed a complaint, and Beth startled so hard, she almost fell again.

With no one to goad him, Roo wouldn't be back. The cows were safe, and if she didn't want to die of hypothermia, she'd better get up to the house and change. Gordon would come soon. He couldn't be dead. She was sure of it.

The cow repeated her complaint, this time without the coo.

"You're welcome," Beth said tartly, and trotted up the path toward Gull Cott.

"Gordon!" Beth rejoiced. It was over. She'd turned back one culler herself, and Gordon had survived whatever clash he'd had with the others. He'd surely met some sort of trouble, because his back-lit silhouette, leaving her porch, moved stiffly.

He tripped as he moved across the bluff toward her.

"Pull yourself together. We've got celebrating to do!"

Why didn't he answer? Gordon could never resist her dares. Now, as he ran toward her, she knew he must be injured, knew—it wasn't him.

Sloan grabbed Beth as she turned to run. One hard arm pinned both of hers while the other arm clutched her neck. He yanked her against the front of him, lifting her off the ground, strangling her yells as she kicked for his legs.

His forearm barred her throat. She coughed once, struggling for air.

"Keep still, Gorgeous, and I'll let you breathe."

Oxygen. She'd felt this airless sinking before. The universe closed in, darker, tighter. Beth let her legs hang still. She nodded and began coughing again.

"I knew you could be reasonable." Sloan turned still and attentive. Was someone coming?

Gordon? But Sloan carried a gun. If only she could get it. Beth drew a deep breath. She had no idea how to fire a gun, but snatching it away from Sloan would reduce his power.

"No big ideas, got it?" Sloan's forearm slammed back against her Adam's apple. "You and me are going on a little trip."

He dragged her backward a few steps. Beth's heels plowed furrows in the mud. If anyone came, they'd by God see signs of a struggle. They'd look for her. Except, of course, for the rain, washing every sign away.

"You gonna behave?"

She couldn't breathe. Her throat burned. She coughed as he kept dragging, and then, she turned her head into the crook of his elbow. Air.

In San Francisco, one of the cops—who? she couldn't think who—had told her just how to get out of this. The most common man-woman attack.

Use his weight against him. That was it.

Beth pretended to launch a last struggle, stomping Sloan's feet, slinging her elbows hard as she could.

"Bitch!"

She couldn't tell which attempt connected before she went limp in his arms.

Sloan fell forward, trying to clutch her boneless mass. Beth rolled, slipped, but still regained her feet before he did. Sloan was shouting, but the thunder roared so loud, she couldn't hear.

There, stuck in the back of his waistband, glimmered the gun. She jerked it loose as Sloan grabbed for her ankle. Beth moved faster. Oh, thank you God for glorious jogging on the beach. *She was faster.*

Not the steps. He'd have a car down there. The path. Beth ran for her wet and muddy, slippery path to the sea. Sloan labored behind her. If only she had a minute to set up, to listen to the language of the waves, she'd jump. Sloan could never follow, but she didn't have that minute, so she threw the gun, letting it take the dive instead, and ran down the path to her cove.

Washed clean by the mud, the rock shone like polished red marble in the moonlight. No particle of dirt remained to create friction, but her mind's warning came too late. Beth's sole hit it, slid sideways, and only a root, pointing seaward like a knotty finger, saved her.

"Hey Gorgeous, where'd you go?"

Her right hand clung to the root. He'd see it, but she couldn't let go. Of its own volition, her left hand wedged under a rock. It shifted and she loosened her hold, lifting her index finger, her middle finger, ring finger, little finger and

finally her thumb. He still hadn't found her. She'd only moved
her hand an inch and grabbed onto another when the first rock
fell. It hit as the second rock came loose in her hand. For a
moment she swung free, feet dangling. The root broke. She
told Gordon good-bye and then she stopped, both feet on a
ledge.

"Hey, Gorgeous, you take up tap dancing or something?"

There *was* no ledge here. Beth searched her mental map of
the cliff face. Maybe flooding had built up a ridge of dirt above
the jumble of jagged boulders, but there was no ledge, certainly not one which could hold her until dawn.

She heard Sloan settle above her, but she refused to look
up. If she did, she'd fall.

"Now ain't this a sorry shame. Just when I was going to
take you on vacation to Mexico and teach you tricks that seal
hugger never would've thought of."

Pebbles and mud squirmed beneath her shoes. Beth plastered her chest and cheek against the cliff face, arms outspread,
trying not to hear his lewd laughter. Grit worked under her
fingernails as she found a hold. It held for at least five hours.
Or perhaps five seconds.

"What I got in mind might sweeten up that smart mouth of
yours, know that? Oh, yeah, we'll have plenty of fun."

If only she didn't move, she'd be all right. If he left her
here, she'd survive. Her cheek stung where the fall had
scraped it, and she began to shiver again. That was a very bad
idea, unbalancing her as it did, but she couldn't seem to stop.
Couldn't he just leave her to die?

"Your face is all scuffed up from falling, and you're bleeding. Can you feel yourself bleeding, Gorgeous?"

The moon peeked out and she imagined she felt its radiance.
Rain dripped down her neck, past the thrown-back hood, into
the neck of her T-shirt and down her back. Her soaked jeans
stole body heat away from her core.

Moisture clung to her eyelashes, starring the fog all around
her. She felt a pulse of hope. She might think of a way out of
this, if only she didn't move.

And then he grunted, shouted. Above her, Beth heard growling. Cash? Had Junior and his Rottweiler come to her rescue?

They were too late. The tiny shelf was disintegrating, falling off in muddy chunks. Only her left toe, driven into the mud, and her right hand, kept her from falling.

She closed her eyes against the swirling silver fog. It shone as if the night rained down cold and merciless stars.

Fists slammed and slapped, but only for a minute. She heard a great groan of effort, like a man lifting a huge tree, and then Sloan screamed.

Sloan plummeted past her. He hit and bounced off a boulder, then another and lay silent.

"Beth?" Gordon's voice was deliverance.

A sob swelled her chest, but she only whispered. "I'm here."

Rock crunched as Gordon knelt at the cliff edge. His hand rested atop her head, gentle as a falling leaf.

If I breath, I'll fall. She might have whispered the words, but she didn't think so. She raised her eyes, *only* her eyes and saw him.

A last wayward stab of lightning lit his face. Blood mimicked the forked pattern overhead, coursing from Gordon's forehead, over his eyebrow. He looked so terribly worried.

"Am I going to die, Gordon?" This time the smallest whisper wafted over her lips.

His hands clamped her wrists and her heels lifted from the ledge. "Not unless I go with you, love. And I'm not about to let that happen."

Epilogue

Bright sky and clear turquoise spills of sea water beckoned Gordon toward a glorious day for swimming, but he did not go.

His wedding gift for Beth couldn't be wrapped in white paper and ribbons. Neither could it wait.

Cloaked in silver invisibility, he stood on Gull Cott's bluff amid tables spread with white linen cloths and shaded with blue umbrellas. From inside a fluttering striped pavilion the aroma of fresh seafood on shaved ice came to him, along with the scent of crusty sourdough bread, champagne, and Maria Rosetti's chocolate truffles.

None of it tempted him like the prospect of privacy with Beth. She had already slipped away from Gull Cott, now he must make certain no one followed until she'd reached the cove.

Guests had begun arriving yesterday. Gordon had curbed his bull's territoriality as long as he could. By sundown, he wanted Gull Cott and Beth for his own.

"Where has that girl gone?" Carol, Beth's stepmother, had taken charge of the wedding festivities and done a magnificent job. He couldn't wait for her to leave.

"I have no clue, Mrs. Caxton." Stefanie, in a bridesmaid

gown of misty green, flashed Carol a practiced smile. "I was helping her with her hair when Charmaine screamed for help."

Stefanie returned to the intricate chore before her as Charmaine tried to explain.

"First Minny insists on bringing her magic wand." Charmaine crouched before her daughter, trying to hold her still. "I knew Beth wouldn't care, but then Minny starts swinging it around and out of the blackberry bushes comes this kitten."

Gordon smiled.

"No, no, no!" Minny's flowery headpiece slipped over one eye. The scrap of fur mewed. "Want my kitty!"

Stefanie and Charmaine dodged the flailing wand and tried to unhook the kitten's claws from Minny's puff-sleeved flower-girl dress.

"She seems completely recovered from her ordeal." Carol settled Minny's crown of baby's breath and roses, and for a minute the tranquil touch distracted her.

Gordon thought the villagers of Grey Gallows might get their way. Minny might not learn of the anguish Karl had caused by staging her "kidnap."

Karl's confession had come before Reynolds even snapped the handcuffs in place. The shopkeeper's sloppy attempt to keep Gordon from alerting Reynolds to the poaching ring was a flop. Karl had underestimated the young sheriff. He, Roo, and Karl's logging truck cohort had strolled into the ambush just outside Sloan's garage. Reynolds regretted he hadn't been able to make the arrest on the final delivery of abalone steaks to their San Francisco and San Diego connections, but it looked as if he'd make the arson charge stick. Investigators had already indicated Al MacDonald hadn't fallen asleep smoking, after all.

Gordon decided the thousands of dollars from seafood restauranteurs must have scrambled Karl's brain. How he could have expected complicity from such an independent soul as Stefanie was beyond Gordon's understanding.

Even now, Stefanie cast her eyes past Minny, sizing up Beth's young friend Eddie Kung. He stared back, agog, but perhaps he stared at the diamond stud glittering in Stefanie's nostril.

"Oh, let her have it, Stef." Charmaine surrendered the kitten and stood up, brushing her skirts into place as Bob Reynolds approached.

"Sheriff Reynolds, you haven't seen Beth and Gordon, have you?" Carol nodded approval at Bob's suit and tie.

Out of his khaki uniform, the sheriff looked particularly young, but Gordon regarded him with gratitude. Because Bob Reynolds knew Sloan's history of drugs and violence, he'd kept Sloan under surveillance. When a dozen respectable citizens—and Junior—branded Sloan's death a boon to the community, Reynolds had taken Gordon's statement at Beth's kitchen table instead of detaining him in the Parish jail. In days Sloan's death had been deemed justifiable homicide, not murder.

"Haven't seen them, Mrs. Caxton. Want me to get up a search party?"

Though the young sheriff was clearly joking, Carol frowned. "No, no. I'll ask Phoebe. She's the maid of honor, if anyone knows, she should."

Even now, Phoebe emerged from Beth's bedroom, setting straight the bodice of her green dress.

"Maid of honor" might have been a title Beth bestowed with fanciful optimism, but the girl looked flustered, after her first kiss from Junior MacDonald.

Gordon had seen the kiss coming since Phoebe had climbed down from her VW bus, yesterday. Last night, during a bachelor party Junior found disappointingly sedate, Junior had confided why he admired Phoebe. "That woman won't do one damn thing I tell her to. I think I'm in love."

Now Carol had Phoebe cornered, but their quick conversation apparently brought no satisfaction.

Any minute now, he'd follow Beth. He ached to fold her against his chest and feel her heart beat hard against him.

As Beth's father appeared in Gull Cott's doorway, Carol turned the full force of her agitation his way.

"Jack, I can't get over the fact that she doesn't want you to give her away. It's simply not correct."

Jack's voice was almost a whisper. "Carol, I gave that child her independence a long time ago. It's the way we both want it." Jack reached for his wife.

"If you say so, but all the guests are here, the music's started, her *gown* is gone, but her shoes and stockings are just flung—"

Jack kissed the fidgeting stepmother-of-the-bride. Gordon admired his masterful style and Carol's sigh.

"If she's gone traipsing down to that seal cove—" Carol managed a final protest.

"Honey, don't you think those two are at least as eager for this wedding as you are?" Jack smoothed a hand over the chiffon covering his wife's behind. "Let's go down to the beach, have a seat, and wait for them."

Trailing silver mist, Gordon found Beth frozen one step before the smooth reddish stone.

"Gordon!"

She'd told him the white dress was designed to hang off her shoulders, holding a span of lace over the suntanned flesh above her breasts, but he still felt tempted to yank the silk the rest of the way down. Around her waist.

"You are so beautiful." He caught her against him and she came joyously, but still he saw it. The face Beth pressed against his neck wore a faint shadow, like sun-sheened waters as clouds pass overhead.

Beth hadn't set foot on the cove trail since Sloan's death. Gordon had held her hand and tried to lead her, but Beth refused to go. Only when he'd begged it as her wedding gift to him had Beth agreed.

He set her away with a chaste kiss, then, careful of her ribboned hairstyle, swept her into his arms and navigated the path.

The concealing fog glittered with such radiance, Gordon actually heard the tinkling of enchantment. He'd prove to her the cove held no darkness, only the most ordinary kind of magic. And love.

He didn't have to ask her to look. As the beach turned level, she heard splashing.

"Oh!" With one shoulder still cuddled against his chest, she pointed. "It's Baby! He's all right, don't you think?"

"Fine, I'd say, since he swam back for your wedding."

The gray-and-white creature slithered ashore with a blatting summons, but when Beth struggled free of Gordon's arms and ran forward to pet it, the thing slithered and puffed back into the water where it displayed dolphin-style jumps for their amusement.

"Oh, isn't he beautiful." Beth turned her back on the shallows, thanking Gordon with soft eyes.

Though heartened he'd cheered her, Gordon couldn't, in all honesty, agree. "No, he's as fat as a little pig. He has a pushed-in nose . . ."

"And you're jealous." Beth clasped her fingers through Gordon's. Now her face was shining.

A sea breeze blew her curls forward over her shoulders. One grazed Gordon's chin and he shivered. The reflection in her eyes held only him.

"Not jealous, just a little superstitious." He took in the vast orb of sea and sky, with Beth at its center, and swallowed the idiot human feelings that threatened to strangle him, "Tell me why you changed, why you decided to marry me."

Beth held both his hands, and a lesser being might have staggered under the onslaught of her kisses.

"Because I only have one life and I need to spend it with you."

In his heart, a glow of warmth sparked into fire only Beth could kindle.

"Or were you fishing for more specific compliments?" Beth's hands skimmed past his wrists, up sleeves that he hadn't yet fastened with the onyx cuff links Beth had been hiding all these weeks. "Want to start with the fact that I can't keep my hands off you?"

"Come swim with me. That's all."

"Look what happened last time I did." But her teasing lips, pink and smiling, said she might.

A burst of spritely music, Gimp's pipes and Lucinda's flute, came soaring on the wind. He wanted this ceremonial nonsense over. He wanted these people gone, and he lacked the power to make them disappear.

"We'd best go through with it." He plucked a blue satin circlet from his pocket. "But the least you can do is let me help you with your garter."

"Where—how did you get that?"

Gordon didn't answer. He knelt. Beth leaned forward, hand steady on his shoulder as he lifted one of her feet and admired the painted pink toenails.

"Were you skulking around in my room?" Breathless, she tried to jest as he pushed the garter over the tanned smoothness of her ankle.

There, her pulse raced. Wild. Out of control.

"Promise me you won't cover your legs with those nylon things. Just today."

Beth's hum might have been assent, but he wasn't certain. He edged the garter up an inch, but his hands shook so, he couldn't think. Then, he found himself kissing the tender flesh on the inside of her knee.

"Higher."

"Your wish is my command."

"No! The garter! The garter has to—Gordon? Oh, why can't I . . . Gordon, I mean the *garter* goes up . . ."

When bagpipes blared the wedding march, Beth appeared on the raked white beach with her arm tucked through Gordon's. All guests turned, agreeing Elizabeth Caxton made a blushing bride. If she appeared a bit unsteady as she swayed toward the makeshift altar, the dark man who was her groom looked stalwart enough for both.

The pastor read selections from First Corinthians and spoke of two lives entwined and those who sat nearest watched the couple ready rings wrought from thick waves of gold. Beth's glinted with an iridescent pearl, the groom's Midsummer gift, it was said, too precious to hide away for safekeeping.

Beth poised Gordon's ring at his first knuckle and they began their closing vows.

"Before ever land was . . ."

"Before ever the sea . . ." Gordon put Beth's ring in place and they continued together.

"I was, and thy soul was in me."

For the space of a heartbeat there was only the applause of waves and the knowing laugh of a gull. Then silence burst into gaiety bright with confetti and the beat of human clapping.

Gordon Henson did not wait for permission to kiss his barefoot bride.